J

Don't
Say
a Word

Don't Say a Word

by

Andrew Klavan

POCKET BOOKS

New York   London   Toronto   Sydney   Tokyo   Singapore

This book is a work of fiction. Names, characters, places and incidents are either the product of the author's imagination or are used fictitiously. Any resemblance to actual events or locales or persons, living or dead, is entirely coincidental.

POCKET BOOKS, a division of Simon & Schuster
1230 Avenue of the Americas, New York, NY 10020

Klavan, Andrew.
    Don't say a word / by Andrew Klavan.
       p.   cm.
    ISBN 0-671-74008-3 : $19.95
    I. Title.
    PS3561.L334D66 1991
    813'.54—dc20   90-26461
                                                CIP

First Pocket Books hardcover printing May 1991

10 9 8 7 6 5 4 3 2 1

POCKET and colophon are registered trademarks of
Simon & Schuster.

Printed in the U.S.A.

This book is for Richard Friedman

I am extremely grateful to the following people:

Maureen Empfield, M.D., and Howell Schrage, M.D., for generously providing me with insights on the treatment of mental illness, the administration of a psychiatric hospital, the use of antipsychotic drugs, and so on;

Tim Scheld, one of New York's best and busiest radio reporters, for helping me get into some of the city's off-limit locations;

Richard Scofield, M.D., for his kindness in providing free medical advice to fictional characters;

my wife, Ellen, as always, for her patience and editorial assistance.

PROLOGUE

The Man Called Sport

The right apartment was tough to find, so they murdered the old lady. The man called Sport knocked on her door. He was dressed in green overalls so he'd look like a plumber. Maxwell stood off to one side, out of the line of the old lady's peephole. Maxwell was wearing green overalls too, but he didn't look like any plumber. No one was going to open the door to let Maxwell in.

Sport was presentable, though. He was a young man with a round, smooth face. He had straight brown hair that fell down in a youthful shock on his forehead. He had a brilliant smile and friendly, intelligent brown eyes.

The old lady's name was Lucia Sinclair. When she heard Sport's knock, she called out through the door.

"Who is it?" She had a high, fluty voice. A rich woman's voice. Sport didn't like it. Back in Jackson Heights, when he was a kid, he'd worked Saturdays as a delivery boy for the A & P. Lucia Sinclair had the kind of voice women used when they told you to put the grocery bags in the kitchen. Sometimes they didn't even look at you when they told you.

"It's the plumber," Sport called out pleasantly.

He heard the little metal cap slide off the peephole. He gave Lucia Sinclair a look at his bright smile.

3

"Rick sent us," he said. "Mrs. Welch downstairs is getting water in her bathroom walls. We think the leak may be coming from your apartment."

He heard the peephole slide closed. He heard the chain lock slide open. He glanced up at Maxwell. Maxwell smiled eagerly. Maxwell was getting excited now.

The door opened and there stood Lucia Sinclair. Not bad looking actually for such a crone, Sport thought. She was small and slender. She had a heart-shaped face, the cheeks pinched but not saggy and wrinkled. Her short silver hair was set in an old-fashioned wave. She wore a loose flannel shirt and pale blue Jordache jeans. Expensive jeans, like the women he used to deliver groceries for. They would bend over their change purses and show off their asses. "Put the bags in the kitchen," they would say. They didn't even look at him.

Well, thought Sport, Maxwell ought to have a good time with this one.

Lucia Sinclair stepped back to let Sport in. She smiled and patted her hair into place.

"I'm afraid I'm a bit of a mess," she said. "I've been doing a little gardening." She gestured gracefully. At the far end of the long living room, there were sliding glass doors. The doors gave out onto a small balcony. On the balcony, there were several potted plants and flower boxes. "*Very* little gardening, I should say," Lucia Sinclair babbled on. "But it does seem to produce a great deal of dirt and I . . ."

She stopped. It made Sport smile the way the words just died on her lips. She stood there with her jaw hanging down. She stared and Sport saw gray depths of fear open in her eyes. She was looking at Maxwell.

Maxwell came in and shut the door behind him.

Sport could remember the first time *he* had seen Maxwell. It was in the Correctional Institution for Men on Rikers Island. Sport had been working as a correction officer there: a guard. It was early afternoon and he was resting his feet. Sitting in a wooden chair, tilted back against the cinderblock wall in the officers' stations near Dorm C. When they led Maxwell in, Sport's lips parted. Sport's chair lowered until its legs clicked against the concrete floor.

"Holy shit," he whispered.

And he thought: There is a man you want to make friends with.

He was way over six feet tall, was Maxwell. His shoulders were hunched and his muscular arms hung down heavy at his sides. He was built like a grizzly bear: that huge, hulking shape; the shambling movements, thick

4

with power. His head jutted forward, like a bear's or like a cave man's head. His great chest stretched his prison greens. He looked like he was about to burst out of them.

But his face . . . That's what caught Sport's attention right away. The look of his face. It was small, squarish, with wispy blond hair lying across the top of it. A large, flat nose like a black's and thick lips too and sunken eyes—brown eyes sunk down so deep they stared out of the shadows at you kind of sadly, as if they were trapped in there.

Christ, Sport thought, it's not like a man's face at all. Not like a man's and not like an animal's either. It was like a baby's face stuck on the top of this great bear's body. All that lumbering force—and a frightened baby's face on top of it.

Just then, as he came into the dorm, Maxwell was scared. Sport could see it. He was scared of being in jail. His lips were turned down in a big frown, as if he might cry.

His eyes kept shifting back and forth over the expanse of cots and footlockers—and men, mostly black men, who turned to stare at him with baleful, speculative eyes.

It was, as it turned out, his first time in. He had just pulled six months for exposing himself in a playground. His lawyer had bargained it down from sexual assault.

And Sport could see with a single glance that there was far more to the man than that.

Lucia Sinclair stood looking at Maxwell now and couldn't speak. Sport saw in her eyes that she knew she had made a mistake. He could almost hear her thinking: *If only I hadn't opened that door, if I just hadn't opened that door.*

Too late, cunt, Sport thought.

He smiled pleasantly again. "Now, if we could just take a look at your bathroom, ma'am."

Lucia Sinclair hesitated as she tried to think her way out of it. The loose skin around her lips shivered. "Yes, of course," she said finally. "Just let me . . ."

She made a move to the front door. Tried to step around Maxwell, reached for the knob.

Maxwell grabbed her wrist. Held it.

"Take your hands—" she began to say.

Then her mouth widened in pain. Her eyes filled. Maxwell held her thin

5

wrist tightly. He twisted her arm slowly away from the door. A small, strange, dreamy smile passed over his lips.

Lucia Sinclair barely managed to whisper, "Please . . ."

Maxwell released her. She stumbled backward and fell to the floor. She slid away from them up against the wall. She didn't get up. She cowered there. Sport liked that. She was not such a big-shot bitch now. She cowered there and rubbed the reddening skin of her wrist. She stared up at Maxwell. Maxwell stood over her. He was breathing heavily, his great shoulders rising and falling.

Sport spoke quietly. "Now if you'd just show him the bathroom, ma'am."

The old woman turned to Sport. Her eyes looked as if they had been jacked open. "Please," she said. The fluty trill was gone. It was just an old woman's cracked, trembling voice now. "Please, you can take anything you want."

"Max," Sport said.

Lucia Sinclair cried out in pain as Max reached down and grabbed her. He grabbed her just under her armpit with one huge hand. The old woman had to scramble to her feet to keep Max from yanking her arm out of its socket. She kept looking at Sport, appealing to Sport. She must've known it was no good appealing to Maxwell.

"Please," she said again. "Don't hurt me. Don't let him hurt me."

Sport raised his hand. He spoke in a soft, reassuring murmur. "He won't hurt you, ma'am. Just go on ahead into the bathroom with him."

"Please," Lucia Sinclair said. She was crying now. A track of tears was on each cheek. Her lips shook. Her whole face seemed to have sunken in and turned gray.

Max pulled her down the short hall toward the bathroom door. She kept calling back to Sport.

"Please. I can't hurt you. I won't even call the police."

Max reached the bathroom door. He flung her through it roughly. He stepped inside after her.

Sport heard her whimper one more time. "Please." And then she gave a hoarse cry from deep in her throat: "Oh, God."

And the bathroom door swung shut.

Of course, there was no stopping Max now, anyway. Not once he got that look on his face, that dreamy smile. That was the thing about Maxwell: he liked doing it; it turned him on. Like when they did the Freak.

Maxwell got a hard-on, an actual hard-on, just from cutting the guy's throat. The Freak was thrashing around on the floor, kicking around and gurgling. He was grabbing at his neck and the blood was spurting out between his fingers. And there was Maxwell, standing over him, his eyes bright, his lips parted, a line of drool running down the side of his chin—and a genuine banger standing up in his pants like a tent pole. Sport was sure Max would've whipped it out right there. Whacked off right there with the guy dancing and shivering underneath him. But Sport was grabbing at Maxwell's shoulder, practically yelling at him, "Let's go! Let's go!" Maxwell finally nodded sheepishly and ran his hand up through his thin blond hair.

Still, he lingered another moment for all that. He stayed to watch the Freak die.

While Max was in the bathroom with the old lady, Sport wandered around the living room. It was quite a place the old woman had. Very ritzy. Very posh. Not much direct sun, but plenty of early-autumn daylight pouring in through the balcony's glass doors. Beautiful coppery rugs on the parquet floors. A dining table all made of glass with silver candle holders on it. Heavy wooden chairs with scrolled arms and legs and tapestries of fruits and vines for their upholstery. Dark wooden bookcases with old, heavy books on them. And real rosewood cupboards and showcases with fancy knickknacks behind the glass: silver goblets, pewter pitchers, small ivory sculptures of horses and Buddhas; photographs in silver frames of a smiling couple, a suburban house, a little blond girl smiling, a little towheaded boy.

Sport paused before the showcases as he strolled through the room. He examined the knickknacks behind the glass, bending toward the glass with his hands clasped behind his back. This was the real class, all right, he thought. The genuine article.

When he was a kid out in the Heights, he'd wanted to be a singer. Not one of these rock-singing faggots either, but a real nightclub singer. A Julio or a Tom Jones or even a Sinatra. He dreamed of wearing a tuxedo and singing ballads. Holding the microphone in one hand, stretching the other out toward the crowd. The women sighing, screaming. The cigarette smoke drifting over him. This was the kind of place he had imagined living in then. Actually, he had imagined a house, a place in Hollywood, down the road from Johnny Carson's house. But a real elegant place like this one with fancy, carved furniture people would admire.

Sport paused before a bookshelf to bend toward a copy of *Little Dorrit* with a brown-leather, ribbed binding. He straightened now with a sigh.

Unfortunately, he had never gotten to wear a tuxedo or stand in a nightclub holding a microphone. And the only woman he had heard screaming was his mother. He could remember—he could sometimes *feel*—her pocked moon of a face pressing in on him. Her hot breath and the hot beer in it washing over his own face.

"I fart better than you sing," she had explained to him in a voice that sounded like a cat caught in a blender. And then she had demonstrated her point. "Hear that? That's you singing. That's how well you sing." She had farted again. "I'm singing," she had screamed. "Listen to me, everybody. I'm singing through my ass." And the hack of her laugh sent the stench of beer over him again.

A sound from the bathroom caught Sport's attention. Sport glanced back over his shoulder at the hallway. He wasn't sure what the sound had been. A thud, something dropping maybe. Or a hollow, wordless grunt; a moan. He was reminded of something Maxwell had told him when they had been getting to know each other out at Rikers. One night as they whispered together in the bathroom after lights out, Maxwell had confided in him shyly, even sweetly. He liked to cut the tongues out of cats, he said, and then break their legs and listen to them try to howl.

Sport shook his head and smiled as he moved away from the bookshelf. That Maxwell. What a sketch.

He wandered over to the glass doors now, the balcony doors. He stood before them, looking out. He rocked back and forth on his heels, his hands clasped behind his back.

The balcony itself was very small. Not much more than a triangular concrete ledge really. The few plants and flower boxes the old lady had been working on took up most of the space. Standing where he was, Sport could look out over the ledge and see the courtyard five stories below. It was a long, thin stretch of grass with a few sculpted hills of pachysandra on it. There were wooden benches here and there. And there was a slate path running down the center of it. The path ran from a gravel arbor under a vine-covered latticework on Sport's left to a small rectangular fish pond on his right. The courtyard's fourth wall was formed by the rear of a church.

Its brownstone wall and stained-glass lancets stood just beyond the fish pond.

Sport raised his eyes from the courtyard. He looked out at the building across the way. Lucia Sinclair's apartment was in the back of her building on East Thirty-fifth Street. The building on the other side of the court was over on Thirty-sixth. It was close, twenty yards away at most. Close enough anyway.

Just then, behind him, there was a tinkling sound. The knickknacks were rattling in their shelves. Maxwell, he thought, was obviously hard at work. He turned and surveyed the apartment again. Hard at work, he thought, getting me a lease on the place.

It was a trick Sport had learned from a drug dealer at Rikers. A high-class blood; a real high roller by the name of Mickey Raskin. Mickey had taught Sport the fine art of short-term apartment hunting. First, said Mickey, read the obits. Find a stiff, preferably without survivors. Next, approach the landlord or super and hand him an envelope stuffed with a year's rent. Tell him you need the apartment for a month, two at most, no questions asked. The only risk, Mickey said, was running into an honest landlord. In other words, it was foolproof.

It was a good method, Sport agreed. But the obit angle, that needed some work. Sport didn't need just any apartment. He needed this apartment, or one right nearby. So he couldn't wait for an obit, he had to create one, as you might say. And in a day or so, when the "obit" appeared, he would show up at the building and ask to talk to the super. I read about the old woman's murder in the *Post*, he would say, and I want to rent her apartment for a month when the police are done with it. At first, the super might be disgusted, or even suspicious. But then Sport would put an envelope in his hands. When the super looked down and saw how thick the envelope was, he would stop being disgusted and he would stop being suspicious. When the police were done—in a week, maybe two—the apartment would be his.

Sport heard the bathroom door open. There were heavy clumping footsteps. Maxwell appeared at the living room's far end.

The big man's chest was heaving. His jutting head moved up and down. The smile was gone from his thick lips and his eyes were glazed and distant. His great arms hung heavily at his sides. His thick fingers were dark with blood. He plucked bashfully at the fabric of his overalls. The overalls had

9

dark stains on them too. Maxwell hung his head and toed the floor sheepishly.

"Okay, big guy?" Sport said with a charming smile.

Maxwell nodded shyly, answered breathlessly, "Okay."

Before joining him, Sport turned for one more look out the glass doors. He nodded. It really was perfect. With a decent pair of binoculars, he would be able to look right into the window across the way.

Right into the apartment of Dr. Nathan Conrad.

PART ONE

The Psychiatrist
of the Damned

Dr. Nathan Conrad sat alone. He rested his hands on the arms of the leather recliner. He leaned his head back. He stared up at the molding that ran along the top of the walls. He thought: Shit.

His head was beginning to hurt. Red spots flashed and spread like stains before his bad right eye. His stomach felt hollow and heavy. There was no question about it: it had been a depressing session.

It was Timothy again. Timothy Larkin. Twenty-seven years old. A talented choreographer with a promising career. He had already worked as an assistant on two Broadway shows. And a year ago, he had landed a job as head choreographer of an outdoor dance performance for the World Trade Center's summer program. About a month after that, he'd discovered he had AIDS.

For the last six months, Conrad had watched the young man waste away. The dancer's frame, once lithe and muscular, had grown tremulous and frail. The chiseled face had gone flaccid and had sunk in on itself. He'd had radiation treatments for various cancers, and his rich black hair was gone as well.

Conrad rubbed his eye to clear away the red clouds. With a sigh, he worked his way out of his chair. After an hour of sitting, his bad leg, his right leg, had stiffened. He had to limp across the tiny office to the little lampstand near the bathroom door. A Mr. Coffee stood on the lampstand. His beloved Mr. Coffee. Mr. Coffee, Esquire. Sir Coffee. Saint Coffee.

His mug was standing by the machine. It was a black mug with white lettering: LIFE'S A BITCH, THEN YOU DIE. He lifted the coffeepot from its holder. He poured the dregs from the pot on top of the dregs in the mug. Setting the pot down, he sipped at the mug.

"Aah!" he said loudly.

Tasted just like sludge. He shook his head, carrying the mug back to his chair. It was his third mug of the stuff this morning.

He found it hard to believe it was only nine-fifteen.

Conrad had taken Timothy on at the request of the Gay and Lesbian Health Alliance. The Alliance internist—a woman named Rachel Morris—had made the referral.

"You know, I can't afford you guys anymore," Conrad had told her.

"Well, you did put your name on the list, Nathan," she said.

"Yeah, but you didn't tell me the rest of the page was blank."

She laughed. "What can I say? You've developed a reputation among the city's more desperate support services."

"Oh, yeah? What's my reputation? And make it good."

"They call you the Psychiatrist of the Damned."

Conrad held the phone in one hand and his head in the other. "I'm flattered, Rachel. I'm deeply moved. But I'm a fancy Upper West Side shrink now. I have a wife and child and Mercedes-Benz to support."

"Oh, Nathan, you do not."

"Well, I have a wife and child. And I would have a Mercedes-Benz if you guys would stop calling me."

"And your wife can support herself."

"She can? Can she buy me a Mercedes-Benz?"

"Nathan!" Rachel had finally cried. "He has no money, his insurance doesn't cover it. He's suicidal and he has nowhere else to go. He needs you."

Conrad considered it for another moment. Then he let out a howl of despair.

Conrad's office was in a rambling Gothic apartment building on Central Park West between Eighty-second and Eighty-third streets. He was on the ground floor in the back. His only window looked out on the depressing airshaft his building shared with the rambling Gothic apartment building next door on the Eighty-third Street corner. He kept the window covered with wooden blinds. No daylight came through it—you could hardly tell there was a window there at all. The office always looked stark somehow, stale and artificial.

The office was divided into a waiting room and a consulting room. Both were small. The waiting room was no more than a rectangular strip. There was just space enough there for a couple of bookshelves, a couple of chairs, and a small corner table on which Conrad provided his patients with the *New York Times* and *Psychology Today*. He never read either himself.

The consulting room was a little bigger, but it was crowded. There was the window on the north wall and a bathroom on the south. But every other inch of available wallspace was taken up by bookshelves on which sat such weathered tomes as *Sexuality and the Child*, *Psychopharmacology*, and the *Complete Writings of Sigmund Freud* in several volumes. There was also a rolltop desk across one corner. Its lid was up and its writing surface was completely covered with papers and journals. Somewhere under all that stuff there was a telephone and an answering machine. Balanced on the very corner was a traveler's alarm clock.

Finally, there was the essential furniture: Conrad's chair—the leather recliner—the couch for analysands, and the big yellow armchair for patients in therapy.

When Timothy had sat in that armchair today, it had dwarfed him. His thin arms had lain wearily on the rests. His bony hands had trembled slightly. His head had wavered as if his neck couldn't support it. A Mets baseball hat, pitifully large, sat at an angle on his head. It was supposed to cover his baldness.

Looking at him, Conrad had to lift himself up through a cloud of pity. Had to set his own sad and saggy face into an impassive mask. He breathed slowly, forcing the air out with his abdomen. He waited for his mind to click into its low, dark state of receptivity. No judgments, no interpretations. Let the connections make themselves. *The way of the Tao is easy,* he recited, *simply give up all your opinions.*

"You know," Timothy was saying softly, "the guilt is worse than the fear. I mean, when you get down to it, I feel so bad but . . . I'm not really all that afraid of dying."

Conrad listened silently. Timothy had been talking about this for weeks:

the guilt and shame that weighed on him as heavily as death. He already knew the causes of it. Now he was just trying to trade that knowledge in for an insight.

He raised his head wearily. Looked hard at Conrad with wide, sunken, black eyes. "What I hate is feeling that . . . God is punishing me. That AIDS is some kind of divine sentence. Punishment for my sins."

Conrad shifted slowly in the recliner. "Which sins are these, Tim?" he asked softly.

"Oh . . . you know." Timothy took a long, painful breath. "The same old sins. My life, my lifestyle. My sexuality." And then, with an effort: "I mean, this is what you get, right, for having sex with men?"

And Conrad asked: "Is it?"

The young man's eyes filled with tears. He raised them toward the ceiling. "I feel as if somewhere in my mind there's some kind of fundamentalist preacher, you know? Like in that Woody Allen movie: some kind of preacher living in my conscience, shaking his finger at me and saying, 'See? See? God is not mocked, Timothy. This is what you get for doing dirty things with other boys.'"

Conrad smiled with as much charm as he could muster. "I hate to sound like a psychiatrist here," he said, "but this preacher character—he doesn't happen to look anything like your father, does he?"

With a laugh, Timothy gave a weary nod. "You know, I think he really would think that. My father. If I talked to him. I mean, maybe he wouldn't say it out loud, but I really think he would believe that I'm . . . being punished because I'm gay."

"It's an interesting theological point," Conrad said. "If AIDS is a punishment for homosexuality, what's childhood leukemia a punishment for? Not sharing your toys?"

Timothy gave another soft laugh.

"The rain falls on the just and the unjust," Conrad said gently.

"Oh, great." With a groan, Timothy laid his head back on the chair. "Who said that? Sigmund Freud?"

"Probably. One of us smart Jewish guys."

For another long moment, Timothy sat like that, his stick figure sprawled in the chair, his head flung back. Then Conrad saw tears begin spilling down his temples. Dripping onto the chair back, dampening, darkening, the yellow upholstery.

Conrad glanced over at the clock on the desk. It was 9:13. Thank God, he thought. Thank God, it's almost over. For a moment, he felt the tide of pity rise in him again. He could hardly stand it. He forced it down.

He looked back at his patient. Timothy remained still, his head back, the tears falling. Hurry it up, Timbo, Conrad thought, you're killing me here.

And finally, the dancer lowered his eyes to the psychiatrist. The tears were already drying. The lips were set. With welling emotion, Conrad saw the young man's eyes go hard.

"I'm glad I've loved the people that I've loved," Timothy said. "I don't want to die ashamed. I'm glad."

Then his lips trembled, buckled. He began to cry again.

Conrad leaned forward and spoke very gently. "Our time is up," he said. "We have to stop now."

Timothy was going to feel better, Conrad thought. He leaned back in his recliner and sipped the steam off the thick coffee. If he had time to work on it, Timothy would come to terms with his guilt and his disease. He would feel refreshed in some mysterious way; at peace.

And then he would die—slowly, painfully, horribly, alone.

Shit. Conrad shook his head. Great attitude, Nathan my friend. And it was only twenty past nine in the morning. He couldn't afford to be this depressed yet. There was still June Fefferman to get through: a sweet, dependent little mouse of a woman whose airline-pilot husband had died last year in a car crash while driving home from the airport. Then after her, he had Dick Wyatt, a vibrant forty-five-year-old executive who had slipped on the stoop of his Brooklyn brownstone one morning and paralyzed himself from the neck down. Then, and maybe worst of all, there was Carol Hines, who had lost her five-year-old son to a brain tumor. Conrad's daughter, Jessica, was just five herself. He hated to deal with Carol Hines.

Conrad squeezed his eyes shut. He made a noise, half sigh, half groan. Psychiatrist of the Damned, he thought. Jesus, where were all those well-heeled, run-of-the-mill Upper West Side neurotics he'd heard so much about? The best he could do for this lot was cure their delusions so they could live out their nightmares.

Outside, he heard the waiting-room door squeak open, close with a thud. He glanced at the little clock again: 9:25. Mrs. Fefferman and her dead husband had arrived five minutes early. Five minutes. He still had time to relax a little before the session began. He gripped the handle of his mug gratefully. He brought it to his lips. Breathed in the smell of it.

17

The phone rang. A piece of notepaper balanced on top of it slid off and floated down to the floor. The phone was a black push-button. It rang again: a loud, shrill blast.

"Uh—how can I put this?" Conrad muttered at it. "Bugger off."

The phone rang again.

With a curse, Conrad rolled the recliner over to the desk. He laid his coffee mug down on top of his paper-in-progress on grief reactions in children. He snatched up the phone.

"Dr. Conrad," he said.

"Yo, Nate. Jerry Sachs here."

Conrad cringed. There went his five minutes.

"Hi, Jerry," he said as cheerfully as he could. "How're you doing?"

"Oh, you know. Not raking in the big Central Park West bucks like some people, but getting by. How about you?"

"Oh," said Conrad. "Fine, thanks."

"Listen, Nate," Sachs pushed on, "I got something over here that I think might be right up your alley."

"Nate" shook his head. He could picture Sachs on the other end of the line. Sitting behind his oversize desk at Impellitteri Municipal Psychiatric Facility. Leaning back in his chair, his big feet propped on the desk, his hand tapping the dome of his belly. His enormous egg-shaped head tilted way back so that his black glasses flashed in the toplight. And that huge onyx plaque in front of him: JERALD SACHS, M.D., DIRECTOR. That plaque had to be about three feet long.

But then Conrad figured Sachs had earned it. His appointment to the directorship was the result of nearly ten hard years of sucking up to the Queens borough president, Ralph Juliana. Conrad had seen Juliana on the TV news: a squat party hack with an expensive suit and a cheap cigar. Sucking up to him could not have been pleasant. Sachs had spent the better part of a decade laughing at the weasel's jokes. Showing up at his parties. Providing him with a "respected psychiatrist" to impress his friends with. Not to mention giving expert opinions in several court cases in which Juliana had an interest. And finally, he had managed to get himself appointed director of Impellitteri. Proud master of its green cinder-block walls, its barely furnished dorms, its squalid day rooms. Fearless leader of its staff of cast-off doctors and semiliterate therapy aides and pit-bull nurses with basset-hound frowns. The King Python in the city's snakepit.

And for all that, Conrad owed him. He had met Sachs some fifteen years ago when they were both interns at NYU Medical Center. He hadn't much

18

liked him then either. But five years ago, Conrad had found himself treating a manic-depressive teenager named Billy Juarez. Billy was destitute and growing violent. He had already punched a teacher who had questioned him about his attendance record. He was starting to talk about buying himself a gun. Billy needed hospitalization and medication and he didn't have the money to get it. He was destined, Conrad feared, for one of the public hellholes. Then the state started funding an experimental program that required removing patients from Impellitteri to a pleasant private sanitorium up near Harrison. The program also included access to lithium. Conrad had called Jerry Sachs and reminded him of their connection. He'd asked for a placement for Billy Juarez and Sachs had come through.

So he owed him. So he said, "Something up my alley, huh?" He couldn't work any enthusiasm into it, but he kept going. "Well, I'm interested to hear about it, Jerry. I am kind of busy right now but I—"

"Come on, Nate!" Sachs said with the gruff, jovial camaraderie that Conrad detested. "You can't just sit over there on CPW treating rich biddies who get bored counting their money. Although I guess you private practitioners know the cure for that, all right."

Yeah, just like you political cocksuckers know the cure for integrity, Conrad thought. But he kept his mouth shut. After a while, Sachs stopped laughing at his own joke and went on.

"No, but seriously, Nathan, this is something exciting. A 330-20."

"A criminal procedure?"

"Yeah, it was just in the newspapers and everything."

"Oh," said Conrad bleakly. "In the newspapers and everything, huh?"

"Yeah, sure. About three weeks ago. The Elizabeth Burrows case? Don't tell me you're too much of a big shot to read the tabloids?"

"Uh . . ."

"Well, the court sent her to us for a thirty-day evaluation, to see whether she's fit to stand trial. She's eighteen. Been diagnosed as a paranoid schizophrenic. She's got command-auditory hallucinations, severe delusions, and a history of violence to boot."

"Sounds like a druggie."

"Not that we can find."

"Really. But she's violent."

"Is she." Sachs gave a low whistle. "Listen. I started questioning her, okay? Everything's going great, better than great. She loves me; she won't stop talking. Then, all of a sudden, kaboom. She becomes, as we say, agitated. I mean she flipped the fuck out, man. Comes after me. Damn near strangled me before I got some help, got her restrained. And she's this little woman, Nate. I mean, you wouldn't believe her strength. Took four aides to throw her in seclusion, plus two more to get her in four-point restraint. When we let her out, we had a security-care aide on her one to one, and I mean this two-hundred-pound SCATA's scared out of her ever-loving wits. Finally, when we'd pumped enough medication in Miss Crazy Lady to snow an elephant, I put her in one of the forensic singletons, all right? And then what? She goes catatonic on me. No movement at all, won't speak, just sits and stares . . ."

Conrad snorted. "Great, Jerry. I'll come right by with my Super Duper Delusional Atomizer. I mean, what the hell do you want me to do for her?"

"Nothing. We're not trying to cure her, man. We need someone to get her talking. Determine whether she's fit to stand trial and make a report."

"So give her to one of your forensic guys. That's what they're there for. Listen, I have a patient in a minute here. Couldn't we . . . ?"

"Oh, tell her to cool her high heels," said Sachs. He chuckled. "No, seriously. Seriously . . . You were involved in that study up at Columbia Pres three years ago, right? Catatonics. Same kind of cases; you did great stuff. I mean, *Science Times* covered that, Nathan. You have a big reputation. . . ."

There was a pause. Conrad sat silently shaking his head.

Then Sachs said, "It's a big case, Nate. Why the hell do you think I got in on it in the first place? The bosses are watching me. The papers too, see. You're the kind of name that'll make a difference to them." And when Nathan still didn't answer, Sachs said, "It's a favor, Nate. Really. Really."

Conrad looked at the clock again: 9:34. Mrs. Fefferman would be getting restless. He ran his hand up into his hair. "What, uh . . . what was she arrested for?"

Sachs let out a loud laugh—half triumph, half relief. "Boy, you really don't read the papers, do you? The Burrows case. Elizabeth Burrows? She killed a man, Nathan. She cut his throat. Christ Almighty, she cut the poor bastard to pieces."

Agatha

Conrad was a small man, short and thin with sloping shoulders. He had a round, melancholy face: deep, soft brown eyes and thick lips that turned down, making him look thoughtful and grave. A few strands of sandy hair still lay limply across the top of his head, but most of it was gone. He was forty years old.

He felt those years, all of them. Except for his hour-long walk to work in the morning, he never exercised. He often felt tired; creaky in the joints. After a lifetime of eating without gaining weight, he was now developing a paunch around the middle. And sometimes—well, a lot of times—well, just about every day—he found himself dozing in his recliner after eating the yogurt and nuts his wife packed him for lunch.

On a day like this, it could be especially tough. Starting with Timothy, he had been in his recliner almost steadily from eight that morning until seven-thirty that night. He had listened to patients all day long with few breaks in between. It had taken its toll.

He'd downed a couple of aspirin after lunch. That had stopped the flashing in his eye, cleared up his headache. But his right leg: it had really begun to ache on him. He was limping as he left his building for the night.

He moved to the edge of the sidewalk and stood waiting for a cab. The traffic breezed swiftly down Central Park West. In the brisk October night, the green lights gleamed brightly all the way up the broad avenue. Across the way, in the park, the branches of the sycamores rattled their dying leaves against the sky. Some leaves fell onto the far sidewalk or tumbled and danced in the air above the park wall. Conrad paused and watched them.

The leg really did hurt, he thought. The knee throbbed. He had to remember to stand up more during the day, walk around, stretch it out.

It was Agatha's fault, he thought, that knee. She was the one who had crippled him like this.

But the thought made him smile as he watched the leaves falling.

He had met Agatha when he was seventeen. That was the first time they had taken his mother away. Mom had been coming out of the Grand Union with a bag full of groceries. She had tripped on something—or maybe just collapsed. In either case, she had fallen to the sidewalk just beyond the parking lot. She had dropped the grocery bag. Red tomatoes, yellow lemons, and silver tuna-fish cans had all gone rolling this way and that, flashing in the sun. Another housewife and the cashier from the hardware store next door had run over to help. But Mom just lay there, just lay there trembling. Her mouth open, drool dribbling out the side of it, she stared into the brown paper sack on the sidewalk before her. She stared at the carton of eggs in there. She watched the broken shells dangling out the top. She saw the yolk spreading on the brown paper beneath them. And she began to scream.

The housewife tried to calm her. The cashier tried to hold her steady. But Mom thrashed and screamed and moaned fiercely. When she looked into that bag, she had seen a carton full of eyeballs. She had seen those eyeballs split open right in front of her. Blood had poured out of them—viscous, scarlet—followed by black spiders clambering up out of the shattered pupils. Mom screamed and screamed. She wasn't used to seeing that kind of thing. As hard as she'd been drinking for the last twelve years, this was the first time she'd ever had the d.t.'s.

Seventeen-year-old Nathan was the one who got to the hospital first. He had just come back from school when he got the call, hadn't even had time to take off his coat. He hopped back into the ancient Chevy he'd worked all summer for and sped off to the hospital. It was he who sat by his mother's bed and listened to her sob in terror and humiliation. He sat and stroked the hair back from her gray face—that thin, once stately face with its thin, patrician nose. She was so proud of her nose. It was not a Jewish nose. "My father never let us live among Jews," she used to say grandly. And she'd lift her chin in the air, showing off her swan's neck, her slim figure.

Nathan held her hand. Her skin was so pale that he could see the dark needle of the IV inside her vein. She cried and cried as Nathan sat there.

Good Ol' Reliable Nathan. That's what his dad liked to call him. His dad—who didn't show up for another hour. Nathan suspected Dad was purposely taking his time leaving his office. He was a busy man, a dentist, but still . . . Dad liked for Nathan to clean things up a bit before he himself arrived on the scene. Then, when Dad got there, he could chuckle weakly and slap Nathan's shoulder. "See there, it's not so bad," he would say. His pale, round face would open on a grin, his small eyes would blink behind his big glasses. "No big deal, right?"

And Nathan would swallow hard and say, "Right, Dad." And Dad would chuckle some more and then turn away miserably.

After an hour, Dad finally did get there. Nathan left him at Mom's bedside and went to the hospital cafeteria for a cup of coffee. He sat at a corner table, brooding over the stained-brown cup from the vending machine. After about ten minutes, he lifted his head. There was Agatha.

She was a candy striper, a hospital volunteer. And as if her pink-and-white-striped outfit were not bad enough, she also had one of the most cheerful faces Nathan had ever seen. Round cheeks that reddened as she smiled, and bright blue eyes that grew brighter. Her auburn hair was tied up under her pink-and-white cap, but Nathan could see how thick it was. He could imagine it spilling down around her face, offset by her complexion, which was as pink and white as her outfit.

Nathan was a shy kid, some might even have said sullen. He had only one friend—Kit, his faithful companion since elementary school. He'd never had a girlfriend at all. He'd had a few dates in a row with Helen Stern, but she'd broken it off with him when he'd gotten "too serious." In general, he considered the opposite sex rather foolish, and more than a little untrustworthy.

He'd never seen Agatha before, and he didn't know what she was staring at. He was made uncomfortable by that steady smile, the bright gaze of those eyes. He almost glanced over his shoulder to make sure she wasn't looking at someone else.

But Agatha—that was the name on the black nameplate above her chest, the one he could barely peek at for fear his eyes would become glued to the full swell of her pink-and-white blouse—Agatha spoke to him directly.

"You know, you can't save her," she said. "No one expects you to be able to save her."

The words struck so close to home he felt compelled to deny them. He stared down at his coffee cup and muttered glumly, "I'm not trying to save anyone."

To his surprise, she reached out and touched his wrist. Her fingers were cool and soft. "You're trying to save *everyone,*" she said gently. "I've seen you. I go to North too. I'm in eleventh. I heard you arguing with Mr. Gillian about the kid with the hall pass last semester."

"Ah, Gillian's a jerk," Nathan muttered. "He practically made that kid cry."

"You could've been suspended for what you called him. And I saw you out in the yard—just before spring break—I saw you stand between Hank Piasceki and that little guy. Hank Piasceki is twice your size. And he can box too."

Nathan couldn't help it—he smiled. That actually had been kind of brave of him. But he tried to wave it off. "I wasn't gonna fight him. Piasceki likes me. I helped him pass Bio last year."

Agatha smiled at him, the light in her blue eyes dancing. "See what I mean?" she said.

Nathan looked up at her. She laughed. He laughed too.

Conrad grew up in Great Neck out on Long Island, about fifteen miles from Manhattan. It was a fresh and pretty suburb of wide green lawns and large white houses. Most of the people who lived there were well-to-do and Jewish, as he was. They were moderately liberal in their politics and largely conservative in their behavior. As for free love, drugs, antiwar protests— though it was the heart of the sixties, these were only beginning to leak through the first cracks in the community. They attracted a few rebels, problem kids, outcasts, that was all.

They did not attract Nathan. He was having none of it. He was going to be a doctor—a surgeon. He had no time for fads and nonsense like that. The first time he saw a senior wearing bell-bottom jeans, he sneered and snorted and raised his eyes to heaven—and then hurried home to crack open those books. Most of his classmates felt pretty much the same way—for the time being at least.

But Agatha was different. She wasn't Jewish, for one thing. And she wasn't all that well-to-do for another. Her father worked for the town highway department and her family lived on Steamboat Road. Steamboat was a long, curving stretch of run-down clapboards, small groceries, auto parts stores, bars, and the like. The town's maids lived here, many of them, and its service station workers, its gardeners: its blacks. And at the far end, near Kings Point Park, there was a small collection of Polish and Irish families. That's where Aggie's green, two-story clapboard stood.

Now Nathan, in those days, paid little attention to differences in culture. All kids went to school and were pretty much the same to him. It wasn't as if he really liked any of them anyway. So it was actually several months before it occurred to him that, Agatha's last name being O'Hara and all, she was probably of Irish ancestry. The thought flitted through his head and was forgotten.

But what he did notice was that life at the O'Haras' on Steamboat Road was not the same as life with the Conrads on Wooley's Lane. Aggie's older sister, Ellen, for instance, had actually dropped out of high school. Just dropped the hell out just like that and was living away from home and working as a beautician up on Middle Neck Road. And then Mr. O'Hara, a bulky, silver-haired rough guy, could sometimes be heard to remark after a beer or two that he thought Mr. President Lyndon Johnson was no better than a two-bit, son-of-a-bitch asshole—and that John F. Kennedy, rest his soul, hadn't been very much better! Whereupon Mrs. O'Hara might shout—really *shout* from the kitchen—"Stop talking filth in front of the children." And her husband might yell back, "Ah, who asked ya?" and storm out of the house, slamming the screen door behind him.

Nathan's head reeled. God knew his mother drank enough. But no one in his family ever *yelled*. Or dropped out. Or voted Republican. What kind of a place *was* this anyway?

And then there was Agatha herself. When she wasn't wearing her candy stripes, it turned out, she not only wore bell-bottoms, but tie-dyed T-shirts too. And suede vests that left her midriff bare. And sometimes no bra though her breasts were large and round and heavy and he could see her naked nipples, for Christ's sweet sake, pressing through the fabric of her blouse.

She smoked cigarettes—at sixteen, right in front of her parents. And alone with him in the tiny apartment she had above the family garage, she offered him his first taste of marijuana—which Nathan sternly declined.

But he was not so prim when, the very first time he kissed her good-night, she guided his hand up inside her shirt. Or when, only two months after they'd started dating, she suggested they make love.

They were both virgins. But Aggie had plenty of experience and an older sister to guide her. That first afternoon, up in the garage apartment, she was calm—serene—as she undressed in front of him. Nathan sat on the edge of an old armchair, his hands clasped between his legs. He shuddered as he watched her.

Agatha was a short girl, shorter even than he was. But she was sturdy and round, with big hips and those breasts, those wonderful breasts, with salmon areolas the size of silver dollars. To this day, Conrad could remember the liquid softness of her flesh and the smell of Ammens baby powder and her small, welcoming kisses. He could remember that first afternoon in detail—and all the afternoons of their first spring together. The little room with the low ceiling. The old convertible sofa that opened into a bed. The cries she stifled with the back of her hand. The song of sparrows gathered on the rusting swingset in the little yard out back.

Mostly, though, he remembered that convertible sofa. That goddamned convertible sofa.

It was a Castro; older, it seemed, than time. The mattress was dirty. It was thin. It rippled and sagged. Nathan could feel the springs and metal support bars of the sofa's mechanism right through it. He could especially feel the metal support bar that jutted up directly into the center of the thing. No matter where Agatha lay—no matter how he shifted her and which way he turned her—the minute he climbed on top of her, that bar was jutting up right into his knees.

It seemed a small price to pay, though. For the texture of those lips, for the taste of those breasts. For the long shock of warmth inside the rippling cleft between her legs. Sometimes his knee was so sore, he could barely make it up the apartment's short flight of stairs. But he'd make it, all right. And moments later, he would be on top of her, in her, thrusting as she cried, and oblivious to the fact that somehow, no matter how he'd arranged it, he had slipped back into the one position the old mattress seemed to allow, with his knee rubbing smack up against that goddamned bar.

Twenty-three years later, when a taxi pulled up to the curb in front of him, Dr. Nathan Conrad had to lower himself to the seat backwards and pull his right leg in after him.

The cab slipped out into the rapid flow of traffic. The driver, a grim-lipped, dark-skinned man named Farouk, glanced up at him in the rearview mirror.

"Thirty-sixth Street," Conrad said. "Between Park and Madison."

The cab eased up to speed. Conrad sat back wearily, gazed out the window. He watched the park wall speeding by, and the spidery branches of the trees above it. Absently, he rubbed at the throbbing knee with his hand. He tried to stretch it, moving his foot back and forth a little in what space there was. He really had to remember to walk around more. It only got bad like this when he was in the chair all day.

He just hadn't been able to stay away from Agatha, that was the thing. He hadn't been able to change beds. Or find another room. Or do anything that took away from the time he spent making love to her.

Finally, just before his eighteenth birthday, the knee had swollen up on him. By the time he overcame his embarrassment and went to the doctor, it was the size of a small pumpkin and still growing. Poor old Dr. Liebenthal. He'd been taking care of Nathan forever—gave him his first tine test, stitched up his forehead when he fell off the jungle gym, all of that. He'd looked at that knee and rubbed his chin and shook his head in deep puzzlement.

"It looks like a whopping bad case of bursitis to me," he had said. "It's the kind of thing you usually see with older folks, though. People who work on their knees, like washerwomen or repairmen—you know? And you say you've got no idea what could've brought it on."

And Nathan had spread his hands and shook his head. "It's a poser, Doc."

Later he and Aggie had sat on the floor and laughed until their bellies hurt. And then they'd climbed back onto the bed and gone at each other again.

The taxi reached the end of the park. Conrad watched as the marble Columbia—a heroic woman standing in the prow of a boat—saluted his passage by the Maine Memorial. Then the cab was sliding down the dark entrance of Broadway, moving over that short shabby stretch before the burst of neon and Times Square.

At Fifty-third Street, the cab stopped at a light. Conrad, his chin propped on his hand, found himself gazing absently out the window at a trio of streetwalkers. There was one black one, two whites. All were dressed in leather skirts that ended high on the thigh. All wore tight, glittery T-shirts, too light, it seemed to Conrad, for the cool fall weather.

Farouk looked up into the mirror hopefully.

"Hey, mister," he said. "You wanna get laid?"

Conrad kept gazing out at the hookers. He thought of Agatha. He smiled.

"Yeah, I would," he said quietly. "Take me home."

Jessie

The cab dropped him off on East Thirty-sixth Street. An elegant block, between Park and Madison. The north side was taken up by the J. P. Morgan library. It was a low, graceful temple of a place, with a Palladian porch flanked by lionesses. Its floodlights, just on, brought its marble facade into relief against the dusk. Friezes and statuary gleamed through the spreading sycamores that lined the sidewalk.

Conrad went into the building just across the way: a rippling prewar brick tower half a block long and fourteen stories high. The ancient doorman struggled off his bench as Conrad pushed through the glass doors.

"Evening, Doc."

Conrad smiled and limped past. Across the lobby, he saw one of the elevator doors was open.

"Going up," he called out. And he hopped toward it, his briefcase rocking at his side.

The doors began to slide shut but a hand reached out and stopped them. Conrad stepped through. The doors closed.

He was standing in the elevator with a young man. Midtwenties maybe. Tall, well-built, handsome. He had a smooth, angular face and a slick crest of black hair. A shy smile but quick, ferocious eyes; an expensive serge suit, navy with gray pinstripes: Conrad pegged him as a Wall Street turk.

When Conrad pushed the button for the fifth floor, the young man turned to him. "Well, I guess we're neighbors then," he said. He had an even voice, self-assured. It had a faint Midwestern twang.

Conrad smiled politely. The young man stuck out his hand. "Billy Price. I just moved in. Five-H at the far end of the hall."

Conrad shook hands with the kid. "Nathan Conrad," he said.

"Oh, yeah. The doctor, the headshrinker. I guess I better watch what I say around you, huh?"

Conrad managed to laugh as if he'd never heard that one before. Then they reached five and the doors opened. They came out and went their separate ways, Price to the left, Nathan to the right.

"Be seeing you," said Price.

Conrad waved over his shoulder.

It was nearly eight o'clock when Conrad entered his apartment. He was figuring on dinner. He figured he'd eat his dinner and his wife would sit with him and talk. He liked to listen to her. He liked the sound of her voice. Anyway, he was too tired to talk much himself.

So they would have dinner and she would talk and then they would go to bed together. And then after about a fifteen-minute nap, he would get up and go back to work on his grief paper until about one A.M. That was how he had it figured.

Then he opened the apartment door and stepped in.

"Daddy!"

The little girl came rocketing out of the kitchen hallway. She ran toward him with her arms open, her long braid flying back.

"Daddy-Daddy-Daddy. Daddy-Daddy-Daddy. Daddy-Daddy-Daddy-Daddy-Daddy!"

Uh-oh, Conrad thought. And then the kid hit his bum leg at full speed. She wrapped her arms around it, pressed her cheek to it, closed her eyes.

"Daddy!" she sighed.

"Hey, my little friend!" Conrad tried to smile, but it was more like a grimace. "Oh, gee. Oh, honey. Jessica, honey, sweetheart, please. My leg. Oh."

Gently, he peeled her off him. She grabbed hold of his hand and started jumping up and down.

"Mommy let me stay up for you."

"Hey. Great," Daddy said. I'll kill her, he thought. First I'll have dinner, then I'll kill her, then we'll go to bed together . . .

"Because remember," Jessica was saying, "you promised to play Chutes and Ladders with me before I went to bed?"

"Uh . . . did I? Uh . . . Oh, boy, that'll be great."

"So Mommy said it was fair because you promised."

"Ah. Well. That *was* fair," said Conrad. "Good for Mommy." First he would kill her, *then* he would have dinner . . .

He set his briefcase down as Jessica dragged him across the apartment to the kitchen. They were almost to the door when his wife stepped out.

Twenty-three years since they'd met, Agatha still had that happy smile, the one that made her round cheeks pink, her blue eyes bright. Her auburn hair was a little bit shorter now, but it still tumbled to her shoulders in breathless curls. And her round figure was a little bit rounder. He could see the curves of it even in her baggy black sweater and loose khaki slacks.

"Hiya, Doc," she said. And she came forward and kissed him lightly on the lips. The smell of roast chicken, hot butter and garlic, came out of the kitchen behind her.

Maybe he would go to bed with her first, he thought.

He couldn't remember what he was going to do second.

The Chutes and Ladders game seemed to go on forever. Jessica would painstakingly count her piece along the spaces—"Wa-un, two-oo, three-ee . . ." Then she would miss the count—"Oooh . . . wait a minute, wait a minute. Where was I?" And she would set the piece back at the original space and start again, "Wa-un, two-oo, three-ee," while Conrad would be thinking: *Four five! Four five, for the love of God, child!* It went on and on.

After a while, though, Aggie brought him a soda water and a few crackers. It took the edge off his hunger and his weariness. He began to relax.

He and Jessie were lying on the swatch of maroon carpet in the center of the living room. Jessica was sitting Injun style, bent over the game board. Nathan was stretched out, his head propped on his hand. He sipped his seltzer and watched her as she spun the wheel and went through the long, slow count again. "Wa-un, two-oo . . ."

Jessie had sandy hair like his—or like his used to be. Hers was thick and long—she wore it in a braid so her mother wouldn't have to fight the snarls in it every night—but the color was his exactly. The rest of her was pure Agatha. The apple cheeks and the blue eyes and the big smile. Margaret, her teacher at Friends Seminary, said she was talented at art, as Agatha was too. She certainly seemed to enjoy it as much as her mother. Almost every day, she came back from the Quaker private school bearing another drawing of a rectangle house with a triangle roof, or a stick-figure woman in a triangle dress, or wavy water or lollipop trees or some other thing Conrad and Aggie could clap their hands and exclaim over. The best of these were hung in the Metropolitan Museum of Jess: the little stretch of hallway formed by the nursery and kitchen walls. Conrad had no idea whether the pictures were good or not. But he did sometimes stand in that little hall and congratulate himself on how colorful and solid they were. They showed none of the tendency toward disjointed abstraction he'd seen in pictures drawn by emotionally disturbed kids. Once or twice, he'd even stood there looking at them and caught himself thinking, "Well, *she* won't ever need a psychiatrist." (Not that there was anything wrong with seeing a psychiatrist, of course. But why *should* she? *Her* mother wasn't an alcoholic. *Her* father wasn't a craven codependent. There was absolutely no reason why she shouldn't be the happiest, most well-adjusted human being who ever existed since time began. Right?)

Well, anyway, the kid really did seem to have Agatha's cheerful disposition. Her generosity. Her avocation to nurture others. Of her two "best friends," one was a sweet but ugly and clumsy girl whom Jessie had seen rejected in the playground. Jessie had invited the child, Adrienne, to join the unicorn game she played with her other best friend, Lauren. Jessie had been taking care of Adrienne ever since. It was exactly what Agatha would have done.

But if Jessie derived a lot from her mother, there were some traits, subtle traits, in which Conrad thought he saw himself. She was easily frightened, for instance, and the slightest criticism moved her to tears. Conrad had been like that as a little boy, and he hoped she would not be forced to harden herself as much, to bury her fears as deeply, to learn to take charge as completely, as he had. (But then why *should* she? *Her* mother wasn't an alcoholic. *Her* father wasn't a craven codependent. There was absolutely no reason she shouldn't be the happiest, most well-adjusted . . .

But be that as it may.)

Also, no matter how tender and affectionate Jessie could be toward her outcast classmates, she was nonetheless grimly determined to be accepted by the more popular girls. They had rejected her—some of them—because of her friendships with girls like Adrienne. But Jessica had continued to invite them over for playdates and parties, hoping to bring them around. In this, Conrad saw a touch of his own brand of ambition: quiet, unspoken, and relentless.

"Wa-un . . . two—oo, three—ee . . ." She was counting her piece carefully along the board again. Her head was bent toward it, her braid falling forward over her shoulder. Her blue eyes were intent on the task.

Conrad smiled. He did not feel impatient anymore. She was working so hard at it. To count, just to count to five, took all her concentration. She was so small, he thought, and the world was so difficult to master.

He reached out and touched her nose gently with his finger.

"Honk," he said.

"Dad-dy! Now I lost count."

"Know what?"

"Yes." She cast her eyes heavenward. "You love me. Right?"

Conrad laughed. "Right. How'd you get so smart?"

"You always say that."

"Sorry. I'll never say it again."

"Daddy. You have to say it. You're my daddy."

"Oh, yeah, I forgot."

The beleaguered child sighed wearily. "Well, I guess I'll just have to count all over again. Where was I?"

He showed her. She began the count again. Her piece was on the last row of the game but one.

"Oh, nooo," she cried.

Conrad looked down. Jessica's piece had landed on a chute. Not just any chute. The longest chute in the game. Her piece slid all the way down to the third row.

Conrad's smile faded. The game, he thought, would never end.

In fact, it was done by eight-thirty. Conrad's leg felt better by then and he'd swung his giggling daughter to the nursery by both hands. He tucked her into her loft bed. He kissed her forehead and pronounced the Ritual Good-night—"Hit the sheet, feet; hit the bed, head; start to nod, bod; start to snooze, youse." Then Agatha came in to sing the Good-night Song, and Conrad was relieved of duty.

He returned to the living room. It was a long room, which Agatha had decorated in three useful sections. The first third, by the door, was a small work station, a desk for Aggie during the day and for Conrad at night. The middle of the room was a play area—the red carpet—with a folding dinner table pushed to the side. The far end, by the glass doors to the balcony, was the sitting area. Two huge brown armchairs and one long brown sofa around a circular, white marble coffee table on a Persian rug.

Conrad collected his soda water and went to the sitting area now. He sat on one of the chairs, his body shifted so he could look out through the glass doors. He saw, in the night, the lighted windows of the building across the courtyard. A woman in her kitchen. A man in an undershirt, watching TV, drinking beer. An old silver-haired woman in a smock, working with clay at a table.

There was a dark window, too, directly across from him. That was where the old lady had been murdered a few weeks ago. Conrad gazed at this one absently. Absently, he listened to Aggie sing:

"Hush, little baby, don't say a word, mama's gonna buy you a mockingbird . . ."

Jessie was probably getting a little old for that one, he thought. But it was part of the Bedtime Ritual; hard to let go of. Conrad himself found it comforting: the sound of Aggie's voice, sweet and shimmering like a little stream.

He thought again about Jessica counting and he smiled to himself. He felt better now; his leg, his head. He just felt better. Nothing like a little game of Chutes and Ladders to burn off the tensions of the day.

He did not hear Agatha stop singing. He was a little startled to see her reflected in the window, coming up behind him. She put her hands on his shoulders. He put his hand on her hand.

"Is she out?" he said.

"Like a light. I took her and Lauren over to the Waterside playground after school. She's exhausted. I don't know how she stayed awake till you got here."

He smiled again. Brought her hand to his mouth and kissed it.

Aggie sat on the back of the chair. Kissed the top of his head. Her auburn hair tumbled forward and he felt it brush his bald flesh up there. He could smell her, her flowery toilet water. He closed his eyes and breathed it in.

"So what's up, Doc?" she asked him softly.

"Hm?"

"You're a depressed kind of a guy. I can tell. What's the matter?"

"No, no, no." He tilted his head back so he could look up into the round, cheerful face. "It's just Thursdays. I schedule too many hard cases on Thursdays. I'm starting to develop a case of the Thursday blues."

"Ah. I see. And how are they different from the Wednesday blues you had yesterday?"

"Uh . . . Wednesday blues are a sort of lavender with patches of aquamarine. Thursday I go for robin's-egg with great swaths of azure."

Agatha laughed above him, her eyes bright. "Oh, Doctor, Doctor? Oh, Mr. M.D.? You are bullshitting your faithful wife and Indian companion."

He looked away from her, out into the dimly lit room. "No, really," he said. "It's only Thursdays."

Agatha brushed at his last strands of hair. "Nathan. Every day has been Thursday around here lately."

"Isn't that what I promised you when we got married? Every day would be Thursday?"

"You promised me every day would be a holiday."

"Uh-oh."

"Nathan." She took his earlobe between her thumb and forefinger. "I hate when you do this thing."

"What thing?"

"This Psychiatrist-I-Am-a-Camera-with-No-Problems thing. This I-Take-Care-of-Everyone-But-No-One-Has-to-Take-Care-of-Me thing. I hate it. And if you don't tell me what's bothering you right away, I am going to squeeze your ear until the top of your head blows off."

"Ah, these cruel little love games, how they make my heart flutter. Ow!"

"Tell. What's bothering you, Doc?"

"Well, my ear hurts for one thing."

"It's hard to be a shrink when you're deaf. Tell."

"All right. All right." Conrad pried her hand from his earlobe. With a small groan, he stood up and went to the glass doors. In reflection on the glass, he saw Agatha slide off the chair's back into its seat. Her baggy black sweater rode up above her navel. She pulled it straight again and watched him. He fixed his eyes on a window across the court: the old woman working with clay.

"I can't help them." He heard himself speak suddenly, more harshly than he'd meant to. "I can't help them. All right? Can we eat now?"

"Your patients? You can't help your patients?"

He turned to her. "You know, I hate this kind of conversation, Aggie, it really doesn't—"

"I know, I know," said Agatha, holding up her hand. "Just shut up and talk."

He rolled his eyes. Turned away, faced the window again. He shrugged. "Yeah, my patients. I'm just . . . I can't help them. No one can, not this kind of patient. Somehow I seem to have become an expert on trauma neurosis. I never seem to get the people who come in and say, 'Oh, Doctor, my life is wonderful, why do I feel so bad?' You know? They talk for five years and then shake your hand with tears in their eyes and say, 'Oh, thank you, thank you, Doctor, you changed my life.' No one ever refers them to me. I get—like—Job. If Job were alive, I would be Job's psychiatrist."

Agatha smiled, tilted her head. "Well, if I were a shrink, you know, I'd say that—if you have a trauma neurosis practice, that must be what you want somehow."

He nodded at the window. "Yeah. Yeah, it is what I want. It was what I wanted anyway. I mean, I'm good at it. People come to me and their kids are dead and their neck is broken and their cattle have boils or whatever. And they talk to me and they learn to live again."

"Sounds good to me, Doc."

"Ach." He felt stupid even as he went on. "What's the point of it? You know? Their kids are still dead. Their cattle still have boils."

He was grateful that Aggie didn't laugh at him. He watched in the window as she pushed herself out of her chair and came to him. She put her arms around his waist, rested her head against his back.

"Did I remember to tell you that you can't save the world?" she said. "Your mother's dead and you can't save her and you can't save the world."

"Please," he said, but not unkindly. "I went through ten years of analysis. I understand everything." He turned around in her arms. He held her, laid his cheek against her hair. "I just don't understand anything," he said.

She raised her face to him, kissed him lightly. "It sounds like you miss the old days of staring into the sun."

He made a face at her. No, he did not miss those days, not at all. They had been in college then, both of them, Nathan at Berkeley, Aggie at San Francisco State. Living together in the seedy one-bedroom right over Telegraph Avenue. Nathan had grown his hair down past his shoulders and wore a long, sandy beard that made him look like a cross between Charles Manson and Jesus. Sometimes he even sported tie-dyed T-shirts, and his jeans were always faded nearly white. He was supposed to be premed, but he spent much of his time studying Eastern religions; he was pre-Zen, Aggie used to say. On the warmer afternoons, he liked to go up to Seminary Hill on the north side of campus. He would sit in the half-lotus position on the rocks overlooking San Francisco Bay. He would watch as the red ball of the sun turned the sparkling water orange and the drifting clouds pink. And he would meditate, counting his breaths, breathing slowly, forcing the air out with his abdomen, waiting for his mind to click into its low, dark state of receptivity. No opinions, no interpretations. Let the connections make themselves. *The way of the Tao is easy. Simply give up all your opinions.*

He had thought he was raising himself to new levels of consciousness. He had not realized until the day his mother died, until the day he'd nearly made himself blind, that he was also, to put it in technical terms, losing his marbles.

"At least I thought I knew something then," he said. He put his hand on the side of Aggie's face. He looked down into her blue eyes. "These people—my patients. Their dead children; their crippling injuries. I mean, it's just . . . so *bad*, Aggie. It's like . . . just this bad, bad thing with nothing good about it. And you can talk God or enlightenment or catharsis or even politics all you want, and the real truth of it is, it sucks and you can't explain it, you can't mitigate it or talk your way out of it. Children die and people get hurt and it just sucks. And when they look at me and say, 'Oh, thank you, Doctor, now I can live with it!' I feel guilty. I feel like I've put one over on them. I mean, how *can* they live with it? How can anything ever mean anything to them again? How can they face it, for Christ's sake?"

Looking up at him, Aggie smiled. "How can *they?*" she said softly.

Conrad closed his eyes and let out a sigh. "How can anyone?" he said. And then he said, "How can I?"

They were both silent a moment. Then Agatha lifted her face to his again, kissed him gently, moving her hand to the back of his neck.

"That's a very important question," she told him. "Let's fuck."

Conrad locked the front door for the night: the dead bolt, the intergrip, and the chain. Then he waited for Aggie in the bedroom, by the windows.

The bedroom was not as long as the living room. Aggie had only been able to divide it in half. The first half, near the door, had her stool and drafting table in it. Drawings, paintings, and designs were spread over the face of the table or stacked on the floor or clipped to the wall nearby. The cover mock-up for *Sam's Kite*; the watercolor illustrations for *A Day With Santa*; pencil sketches for *Count the Bunnies*; others only just begun.

In the other half of the room was the bed, a TV, a TV chair. And the wall of windows. Conrad stood by those windows, looking out. He didn't notice anymore what was happening in the building across the court. He was thinking of his own words, replaying them in his head.

How can they live with something so bad, how can they face it? How can anything ever mean anything to them again?

Christ, he sounded just like a fucking forty-year-old, like he was having a midlife crisis. The next thing he knew they'd find him in some New Jersey motel, dancing with a sixteen-year-old and wearing a lampshade on his head. Why did she have to start him talking like this in the first place? There was nothing he hated worse than hearing himself complain about . . .

Something caught his eye. A light in one of the windows across the court. In one of those darkened windows just opposite him. It was not an electric light; more like a burst of flame, a match flaring. Just for a second. An orange flash. And then gone quickly, as if someone had put his hand in front of it or blown it out.

The bathroom door opened behind him. Conrad glanced over his shoulder. Aggie had come out wrapped in his white terry-cloth bathrobe. It was too big for her and came up around her ears like a high collar. Her blue eyes blinked out from it gaily.

"Sweetheart?" he said. "Isn't that the apartment where that old lady got killed?"

"Which?" Aggie, who loved gossip of all kinds, was immediately attentive. She approached him as he gestured toward the dark window. "Yeah, that's it. Lucia Sinclair's place. Or 'Park Avenue House of Death,' as we faithful readers of the *Post* call it. Why?"

"Has anyone moved in there?"

"Not that I've heard. And I would've heard."

"Huh," Conrad said. "I thought I just saw someone light a match in the window."

Aggie shook her head with grave authority. "The murder didn't even happen three weeks ago. I can't believe the police would let anyone rent it yet." She wrinkled her nose. "I can't believe anyone would *want* to rent it yet, after what they did to that poor woman. Remember the papers said they kept her alive while they . . . ?"

Conrad laughed and turned to her, holding up his hand. "I'm sorry I asked." He touched his right temple. "My eye was bothering me today. It was probably just a scintillation."

37

"Okay," Agatha said. "If you don't want to hear the local news . . ." With a single graceful motion, she shrugged off the bathrobe. It slipped down to her feet. Conrad's eyes ran slowly over her body. "Just forget the whole thing," she said softly. "And close those curtains." She stepped out of the tangle of terry cloth around her ankles. She came toward him. She whispered, "You never know who might be watching."

The Woman in the Chair

The Impellitteri Municipal Psychiatric Facility was set a few blocks off
Queens Boulevard, not far from the county jail. Lit by small spotlights, it
seemed an enormous gray cube floating in the dark. The rain ran down the
lights, and shadows of the rain played over the building's stone surface. To
Conrad, as he drove into the parking lot, the building seemed to drift and
waver under the downpour.

He had told Jerry Sachs he would be there at seven-thirty that Friday
evening. It was seven-thirty on the dot as he parked his Corsica—a jaunty
silver-blue sedan—in one of the RESERVED-MD spaces by the front door.
When he shut the engine off, the rain sounded loud and hard on the
rooftop.

He wished he were home. He wished he were playing Chutes and
Ladders.

He took his briefcase off the floor, brought it to his lap, and snapped it
open. He lifted out his little Sony cassette recorder. Pressing the red
button, he held the recorder up with the built-in microphone near his
mouth.

"Friday, October twelfth," he said. "First session with Elizabeth
Burrows."

He rewound it, played it back. His own voice came up to him clearly:
". . . session with Elizabeth Burrows." He slipped the recorder into his

inside jacket pocket. He glanced out the window, through the streaking rain, at the hospital's vaporous facade.

She killed a man, Nathan. She cut his throat. Christ Almighty, she cut the poor bastard to pieces.

Conrad let out a long breath. "Uh boy," he said aloud.

He took his briefcase by the handle, pushed the door open, and ran through the rain to the hospital steps.

"Well, I'm afraid she's not one of your typical Upper West Side matrons," Sachs said. "She's been in institutions off and on since she was ten years old. And there have been several violent episodes both in and out. Her records from the Manhattan Children's Center show she once slashed another child's face open with a kitchen knife. And the DA told me the police have arrested her twice before on assault and battery charges. You'll be getting your sweet little fingers dirty on this one, Nate."

Sachs tilted back in his chair and grinned a wide pink grin. He was a big man, half a foot taller than Conrad at least. His face was broad and fat. His shoulders stretched the limits of his white shirt, his belly stretched it taut above the belt line. When he moved, he breathed hard and he was damp with sweat all over. There were dark sweatstains under the arms, and his head—large, bald, and pink—gleamed with it. His thick black glasses were perched up above his eyebrows. Conrad kept waiting for them to slip through the sweat down onto his nose.

Sachs laughed, a loud, mirthless laugh. "One time," he said, "she beat the living shit out of a Dutch sailor. Swear it to God. She was wandering around Times Square apparently and the poor bastard goosed her." He laughed again, his voice cracking. "She broke both his arms and stomped one of his testicles to pudding. She was sixteen years old at the time. And she's just a little thing, too, wait'll you see her. It took three cops to pull her off the guy. And when she came to, she seemed surprised. She said it wasn't her who did it. It was her friend, her secret friend."

Conrad leaned forward. His chair's wooden top rail had been pressing into his back. "Her friend?" he said. "You mean, like, another personality?"

"Nah, more like a voice, command-auditory, telling her to do things, though it seems to have some kind of visual component too. Whatever it is, it sure agitates the hell out of her. She goes wild; she has fantastic strength. Definitely capable of real nasty stuff, savage violence. Which is apparently what happened with this other poor bastard, this token clerk she cut to ribbons. She said her 'secret friend' was responsible for that one too." He

40

chuckled, his big head bouncing up and down. "I tell you, Nate, you're gonna wish you were back on Park Avenue so bad . . ."

Conrad smiled. "I already do, Jerry, believe me." He shifted in his seat—the chair really was killing him. The rest of Sachs's office looked comfortable enough. A vast space with brown linoleum floors and bright orange walls. There was a brown sofa along the wall to Conrad's left. A half-size refrigerator in one corner, a graceful coatrack with Conrad's trench coat dripping in the other. And of course, behind the vast cluttered expanse of Sachs's desk, in front of a broad window overlooking the parking lot, there was Sachs's own enormous leather armchair. Its back was so high the headcushion curled up over the director's gleaming head like a vulture. That looked plenty comfortable.

But the chair in front of the desk—Conrad's chair—was wood. Small, round backed, hard. There was a butt-shaped depression in the seat of it. Maybe it was supposed to make the unyielding wood more comfortable. All Conrad knew was that it felt as if he were sitting on an anthill. There was no pleasant spot on it anywhere.

"This token clerk," he grunted through his pain. "This is the current case."

"Yeah. Same kind of situation as the sailor. This guy, this . . ." Sachs leaned in over his desk, floated a big hand over some papers there. "Robert Rostoff. He apparently got Elizabeth to take him up to her apartment. But when he made a pass at her: whammo." Sachs reached up and pulled three times on his nose to clear it. "She really cut him up but good. Took his eye out, cut his dick off. Bad news for Bob all around."

Conrad's butt searched for some softness in his chair's butt-shaped depression. He did not think he was going to be able to take a month of this.

"And she wasn't on drugs?" he asked.

"Not according to the reports."

"Was she on anything, any medication?"

Sachs waved at his papers again. "Haldol, yeah. But only ten milligrams, five BID. She'd been taking it on an outpatient basis for two years. I've got it tripled now."

Conrad nodded.

"The thing of it is, she really did seem to be in remission," Sachs said. "She was living independently, seeing her shrink, working a menial job at some counterculture day-care center or some shit like that down in the Village. Everything was tickety-boo, know what I mean? Then suddenly—

Bobby goes bye-bye. And here she is." Sachs coughed—and finally the glasses did slide down his forehead. They landed on his nose with a little splash of sweat. "She was apparently still taking her meds at the time too."

"She just broke through? Had she been having any reactions? Dystonias? Convulsions? Anything?"

Sachs shook his head. "No. Though I didn't get a chance to ask her much before she went wild on me."

"And now she's catatonic. Has she eaten? Slept? Got up to go to the bathroom?"

"We can feed her orally. She has fallen asleep. She hasn't gone to the bathroom or defecated. She's urinated on her chair. We cleaned her up though—don't wanna make it too hard on you." He tried to give another of his hearty chuckles, but it died somewhere in his throat. He seemed, Conrad thought, to be running out of steam.

"You've still got her medicated," Conrad said.

"Yeah, by injection." Sachs spread his hands, dropped them onto his thighs with a loud slap. His smile was still wide but it looked strained now. A line of sweat trickled down his pink cheek into his graying collar. "The thing is, though: she won't talk. I mean, this was a willing patient, Nate. She'd had a good experience with her last doctor, the state guy who got her out of Manhattan Psych, got her stabilized. She was user friendly, man. Ready to talk. She *wanted* to talk. Now, suddenly, not a word." He wiped the sweat from his lips with his palm. "So, uh, what do you think, Nate?"

For a long moment, Conrad could only look at the man. The Humpty-Dumpty head, the shiny pate. The dark eyes blinking somewhat desperately behind the thick glasses. Conrad guessed it wasn't pleasant to have the Queens borough president breathing down your neck. To have thirty days to make a high-profile case look good when your subject had gone mute on you.

Conrad reached down and took hold of the briefcase on the floor beside him. "Let's go have a look at her," he said finally.

Anything to get the hell out of that chair.

An elevator took them to the fourth floor: the Women's Forensic Ward. A female correction officer was there, sitting at the gunmetal desk outside the ward's double doors. The obese black woman lifted fierce dark eyes to the ID card clipped to Sachs's lapel. She nodded and Sachs stepped forward to unlock the doors with a large master key.

Conrad followed Sachs into the ward.

There was a long hallway before them, cavernous and dim. Fluorescents flickered purple in the high ceiling or hung gray and dead. As the two doctors walked together, the shadows obscured the far walls. The corridor seemed to vanish in a sickly dusk.

It was dinnertime now. Passing the cafeteria, Conrad saw the women at their meal. About ten black women sat hunkered over their plastic trays. Shapeless women in the shapeless, shabby street clothes the city issued them. They were shoveling bread and potatoes into their lax mouths, letting the crumbs dribble down their chins.

Out here, in the hall, it was quiet. Only aides passed back and forth and they passed silently. Black women, gray figures, they emerged one by one from the shadows ahead. They nodded at Sachs without speaking, without smiling. They passed into the shadows behind as Conrad glanced over his shoulder to watch them go.

Sachs stopped before a door marked 3: a thick wooden door, its vertical strip of window laced with wire. Sachs glanced at Conrad; chuckled; shook his head. Conrad realized it was supposed to be ingratiating.

Sachs slipped his master key into the lock. The door swung in and Sachs stepped through. When Conrad followed, the larger man was standing in the center of the room.

It was a small room, a cell really. Dim, with a single light burning in the ceiling above. A metal bed was pushed against the wall to Conrad's left. A small water basin stood on a plastic table against the wall opposite. There was a nook in the far corner—for a toilet, Conrad guessed. To the left of that, in the far wall, there was a large double-hung window with heavy grating over the glass.

In a chair in front of the window, there sat a young woman.

Conrad stopped when he saw her. His lips parted. My God, he thought.

Sachs lifted a hand toward her, like a butler making a formal introduction.

"This is Elizabeth Burrows," he said gravely.

Nathan stood without speaking.

My God, he thought. Look at her.

Don't You Want to
Touch Me?

She had a face from a painting, an angel's face. Her strawberry-blond hair hung down, straight and silken, long past her shoulders. It framed her high cheeks and her high brow, both of them alabaster and luminous. Her large, crystalline, green eyes stared out at nothing.

She was sitting very still in a wooden chair. She sat upright, her head erect. Her eyes were fixed directly before her. She wore wrinkled brown corduroy pants and a man's short-sleeved shirt. But even in the city-issue clothing, her figure seemed slender and graceful: she hadn't had time to get fat on the starchy hospital food. Her bare arms were very white. Her white hands lay folded in her lap.

Slowly, Conrad let out his breath. Man oh man, he thought. He blinked and straightened. He made himself speak.

"Hello, Elizabeth," he said, "it's nice to meet you."

She said nothing. She didn't move. She stared straight ahead. Conrad narrowed his eyes as he looked at her.

Three years before, he had been asked to participate in a study at Columbia Presbyterian. They were testing a new approach to withdrawal reactions that involved a style of therapy he and another doctor, Mark Bernstein, had pioneered. The idea was to rely less on medication and more on sparking some form of interaction with a therapist. Using a combination of drugs and active, even radical, engagement techniques, Conrad was rapidly able to lure several patients into a new relationship with reality. In one or two cases, he could even report important remissions.

In the course of the study, Conrad had worked closely with over a dozen withdrawn or catatonic patients. He had seen a forty-two-year-old man stay locked in the fetal position for days and days on end. He had seen a teenage girl posed perfectly still with her arms out and one leg raised, like a ballerina about to be lifted into the air. He had seen patients who shuddered like a plucked string and patients who stared and drooled without moving. There had been one woman, Jane, a childhood rape victim, who wandered around saying "No" very firmly over and over again at intervals of exactly three seconds.

But Conrad had never seen anyone like Elizabeth Burrows.

It wasn't just her beauty. It was her composure, her seeming serenity. Her hands rested in her lap so peacefully, her bare arms flexible and relaxed. Her gaze was distant but her eyes went down deep. Conrad had the momentary sense that he could see her in there, still alert, still aware.

He turned to Sachs, forced a smile. "Why don't you leave Elizabeth and me alone together so we can get to know each other," he said.

Sachs hesitated a second. He had a lot riding on this, Conrad could see it. But he had no choice. He forced a thin smile of his own.

"Just call if you need an aide or . . ."

He placed his key in Conrad's hand and went out, closing the door behind him.

Conrad turned back to Elizabeth, still smiling. "I'm going to turn on a tape recorder," he said. He lifted the machine out of his pocket. He pressed the button and set it on the table next to the water basin. Then, with two steps, he crossed the room. He lay his briefcase on the bed and opened it. He didn't look at Elizabeth as he rummaged through it, but he thought he felt her eyes shift toward him. He thought—he sensed—that she was looking at him.

He removed a penlight from the case. When he faced her again, she was sitting still, staring straight ahead.

Conrad stepped up to her. "Excuse me," he said. He leaned forward and gently, quickly, retracted her eyelid with his thumb. He beamed the flash into her eyes, first the right, then the left. The pupils contracted as the light hit. He felt the normal blink reactions under his fingers.

He slipped the flash into his pocket and took hold of her right wrist. The white skin felt warm. The pulse beneath his thumb was steady and even. He lifted her arm to the height of her shoulder. He watched her face. He let the wrist go.

The girl's hand dropped a little, then hung in the air uncertainly. Her pale lips tightened. Then her hand floated slowly back to her lap. She clasped it with her other. She sat quietly, staring.

At the other end of the bed, there was another wooden chair. Conrad got it now and set it down in front of her. He turned its back toward her and straddled it. He leaned on the back, smiling at her.

"Actually, it was supposed to stay in the air," he said. "Your arm, I mean. True catatonics generally have what we call waxy flexibility in their limbs. They'll stay in whatever position you pose them."

It was a risk, he knew. He might be wrong. Even if he was right, the challenge might spur a violent reaction. She was a small, almost frail, girl, as Sachs said. But if her "secret friend" came to her, Conrad had no doubt that she could put him in the hospital, if not the morgue.

At first, though, she didn't react at all. The words hung between them in the silence. He sat watching her. She sat still.

Then, slowly, Elizabeth turned her head to him. Conrad heard his heart beating in his ears as her deep green eyes slowly came into focus. The sweet features framed by the hanging hair began to seem animated. A tint of rose seemed to come into the white skin. She looked for all the world, Conrad thought, like a department store mannequin coming to life.

She raised her hand to her throat, unbuttoned her shirt, and bared her breasts to him.

"You can touch me," she whispered, "if you'll leave me alone."

"Uh . . . ," Conrad said. It was all he said. In spite of himself, his eyes flicked down over her. Her skin was smooth and white all over. Her breasts were small but gracefully shaped, and the sudden pink tips of them would have made him breathless, if he'd allowed it.

But he raised his eyes to her face. "Please button your shirt, Elizabeth," he said.

Her lips parted. Her own eyes narrowed. "Don't . . . don't you *want* to touch me?"

Oh, boy, Conrad thought, don't ask. "I want to help you," he said evenly. "And I don't think that's the best way to go about it. Please button your shirt."

Still looking confused, Elizabeth pulled the two halves of the shirt together. Conrad glanced away, afraid to let his eyes rest on her.

The poor bastard propositioned her, she just beat the living shit out of him. He could hear Sachs and his horsey laugh. *And Robert Rostoff, he made a pass at her: whammo. She cut him up but good.*

And what did you do to her, Jerry? Conrad thought. What did you do that made her go wild on you?

Don't you want to touch me?

When he looked at her again, he was relieved to see she had buttoned the shirt. She had returned her hands to her lap. She had fixed him with a wary, but also curious, gaze.

Conrad leaned forward, spoke carefully. "Elizabeth . . . you're accused of murder. Do you understand that?"

She did not answer right away. She gave a small, negative shake of her head. "I don't . . . I don't want to talk to you," she said. There was a faintly automatic, singsong quality to her voice. It made her seem distant, as if she were commenting on events that didn't concern her. "I don't want to talk to you. You might be one of them."

Conrad nodded, said nothing.

The girl reared back haughtily. "I mean, they *all* pretend they're nice at first. Sometimes they' fool me. But I know what they really want. *I* know."

She looked at him from her high perch. She smiled, superior with her secret.

"All right," said Conrad, "what do they want?"

She leaned toward him. "They want to take my mother out."

"Your mother," Conrad said with an encouraging nod.

"Yes. That's what Robert Rostoff told me."

"Robert Rostoff. The man who was killed."

"Yes. He told me, he warned me. That's what they were going to do."

"And it made you angry."

Elizabeth began to nod, but stopped. "Oh, no," she said carefully. "Not me. *I* wasn't angry. It was the Secret Friend. He got very mad. He did a bad thing. Very bad. That's why I'm here. But it wasn't me. It was the Secret Friend."

Conrad waited a moment to see if she would say more, but she didn't. She gazed past him, chewing her lip. She seemed to be trying to remember something.

47

Conrad prompted her. "The Secret Friend didn't want them to take out your mother."

"Yes. That's right. Yes."

"Why not, Elizabeth?"

"What?" She blinked and shifted her gaze back to him. "Well . . . because there would be worms coming out of her eyes by now," she told him simply. "Worms and . . . and bony fingers coming out from her flesh." She made a face, shuddered. "And her flesh would be all like rags with the bones coming out of it, and there would be her empty eyes with the worms in them . . ."

Conrad felt a small chill on the back of his neck. He actually glanced over his shoulder to make sure no one was there, that no one was sneaking up behind him. (No one with worms, anyway, coming out of her eyes.) There was only the dimly lit little cell. The wooden door with the thin vertical window. The washbasin, the shadow of it stretched on the plastic table. The taut and empty bed.

He cleared his throat as he looked back at her. "Your mother is dead, you mean," he said.

"Yes. Oh, yes. And if they took her out, you know, her soul might fly away. And then there might be nothing left of her anywhere." She shook her head sadly. Looked at him earnestly. "Everyone has a soul, you know. Everyone. Even me. I can feel mine sometimes. I wouldn't want it to fly away. I can feel it right there inside of me."

Elizabeth lifted her hands from her lap. She lifted them to her shoulders, crossing her arms over her breasts. For a moment, Conrad was afraid she would undress herself again. But instead, she hugged herself tightly. She closed her eyes. She lifted her face to the light as if it were the sun. Rocked herself gently back and forth beneath it.

"I can feel it right now. I can feel my soul," she murmured. "It's still in here. I'm still in here."

Conrad sat without moving. He watched her. He couldn't take his eyes off her. Moment after moment, she rocked herself under the lamplight, hugging herself with her crossed arms. And then, as Conrad stared, the expression on her face began to change. Her mouth was tugged down, her chin wrinkled. Her lips began to quiver as if she were on the brink of tears. . . .

With a sudden gasp, she opened her eyes and looked at him. Conrad felt it like a blow. He started back a little in his chair. Those eyes, those crystal green pools, had cleared to their very bottoms. He saw her agony in them. Naked and bright: the hard fire of pain at the center of her.

"Oh, God," she barely managed to whisper. "I'm still in here." One of her hands reached for him, took hold of his. He felt the heat, the desperate pressure of her fingers on his palm. "Oh, God, oh, God," she cried to him softly. "Please. Please, Doctor. I'm still in here."

The Cemetery

In the evening, Conrad went to the cemetery. It was a small and shabby place. Its old monuments and Celtic crosses stood skewed and chipped in the purple twilight. A chilly mist, rank with the city, wove its tendrils between the graves.

The spot he wanted was in the back, near the slanting iron fence. It was marked by a statue of a mourning woman. The cowled figure bowed over the gravesite, one hand gesturing down to it. Conrad went toward her, walking through the mist, among the stones.

As Conrad came near, he saw that the grave beneath the statue had not been filled in. He had expected that. Still, as he came to the edge, he felt a cold spot in his stomach. He looked down into the pit and saw the coffin lying at the bottom. It was a heavy gray box with a cross carved into the top of it. He raised his eyes and saw for the first time something odd about the statue above him. The mourning woman was smiling. She was staring down at him with a mad, bright-eyed smile. Seeing it, the chill of fear in Conrad's stomach grew. His limbs felt weak and rubbery.

And then a sound came from the coffin below him.

Conrad wanted to run. He couldn't. He didn't want to look. He had to. He lowered his eyes to the open grave. The noise came again: a distant, inquiring murmur. Conrad knew the coffin was about to open—he had seen it happen in the movies a dozen times. But he still couldn't run, couldn't even turn away. He stood helpless as the lid slowly, steadily lifted. He began to moan with fear. He began to tremble.

The coffin opened and he saw her. He cried out wordlessly. She reached for him with her arms: two shafts of rotted flesh. She smiled at him as her eyes cracked open like eggs and the spiders came crawling out of them.

"I'm still in here, Nathan," she whispered to him. "Don't you want to touch me?"

With a cry, Conrad sat up in bed. His heart was hammering in his chest. He was gasping for air. Even now, it took a moment before he realized it had been a dream. The outline of the TV set came into focus in the dark. The drift of the curtains, the smell of the October rain. He saw his wife beneath the covers and laid his hand on the rise of her hip.

"Shee-yet," he said softly. He lay back against his pillow, feeling the sweat there. "Shee-yet."

The dream stayed with him through the morning. The dream—and the girl. It was Saturday; his turn to take Jessica to her violin group. All the while he was getting her ready, talking and joking with her on the bus to Eleventh Street, listening to her play with the other children, he was thinking about the dream, about Elizabeth.

Conrad liked going to the group. He liked the old music school. He liked to walk through the halls and hear the sounds drifting out of the classrooms. The halting pianos, the screechy violins. He liked to glance in the dance room and see the girls in their leotards, practicing leg lifts at the barre. Children learning music, dance: it made him feel warm and melancholy.

He had never learned to play an instrument himself. He could remember his mother saying to him once when he was in his teens: "Why *don't* you learn to play an instrument, Nathan?" He could remember her sitting in the armchair in the family room at the back of the house. The window was behind her. The cherry tree just outside it cushioned her on a background of pink and white blooms. She was sipping at a glass of grapefruit juice—grapefruit juice secretly laced with vodka—and she pouted at him. And she said, "Why *don't* you learn to play an instrument?" It was the usual tone of voice she used for such advice. That same vaguely despairing tone in which she would say, "Why don't you take up a sport, Nathan?" or "Why don't you join an after-school club?" That faint, distant, unhelpful little voice.

And then his father, seated on the sofa, glanced up from his newspaper.

51

Chimed in: "I always felt that if you can't do something well, there's no sense in taking the thing up at all." Yes, and that was his usual advisory tone; his deep, wise-man's voice. That was the voice in which he would sometimes tell his wife, "Well, of course I want you to give up drinking, dear. I just don't think you ought to try it all at once, that's all. A little at a time, that's the secret." A man full of good advice was dear old Dad.

But the truth was, it wouldn't have mattered what they said, or how they said it. It wouldn't have changed a damned thing if his mother had bought him a Stradivarius and laid the instrument in his hands with her blessing, or if his father had put an arm around his shoulders and cried, 'Go forth, my son, to strive and achieve.' Nathan would still not have learned to play an instrument; he still wouldn't have taken up a sport or joined an after-school club. He wouldn't have done any of those things because they would've kept him away from home more. They would have left his mom alone more. Alone with her not-so-secret bottles of vodka and gin. Wasn't that why she was making her faint little suggestions in the first place? To get rid of him? He thought so at the time in any case.

So—in any case—he enjoyed being here at the school now with his daughter. It made him glad for her—and a little envious of her too in a proud, pleasant way. He would sit cross-legged on the wooden floor of the upstairs dance room, a broad space with mirrors along the wall. The children would gather with their violins in a circle around the smiling young woman who taught them. They would saw their ways through "Twinkle Twinkle, Little Star," and "Go Tell Aunt Rhody," and "Song of the Wind." And Conrad would watch his daughter and nod with approval. He was careful to show that approval on his face because she sometimes glanced up at him as she played. She would steal a look at him, then force down a secret smile when she saw him nodding.

But today his mind wandered. It kept going back to the dream, to the girl. He could still remember the clammy fear that had gone through him as he stood at the graveside. He remembered it—and then thought of the little chill he had felt when Elizabeth Burrows first described her mother.

There would be her empty eyes with the worms in them.

That tingle of irrational doubt. The frisson of meeting up with madness.

He nodded and smiled quickly as Jessica snuck a peek at him. The group was playing "Oh, Come, Little Children." It was one of the tougher beginner's pieces. It had a complicated double upbow stroke at points. Last week, Jessie had been one of those who had to sit down while the more advanced students played it. But she'd been practicing all week long. Now, while a few kids still sat, she stood and played with the others. Conrad slipped her a wink when she glanced at him. She fought back her smile and returned her attention to the violin.

Conrad kept watching her, but with distant eyes. He was thinking again about Elizabeth.

They want to take my mother out. It made the Secret Friend angry. He did a bad thing.

There was always, in Conrad's experience, that little chill, that shudder, when you first entered a mad person's world. It was like edging forward into alien territory—and then suddenly stepping into quicksand. . . .

Oh, there would be worms coming out of her eyes by now. And bony fingers coming out from her flesh. . . .

You found yourself sinking into a subterranean jungle, a place of threatening shapes and shadows, of chthonic vampires reaching for you out of the morass. . . .

And her flesh would be all like rags with the bones coming out of it, and there would be her empty eyes with the worms in them. . . .

And yet, that world, that jungle—it was all made of the same materials as your world was. It was just as internal. The logic of it was just as complete. The true shaping hand was just as authoritative and unreliable and unknown. So it made you shudder because it made you remember that you also lived in an ignorance that might be madness. . . .

The Secret Friend did a bad thing. That's why I'm here.

The song came to an end. Conrad recalled himself just in time to give Jessica a thumbs-up. She was bouncing on her toes and grinning, giddy with her achievement.

"Tell me more," he said to her. "Tell me more about this secret friend."

He had not planned to see Elizabeth again until Wednesday. But Mr. Blum, his four-thirty session, had come up with another of the many diseases that helped him explain to himself why his wife had betrayed and deserted him. He'd called in the morning to cancel. Conrad, on an impulse, immediately phoned Mrs. Halliway, his five-thirty. He worked her in to a seven P.M. Tuesday slot and so had a chunk of evening free. Almost to his surprise, he found himself driving out to the Impellitteri facility.

He found Elizabeth just as she had been on Friday. Wearing the same clothes, sitting in her chair by the window, hands in her lap, eyes on the distance. Sachs had told Conrad that she hadn't spoken again since his session with her. But she had been eating by herself and had gotten up to go to the toilet, though she always returned immediately to her chair. Sachs had not wanted to risk upsetting her again. He'd ordered the aides to keep watch on her but otherwise to leave her alone unless she asked for something. Conrad found this an act of extraordinary sensitivity and intelligence for Sachs. The jerk was obviously eager as hell to have this thing work out.

As for Conrad, though, he wasn't expecting much. He was pleased the patient had dropped her silence with him, but he figured he was in for weeks of paranoid sparring, delusional rambling. He doubted he'd ever get much past that with her, in fact.

Still, when he came into her room, she did steal a glance at him. And while she didn't exactly smile, Conrad thought he saw some small flickering of pleasure in her eyes.

He took his cassette recorder out of his pocket, pressed the red button, and set it on the table. Then he placed his chair in front of her and straddled it as he had before. He smiled. "How are you today, Elizabeth?"

She looked at him again, then looked quickly away. She didn't answer.

"Your hair looks nice," he said. He noticed she had brushed it. The straight fall of strawberry-blond was smooth and shining.

Again, he detected pleasure at the compliment. But she would not speak.

After a few seconds, he said, "You're not talking to me, is that it?"

This time, her glance at him was longer. It was still wary, but now, Conrad thought, there was something playful in it.

"You might be one of them." The girl spoke softly, almost whispering. "Anyone might be. I don't know."

"Is that why you haven't said anything all weekend?"

She inclined her chin slightly. "Dr. Sachs *is* one of them. I know that. And the others . . . I can't tell." She paused, pressed her lips together as if trying not to go on. *"He* can tell," she said then.

"Who's that?"

"Him. You know."

"Your secret friend."

She nodded.

"And what does your secret friend tell you about me?" Conrad asked.

Now she did smile. And it made Conrad catch his breath a little. The pink at the inner edges of her pale lips, the slight flush beneath the white skin. The way her small, perfect features brightened. Elizabeth looked down shyly.

"You didn't touch me," she said.

"That's right."

"He doesn't come when you're here. You don't make him angry. You don't . . ." She raised her eyes to him but her voice trailed away.

"Don't what, Elizabeth?"

"You don't want to take my mother out."

"That's right. So I'm not one of them?"

"No. I don't . . . I don't think so."

Conrad nodded slowly for a few seconds. Stalling. Trying to gauge how far he could go. Finally, on impulse, he leaned forward a little and said, "Tell me more. Tell me more about this secret friend."

It was a long moment before she answered. Very long. Elizabeth gazed at him thoughtfully. Conrad waited to see which way she would go. Probably, he thought, she would joust with him some more. Or, probably, she would fall silent; she would smile slyly and clutch her delusions to herself, protect them from him as if they were her children.

Or maybe . . .

Conrad felt a little jolt of adrenaline go through him as he watched her.

Maybe the demand would set her off, he thought. Maybe it would conjure up her Secret Friend in person.

He had a momentary vision of her leaping out of the chair at him. Her teeth bared, her claws extended, her hands reaching for his throat. He breathed steadily, forcing the air out with his abdomen.

And then Elizabeth did the one thing he had not expected at all.

She began to tell her story.

The Secret Friend

The first time he came, he was a little boy [she said]. He always changes, you see. He's always different. The first time, he was a little boy with a striped shirt and red hair and freckles. Billy his name was. He played with me at the Sunshine School and then he came to see me at the apartment. I was living with my mother then.

I used to like to play with him at the Sunshine School. I was very lonely. My mother and I didn't live in a very nice place and no one nice ever came to visit us. There were never any children at all. Sometimes I would go downstairs and visit Katie Robinson, but she was old. There were no children and I hardly ever got to go out except when my mother took me to the store or to see her friends.

The building was dark all the time. It smelled bad. And lots of times, I remember, I saw rats there. They were downstairs, right underneath the staircase. Upstairs, our room was dark too. The only windows looked out at a brick wall. And it was dirty all the time, with garbage in the trash can and on the floor around the sink. Old dishes, bits of food. It smelled. And there were big roaches and those water bugs. I hated those especially. They were so big. Once, when my mother hit one with her shoe, it cracked so loudly. It squished yellow gunk all over. I hated them.

I didn't have a bed. My mother had a cot by the window. But I slept on the floor, in a sleeping bag on the other side of the room. That's why I hated the bugs because they would crawl right in front of my eyes. I was afraid that the rats would come too, but they never did.

Anyway, Billy started out at the Sunshine School like I said. That was a place I went to when my mother had men. I mean, really I imagined it—the school, I mean—but Billy came out of there. It's very confusing sometimes. I don't like to think about it really.

The thing is, the men would come and my mother would, you know, make love or have sex or whatever you call it. My mother would tell me to go to sleep during it. I would roll over and face the wall. They would say I was asleep but I wasn't really. They made terrible sounds, like wild animals in a forest. When they were done, they would smoke drugs. Did they tell you my mother did that? She did. She smoked drugs and she . . . whatever you call it . . . put them in her arm with a needle too. Injected them. The men would give her the drugs a lot of the time. I guess that's why she had sex with them.

Sometimes though . . . sometimes a man wouldn't give her the drugs unless she let him touch me too. My mother would let him. She would sort of walk away and look out the window. I would cry. I would beg her not to. But she would look over her shoulder and say, "Shut up. Just shut up." And the men would put their hands in me. You know where. I used to feel bad about it. I don't really think about it anymore. That's all you doctors are ever interested in though so I'm telling you. Even the women want to hear all about it. Personally, I think it's just disgusting.

But anyway, what I'm trying to tell you about is that that's how I started the Sunshine School. I didn't go to regular school then. I went for a little while, but then my mother said the teachers wouldn't mind their own damn business. After a while, we moved to the new place on Avenue A and I didn't go to school anymore at all. I was sorry about that. I liked school. So when my mother was doing things with men, I would roll over in my sleeping bag and close my eyes and go to one that I could imagine.

Like I said, it was called the Sunshine School. There was a big green yard there and I would play with the other kids on it. My mother was the teacher and she would stand to the side and watch us and smile. Billy—the little boy with the red hair and the striped shirt—he was there. We would play tag together. He looked like a boy I had known at the other school, the old school. I liked him.

Billy liked me too. That's why he got so angry that night. That night—this night Billy came to the apartment—one of my mother's men really hurt me. He was a short little man with a greasy mustache. He had some kind of foreign accent or something too. He came that night and did, you know, his sex with my mother or whatever. But he wouldn't give her the drugs she wanted. He said he wanted to do something to me too.

I was nine then. I remember because the day before had been my birthday. When I heard what the man said—about wanting to touch me—I pretended to be asleep. My mother even said to him, "Oh, leave her alone, she's asleep." But the man wouldn't give her the drugs and finally she let him. He came over and put his hands on me and told me to wake up. I started to cry. I asked my mother to stop him but she just told me to shut up as usual. But the man was rough. He didn't just touch me. He put his thing in me, you know, his penis, whatever you want to call it. It hurt a lot. I mean, it's not like a big deal or anything. I don't even think about it at all anymore. But at the time, it did hurt me and I cried. But my mother wouldn't stop him. She turned away. She wouldn't watch.

Anyway, I guess that's why the Secret Friend came.

The man was gone by then. He gave my mother the drugs and left. My mother put the drugs in her arm and then she lay in the bed, sort of sleeping. I went to the bathroom to clean up. I ran a bath and sat in it for a long time.

When I was done, I got dressed in my nightgown. It didn't hurt that much anymore, but I was still crying and sniffling a little. I came out of the bathroom quietly so my mother wouldn't look at me. She got angry at me sometimes when I cried or complained or anything.

Anyway, I came through the door—and he spoke to me. I could hear his voice right in my ear.

"Your mommy did a bad thing," he said. He was angry. I could tell by the way he sounded.

I shook my head. I whispered to him. "It wasn't Mommy," I told him. "She had to do what the man said. It's because of the drugs, because she needs the drugs so much."

But the Secret Friend said, "Your mommy is bad. You have to punish her."

But I said, "No. No, Billy." Because I knew it was Billy. I knew he was there, wearing the same blue-and-white-striped shirt as always. Holding a kickball under his arm. (Sometimes at the Sunshine School we played kickball with the other kids.) I said, "No, Billy. Mommy can be good sometimes too. Really. She can."

But Billy wouldn't listen. "Then *I'm* going to punish her," he said. "And then she'll be sorry."

There was nothing I could do. I closed my eyes so I wouldn't see, but that didn't work. I could see anyway. I saw Billy go over to my mother's bed. My mother was lying there on her back, smiling up at the ceiling. I said, "Please, Billy, don't." But Billy didn't listen. He dropped the kickball and it went bouncing away from him, across the room. Then he grabbed the pillow out from under my mother's head. I couldn't do anything. "Please, Billy!" I said. He pressed the pillow down over my mother's face. He pressed it down hard and he—he held it there. My mother tried to get up. She tried to push the pillow away. I saw her feet start kicking and her body twisted around. She grabbed at Billy's arms and she hit him and scratched him. I thought Billy would let go, I thought he would have to let go. But he was so strong. Billy—he was so strong. He had some kind of . . . special powers or something. My mother couldn't get up. She kept fighting but she couldn't. And Billy just held the pillow over her face. He was so mad. He wanted to punish her. I said, "Billy!" But I couldn't do anything.

Then, after a while, Mommy stopped fighting. She stopped trying to get up. Her hands fell back onto the bed. She just lay there.

Billy let go of her then. He put the pillow back under my mother. My mother just lay there with her mouth open. Her eyes were open too. She looked like she was staring at the ceiling, amazed.

"Now she'll be sorry," Billy said.

After that, he went away.

I got into my sleeping bag and went to sleep.

Conrad's expression never changed. He leaned on the back of his chair. He kept his eyes on Elizabeth's face. He kept his own face relaxed. He looked impassive and yet sympathetic, intellectual yet understanding. Silently, he was thinking: *Holy shit! Whoa! Jesus, holy . . . oh, my . . . whoa!*

She had been speaking all this while in that blank singsong. A childish voice, almost sweet. Her eyes had been wide and empty and innocent. When she said "And then, after a while, Mommy stopped fighting," she shrugged slightly, and even flashed a nervous little smile. She seemed to feel the whole thing was a rather puzzling incident that had happened to someone else.

She tilted her head at him now. Looked at him as if she expected him to remark upon the weather.

"I see," he said quietly. *Uh boy. Oh, Jesus,* he thought. "And when did you see the Secret Friend next?"

"Oh, right away," Elizabeth said easily. "Or, I mean, a few days later. He was in the truck going out to the cemetery."

"Tell me about that," he said. He tried to breathe steadily, forcing the air out with his abdomen. He had to stop after a while though. It was making him nauseous.

[Elizabeth went on] Well, in the morning, the morning after . . . after Billy came, I went downstairs to see Katie Robinson. Katie was an old black woman who lived on the floor below us. She was always nice to me whenever I visited her. Once or twice, she even gave me a candy cane or a small toy. I knocked on her door and when she answered, I said, "My mother won't get up. I think she's dead." I remember Katie Robinson said, "Oh, my, my." Then she called the police.

While she was doing that, I ran away. I knew the police wouldn't believe me about Billy. I thought they would put me in jail. I went up to the newsstand and stood outside around the video games. I didn't have a quarter but there was a boy playing Space Invaders. So I stood there and watched him until he left to go to school. When I went back, there were still police cars outside so I hid in the alley. There was an alley right next door where the landlord put old trash. There was a gate in front of it, but I could slip through between the bars. I hid behind some old trash cans, but no one came to look for me anyway. Sometimes, while I was hiding there, I cried. I felt bad about my mother.

It was spring, it was warm, so I didn't mind staying out there. I didn't go back into the building until it was almost night. The police had left by then. I went back to see Katie Robinson. She was very worried. She said the police had been looking all over for me. I said I didn't want to go with the police, they would put me in jail. But Katie Robinson laughed and said that was silly. She said they didn't put little girls in jail. She said they would find someone else to take care of me. I felt a little better after that.

I was very hungry by then. I had stolen two oranges from a grocery for breakfast, but I hadn't eaten since and now it was dinnertime. Katie Robinson let me have some of her cereal. She said I could stay with her for the night and in the morning she would call the police again. I got my sleeping bag from upstairs and brought it down to her place.

That night, as I was going to sleep, I asked Katie Robinson, "Where did they take my mother? Where is she now?"

"Well," Katie Robinson said. "Right now, she's probably over at Bellevue Hospital, over at the morgue there."

"Will they keep her there forever?" I asked.

"Oh no," said Katie. "After a while, they'll probably take her out to the island. Hart Island, it's called, and it's a beautiful place, and they got a whole cemetery out there just for people like us who don't have a lot of money to be spending on funerals and like that. It's a place they call Potter's Field and they'll give your mother a real nice funeral there and lay her to rest real pretty, I'm sure."

"Can I go?" I asked her. I wanted to see my mother's nice funeral. I wanted to tell her I was sorry about what Billy did and to say good-bye. But Katie Robinson said regular people weren't allowed out on Hart Island. That made me feel bad again. That night, when I was supposed to be asleep, I lay awake and cried. I was afraid my mother would think that I had done it to her and that she would tell everyone in heaven. I wanted to explain to her about Billy, about how I couldn't stop him.

The next morning, before Katie Robinson woke up, I crawled quietly out of my sleeping bag and snuck away. I knew what Bellevue looked like because my mother had had to go there once. She had been bleeding too much. Her, you know, woman bleeding. Her period or whatever you want to call it. But anyway, I remembered what Bellevue looked like. So all I had to do was ask Mr. Garcia at the grocery which direction it was in and then I could find it. It was right up on First Avenue, that big wide avenue that goes by the highway and the river.

It was a long walk, but it was still very early when I got to the hospital. It was not a nice-looking building. It was big and dirty; brown and dark and all ghosty. I was a little kid, you know, and it looked to me like some kind of big monster hunching up out of the grass. The morgue was sort of off to one side and around back. It was a more modern building, just a box of glass and green cinder block.

There was a parking lot in front of the door. I was walking across it. I was going to go inside and ask where my mother was. But as I went, I heard someone, a man, say something about Hart Island. "Another load for the Island," he said. The voice was coming from around in back.

I walked over to the edge of the building. I peeked around the corner. There was a white truck parked back there, a small white truck with a square back—a square van section, you know, with Bellevue Hospital or something written on the side. It was backed up to the building, to a metal door. The metal door was open and so was the back door of the van. I could hear the men's voices still. They were coming from inside the building. Then, a second later, the men came out.

There were two of them. One was dressed all in blue, I remember; in a blue work shirt and jeans. The other one had a plaid shirt on. They came out of the metal door. They were carrying a box between them. I knew right away that it was a coffin.

They lifted the box into the back of the truck. Then the man dressed in blue said, "That's the last of them, Mike. Come on in for a sec and sign 'em out and you're on your way." The two men went back into the building through the metal door.

I knew what was happening—I mean, I could guess it. They were taking the poor people out to Hart Island for their funerals. I thought, my mother must be in the truck. Peeking out from behind the building, I suddenly got very excited. My heart started beating very hard. I felt like I was going to do something.

I didn't move, at first. I was too scared. I knew the two men would be coming out any second. I didn't want to move at all. But then, very softly, I heard someone call me. "Elizabeth." Like that: very soft. "Elizabeth." It was coming from inside the truck.

I didn't have time to think. I just ran forward as fast as I could. The van was high for me, but I was so excited, I grabbed hold of the edge of it and jumped right in. There were a dozen or so boxes in there. Coffins. I looked around, but I didn't see anyone else. I didn't hear the voice anymore.

Then the men came back. I saw one of them—the one in the plaid shirt—come to the morgue entrance. He turned back over his shoulder and waved. "See you later, Lou," he called. I just stood there frozen, staring at him.

But then I heard that voice again. "Elizabeth." That's all it said. So quietly. But somehow I knew what it wanted me to do. I crouched down, hiding behind two boxes that were piled one on top of the other. I heard the man's footsteps coming across the parking lot, back toward the truck. Then I heard the back door rumble. The light in the truck started to go out, it started to get dark. I wanted to stand up, I wanted to call out to him, "Wait. I'm still in here." But I didn't. I couldn't. I don't know why.

And the door closed. And it was dark in there. With just the boxes around me. It was very dark.

I remember I called out once. I tried to call out. I just said, "Help. Help. I'm still in here." But the engine started up just then. It was very loud and I don't think anyone could hear me over it. I wanted to pound on the back wall but there were boxes piled against it. I didn't want to go close to them. The truck started moving. I sat down in the middle of the floor. I cried. I tore at my hair and I cried, "Mommy. Mommy. Mommy . . ."

That was the scariest part: I couldn't see anything then. I knew the boxes were there all around me, but I couldn't see them. I couldn't see what was happening to them. I guess I mean . . . if they were still closed. I was afraid someone might come out of them. They were just wood, hammered together, with two planks on top. It would have been easy for the planks to come off, for someone inside to come out. Even my mother. My mother might come out of one of them. She might be angry at me. She might think I was bad. And it would be too dark to see her until she was right next to me, her dead face, grinning. I cried and cried. I whispered, "Please, please, please."

Then, though, I began to see a little. Shadows. Shapes. I could see the boxes, about a dozen, maybe fifteen, stacked two up against the walls, to the side of me, behind me. Some of them were very small. I mean, just a little bigger than cigarette cartons. I kept turning from one side to the other, watching them, making sure that none of them moved or opened. I was still crying pretty hard. My face was all wet and there was snot running down onto my lips.

And then someone whispered right into my ear: "Elizabeth."

I screamed and spun around. I couldn't see her in the dark, but I knew she was there, she was sitting right beside me. Mommy. My mommy. Don't be mad, Mommy, it wasn't me, it was Billy. That's what I said. But Mommy didn't say anything anymore. She just sat there, invisible in the dark. And I could feel her staring at me.

I backed away, backed up against the coffins. Oh, Mommy, please . . .

"Elizabeth." She whispered my name again. "Elizabeth."

I kept turning this way and that. Trying to find her. I knew she was there. Her hair all tangled around her face like seaweed. Her eyes like glass, staring and staring at me. I knew. She was smiling. This soft, kind-of-dreamy smile. I couldn't say anything. I just wiped the snot off my face with my sleeve and shook. My whole body shook and my teeth chattered.

But then—something happened. Mommy—my mother—she changed. Her voice changed, the sound of her voice. All of a sudden, it was . . . different. It was . . . it was more the way she was at the Sunshine School. When she would stand near the yard and watch the children play and she would call to them. She was nice, I mean. Her voice was nice and she said, "Don't be afraid, Elizabeth. It's me. I'm here."

And it was funny. I mean, it was strange. It *was* her, it was her voice. But it was, like—it was Billy's voice too. I mean, it was coming from the same place. It was, like, the same person speaking in different voices, sort of, inside my head, right in my ear. And the voice said, my mother said, she said very sweetly, "Don't worry. Don't worry, Elizabeth. You're not alone anymore. I'm here. I'm your friend. From now on. I'll be your secret friend."

And I felt better after that, a little. I sat in the dark truck and I wasn't so afraid. After a while, I even crawled around—crawled from place to place with the truck floor bouncing under me. I crawled around and looked more closely at the boxes. Each of them had a white tag taped to one end. There was a name typed on the tag and a number, and spaces for the dead person's age and religion too. I read all the tags, looking for my mother's name, but I couldn't find it. At first, I thought maybe she wasn't here and that maybe Katie Robinson was wrong about what they would do with her.

But then—then I saw one box—marked UNIDENTIFIED WHITE FEMALE. I can still see it so clearly in my mind: the name and the number typed in next to it, and then question marks in the age and religion spaces. I realized, that must be her. They must not have known her name because I wasn't there to tell them. And that must be her and they're taking her off to her funeral.

I laid my head on top of the coffin. I pressed my cheek against the rough wood. The truck bounced along and I hugged the box tightly. And the voice spoke to me out of the box.

"I'm with you, Elizabeth," it said. "I'm still with you. I'm still in here."

Jeepers creepers! thought Conrad. He nodded at her sympathetically.

The girl hugged herself gently, rocked herself, and smiled. "I'm with you," she murmured again. Tears were still coursing down her cheeks. "I'll always be with you."

Conrad waited a moment until her chin sank down to her chest, until her tears slowed. Then he asked, "What happened next?"

Slowly, Elizabeth raised her eyes. She dried her cheeks with her palm. She let out a shuddering breath. "Oh, well . . . We drove and drove. It seemed like a very long time," she said. "Then, I heard rumbling noises and voices. . . . I think we must've been on a boat, on the ferry going out to the island. Finally, the man in the plaid shirt lifted the back door. The light was so bright. I had to hold my hand up in front of my eyes. And the man—he just started screaming. 'Oh, Jesus! Holy Mother! Oh, God! Oh, God!' I think he thought I was a ghost."

At that, Elizabeth laughed. A strangely normal sound. Her cheeks flushed with her smile. Her hair rippled as she tossed her head. Watching her, Conrad felt his body stir. It made him ache to see that quick picture of the woman she might have been.

I'm still in here.

She went on, "Other men came running over. One of them, a white man, climbed into the truck and carried me down.

"We were in a dirt lot at the end of an old dock. The water was behind me, and in front of me, in the distance through some trees, I saw some gray barracks surrounded by barbed wire.

"There were more men now, crowding around me—mostly black men, wearing dark green clothes. And then there were a few white men too, only they were wearing white shirts and blue pants. The white men also had badges on their shirts, and they had holsters with big guns on their hips.

"All the men made a big fuss over me. They were prisoners—the men in the green suits, I mean—they were convicts from one of the city jails. They were the men who worked in the cemetery. They were the ones who buried the bodies of the poor people. The other men, the men with guns, were their guards.

"I told the men I had come to see my mother's funeral. I explained that she was in the box marked 'Unidentified White Female' and I told them the number of it; I'd read it so many times during the trip I knew it by heart. The men sort of looked at each other. One man—this small white man with a round head and a funny-looking eye—I think he was the man in charge. His name was Eddie. He gave me to one of the other guards and he climbed into the truck for a while by himself. When he came out, he took me by the hand and led me to a tree at the edge of the lot. He told me to sit there and wait.

"I sat and watched as the prisoners unloaded the truck. They brought the big boxes out first, then the little carton-sized ones. Eddie wrote names and numbers on the side of each coffin. Then the prisoners loaded them onto another truck, a dump truck, and they drove them away down a small asphalt road. I waited under a tree. One of the guards waited with me.

"After a while, Eddie came back with the dump truck. He helped me into the cab and drove me down the little asphalt road too. On one side, the road went by the shore, a pebbly beach with the water lapping at it. On the other side, on the island, there were just trees, thick green trees all tangled with bushes and weeds and vines. Sometimes, I'd look over and see buildings set back there, old brick buildings set back behind the trees. They were abandoned. They had broken glass in their windows. They were peering out at me through the branches.

"And then the trees were gone. We came into an open dirt field. And I saw a ditch.

"It was a long trench with a pile of earth and broken weeds on one side of it. All the boxes had been put into it. They were piled up on each other, three at a time. Eddie told me that they had put my mother's box right on top so I could see it. He stood next to me and held my hand and we watched as they covered the tops of the boxes with dirt."

An image rose in Conrad's mind: a memory of his dream. For just a second, he saw the mourning angel's smile again. He saw the coffin opening. He rubbed his eyes, chasing the image away.

Elizabeth continued, "Eddie said some things. A prayer, I guess. He asked God to take good care of my mother because I must have loved her very much, he said, to come all that way out to Hart Island. And all the time he was talking, I was looking down at my mother's coffin. And I was thinking . . . I was thinking that I was glad. I was glad that Billy had done what he'd done. Because now, you see, now Mother was nice. Mother was my secret friend now. Not like before when there were men and drugs and she was mean. Now she was nice. She would always be nice. Do you see?"

She gave a solemn nod. She fixed him with her eyes. She leaned forward in her chair as if to tell him a great secret. "That's why the Secret Friend got so angry," she whispered. "You see? My mother is better the way she is, much better. And if she came back, she might be mean again, and . . . and dirty the way she was before. The Secret Friend doesn't want that. That must be why he cut that man, that Robert Rostoff. That's why he cut him and . . . and cut him—his eyes and his neck and his chest; his face and his belly and his thing and . . ." She stopped herself. A breath came hissing out of her.

"I think . . ." Conrad had to clear his throat. He said, "I think that's enough for now."

Good Morning, Dr. Conrad

"I have to be honest with you: I just don't have any answers."

It was Friday evening now. Conrad was sitting again in what he had come to think of as The Painful Chair. Somehow, Sachs had managed to steer him to it again. The curved top rail was searing his shoulder blades. The hardwood seat was eating into his buttocks like red ants. Conrad kept shifting from one side to the other as if he were doing some sort of seated dance.

Across the desk from him, Sachs kept nodding his huge bald head. Almost as if he were listening, Conrad thought.

"First, with you, she won't talk at all," Conrad went on. "And then suddenly, in two sessions, she's telling me everything. I mean, she's laying out her whole background for me—schizo stuff, but you know, cogent in its own way. I . . . I just don't know how much of it is true, how much is delusional—and how much, if any of it, is just a fake to get out of going to jail. I mean . . ." He sighed. "Lookit, Jerry. Given her case history, a diagnosis of paranoid schizophrenia seems unavoidable, okay? How much of the story about her mother is true . . ." He shrugged. "You got me. Again, my guess is, Elizabeth suffered a severe trauma at her mother's death, which led to an early first break of the disease. As for getting locked in a truck with

67

her mother's coffin—well, it sure sounds like a fantasy to me, but . . . All I can say is that it accurately charts her fixations. She objectifies her own sexuality in terms of her mother's body. And she refers to any attempt to arouse her sexually as an exhumation of her mother's corpse—a plot to 'take her mother out' of the ground. And that seems in turn to stir up her rage at her mother's failure to protect her from molestation—and so the rage materializes in terms of her dead parent returned finally to play the protector role: the Secret Friend."

Sachs did some more solemn nodding. He pulled his glasses off the top of his head and gestured with them pompously. Conrad shifted his aching backside, praying for the end of this.

"Well, the big point here is whether she's capable of standing trial," Sachs said. "Is her memory good?"

"Yeah, it seems to be excellent. I've gotten her to repeat her stories, and the details are always the same. But her affect is all off, totally inappropriate; she's got paranoid ideation coming out the ears. . . ."

Sachs leaned forward in his chair. "Can she assist in her own defense, Nathan?"

Conrad opened his mouth to answer, but something in Sachs's demeanor—some eagerness—made him hesitate. Then, finally, he said, "No. Hell, no. She's acutely schizophrenic, Jerry. Paranoid schizophrenic. That's my diagnosis. No."

"And you would testify to that?"

Again, Conrad hesitated. But then he said, "Yeah. Yeah, sure I would. I mean, she can't stand trial. There's no way."

That was obviously the answer the director of Impellitteri wanted. He leaned back in his tall—his soft—recliner. He slipped his glasses back on his great domed head. He clasped his hands on his great domed belly. A pink smile played at the corner of his wide mouth. "Good," he said. "Good."

Conrad just couldn't take it anymore. He stood up. He let out his breath as the blood rushed into his aching posterior. "Well . . . I've got to go but . . ."

Sachs practically jumped to his feet. He extended a hand the size of a hamhock. "Well, great work, Nate," he said. "The great Nate, that's what we'll call you." Conrad winced as his own hand was squeezed in the enormous paw. "I mean, the thing is, the girl has really come to trust you, hasn't she? She's talking to the aides a little. She's taking her medication, eating well. Next thing you know you'll have yourself a little romantic transference neurosis going on, you'll be in fat city." He laughed and slapped Conrad's arm. "She's a pretty one, Nate," he said.

Before Conrad could answer, Sachs had his heavy arm around his shoulders and was quickly propelling him toward the door.

Next thing you know you'll have yourself a little romantic transference neurosis going on, you'll be in fat city. She's a pretty one, Nate.

God, Conrad thought, the man is unspeakable.

He drove his little Corsica across the Fifty-ninth Street Bridge, heading back toward Manhattan. The clustered skyscrapers of Midtown gleamed in front of him out of the gathering dark. Cars went by him, whooshing at the open window.

A little romantic transference neurosis . . .

God, God, God.

He drove straight through the dodging traffic. He clung to the right lane. He gazed at the taillights swinging and weaving ahead of him. The cold autumn air played over his face. He thought about Elizabeth.

He had spoken to her every day that week. On Tuesday, he had once more shuffled appointments in order to go see her. On Thursday, he'd done it again. He had listened as Elizabeth talked about her childhood. About orphanages and foster homes. About tough children who taunted and beat her. And about the voices that called to her though no one else could hear.

And he had listened as she talked about the Secret Friend, about the things the Secret Friend had done.

There was the incident at the Manhattan Children's Center, for instance. Elizabeth had been lonely there, the way she had been at home. She held whispered dialogues with Billy, the red-haired boy from the imaginary Sunshine School. Billy had grown older now, just as she had. His personality, however, had apparently not changed very much.

There had been a black girl at the Center who bullied Elizabeth—or so Elizabeth said. The black girl had made Elizabeth do some of her chores and had stolen some of her food. One day, the black girl threatened to make Elizabeth submit to what she called "feelies." That made Billy—the Secret Friend—mad. Billy stole a knife from the cafeteria. He attacked the bully-girl that night and slashed open her cheek. Elizabeth was eleven at the time. According to a report in her files, it had taken four adult male custodians to wrestle her down and get the knife out of her hand.

Another time, one of the custodians had tried to slip into Elizabeth's bed at night. Elizabeth said that the Secret Friend had turned into a lion and pounced on him. By the time the lion could be subdued, the custodian's face was a mask of blood. The Center's report said bits of his flesh were caught between Elizabeth's teeth.

As for the Dutch sailor, Elizabeth's dead mother had returned to teach him a lesson:

She broke both his arms and stomped one of his testicles to pudding. It took three cops to pull her off the guy.

Conrad had listened to all these stories. He had spent a good deal of time thinking about them, reading the girl's files. He had tried to separate the reality from the delusions and hallucinations. But his mind kept wandering. He kept thinking about other things. The sound of Elizabeth's voice. The look of her.

She was becoming a little more animated around him now. She no longer spoke in that blank singsong all the time. Occasionally, it gave way to her own smoky murmur. And occasionally, she laughed. And when she laughed, her high white cheeks turned pink and her green eyes glittered. The sound of her, the sight of her like that, made his breath catch.

She's a pretty one, Nate.

Every time he drove to Impellitteri, he hoped he would hear her, see her that way: murmuring, laughing.

You're in fat city.

And he had dreamed about her again. On Wednesday night. He had dreamed she was standing in the doorway of a house. She beckoned him and he went toward her. As he neared, he saw that it was the house that he had grown up in. He knew there was something terrible in the house, but he kept going forward anyway. She withdrew inside and he knew he had to follow her. But before he reached the door, he woke up. His heart was hammering. His pillow was drenched with sweat.

Then, the next day, Thursday, yesterday, he had had a fantasy. He'd been wide-awake when he had it. He was with a patient, in fact: Julia Walcott. Julia was in the armchair, talking about the amputation of her leg. Conrad was breathing steadily, completely tuned in to what she was saying. And then he wasn't. He was thinking about Elizabeth. He was thinking about her lying naked on a bed. Her white arms were reaching up toward him. She was grateful to him for curing her. She wanted to show how grateful she was. "Don't you want to touch me?" she whispered. Conrad had had to battle hard to get his mind back on Mrs. Walcott.

Now, in his car, he shifted uncomfortably. Remembering the fantasy, he was getting an erection.

DON'T SAY A WORD

The Corsica came off the bridge, turned into the crush of cars on Second Avenue. Conrad reached out quickly and turned the radio on. He listened to the news as he drove the rest of the way home.

When Conrad came into his apartment, he found Agatha sitting at the dining room table. She was bowed forward unhappily. Her auburn hair was spilling down. She was supporting her head in her two hands.

"Maa-meee . . ." A despairing little wail drifted through the nursery wall behind her.

"Sweetheart, go to sleep," said Agatha. She said it through her teeth.

"But I *can't* sleep," said Jessica tearfully.

"Then close your eyes and lie quietly," Aggie said more gently. It was a good imitation of patience, Conrad thought.

Conrad closed the door. Agatha looked up and saw him. "Oh, thank God, the cavalry," she said. Conrad managed a smile. "Would you please go in there and murder our child? We have been doing this for the past hour and a half."

Conrad nodded wearily. He set his briefcase on the floor and headed into Jessica's room.

The nursery was Agatha's masterpiece. She had painted it beautifully. The walls were sky blue. There was a rainbow painted on one, a crystal palace on another. Clouds and unicorns all around. The walls grew darker toward the ceiling. The ceiling itself was night black. It was studded with stars and the faint, ghostly outlines of constellations.

Just under these stars lay Jessica. She was atop the loft bed, level with Conrad's chin. When he came in, she was lying curled up on her side. Her Big Bird quilt was in a tangle at her feet. She was wearing a pink nightgown and had a pink stuffed turtle tucked under her arm. It was a Turtle Tot, as Conrad recalled, and it was named Moe. Jessica was hugging Moe hard. She had a frown on her face. She had tears brimming in her eyes.

"Hello, Daddy," she said miserably.

Now Conrad smiled in spite of himself. He pulled Jessica's Big Bird quilt up and tucked it in under her chin. He kissed her softly on the forehead.

"What's an awake child doing in my house?" he whispered.

"I can't sleep."

"Well, you know, we gotta wake up kind of early tomorrow. We're gonna take a drive in the country. See all the leaves changing colors."

"I know. But I'm scared," Jessica said.

"What are you scared about?"

She gave a pitiful sniffle. "I'm scared about Frankensteins," she said. "There was a Halloween show on the Disney Channel and there were Frankensteins in it and now I'm scared about them."

"Uh-oh," Conrad said.

"And Mommy already told me there are no Frankensteins in real life. But I'm not scared about them in real life."

"Oh. Well, where are you scared about them?"

"In my mind."

"Ah."

A single tear fell from the child's eyes. It rolled over her nose and was sopped up by the plush of the faithful Moe. "Mommy says they're only in my mind. And when I close my eyes, I can see them in there. That's what I'm scared about."

For a moment, Conrad could only nod at her. "Wow," he said finally. "That is a tough one."

"I know. And I can't sleep."

"Whew." Conrad scratched his jaw thoughtfully. "How about if I sing you a song?"

"You can't sing, Daddy."

"Oh, yeah. I forgot. Okay. Let me think." He scratched his jaw some more. His daughter watched him solemnly. Moe absorbed another tear. "All right," Conrad said finally. "I've got it. We'll chase the monsters away."

Jessica sniffled. "How can you chase monsters away if they're only in my mind?"

"It's very simple," Conrad said, "but it'll cost you a hundred and twenty-five dollars an hour, okay?"

"Okay."

"Okay, now, close your eyes."

"But then I see the monsters."

"Well, you gotta see the monsters if you want to chase them away, right?" She nodded. She closed her eyes.

"You see them?" Conrad asked.

She nodded again.

"Now," said Conrad, "imagine a torch."

She opened her eyes. "I don't know what that is."

"It's a stick with fire on top of it."

"Oh. Oh, yeah." She closed her eyes again. "Okay."

"Okay, now wave the torch at the monsters."

"Why?"

"Because Frankensteins hate fire. They always run away from fire."

"How do you know?"

"I saw the movie."

"Oh."

"Now stick the torch in their faces. You see them running?"

Slowly, her eyes still shut, Jessica began to smile. "Yeah," she said. "Yeah."

Conrad leaned forward and kissed her forehead again. "Good night, sweetheart," he whispered.

"Good night, Daddy."

He walked back into the living room. Agatha lifted her face from her hands. She shook her head at him. "You're my hero," she said.

"For chasing away imaginary monsters?"

She smiled lazily. "It's a living."

He made love to her that night troubled by a fierce sense of longing.

He had never made love to any other woman. He had eyed enough of them on the street. He had fantasized, he sometimes thought, about all of them: naked, crying out for him. There were certain days in early spring when he thought he would die if he didn't possess some young creature passing by him in her new flowery skirt. But in the event, it was always Agatha. It was her eyes, welcoming and faintly amused. Her breasts, the feel of her breasts, which made him ache for their old days together. It was the way she sucked her breath in sharply when she came, the way her eyes filled. In the event, that was usually enough.

That night, though, he made love to her, and the ache, the longing, wouldn't go away. He kissed her, he whispered her name. Her fingers brushed at his neck, dug into his back. And he felt empty, almost homesick. As if there were something that had eluded him in life. Something he wanted desperately but could never have.

Agatha arched her back, sucked in her breath. Her eyes filled. Her tears spilled over. And Conrad, with a whisper of panic, felt himself losing his erection.

He seemed to know instinctively what he had to do. He closed his eyes. He murmured, "Aggie. I love you." And he thought about Elizabeth. He thought about the whiteness of her flesh, the flush of her cheeks. The sudden nakedness of her small, exquisite breasts as the unbuttoned shirt was pulled away from them . . . "Don't you *want* to touch me?"

73

The husband and wife came together and lay breathing hard in one another's arms.

It was just past ten. Even with his eyes closed, Conrad could tell. He could hear Mr. Plotkin spitting.

Leo Plotkin was a retired garment worker who lived in the apartment directly above the Conrads. He was a cranky old Jewish guy who hadn't spoken to Conrad since he'd seen him carrying a Christmas tree into the elevator. At a minute past ten o'clock, like clockwork every night, Conrad and Aggie could hear him spitting. His loud hawks came directly through the heating duct from his bathroom into theirs. Conrad called it The Ten-O'Clock *Cheh.* You could set your watch by it.

When he heard it tonight, Conrad opened his eyes and looked at Aggie. She glanced back at him and laughed. She nestled close to him, her head on his chest. He looked down at her hair for a long moment. He breathed in the scent of it.

"Can I ask you a really stupid question?" he said after a while.

Agatha lay with her head on his chest. She was playing quietly with his nipple. He was breathing in the scent of her hair.

"That depends," she whispered. "Can I ridicule and belittle you for it?"

"I'd be disappointed if you didn't."

"Then shoot."

Conrad took a deep breath. Then he said, "Do you think—I mean, laying aside all the God stuff, and the, you know, supernatural business— do you think human beings have souls?"

"Oh, jeez," Agatha said. "You know, I deal with publishing people most of the time—but I suppose it's possible in theory. What exactly do you mean?"

"Well, I mean, do you think you could talk to a person, like a psychotic, you know, or an advanced Alzheimer's patient—or say a person with multiple personalities—someone whose ego is shattered beyond rec-cognition—and yet still find some essential individuality in them? Some—*self*—that remained no matter what?"

"Nah."

Conrad laughed. "Oh."

She turned her face up and gave him a quick kiss under the chin. "If you go crazy on me again," she whispered, "I get the car and the apartment."

He nodded, smiling.

And Agatha said softly, "There's no soul. You just die. You're forty. Life is hard. Go to sleep." She kissed him again. Then she rolled over. Within seconds, her breathing deepened and he knew he was alone.

He stopped smiling. He gazed up at the ceiling.

If you go crazy again.

It was odd how it happened, he thought. Going crazy, breaking down. It was odd how it seemed to you that you were growing, getting wiser. That you were having revelations into the ways of the world. That you were suffering, but also achieving a measure of enlightenment. And all the while, in fact, you were standing still. Standing still while the garrote of your neurosis tightened around your neck.

That day after his mother died he had felt fine. Strong, in fact. The Nathan of those days—the long-haired college kid in the colorful T-shirts—felt he had risen above such base emotions as grief. Oh, sure, he was not above some petty emotions. He was a little annoyed, for example, that his father had waited so many hours to call him. (Dad said he didn't see the point of waking him up for bad news.) And of course, he was . . . *saddened* by the loss of his mother. But grief? That was for the unenlightened.

Mom had stumbled into the kitchen to make herself a cup of tea in the middle of the night, Dad had told him. She was drunk, of course. She was wearing a flowing silk nightgown. Nathan remembered it: it was white with a print of violet chrysanthemums. She had turned on the gas burner, Dad said. And she had reached out to lay the teapot on. As she did, the burner's blue flame licked up and caught at her loose, flowing sleeve. Dad said the nightgown must have gone up like paper. But Nathan couldn't help thinking, maybe if she had been sober, she'd have gotten out of it. Maybe if someone had been there other than Dad . . .

Dad said Mom had lingered through the night. Nathan didn't like to think about that. He didn't like to think about the sound of his father crying over the telephone either. Other than that, though, all in all, he felt strong. He was at peace, he told a doubtful Agatha. He was perfectly serene. Through his meditation, through his study of Zen, he was transcending the dualism of life and death, he told her. Time itself, in which his mother had perished, was a mere illusion. Anyone could see that.

Before catching the red-eye back to New York, he went up to Seminary Hill to meditate.

It was his favorite time of day. Just sunset. The sun was falling into the bay on a cushion of clouds. The clouds were pink and lavender and green.

They rolled and turned and expanded with the wind. Nathan sat on a large flat rock. He arranged his legs in the half lotus—the full lotus was too hard on his knee. He counted his breaths, pushing them out with his abdomen. He let his mind sink away. He stared into the sun. He sank into samadhi, the state of perfect concentration.

It was a half hour before anyone found him. A professor of Southern literature, an attractive young woman, was the one. She had strolled up the hill to watch the stars come out. She stopped on the grassy slope when she first spotted him. She figured he was a drunk. He was stumbling around in the twilight, his hands out in front of him. Annoyed, but cautious, the professor was about to turn around, head back to the street. But then she heard him cry out. It was a high-pitched cry of anguish. She leaned into the twilight and listened. She heard him sobbing. She took another step toward him.

"Are you all right?" she called.

"My eyes!" he cried out to her. "Jesus Christ! My eyes!"

The young teacher had put her caution aside. She had run to him, taken him by the shoulders.

"Oh, my mother," Nathan had sobbed. "Oh, Jesus. Oh, Jesus. My eyes."

He was completely blind for two days. He attended his mother's funeral with his head wrapped in bandages. Agatha had to lead him to the graveside by the arm. He had looked down into the open hole and seen nothing. He had had to imagine the coffin. His mother inside the coffin. His mother's open eyes, staring at him.

I'm still in here.

Lying in bed now, Conrad reached out and patted his wife's hip. Poor Aggie, he thought. Even then, it had taken her weeks to convince him to go see a psychiatrist. When he finally did, it had taken him another six months to admit he had had a breakdown. It had taken ten years for him to feel he had recovered from it. By then, of course, he was a psychiatrist himself.

And the eye, like his knee, still bothered him sometimes. Long days and little sleep made it ache. He would see red flashes—like afterimages of the clouds around the setting sun.

If you go crazy again . . .

He let his hand slide off of Aggie. He stared up at the ceiling. Until it happened, until he had cracked, he had not known. He had not realized there was anything wrong at all.

He closed his eyes. He breathed slowly. There she was. There she was before him. Her long silken hair like gold. Her high cheeks, her white, white skin. The opening halves of her unbuttoned shirt. Elizabeth.

Don't you want to touch me?

She was so beautiful, Conrad thought. He began to drift into sleep. She was so beautiful.

The radio alarm went off at eight A.M. A newscaster was saying that a private plane had crashed in a residential area near Houston. Conrad turned the radio off. He sat up in bed.

He had slept soundly. His knee was stiff. He stretched it out, grimacing. He slid it carefully over the side of the bed. He got up and limped gingerly into the bathroom. He took a shower, letting the warm water pound at his knee. He had had another dream, he thought. Something about a hospital. He tried to remember but the images drifted apart like clouds. He got out of the shower. Dried himself and wrapped the towel around his middle. He stepped out of the bathroom and there was Agatha, waiting. She smiled at him, her eyes half closed.

He kissed her. "How'd you sleep?"

"Mm, good. The sleep of the sexually satisfied."

She went past him into the bathroom. He headed back to the bedroom. His knee felt better now.

He looked out through the bedroom curtains. The day was gray but it wasn't raining. That would be all right, if the rain held off. He went to his closet and got dressed while Agatha showered. He put on jeans and a peach, button-down cowboy shirt. Probably should wear a sweatshirt for a day in the country, he thought. But he wasn't comfortable in sweatshirts. He wasn't comfortable in anything really, except gray suits.

As he finished buttoning the shirt, he returned to the window. He pulled the curtains open.

Aggie came out of the bathroom then. He turned and caught a glimpse of her as she went by the door. She was heading for the kitchen, belting his white bathrobe around her. A moment later, he heard her voice calling, "Wake up, munchkin. Rise and shine."

He went into the living room. Agatha was setting cereal boxes down on the dining table. Raisin bran for him, granola for her, Rice Krispies for the kid. She returned to the kitchen, singing out as she went, "Wake up, sleepyhead. We don't wanna get caught in traffic."

Conrad sat down at the table. Aggie returned with bowls and the milk.

"Those rotten Frankensteins kept her up so late," she said. "It'll be noon before we get out of here." She went back to the nursery.

"Sweetheart. Wake up now."

Conrad smiled. He poured some raisin bran into his bowl.

"Nathan?" Aggie spoke from behind him. "Is Jessie awake already?"

"What do you mean?" He reached for the milk. He sniffed at it to make sure it hadn't gone sour.

"She's not in her bed," said Agatha.

Conrad poured the milk on his raisin bran. "What do you mean?"

"I mean she's not in her bed," said Agatha. She walked across the living room toward the bathroom. "Did she wake up already? Jessie?" she called.

Conrad set the milk down and listened. He heard Aggie's voice from the bathroom. "Jessie?" she said again.

Conrad pushed his chair back. He got up and went toward the nursery. "What do you mean she's not in her bed?" he muttered. "Where would she be?"

He heard Aggie calling in the bedroom now, "Jessie? Are you in here? Sweetheart?"

Conrad went into the nursery. The loft bed was empty. Jessica's Big Bird quilt was pushed down to the bottom of the mattress. The stuffed turtle was gone.

She must be in her closet, Conrad thought. She went in there sometimes to play with her toys in private.

He went to the closet and looked in. There was an open space cleared on the floor for her. It was surrounded by stuffed animals. But Jessie wasn't there.

He went back into the living room. Agatha was waiting.

"Did you find her?" she asked.

"No, did you look in the bedroom?"

"Yes. She's not there." Agatha gave him a puzzled little smile. "Where'd she go?"

"She must be in the bedroom," Conrad said. "Where else can she be?"

Conrad went into the bedroom himself. Agatha followed him. As soon as he looked in, he could tell the room was empty. Still, he glanced into the closet. He checked on the far side of the bed by the window. He looked up at his wife, puzzled.

"Nathan?" she said.

"Where is she?" said Conrad.

Then Aggie's mouth opened. "Oh, Jesus, the balcony," she said.

"She knows not to go out there," said Conrad. But when his wife hurried out of the room, he followed after her quickly.

Aggie got there first, opened the glass doors. She stepped out onto the balcony. Conrad came up behind her. He saw her take a deep breath as she stepped to the rail. She looked over it into the courtyard below. Conrad stood behind her. He waited for her to turn, dreading it.

When she did turn, he was relieved to see her.

"No," she said. "It's all right." Then she looked at him. "Where . . . ?"

They both went back into the living room. They turned this way and that, looking aimlessly.

"Jessica," Aggie called. "Are you hiding?"

"Jessica," Conrad called in a commanding voice. He looked behind one of the chairs. Aggie went to the front closet and looked in there.

"Jessica," Aggie said. "Don't hide, sweetheart. You're scaring Mommy." She turned away from the closet. Conrad saw her face was tense now. Her brow was creased. Her lips turned down. "Jessica."

Conrad, on an inspiration, bent down and looked under the dining room table. He expected to see Jessica crouched under there, grinning, gripping her Turtle Tot. He expected to hear her shout "Boo!" and start giggling.

She wasn't there.

"Jessica," Aggie said again.

Conrad heard her voice tremble. The sound made him swallow hard.

"Sweetie," she said, "don't hide, okay? Really. I mean it, sweetheart, it scares me."

She looked at Conrad again. She clutched the front of the bathrobe closed at her throat. "You don't think she went out in the hall, do . . . ?"

Then she stopped. Her eyes had shifted. They had moved from him to the front door. Conrad saw her cheeks go ashen. He saw a look on her face of such blank, stupid terror that his own heart seized in his chest like a dry engine. His limbs felt weak.

"What?" he said. "What's the . . ."

"Nathan." The word barely escaped her lips. "Oh my God . . . Nathan . . ."

Conrad turned. He turned and followed Aggie's gaze. He looked at the door. "Jesus," he said.

The chain lock hung limp. It was in two pieces. It had been cut in half. Conrad felt his throat close.

"Nathan. . . ." Agatha barely whispered his name again.

Conrad ran to the door. He put his hand on the knob. The door swung open. Both the other locks had been undone as well. Conrad looked out into the hall. No one. There was no one there. Behind him he heard Aggie call in a wild tremolo:

"Jessie! Jessie, come out right now, sweetheart! Please, sweetheart! You're scaring Mommy! Please . . ."

Wild-eyed, Conrad turned back to her. One of her hands still clutched her robe. The other now covered her mouth. She stared at him.

"Oh, Jesus," she said. "Oh, Jesus, Nathan. My baby. Call the police. Oh, God."

Her knees buckled. She reached out quickly. She grabbed hold of the back of a chair.

Conrad ran back into the room. He ran to the phone on the table beside him.

"Oh, God," Aggie said.

Conrad grabbed the phone. He reached for the buttons. But he stopped. There was no dial tone. Where the hell was the dial tone? Quickly, he started punching the buttons. No sound. What the hell was . . . ?

And then there was a sound. There was a voice. On the phone, on his phone. There was a clear, strong voice. It spoke to him wryly, calmly. It was in complete control.

And all it said was: "Good morning, Dr. Conrad."

PART TWO

PART TWO

Don't Say a Word

It had been easy to take the kid. There had been nothing to it at all.

A little after three A.M., Sport had left the Sinclair apartment. He'd taken the elevator down to the basement. He'd unlocked the door to the courtyard with a duplicate key he'd had made earlier. Outside, he strolled across the courtyard from his building to Conrad's. It was a nice night, he noticed. Cool air. Clear sky. A strip of dim stars shining between the two buildings; he hummed to himself a little as he glanced up at them.

The lock to the other building's courtyard door was the only tough one he hit. The bolt was too heavy. His pick wouldn't make it turn. He had to use a needle-nose pliers for leverage. He hummed "All or Nothing at All" as he wrestled with the inner latch lever. For Sport's money, Sinatra had sung the shit out of that song. The lever went back, the bolt lifted. It didn't take more than sixty seconds.

He entered the basement and flicked on a small flashlight. He followed the beam to the master phone box. Dolenko, who was handling the electronics, had given him a little transmitter. It was just a black plastic box about the size of his palm. It had two alligator clips attached. Dolenko had explained how to hook them up to Conrad's line. It turned out to be simple. The clips in the master box were clearly labeled: 5D. The transmitter hooked right on. Easy as that.

Afterward, Sport just took the stairwell up, avoiding the doorman in the lobby. He climbed quickly toward the fifth floor.

He was dressed in dark clothing: black slacks and a navy-blue windbreaker. The pockets of the windbreaker bulged and sagged with his tools. He was also carrying a blanket under his arm. All the same, he figured he looked natural enough. If he met someone on the stairs, he would just wave and smile. Of course, there wasn't much chance of that at three A.M. As it happened, he met up with no one.

On five, he came out of the stairwell and walked quickly to the Conrads' door. Now this, he thought, might be a little tricky. Right out in the hall like that, working on the locks. But no, again, it was no trouble at all. The intergrip was well-oiled and snapped back quickly. The latch was a joke. It popped almost the moment he slipped the pick into the hole. He pushed the door open slowly to get at the chain. He had brought heavy fence cutters to take care of that.

He eased the cutters through the crack in the door. He positioned the jaws carefully between two links. He brought the heels of his palms down hard on the handles. The chain snapped. It was like a rifle shot—surprisingly loud.

"Shit!" Sport whispered.

He held his breath. Someone must have heard that. He crouched in the hall. The chain dangled down in two pieces. The Conrad apartment was silent. After a while, Sport gave a soft snort and shrugged. Guess not, he thought. He went inside.

He closed the door silently. Walked quickly to the nursery. He found the kid in her loft bed, asleep. She was lying on her side, facing him. Her mouth was open. She had a pink stuffed animal of some kind under her arm. A pretty kid, Sport thought. Just as snug as a bug in a rug. He smiled. The idea of snatching her while her mama slept only a few yards away was pretty funny.

He took a jelly jar out of his pocket. There was half an inch of clear liquid in it: chloroform. He took out a washcloth and dampened it at the mouth of the jar. When he put the cloth over her mouth, the kid woke up for a second. Her eyes fluttered open. They gazed at him sleepily. Then she must have felt herself suffocating because her eyes got wide and frightened. Sport grinned and held the cloth in place tightly. Then the kid's eyes fell closed. Sport felt her go limp under his hand. He laughed silently.

He unfolded his blanket on the floor. Then he dragged the girl down from the bed and put her on top of the blanket. He put the stuffed animal there next to her. Something to keep her happy and quiet until they could kill her. He wrapped the blanket around her. It covered her from head to foot.

Then Sport hoisted the kid up over his shoulder. He had decided to leave Maxwell back in the Sinclair apartment. The big man moved about as quietly as a tank battalion. Also, once he got his hands on the little girl, he might get excited and ruin everything. But now he wished he had brought the big guy along. Christ, but the kid was heavy. He might sprain his back if he wasn't careful.

He carried her to the door, down the hall. By the time he got back to the stairwell, he was huffing under her weight.

When he got to the bottom of the stairs, he had to rest for a moment. He was inside the stairwell on the basement level. He sat the kid's blanketed form against the stairwell wall. He leaned there himself, sweating and gasping for breath. After a few moments, he reached for the stairwell door. As he did, he heard a toilet flush—just in the basement, just outside.

Sport froze. It was the doorman. He must've come downstairs to take a leak. Suddenly Sport's heart was racing. He stared wide-eyed at the stairwell door. Sweat beaded on his forehead, ran down into his eyes. He heard the doorman's footsteps just beyond the door. He reached into his right pocket, felt for his switchblade. It was there, tumbling around with the cutters and the pick case. He grasped it, but it only made things worse. It only made him start to tremble.

Fucking coward, he thought. He thought it in his mother's voice, that cat's yowl. Fucking nutless crybaby coward.

The doorman's footsteps came closer. Sport imagined plunging the knife into the man's belly. He imagined how it would feel. The flesh resisting, giving way. The blood. His arm felt weak and rubbery. He couldn't do it. He knew he couldn't do it.

The doorman's footsteps went by the door. A moment later, Sport heard the elevator doors open out there. He heard them slide closed again. There was silence. Sport took a deep breath. He pushed the door out, peeked through the crack. The basement was empty now.

Sport grinned. He let go of the knife. Propping the door open with his foot, he hoisted the kid back up onto his shoulder. He carried her out to the courtyard, across it to his own building.

He was back in the Sinclair apartment—his apartment—seventeen minutes after he'd left. It was that easy.

* * *

There were three of them in the apartment, aside from the kid. There was Sport and Maxwell and Dolenko. The Freak had brought Dolenko in on it. Dolenko had been the Freak's friend when the Freak was still alive, before Maxwell killed him. Dolenko had met the Freak in one of those after-hours bars the Freak liked to go to. In the old days, the Freak had taken Sport to those bars. It was just a lot of faggots in leather jackets, as far as Sport could tell. Guys dancing the conga in their jockstraps. Even live sex shows sometimes. Once Sport had seen them gang-bang a girl right on the bar. The girl's hands were tied and her head was covered by a leather mask. Everybody in the bar applauded. Sport shook his head when he saw it. Fucking faggots, he thought; they'll do anything. But the Freak liked that kind of stuff.

After going to the bars, Sport and the Freak would go back to their place in Flushing. The Freak and Sport had shared a house then, just the two of them. They would go back to the house and hang out together, making fun of the faggots they'd seen. They would dance around together in their underwear or even naked, the way the faggots did. It made Sport laugh to imitate them. Sport had a good time hanging around with the Freak.

But then the Freak had met Dolenko at one of the bars. Dolenko was an electrician with the city's Department of Transportation. He was thin and muscular. When he took off his shirt, you could see every sinew etched in his skin. It looked as if he were always straining at something. His thin face looked like that too. The short salt-and-pepper hair stood up. The tendons of the neck stood out. His eyes bulged and his mouth twitched and twisted.

This was partly because Dolenko was a cokehead. He was always buzzed, always hyper. But the Freak had taken a liking to him. And pretty soon, the Freak and Dolenko were hanging together almost all the time. The Freak hardly came home to Sport anymore at all.

"What're you, some kind of faggot?" Sport had asked the Freak. "Hanging with him all the time."

But the Freak gave one of those indifferent tosses of his thick red hair and said, "Fuck you. He's a sketch. I like him." And that was that.

That was partly why Sport had taken up with Maxwell in the first place: to get back at the Freak for hanging with Dolenko. After Maxwell had come to Rikers, Sport had gone out of his way to befriend the new prisoner. Maxwell hated the Island: the bars, the ceaseless noise, the hard stares of the men. He was like a frightened animal in a cage and he was glad to have a correction officer show him some kindness. Sport told Maxwell to look him up whenever he got free. And that was exactly what Maxwell had done. So, while the Freak and Dolenko were hanging together, Sport had started hanging out with Maxwell.

"Look at this guy," Freak had said when he saw Max. "He's a fucking monster, Sport. He's Frankenstein's fucking monster, man. You're hanging around with Boris Karloff."

"I like him," Sport had answered, smiling. "He's a sketch. See what I mean?"

Things had been tense among the four of them at first. But it all smoothed itself out after a while. One day, Sport told the Freak about what Maxwell liked to do to cats. The Freak thought that was hilarious. He bought Max a kitten and made Sport and Dolenko sit around the breakfast table while Maxwell killed it. Maxwell cut out the kitten's tongue so it couldn't yowl, then broke its legs one by one, then strangled it. But the real joke was, the Freak got him to do it without his pants on. Then, when Max got real excited, the Freak grabbed hold of Max's short, thick dick and jerked him until Max cried out and spurted all over the place.

"You faggots," Sport had shouted at them. But he'd been laughing too. And the Freak had laughed and laughed until he was weak.

After that, they all got to be pretty good friends.

Now there were only the three of them left. Sport was sorry about that. He missed the Freak. He was sorry Maxwell had had to cut his throat. It never would've happened, he thought, if the Freak hadn't started hanging out with Dolenko.

When Sport returned from Conrad's, he put the kid in the bedroom. He hadn't gotten much furniture for the Sinclair apartment, but there was a mattress in the bedroom and a TV. There were heavy curtains covering the windows. There was a small lamp on the floor. It threw long shadows over the white walls.

He lay the kid on the mattress and unwrapped her. She lay motionless on her side. She was wearing a long flannel nightgown. It had red ribbons at the throat and there were valentines all over it. The nightgown had ridden up over her waist. She was naked underneath. The sight of her nakedness made Sport queasy. He tugged the nightgown down. He shook his head. He lay the pink stuffed animal next to her.

All the while, Maxwell stood behind him and watched. Dolenko was not there. He had gone out to fix things at Conrad's office and had not come back yet. Maxwell stood looking over Sport's shoulder. His eyes were bright. His great grizzly-bear arms swung restlessly at his sides. He had that strange look on his face, that dreamy smile. Sport didn't like that. Once Maxwell got really excited there would be no stopping him.

So, when he was done with the kid, Sport turned to him. "Listen, Max," he said. He had to crane his neck to look at him. He pointed a finger up at that small, baby face with its sunken eyes and pouting lips. "You have to leave her alone for now, all right? You can't do her yet. That would ruin everything. Understand?"

Maxwell massaged his palm. He stared down at the child on the bed. He looked embarrassed. "I could touch her," he said. "That wouldn't ruin it."

"No," Sport said firmly. It was like talking to a dog. "You can't touch her. You'd just get excited and then you'd lose control. It would be all over before you even knew it. Now you know I'm right, don't you? Don't you?"

For a moment, Maxwell's eyes shifted from the girl to him. It made the hair stand up on the back of Sport's neck. He thought about the Freak kicking and shivering and bleeding to death on the floor as Maxwell looked on. Maxwell and his hard-on.

But then Maxwell turned away. "I'm just watching anyway," he said.

"Attaboy," said Sport. He slapped Max on his thick shoulder. "You can keep watch on her for me, okay? But leave the door open. I'm gonna try and catch an hour of sleep."

Maxwell nodded gratefully. He placed a chair against the wall and sat down on it. With his shoulders hunched, his heavy hands dangling between his legs, he leaned forward and watched the girl. Sport went out to the living room. He left the connecting door open. All the same, he decided to wait for Dolenko to get back before he went to sleep.

In the living room, there were two sofas, a coffee table, and three director's chairs. There were also a couple of standing lamps. Other than that, the broad expanse of parquet floor was bare. All of Lucia Sinclair's furniture was gone. The lordly chairs and impressive bookcases. The rosewood showcases with their porcelain knickknacks. Lucia Sinclair's grandson had taken care of them. He had flown in from San Francisco for the funeral and stayed to deal with the furniture. The same day the police took down the yellow crime-scene tape, he had cleared the apartment out. Just ten days after the old lady died, her fancy apartment was empty. One day after that, Sport, Maxwell, and Dolenko had moved in.

When Dolenko returned from Conrad's office, Sport lay down on one of the sofas. He closed his eyes and tried to sleep. He imagined himself singing in a nightclub. That was the way he relaxed his mind. He imagined himself in a tuxedo, smoking a cigarette and singing "All or Nothing at All." Women sat at their tables and sighed. Their men looked on with grudging admiration. After a while, Sport's thoughts got confused. He was still trying to sing in the nightclub, but he kept farting loudly. It was awful. It sounded like a trumpet. The audience was laughing at him. The women covered their red mouths with white hands. The men slapped the tables and guffawed. He couldn't stop. Then Dolenko jogged his shoulder.

"She's waking up, Sporty," Dolenko said. He gave Sport another shake.

Sport opened his eyes and sat up suddenly. "What?"

"She's waking up, man."

"Oh. Okay. Okay."

Sport rubbed his face with both hands. He looked up dazedly at Dolenko. Dolenko was standing above him, bouncing on his toes. He was nodding rapidly for no reason. He was chewing gum fast. The muscles in his jaws stood out, working hard. His coked-up eyes shifted back and forth quickly.

"Thanks, Dolenko. Thanks," Sport said. He looked at his watch. It was five-fifteen.

He got up and went into the bedroom.

The kid was stirring on the bed. She had rolled over onto her back and was rubbing her eyes with her hand. Maxwell was standing in front of his chair. He looked down at her with big eyes. Sport could hear him breathing.

The girl opened her eyes and looked around her. She blinked. "Mommy?" she said. Then she turned and saw Sport and Maxwell. "Where's Mommy? Mommy." She started to sit up. "Ow!" she said. She held on to her head with one hand. She looked up at the two men. Her lip began to quiver. Her cheeks turned red.

"It's all right, sweetheart," Sport said. His youthful face crinkled with humor and kindness.

"Where's my mommy?" said the little girl.

Sport gave her one of his sparkling smiles. "Listen, sweetheart, your mommy can't be here right now, okay? But we're gonna take good care of you. We've got a TV here and everything. It's gonna be great."

"I want my mommy. Please." The girl began to cry. "Where *is* she?"

Shit, Sport thought. He kept smiling. "Now, don't cry. We're gonna take good care of you," he said. "Here, why don't we turn on the TV and . . ."

But the girl began to cry harder. She sucked in her breath hard. She cried out, "Mommy! Mommy!"

"Aw, shit," Sport muttered.

Quickly, he went into the other room to get the chloroform. He could hear the kid bawling behind him. She was sobbing so hard she could hardly get the word out: "Mommy! Mommy!" She just kept saying that.

Sport dampened the washcloth and brought it back to the bedroom. When he got there, Maxwell was standing close to the bed. He had his hands lifted in front of him. He was breathing hard; it made a funny sound in his throat. The child was cowering against the wall, clutching her pink stuffed animal in her arms. She was staring up at Maxwell and she was crying so hard she couldn't talk at all. When Sport hurried back in, she turned to him and just managed to sob out, "Please. Please. I just want my mommy."

Sport stepped up to her. She recoiled, but he grabbed the back of her neck with one hand. He tried to put the washcloth over her mouth with the other. But she pulled back, shaking her head.

"No. No," she sobbed. "Please."

Sport forced the cloth over her mouth. She pulled away again. She gasped, sobbing. Sport pulled her head back toward him, stuffed the cloth up to her mouth. He felt her pitch forward. She threw up on the bed, a great yellow gob.

"Ah, shit!" Sport said. He pulled back a second to get away from the mess.

"Oh, no," the little girl cried, looking at the vomit. "Oh, no." Her lip was bleeding. She sobbed again.

Sport shoved her head back into the cloth. "Now, just be quiet," he said.

This time, the little girl couldn't get away. She looked up at Sport above the cloth. The tears poured out of her eyes. Then her eyes closed and she went limp. Sport let her fall back onto the bed. He waved his hand in front of his face to clear away the smell of vomit.

Cursing, he pulled the dirty blanket out from under the girl. He rolled it up with the vomit inside and threw it into a corner. Then he looked up and saw Maxwell.

Maxwell's hands were still out in front of him. His cheeks were red. He seemed frozen in place. And look at this, Sport thought, a fucking dick like a flagpole.

He straightened and slapped Max's shoulder. He tried to keep the anger out of his voice. "Come on," he said.

They left the kid in the bedroom and closed the door.

When morning came, Maxwell was still sitting in front of the door, staring at it. He was sitting in one of the director's chairs. He was hunched forward, rubbing one hand with the other. He kept staring at the door.

Sport and Dolenko were across the room. They were at the glass doors that led out to the balcony. Sport was sitting in a director's chair, holding the portable phone on his lap. Dolenko was standing beside him. He had the binoculars plastered to his bug eyes. He had them trained on a line of windows in the building across the court. He was bouncing up and down on his toes.

Dolenko giggled as he looked through the binoculars. He had a high-pitched giggle like a girl's: Hee hee hee. "Look at this. They don't even know. He's sitting down to have breakfast." Even his voice sounded sinewy and strained. "Oh, this is great. Tits is going in the nursery." Hee hee hee: he giggled again. "They're looking for her. Where is she, Pa? I dunno, Ma. Where could she be?" Hee hee hee.

Sport snorted. He shook his head at Dolenko's goofy sense of humor, but it did make him smile. He sat slumped in the chair and looked out through the doors. Even without binoculars, he could see the Conrads clearly: their two small figures moving in the apartment across the way. They moved more and more frantically.

Dolenko bounced up and down faster. "They see the door! They see the door!" he said.

Sport laid his hand on the phone-pack's receiver. Whatever else you said about Dolenko, he thought, you had to admit he knew his electronics. Originally, Sport had wanted to bug Conrad's apartment, maybe even place some hidden cameras in there. When that turned out to be unfeasible, Dolenko had come up with the transmitter idea. Now, Conrad's phone was hooked right into Sport's portable cellular. Sport could call in—but Conrad couldn't call anyone but him.

Sport lifted the receiver to his ear.

A moment later, he saw Conrad running toward his telephone. He heard the click as the doctor picked the phone up. He heard the doctor pressing the buttons, hitting the plunger. Then there was a moment's silence.

Sport took a breath and spoke quietly. He was excited, but he tried to keep his voice even and steady. "Good morning, Dr. Conrad," he said. "My name is Sport."

There was a pause. And then Conrad sputtered, "What the hell—"

Sport cut him off. "Listen to me. Don't say a word. I have your daughter."

The pause was longer this time. Then: "Who are you? Who the hell are you?"

"I've been working on your apartment for several days, Dr. Conrad. I've planted cameras there—I can see what you do. I've planted microphones and I can hear what you say. In fact, that's a very nice shirt you have on." Sport squinted. "Orange suits you. And you should wear jeans more often."

"Look at him. Look at him: he's looking for the cameras," Dolenko whispered. Hee hee hee. "He's looking around like: Wo, shit! Where are they?" He laughed.

Sport waved at him to be quiet. He kept his eyes on the window across the way, on Conrad's figure. "If you try to go out," Sport went on, "if you try to contact anyone in any way, I'm going to kill your daughter. If you try to dismantle my equipment, if you do anything suspicious at all, I'll kill her."

"You bastard. Where's my daughter? I want to talk—"

"Oops," said Sport. He smiled. "That was a mistake. If you make another mistake, your daughter will suffer. If you make a mistake after that, your daughter will die." He waited a moment. He wanted to see if the rich Park Avenue doctor was going to open his big mouth now.

"All right," Conrad said after a moment. "What do you want?"

Sport's smile widened. His eyes were bright. "Now you're getting the hang of it, Doctor. Listen: Do you have any appointments today? Are you expecting any calls?"

Silence on the line. Then: "No. No."

"Tell me now, because if anyone pops up later, it'll spell oopsy-daisy for our dear little Jessica."

"No. We were going . . . There's nothing. No."

"Good. I want you to just stay where you are and don't do a thing. You can eat and you can shit—and even when you shit, I'll be watching you. At seven o'clock this evening, I'll call you again. Then I'll tell you what you have to do to get your daughter back alive."

"Listen—" said Conrad.

Sport placed the phone back on the pack. He laughed quietly. Hee hee hee, said Dolenko beside him.

Maxwell sat hunched in his chair, staring at the bedroom door.

Tough

Slowly, Conrad put the phone down.

"Nathan?"

He took a deep breath.

"Nathan, what . . ."

Finally, he managed to turn to her, face her.

"Oh, Jesus, Nathan," she said, "what is it?"

Aggie was leaning toward him, clutching her hands between her breasts. Her eyes were wild but she wasn't crying. She seemed to be pleading with him. "Nathan?"

It was a moment more before he could speak. He cleared his throat. "Someone's taken her."

"Taken . . . ?"

"Listen to me, Aggie." He stepped forward. Took her by the shoulders.

"Taken her? Taken my baby? Why would they . . . ?"

"Ssh, Aggie, listen . . ."

"But why would they take my baby? Why would they . . . ?"

"I don't know. Aggie, listen to me, I don't know."

"They have to bring her back. Won't they bring her back? Do they want money? We can give them money, they can have all our money, Nathan. Did you tell them? You have to tell them that, so they'll bring her back. Nathan . . ."

"Oh, Jesus!" Conrad threw his arms around her, pressed her to him. Tears sprang into his eyes but he sneered them down. He held Aggie tight. She only trembled against him. She kept talking into his chest.

"They can't just come in here, can they? Into our home? Into our apartment? Take my baby. They don't want to hurt her, do they? I mean, she's just a little girl."

"Ssh." Conrad whispered it into her ear. Kissed her cheek desperately. "Ssh."

"Should we call the police? Maybe if we call the police . . ."

"We can't. They're watching us, listening. Somehow they . . . They've been putting cameras in the apartment. Microphones. They can see what we do, they can hear us . . ."

"But we have to . . . we have to do something . . ."

"We have to wait. This man—Sport—he's going to call us at seven. He'll tell us what to do. If we don't just wait . . . if they see us do anything . . . they'll . . . they'll hurt her, Aggie . . ."

"Oh, no. Oh, God."

Conrad squeezed his eyes shut, holding her tight. "Ssh," he whispered in her ear. "Ssh."

After a moment, Agatha slowly pulled away from him. She looked up at him. She still wasn't crying. But her eyes were wide, like the eyes of someone who's been punched in the stomach. She shook her head at him, exploring his face, looking for something from him, anything.

Conrad touched his wife's cheek. "It's going to be all right," he said.

"Why is this happening? Nathan? Why is this happening?" Finally, the tears started. "Oh, Jesus. My baby girl. Jessie. Oh, God."

She wept, trembling, covering her mouth with her hand. Reaching out with the other hand blindly, she found a chair. She pulled it to her, sank down into it. She sat at the dining table and cried. Wearing his white bathrobe, her hair hanging down in tangles, her round cheeks mottled and damp, she looked old and lost. She rubbed her hands together on the table.

Conrad turned his eyes away from her. He ran his fingers through his thin hair. She kept crying and wringing her hands. He couldn't look at her. After another moment, he left the room. He went quickly into the bedroom. His medical bag was on the floor of his closet. He knelt down and opened it. Rummaged through it until he found a container of Xanax.

Clumsily, he shook two of the pills out into his hand. "This will help," he whispered to himself. The pills were purple ovals: one milligram apiece.

He shook out two and put the cap back on the container. Then he opened it again and shook out another pill.

He got a glass of water in the bathroom. He carried the pills and the water back to Aggie. She was still sitting at the dining table. She was staring at the wall. She was silent, but the tears ran steadily down her cheeks. She kept wringing her hands.

"Here," Conrad said. He set the water and pills down in front of her. He looked away from her. He looked at the door where the chain hung down, cut. "This will help," he said.

Aggie looked up at him, dazed. "What?"

"It's medicine. It'll help you."

Aggie looked down at the purple pills. She looked up at him again. Still crying, she laughed. Then she stopped laughing. Suddenly, as if she were slapping his face, she hit the glass of water with her hand. It flew off the table, hit the maroon play rug. The water spat out on the rug leaving a dark stain. The glass rolled noisily onto the floor.

"Goddamn you, Nathan," Aggie said. It was a voice Conrad had never heard from her before. Guttural, trembling. "Goddamn you."

When she looked up at him, Conrad's stomach felt hollow. His legs felt weak. He sank into the chair across from her. "I'm sorry. Oh, Jesus, I'm sorry, Aggie." He reached out to take her hand but she pulled it away. She wouldn't look at him. Conrad's throat tightened. He had to fight down the tears again. "I couldn't stand to see you . . . ," he said. "I couldn't . . ."

He couldn't say any more. He looked down at the table. After a few seconds, Agatha turned to him. Her tears had stopped. She looked weary, bowed with weariness. She reached out and took her husband's hand. Conrad grabbed her hand in both of his.

"I know," she said softly. "I know."

In the first hours after he talked to Sport, Conrad thought he would go out of his mind. He and Aggie sat in the apartment. Their own apartment. Staring at the walls. Staring at the windows like prisoners. They didn't talk. They didn't know what to say. They didn't want *them*—Sport; whomever —to hear. They just sat there. They sat on the sofa, holding hands. Conrad sat thinking. He was thinking about Sport.

He was thinking about Sport's voice.

If you make a mistake . . .

The sound of Sport's voice. He was thinking about its sweet, untroubled, mocking charm . . .

. . . it'll spell oopsy-daisy for our dear little Jessica . . .

He did not recognize the voice; he could not place it. But he thought he recognized that tone well enough. He thought he had heard that tone once or twice before. On the wards of hospitals. From the unshadowed corners of sealed white rooms.

If you make a mistake . . .

After a while, Conrad stood up. He started to pace. He had to think. He had to think about Sport. He had to think about what Sport had said.

Good morning, Dr. Conrad.

He had called him Doctor. He had known who he was. Maybe he was a former patient. Maybe he just wanted some attention. Or drugs—maybe he thought a doctor could help him get drugs. He had to want something. Drugs. Money. Something.

Conrad paced. He thought about seven o'clock when Sport and he would talk again.

Then Agatha began to cry. He stopped pacing. He sat down and held her. They held each other. They urged each other to stay calm, to eat, to keep up strength. They didn't eat. They couldn't. They waited. The hands of Conrad's watch seemed not to move. The gray daylight at the window seemed not to change.

The deadness of time seemed to swell up inside Conrad. There were moments when he wanted to tear his skin to get at it. He wanted to charge out the door, shouting for the police. He wanted to reach through the phone line and drag Sport through it, shake him: "Where's my daughter?" There was even one moment, after about two hours of this, when he had a fleeting fantasy of getting a kitchen knife and killing both his wife and himself. Anything to make it end.

But that was the worst of it. After that, it seemed, the nature of the day began to change. The very nature of time, it seemed, began to change. It began to move, it began to get quicker. Husband and wife went into the bedroom together. They sat on the edge of the bed and watched TV. Cable news. A new report every half hour. Upheavals in Eastern Europe. An oil-tanker fire in the Persian Gulf. Half hour by half hour, the day began to go by. Conrad stared at the TV, at the news. He thought about Sport. He remembered Sport's voice—and he remembered his own voice. He had sounded scared; he had been scared, and he had let the sound of it into his voice.

He grit his teeth at the thought. His breath came trembling out of him. He stared at the TV. Actor Mel Gibson was making a new movie. There was snow in the Western states. Colder weather was coming to the East. The light changed at the window, turned to steel. Conrad and Aggie lay down on the bed. She slept for a while and he held her. He stared at the ceiling. He thought about Sport. He thought about seven o'clock.

When Aggie woke up, she decided to get dressed. She stood in a corner and Conrad held his bathrobe up in front of her. Quickly, she put on a pair of jeans and a sweatshirt from the Mohonk Mountain House. She looked around the room as she dressed, trying to spot the cameras. When she went to the bathroom, she covered her lap with a towel. Even so, her eyes stung with humiliation.

At five o'clock, they made dinner. They stood at the kitchen counter side by side. They made sandwiches: ham and cheese. Agatha was slicing French bread when she broke down and started to cry again. Conrad almost snapped at her. He wanted to yell: Stop it. Don't you know you're killing me? Instead, he put his arm around her shoulder. Crying, she went back to cutting the bread.

At the very end, time slowed again. It almost seemed to stop. The light died outside and night came to the window. Up until then, Conrad had been watching the light. When it's dark, he'd told himself; when it's dark, he'll call. Then, when the light was gone, there was nothing else to watch. For that last half hour, he and Aggie sat at the dinner table. They pushed their plates aside though there was still food on them. They held hands. They tried to smile.

At five of seven, Agatha took his hands in both of hers. She tried to smile, but she was crying again. "Tell them, Nathan . . . ," she managed to say. "Tell them . . . we'll do anything. Make sure you tell them."

Please, he thought. Please stop. But he patted her hands and tried to smile too. "It'll be all right," he said hoarsely. Agatha tried to nod.

He glanced at his watch. It was seven o'clock exactly. The phone rang.

Conrad stepped to the phone. Aggie was at his shoulder. He took a breath. The phone rang again. He picked it up. There was silence on the other end. He said nothing. He waited.

"Don't you even say hello, Doctor?" Sport said. "Manners count, you know."

Conrad took a moment before he answered. He'd had nearly eleven hours to think about this. He wanted to get it right. "Hello, Sport," he said. And it was good. It sounded calm and strong. The Doctor is in. "Hello, Sport. Let's talk about my daughter."

There was a hesitation. Conrad could hear it. Then Sport said, "I'll tell you what, Doctor. I'll talk. You listen. That's the way it is with shrinks, isn't it? I talk, you listen?" He chuckled quietly. "So you listen, and I'll tell you exactly what you're going to do to—"

"No," said Conrad. He pressed the phone tight against his ear. He stuffed his free hand in his pants pocket so the son of a bitch wouldn't see it shaking. "No," he said, "I'm afraid that's not good enough, Sport."

"Nathan!" Agatha whispered sharply.

He turned his back on her. Pressed the phone tight against his ear.

On the other end of the line, the fluid voice turned hard and dark. "Careful, Doctor. Remember what we said about mistakes."

"I do remember, Sp . . ." Conrad had to stop, had to swallow to get his voice back. ". . . Sport. But all the same, before we go on, before you tell me what has to be done, I want you to let me speak to my daughter."

"Hey, Doctor. I don't think you get this. What you want doesn't matter. What you want is shit."

"Well, I understand that you feel that way, Sport. But all the same—"

And suddenly Sport was shrieking. "Don't give me that headshrinker shit, you cock-sucking fuck, that power shit, I'll cut her belly open like a fish, I'll gut her like a fish, you hear me, Dr. Fuckhead! You hear me?"

Conrad could hardly speak at all now. His mouth opened but only a faint, wordless noise came out. He closed his mouth. He grit his teeth. He forced the words through. "If I don't . . . If I don't talk to her . . . Sport . . . I'll assume she's dead."

Aggie let out a little cry. Conrad pushed on.

"And if she's dead, I go to the police."

"Yeah, horseshit, little man, let me tell you what you just bought for—"

Nathan hung up the phone.

He stood there, his hand still on the receiver. He stood and stared at it. I have to let go now, he thought. They're watching. I have to let it go. His hand slowly opened. He pulled it away from the phone.

"Nathan!" Aggie finally found her voice. "Nathan, my God, what've you . . ."

"Listen." He turned to her, gripped her shoulders hard. He looked hard into her wild eyes.

"Nathan, my God, my God . . ." She was babbling in a shrill half-whisper.

Conrad spoke loudly and clearly. He wanted to make sure Sport could hear. "Listen, Aggie. We're going to the police. We have to go to the police."

Ring! he thought. You son of a bitch! Call me back! Ring!

He had had nearly eleven hours to think about this. He had decided what he had to do. Whoever *they* were, they had done something desperate. Whatever they wanted, they must want it desperately. Drugs . . . money . . . a doctor's attention . . . something he had, something they had to get from him. Whatever it was, it was his one bargaining chip. If he didn't use it, if he didn't insist on talking to Jessica—what reason would they have to keep her alive?

"We've got to go to the police," he repeated.

The phone remained silent. Aggie looked up at him, shaking her head: no, no . . .

"We've got to." He let her go. He started walking to the door.

The phone rang.

Conrad stopped. He turned slowly. The phone rang again. Aggie stood staring down at it.

Conrad walked back to her. Just as the phone began to ring a third time, he picked it up. He shoved one shaking hand back into his pocket.

"What," he said.

The silence on the other end seemed to him like a Texas highway: it seemed as if it would never change, never end. Then, low at first, slowly growing louder, Sport began to laugh again. That malevolent, fluid chuckle.

"Oh," he said. "Oh, tough. Tough doctor. Tough Daddy. Oh, yeah. How about I bring her to the phone and let you hear her scream? How would that be?"

"No," Conrad said. Smooth and calm. "Whatever it is you want, you won't get it if you hurt her."

Sport kept laughing. "I hear you. I hear you, I get the whole picture. You're a tough little Dr. Dad, you are." There was a pause. "You know, I like that actually," he went on then. "I mean it, really. That's the kind of thing I like: it reminds me of myself. You know? I mean, you and I would probably get along under other circumstances."

The hand in Conrad's pocket closed into a fist. *Got him,* he thought.

"Okay," Sport said. "Hold on, tough guy."

There was a click, and then a low hum. Conrad listened hard but there was no other sound.

"Nathan . . . ," Aggie whispered. "What's happening?"

100

He turned to her, put his hand on her shoulder. Her face was pale and lined, her eyes were still hectic. Her hair hung down around her cheeks in tangles. He smiled at her.

There was a click on the phone. "Daddy?"

"Jess?"

"Daddy." She started to cry. "I'm scared, Daddy."

The tears returned to Conrad's eyes. "I know, baby. It's all right."

"I don't want to stay here, Daddy. They're bad men. Why can't I come home? I want to come home."

"It's gonna be all right, Jessie. You'll be home very soon." He shut his eyes tight.

"Oh, God, Nathan, please . . ." Aggie reached for the phone with both hands.

But Conrad kept it away from her. Already, he could hear Jessica crying out, "No! I wanna talk to my mommy. I want my mommy. Please. Please . . . *Daddy!*" And then her wordless sobbing grew fainter as she was carried away from the phone.

"Now," said Sport a moment later, "here is what you are going to do, Doctor."

Conrad covered his eyes with his hand. He knew they were watching him, he knew he was on camera, but he couldn't help it. A tremor went through his body as he wiped the tears away.

"You are going to visit one of your patients," Sport was saying. "A woman named Elizabeth Burrows . . ."

One Simple Question

You are going to be followed. Every moment, you are going to be watched.

Conrad slipped his trench coat on. He walked with Agatha to the door.

I'll kill her if you stop. I'll kill her if you turn in the wrong direction. If you make a play, if you make a noise, if you make a mistake . . . she'll be dead.

At the door, Agatha looked up at him. She did not ask him if it was going to be all right. She just looked up at him. Her eyes seemed vast and dark. He touched her cheek. He leaned down and pressed his lips to hers.

"Don't let them see you cry, Aggie," he said.

She smiled tightly. Shook her head. "No."

"Don't open the door for anyone."

She couldn't speak.

"I'll be back."

She nodded, her eyes swimming.

He took a deep breath and stepped out into the hall. He heard the apartment door close behind him.

There'll be someone behind you every step of the way, Sport had told him. *Who knows, right? Could be your doorman, could be your best friend. Could be the butcher or the baker. But there'll be someone there.*

Conrad walked slowly to the elevator. He pressed the button. The light above the door started moving down from the penthouse: 12 . . . 11 . . . 10 . . . Conrad stood before the door and looked up and down the hall. No one else was there. His eyes came to rest on the door to apartment 5C. His neighbors' door. Scott and Joan Howard were behind that door; a retired jeweler and his wife. The door seemed to pull Conrad toward it. "Call the police, Scott." He could hear himself saying it. He even leaned toward the door as he stood before the elevator.

But then his hand went up to his throat.

That's a very nice shirt you have on. Orange suits you.

And behind him, another door opened. Conrad spun around. Billy Price came out of his apartment, carrying a box in each hand. Conrad remembered meeting him on the elevator: his new neighbor; the Wall Street type with the stale sense of humor.

The young man flashed his shy smile. "Hey, Doc. How's it going?"

Conrad smiled and nodded once.

"Another Saturday shot to hell," Price said. He opened the door to the garbage room, held it open with his shoulder. "Can you believe I'm still unpacking boxes?" He tossed the boxes inside.

Conrad watched him. No, he thought. No, I'm not sure I can believe that. He kept smiling.

"Where's the little girl today?" Price asked.

Conrad tried not to gape at him. "Uh . . . out, she's . . . out with friends . . ."

"Oh," said Price. "Well. I'll be seeing you. Right?" He winked and started walking slowly back to his apartment.

The elevator door opened. Conrad stepped quickly inside.

"Right," he said.

There'll be someone behind you every step of the way. Could be your doorman, could be your best friend. Could be the butcher or the baker. There'll be someone there.

Alone in the elevator, Conrad watched the light move over the door: 5 . . . 4 . . . 3 . . . If someone was watching on the outside, they would know if he stopped the elevator, if he got off.

He didn't. He rode down to the lobby.

He got out and walked toward the doorman. It was Ernie tonight. A tall, thin Hispanic with a broad, white, friendly smile. Ernie pulled the glass door open. As Conrad went by, Ernie smiled and winked at him.

"Seeya, Doc," he said.

Conrad smiled back.

Outside, the night was cold and faintly damp. A thin mist hung over the facade of the Morgan Library across the street. The spotlights trained on it brought its friezes into relief, sent its niches into darker shadow. The outglow from the spotlights hung in the sycamores, in their dying yellow leaves.

People were passing under the trees. A black man in a leather jacket, a girl on his arm, laughing; a silver-haired man in a dark suit; an old woman with dyed-red hair walking her cocker spaniel. A young homeless man was sitting on the library steps, his head bowed to his raised knees.

Conrad paused a moment and looked at them. He felt sweat gather at his temples. A drop rolled down his cheek, down his jaw.

I'll kill her if you stop. I'll kill her if you turn in the wrong direction. If you make a play, if you make a noise, if you make a mistake . . . she'll be dead.

He started walking again, toward the garage next door.

"Howya doin', Doc? Time to fire up the old Rolls?"

Conrad looked into the face of the garage attendant, Lar. It was a familiar face; pug nose, shiny Santa Claus cheeks. Lar worked here most nights. He always saluted Agatha when he saw her. And when he saw Jessie, he pretended he was going to steal her nose. Now, as Conrad looked into his small, squinty eyes, the eyes shone right back at him, like black marbles.

"That'd be great," Conrad said.

Lar saluted and waddled off into the garage.

Conrad waited, his hands in his trench-coat pockets. Nervously, he glanced over his shoulder. His heart gave two quick beats.

Across the street, just beside a frail ginkgo, a figure stood, looking at him. Conrad's mouth opened. He stared at the figure.

Slowly, casually, the figure turned and strolled away.

With a screech of tires, Conrad's silver-blue Corsica came shooting up from the garage depths. It stopped short in front of him. The attendant climbed out.

"Thanks, Lar," Conrad said hoarsely. He slipped behind the wheel of the car.

Now, Doctor, this is what you are going to do. It's seven oh five now. As soon as you hang up the phone, you are going to put on your coat and walk out the door. You're going to drive out to the Impellitteri crazy house. The drive ought to take you twenty—twenty-five minutes, tops.

The Corsica traveled slowly across Thirty-sixth Street toward the Midtown Tunnel. At the corner of Lexington, Conrad stopped at a light. A green Grand Am pulled up alongside him. Its engine grumbled. Conrad glanced over and saw a muscular young man behind the wheel. The young man had a crew cut and wore a white T-shirt. He looked over at Conrad and smirked. He gunned the engine, made it roar.

Conrad swallowed hard and turned away. He glanced up in the rearview mirror. He could not see the driver of the car in back of him. Just a pair of headlights . . . and the silhouette of a head, looking at him.

The light changed. He pressed the gas. Cruised toward the tunnel.

Okay, Sport had said. *So now it's seven-thirty. You go into the crazy house and you go see Elizabeth. Go right in. Don't talk to anyone, don't waste any time. You haven't got any time, Doctor, you understand what I'm telling you? Just go see Elizabeth. Talk to her. Just like you usually do. No drugs, that doesn't work, her mind's gotta be clear. Just talk to her, get her to relax. Get her chatting with you. I'm giving you maybe a half hour for that, maybe even forty-five minutes if you want to cut it close. Okay, so now it's eight-fifteen. She's talking, she's relaxed, she trusts you. Right then, just when it's good, you know? Right then, I want you to ask her one simple question.*

Several roads joined and dipped down toward the mouth of the tunnel. The Corsica entered the swift stream of converging cars. In another moment, Conrad was squinting against the underground glare of lights. Tunnel lights on the filthy yellow tile of the walls. Headlights coming at him from the opposite lane. Red taillights and flashing red brake lights in front of him.

A transit worker strolled along the walkway to his right; he glanced over at Conrad's car as it passed. A Coca-Cola truck bore down on Conrad from behind. Up ahead, the man driving the blue Chevy looked up into his rearview mirror; Conrad could see his eyes.

"Elizabeth, what is the number?" That's the question. That's all you have to say. That's all you have to ask her. Once you've got her going, once she's talking to you, all you have to do is lean over, you know, being friendly and shrinklike and say, "Elizabeth, what is the number?" Nothing to it. Simple as that.

He emerged from the tunnel into the misty night. Edged forward in the cramped line of cars to the tollbooth. Passed through the gate onto the Long Island Expressway.

He gripped the wheel hard. He could feel the sweat coming through his shirt now, on his back, under his arms. The Corsica sailed forward over the wide highway. Surrounded by cars. Cars passing him. Falling behind him. Pulling up alongside. Dark silhouettes behind their wheels.

Headlights like eyes.

It was seven thirty-five when he pulled into the Impellitteri parking lot. He was five minutes behind Sport's schedule.

Nine o'clock. That's when you have to be back. Not a minute after nine. Not a second. I won't wait one second, Doctor. Nine o'clock and you're through, your daughter's through. Remember that.

Conrad parked the car in the reserved space right under the building's wall. He tapped the inside pocket of his trench coat, felt the cassette recorder in there. He had brought it along to make sure everything looked normal to her.

Elizabeth, what is the number? Just one simple question.

He slipped out of the car and shut the door.

Out here, away from Manhattan's sheltering buildings, the night was cold. The mist chilled his skin, his sweat-damp hair. He shivered.

He stood where he was a second, trying to compose himself. His hands were shaking badly now. He couldn't catch his breath. Slowly, licking his lips, he raised his eyes to look at Impellitteri.

The clocktower. That's what Sport had told him. *After she gives you the number, come to the clocktower on Leonard Street. Do you know it? It's way the hell downtown so leave yourself at least a half hour to get there. That means you've got to be out of Impellitteri by eight-thirty at the latest. Get the number and get out by eight-thirty. That'll just give you time. Nine o'clock. That's when you have to be back. Not a minute after nine. Not a second.*

Breathing hard, Conrad gazed at the stark stone cube gleaming gray in the night. The thin mist drifted over it. Droplets of the mist danced and fell in the beams of its spotlights. Where there was light behind the windows, it etched the wire grates that laced the glass. Where there was no light, the windows stared down at him lifelessly.

I don't want to stay here, Daddy. They're bad men. Why can't I come home? I want to come home.

"Oh, God," Conrad whispered. She was so afraid.

Why can't I come home, Daddy?

She was so afraid and he didn't know anything. He didn't know who had taken her or why. He didn't even understand what they wanted.

DON'T SAY A WORD

I don't want to stay here, Daddy.

My baby, he thought. My little girl.

And then he forced the thought away. He had to concentrate. Calm, professional, competent. The Doctor is in. He pressed his hands to his sides to stop their trembling.

Elizabeth, he thought, *what is the number?*

One simple question. That was all he needed to know.

He walked into the hospital.

The lobby was sunk in shadow.

In the ceiling, the purple fluorescents sputtered and hummed. The nurse behind the reception desk, the security guard at the hall entrance—both were figures in silhouette.

Don't talk to anyone. Don't waste any time.

Conrad took out his hospital ID card. Held it up to the reception nurse as he went past. She nodded at him without smiling. Watched him as he walked by. He clipped the card to his trench-coat lapel. It gave him something to do as he walked under the eyes of the security guard.

He came to the elevator, the wide silver door. Pressed the button.

"Yo." A voice shouted from down the dimly lighted hall. "Yo, Nate."

Shit! Conrad thought. He didn't turn. The elevator door opened. He stepped inside.

"Nate. Hey, Nate-o! Wait up!"

Don't talk to anyone. . . .

Conrad needed his master key to take the elevator to the fourth floor. He fumbled with his key chain, trying to find it. *Come on,* he thought. *Come on.*

Don't waste any time.

Jerry Sachs's voice grew louder as he came down the hall.

"Nath-an! Hold the 'vator."

The elevator door slid shut. Conrad put the key in the slot and turned it. He looked up at the lighted numbers.

Then the elevator door opened again. Jerry Sachs stepped in.

The big man was painfully out of breath. Sweat was gleaming on his high pink pate. The front of his pink shirt was dark with it. So were the underarms of his pea-green suit.

"Jesus, Nathan. Didn't you hear me? Get three for me, willya? Whew!" He wiped his broad face with a broad hand.

"Sorry, Jerry. I was . . ." Conrad's voice trailed off. He pressed the button to three. The elevator shut again. It started up.

Conrad studied the lighted numbers as they moved slowly: L . . . 2 . . . Sachs looked down at him jovially.

"So," he said. "Saturday night out, huh? A late date with Nate. I bet you Central Park West types aren't used to these doctor's hours." He guffawed.

Conrad turned and looked up at him. Looked through the thick black glasses, into the wide eyes distorted by the lenses. Stupid eyes, he realized suddenly. Venal and coarse, yes—but stupid, mostly, and frightened of the smart and complicated world.

"Jerry," Conrad said sharply. My daughter's been kidnapped. My house is under surveillance. Please. You've got to call the police.

But he didn't say it. He couldn't force the words out.

There'll be someone with you every step of the way. If you make a play, if you make a noise, if you make a mistake . . . she'll be dead.

"I guess it is kind of late," he said softly.

The elevator stopped at three. The door opened.

"Later, Nater."

Sachs stepped out. Conrad rode to the fourth floor alone.

It was seven-forty now. He had fifty minutes to get it done. He passed the correction officer—that same massive woman—at her desk. He unlocked the ward doors. He walked down the hall toward room number 3.

Aides came toward him in the shadowy hall. Others came up behind him and passed by. Conrad avoided their eyes. He clutched his key chain. He looked down at his key chain, at the thick master key.

What is the number? he kept repeating to himself. *Just one simple question.*

He reached the door and slid the key into the lock. . . .

And as he did, panic mushroomed inside him. His face went clammy. His hand started to shake so hard it made the doorknob rattle.

I can't . . . do this. I can't do this.

He couldn't breathe. He looked around him and the hall, the lights, the shadowy people, seemed to tilt and fade. . . .

I can't do this. Aggie . . .

He had left her. . . .

Aggie.

He had left his wife alone.

With them.

With *them*—and who the hell *were* they? They were watching her, listening to her. And they could come right in. They could pick the locks as they had before. Christ, they could just knock—Aggie would do anything they told her to do. She would do anything to save her baby. How could he have left her there? What kind of man . . . ?

I can't . . .

And now he was going in to see a patient. A severely disturbed woman who had begun to trust him. He was going to ask her a question—and he did not know . . . *anything.* Whether they knew her, whether they could help her . . . Whether their question would hurt her or drive her wild. It might destroy what was left of her sanity—and he didn't know. He didn't know.

What number? Why Elizabeth? Why *me?*

For Christ's sake, why me?

I don't want to stay here, Daddy. They're bad men. Why can't I come home?

He should have refused. He should have called the police. He should have negotiated. . . .

His vision blurred. His hand kept shaking. Oh, God, he thought, they're going to kill my daughter.

And he couldn't help her. He was powerless against them, he was nothing, he couldn't help, he couldn't . . .

"Damn it, damn it, damn it!" he whispered.

He stared at his hand, trying to focus. He fought to control his breathing, to push the breath out with his abdomen, ease it out. The Doctor . . . The Doctor is in.

"Goddamn it!"

He swiped quickly, angrily at the sweat on his face, the tears in his eyes. He gripped the key hard until the edges of it dug into his fingers. Until the quaking of his hand slowed to a steady spasm.

What is the number, Elizabeth? That was all—all he had to say, all he had to ask her. He could do that. He could stay in control long enough to do that. He could get to the clocktower on Leonard Street and tell them the number. They would give him his daughter back alive.

Simple as that.

With a fierce effort of will, he swept his mind clean. He turned the key until the knob turned too. The heavy wooden door swung into Elizabeth's room. Conrad moved in after it. He pulled the key free. The door swung shut behind him with a hollow thud.

And then he stopped. Just over the threshold, he raised his head and stopped. His mouth opened. His hands went cold.

Oh Jesus. Oh Jesus. Oh Jesus.

The room was empty.

At-Home Mother

The big closet in the nursery was Jessica's private play-space. Agatha had cleared the floor for the purpose. Jessica liked to sit in there when she wanted to be alone. She would draw or make puzzles. Or she would play with dolls, absorbed in their story, speaking their dialogue quietly to herself.

Ranged around the closet walls, like an audience, sat her stuffed animals. Teddy bears, alligators, martians, clowns. Kermit the Frog, Goofy, Strawberry Shortcake. Her friends—that's what she called them. As in "Can I bring a friend to the park?" or "Can you sew my friend's eye back on?"

Agatha was standing now in the closet doorway. She was looking down at Jessica's friends. There were so many, dozens of them. Jessica hated to throw them away. And when she looked up at you with trembling lips and said, "Oh, don't throw my friend away, Mommy"—well, what were you supposed to do?

Aggie smiled a little at that—smiled without knowing it, lost in thought. It really did seem as if they'd kept every creature they'd ever gotten. Goofy—he'd been Jessica's favorite for almost six months when she was three. And Miss Piggy, right up near the front—she'd shared Jessica's bed through most of last spring. And then there was Snow. Way toward the back of the closet. White Snow.

111

"Wi no," Agatha said aloud.

He was a small teddy bear, gray now, even black in some places. He was missing one orange eye. His right paw was leaking foam. A patch of purple stitching marred one side—it had been an emergency and purple thread was all Aggie'd had. Still, it was sad to see old Snow shunted to the back like that. Half buried under Sebastian Crab and a Pound Puppy. Supplanted by a dozen other characters Jessie had seen on TV or at other kids' houses.

White Snow had been there first, been there before any of them. He was the very first, in fact. Aggie's mother had brought him to the hospital the day Jessie was born. She'd tucked him under Aggie's arm where she lay in bed. She'd said, "About time," and she'd nodded once firmly. Aggie could only shake her head wearily in response. Here she had been the first of her clan ever to graduate from a four-year college; she had left a drab career in social work to win glamour, money, and even a little fame as an artist; she had married her mother's own ideal of respectability—a Jewish doctor, for heaven's sake—and this, this now, was the first time the crusty, disappointed old woman had shown the slightest sign of pride or even interest in one of her younger daughter's accomplishments.

A teddy bear. White Snow.

Of course, the baby didn't care about the bear in the beginning. For more than a year and a half, the faithful creature just sat nameless and ignored in one corner of her playpen. But one Sunday, just after Christmas, when Jessica was nineteen months old, his time arrived. Nathan was reading in one of the armchairs. Aggie was lying on the sofa, calling out clues to the *Times* crossword puzzle. Jessica was on the floor, "cribbling" with a crayon on one of Aggie's drawing pads.

Suddenly, the child looked up. Her eyes opened wide, her jaw dropped. Her finger shot out, pointing urgently at the balcony doors.

"Dis is . . . ? Dis is . . . ?" she cried. "Dis is . . . ?"

Nathan glanced over at the doors. He grinned. "Hey! Dis is snow. Snow."

"Noe!" said Jessie. She spoke the word with amazement. She lowered her hand and stared at the big flakes tumbling out of the sky. "Noe!"

"Yeah," said Nathan. "Pretty neat, huh?"

"Noe!" Jessie wrestled her way to her feet. Toddled over to the playpen as quickly as she could. Agatha laughed. When she hurried like that, she looked, Nathan said, like a robot stumbling downhill. But she'd made it to the pen, reached inside, and plucked out her old teddy bear. She held it up to Nathan. Her voice was strained with urgency. "Noe!" she cried.

"Yeah, that's right!" Nathan laughed. "Snow is white. White snow."

"Wi noe!" Jessica cried out in triumph. "Wi noe!" And she clutched the bear to herself fiercely. Rocked it back and forth in a tremendous hug, cooed over and over in its ear, "Wi noe. Wi noe."

From that time—oh, for at least a year—she had dragged that bear around with her everywhere. She had taught White Snow the new words she learned. Showed him the pictures in her books. Tucked him into bed for his naps. Held him under her arm when she went to sleep. Aggie even remembered having to give the old bear a good-night kiss every night when he and the child were set down in her crib.

Aggie moved to him now at the back of the closet. She knelt down in front of him. She wanted to straighten him a little. Take Sebastian Crab and the Pound Puppy off him. Maybe move him up a little toward the front. Not too much. Not so much that Jessica would notice it. . . . That is, when she came home . . . when Nathan brought her back . . .

Agatha stifled a sob and took the old bear into her arms. She held it tightly. She rubbed her cheek against its worn, patchy gray fur.

"Wi noe," she said to him.

Her eyes filled. Her vision blurred. She clutched the one-eyed bear to her chest. She could remember—she could feel—the warm weight of the newborn there. The doctor had whapped it onto her swollen breasts like a caught fish. Aggie had still been panting from the labor. She had kept saying, "Oh. A baby. Oh. A baby." Over and over again. They had had to wait so long. Until Nathan was all well. Until his practice was set up. Until there was money. Until he felt sure. She had looked up and she had seen Nathan standing over her. He had been crying and smiling at once. "Oh," she had told him. "Oh, Nathan. A baby." And then later, her mother had come to the hospital and given her the bear. White Snow.

Aggie sniffed her tears back fiercely. She daubed at her eyes with the bear's ear. Don't let them see you cry, she thought. Let those sick bastards rot in hell before they see you cry, Aggie. She could feel their cameras everywhere around her—*on* her, like a stranger's hands. She could imagine them—silhouetted figures with hot, white eyes—watching her. Watching her.

Who are you, you bastards? Why are you doing this to us?

113

It took a few more moments before she could relax her hold on the teddy bear. Then she slowly lowered him to the floor, set him in his place. His place in the back of the closet. A place of his own. She rested him against the wall, seated him erect.

Don't worry, she thought to him. Nathan will get her back. He'll get her and bring her back, truly. He's doing it right now.

She had told herself that a hundred times, a thousand times in the half hour since he'd left. Nathan was out there, getting her, right this minute, right now. He hadn't told her where he was going. They wouldn't let him, he said. But whatever they wanted him to do, he would do it; whoever they were, whatever they were trying to get from him, he would hand it over and bring back their child. She kept telling herself that. Soon, she kept thinking—in just a couple of hours—by nine-thirty at most, he would walk in, carrying their daughter in his arms.

She looked down once more at the shabby gray bear. It's going to be all right, she thought. Just hang on. Nathan will bring her back. Everything's going to be all right. . . .

And just then, the doorbell rang.

Aggie's breath caught. She didn't move at first.
Don't open the door for anyone.
The doorbell rang again.

Aggie raised her eyes, searched the closet ceiling, appealed to the cameras hidden there. What should she do? What did they want her to do?

There was knocking now. Soft, but steady and insistent. What if it was them? What if they wanted to come in? What if they got angry at her for not coming to the door?

The knocking paused a second. The doorbell rang again. Then there was more knocking.

"Mrs. Conrad?" It was a man's voice, calling to her.

Slowly, Agatha rose to her feet. She moved out of the nursery as if in a trance. Her feet drifted forward as if she were being drawn on by some mysterious force. Her eyes continued to dart from place to place. Searching for cameras. Glancing at the phone: Call, you bastards. Tell me what to do. Let me know what you want. For Christ's sake, I'll do it, just call.

"Mrs. Conrad?" The soft, steady rapping continued.

Agatha reached the door. She stood before it, running her fingers up through her hair. What do they want me to do? She couldn't decide.

Very slowly, she lifted her hand. As quietly as she could, she slid back the cover of the peephole. She leaned forward, peeked out.

The man in the hall waved at her. He was a handsome young man with slick black hair. "Hi, Mrs. Conrad," he said. "It's me."

She wasn't able to place him for a second. Then it came to her. Price. He was the new neighbor, Billy Price, from 5H. She hadn't spoken to him except to say hello around the elevator. The building gossip was that he was a twenty-five-year-old stockbroker originally from Topeka, Kansas. Unmarried. Harvard educated. Three younger brothers, parents still living.

"Uh . . . hi . . . ?" She had to clear her throat. She moved close to the door and spoke to it. "Could you come back later, Billy? This isn't a good time. I'm not dressed."

"Doesn't bother me any," said Billy Price. He laughed boyishly. "Come on, Mrs. Conrad. Agatha, isn't it? You gotta let me in. I know you're by yourself but . . . really."

Aggie didn't answer. She glanced back at the phone, back at the door. Call, she thought. Tell me. What do you want me to do?

You gotta let me in.

Why would he insist like that? And how could he know she was by herself? Maybe he'd seen Nathan go out but . . . he'd seen her with Jessica before, he knew she had a daughter. How could he know Jessica wasn't here now?

"Oh, A-ga-tha." This time he sang her name out. It sounded threatening, dangerous.

If he wasn't one of them, why didn't they call?

"Let me ii-in, Ag-a-tha."

Without thinking, Aggie shot out her hand. Pulled open the door.

Billy Price stepped inside immediately. Aggie had to step back to get out of his way. He smiled shyly, closing the door behind him.

"Hi. Remember me? Billy Price? From down the hall?" His eyes went up and down her. She was still in her jeans and sweatshirt. She hadn't put on a bra. When he looked at her, she felt her naked breasts under the shirt. He smiled that shy smile again, but when he raised his eyes to hers, she could see that they were not shy at all. They were hot; they were laughing at her. "I really am sorry," he went on. "I just wanted to borrow the yellow pages, I haven't got mine yet. And . . . the truth is, I knew you were home and I . . . Well, I haven't had a chance to get to know you so I . . . I thought I'd come by. You know?"

"Well, I . . ." Aggie tried to form the sentence, but her mind was racing. Was he one of them? Why was he toying with her? "It's—in the kitchen. The phone book. I'll get it."

"Oh, there's no hurry," said Billy Price. He took another step toward her. He was too close now, she could feel his warm breath on her face. "Really. I thought, you know . . . What I mean is, I've noticed you around the hall, Agatha, and I thought . . . well, with your family out and all, this might be a good time for us to, I don't know, talk, sit down together. Get to know each other."

Then, with the screech of a buzz saw cutting through stone, the phone rang behind her.

Aggie jumped. She gasped. "Sweet Christ!" she said. She spun around. The phone rang again.

Breathing hard, she glanced back at Billy Price. He was staring at her. She forced a smile.

"Why, it's the phone," she said. "Won't you excuse me?"

Her heart was knocking at her chest as she staggered to it. She turned her back on Price. She picked up the receiver.

"He . . . Hello . . . ?"

And a voice shrieked wildly in her ear, *"Who's that, you cunt, you cunt! I told you no one comes in! I'll cut her open, I'll cut your little girl in fucking half, you stupid cunt! Tell me who it is now, now, now, now, now!"*

"I . . . How can I . . . I . . ."

"All right, cunt!" And then the man said, "Get me the girl."

"No, I . . ."

Through a haze of terror, Aggie heard her daughter's voice in the background: "Let me go! No! Please. Please . . ." She started crying.

"Please," Aggie whispered. "I just don't know how to say it . . ."

The man's voice was suddenly calmer, quieter. Aggie could still hear Jessica crying. But it was a cry of fear—Aggie could tell; she wasn't in pain. Not yet.

"Jessie," she whispered.

"Listen," the man on the phone said breathlessly. "I'm your friend. Okay? I'm your friend Louise. You understand me. You say, 'Oh, hello, Louise.'"

"Oh, hello . . ." Agatha's voice cracked. She tried again. "Hello, Louise."

"Good. Now say, 'Let me call you right back, Louise. So-and-so just dropped by for such and such a reason."

"I . . . I . . ."

"Say it, you dumb slash!"

"Yes, uh, let me . . . let me call you right back, Louise. Uh . . . Billy Price, my new neighbor from down the hall, he . . . he just dropped by to borrow a phone book. Just to borrow a phone book."

"Good," said the man. "Now, you get that miserable fuckhead out of there in jigtime, cunt, slash, fucking cunt. You've got sixty seconds. Then I cut her." He slammed the phone down.

Agatha lowered the receiver to its cradle. She turned to face Billy Price. Price was still staring at her.

"I'll get the phone book," she whispered.

"Uh . . . really," Price said a little uncertainly. "Really, there's no hurry."

"Yes," said Agatha. "Really. There is."

She left him standing there and rushed into the kitchen.

The phone book was always in there—Aggie did most of her talking on the kitchen extension. She had left the book on the windowsill this time. It had been buried under the big cookie tin, a box of Baggies, and a half-eaten bag of pretzels. She held all these in place with one hand. With the other, she started to wrestle the big book out from underneath.

Who's that, you cunt, you cunt! I told you no one comes in!

She could still hear his voice. That terrible voice. It was burning in her ears, branded on her mind.

Tell me who it is now, now, now, now, now!

She pulled the book free. The cookie tin and all the rest settled down onto the sill. She turned around, ready to carry the book back into the living room.

Why didn't he know?

"Jesus," she whispered aloud. But she didn't stop. She couldn't. There was no time. She walked toward the kitchen door, carrying the phone book.

But why? she thought. Why *didn't* he know who it was? Price had said it, he had announced himself. *Hi. Remember me? Billy Price? From down the hall?* He'd said it the moment he'd stepped inside. Why hadn't the man on the phone heard him? Why hadn't he heard it through his microphones?

She came out of the kitchen, down the short hall.

Maybe he just wasn't listening. Maybe he hadn't been near his machines. . . .

She came into the living room. There was poor Price, looking rather bewildered. Hands in his pockets, feet shuffling, eyes aimlessly scanning the walls.

He'd been hysterical—the man on the phone. He'd been panicked. He hadn't known who it was because . . .

She lifted the heavy phone book in both hands. She held it out as she approached Price. She forced a friendly smile. "Here you are," she said.

There are no fucking microphones, she thought. There are cameras—he can see us all right. He saw Billy Price come in. He can see whatever we do. But he can't hear us. He couldn't hear us talking through the door—that's why he didn't call then. He called when he *saw* Price. He *had* to call, he had to scream at me over the phone, to find out what was going on. He couldn't just listen. *There are no microphones.*

"Oh . . . uh . . . well, thanks," said Billy Price. "Thanks, uh . . ." As she reached him, he lifted his hand for the phone book. He looked into her eyes, trying one more time. "I guess this means I'm not invited in for tea, huh?"

Agatha smiled more broadly. Tilted her head in a warm, neighborly manner. "Listen to me, you creepy little son of a bitch," she said. "I need you to cut the shit right now and help me. My daughter has been kidnapped. My apartment is being watched. Call the police. Tell them. Right now."

Price's smile stayed frozen on his face. He looked at her blankly. Then, slowly, the smile melted away. His mouth fell open.

"Get that look off your face, son, they can see you," said Aggie, smiling sweetly. "Smile. Take hold of the book."

She stuffed the phone book into his hands. He took hold of it. She gave a tinkly little neighborly laugh.

"Now don't think I'm joking," she said. "Don't think at all. Just trundle back to your pad or whatever you call it, and dial 911 as if a little girl's life depended on it." She was pushing him toward the door now—leaning on the phone book so that he was forced backward. Price had managed to fix a sickly smile on his lips and was staring at her glassy-eyed.

She reached around him and opened the door.

"If the police come here, my daughter will die. Tell them that. Make sure they understand. Now say, 'Thank you and good-bye, Mrs. Conrad.'"

"Thank you and good-bye, Mrs. Conrad," Price said flatly. She pushed him out into the hall and shut the door in his face.

* * *

Agatha swung around and stared at the phone. If she was wrong—if there *were* microphones—if they *could* hear her—it would ring. Suddenly, it seemed to her that it *must* ring, that she had to be wrong. It had all happened so fast, there hadn't been time to really think it out. There were so many other possibilities. Of course she was wrong. Of course it would ring. It would ring right now and she would hear that horrible voice again, that vicious man. She would hear her daughter, crying. Screaming. She stared at the phone. The phone was silent. But if she'd been wrong . . . If she'd guessed wrong . . .

And still, the phone didn't ring.

She started to walk back across the room. She went on tiptoe, so as not to disturb the sleeping beast—the silent phone. She went slowly, hardly breathing. Back toward the hallway. Back into the nursery. She wanted to get as far away from the phone as she could. If she could get away from it, maybe it would not catch her.

And yet the phone was not ringing. It still didn't ring. She had been right. They *couldn't* hear her. There were no microphones. Only cameras. She had been right. And little by little, the surging terror fell away. Her mind began to focus, to clear. She went into the nursery. She went to the closet. Somehow, she felt safer there, among Jessie's friends. She felt protected from the phone.

She went to the back. She reached down and picked up the old gray bear. She held it close. She rocked it back and forth.

We did it, old Snow, she thought. We've gotten to the police. They're going to arrest those men. They're going to bring back Jessie. I know it.

She held the bear tighter. "Dear Jesus," she whispered aloud, "help us please."

In the other room, the phone began to ring.

Street Clothes

Conrad stared at the empty room. He thought he could feel time—feel it racing at him while he stood there, motionless. It was . . . what? Seven forty-one? Forty-two? He couldn't look at his watch somehow. But he knew he had to be out of there, on the road, by eight-thirty. And as he stood, sweeping the empty room with his eyes, he could just feel the moment approaching him. He looked at the water basin undisturbed on the plastic table. The empty chair before the grated window. The empty bed, its cover pulled tight. He could feel time bearing down on him like a locomotive.

What did he do now? Where was Elizabeth? Where the hell *could* she be? She was a violent patient in a forensic ward, for Christ's sake. She should've been here.

He spun around to the door. He reached for the knob.

And then the door opened toward him. And Elizabeth was there.

She came into the room and paused. She stood before him proudly. She posed for him, a sly, proud smile on her face. She was dressed differently, that was the thing. She was wearing street clothes—not city issue—her own. It was nothing much. Just an old pink shift that fell around her shapelessly. But the vagabond look of the rumpled cords and shirt was gone. And her hair was tied back with a pretty black ribbon. Her lips were tinged with orange-red lipstick that went well with her light skin. And there was liner highlighting the depths of those deep green eyes. Even Conrad, even then, could see: a lovesick boy couldn't have invented her—she was that beautiful.

A therapy aide came in behind her. A small, pretty Hispanic woman. She stood to one side to let Elizabeth show herself off. When Conrad didn't say anything, the nurse said, "She wanted to get dressed for you. She is excited that you are coming. She is very pretty, huh?"

"Uh . . . what?" Conrad blinked, shook his head. "Yes. I mean, yes, of course. Elizabeth, you look . . . lovely. Really. You really look . . . wonderful."

Elizabeth smiled, her cheeks flushed. "They're just my old clothes. The ones I was wearing when I came here."

"You look . . . beautiful. Really," Conrad managed to say.

Elizabeth laughed. She seemed about to say something more. But she paused, glanced at the aide.

"All right, all right, I will go now," the woman said.

"What?" said Conrad. "Oh. Yes. Please. Thank you."

The aide withdrew, pulling the door shut behind her.

But Elizabeth still didn't speak. And Conrad stood before her stupidly. He rubbed his hands together.

"Uh . . . well . . . ," he said.

Talk to her. Just like you usually do. Talk to her, get her to relax. Get her chatting with you. I'm giving you maybe a half hour for that.

"Uh . . . well, Elizabeth," he said again.

"Doctor," she said. She took a deep breath. "Doctor, I've come to a decision."

Conrad waited. He could feel the time rushing at him. With a slow, steady step, Elizabeth walked past him to her chair by the window. Conrad turned after her. He watched silently as she lowered herself into the chair. She sat in her usual position: her head erect, her hands folded quietly in her lap. Conrad felt a drop of sweat fall from his hair, trickle down the side of his neck. Come on, he thought.

I'm giving you maybe a half hour.

"I've decided to tell you about Robert Rostoff," Elizabeth said.

"Robert . . . ?"

"Yes. The man that . . . he killed, that the Secret Friend . . . killed. The thing I'm here for." She looked up at him. Her mouth was set, her eyes were earnest. "I haven't told anyone," she said. "Not the whole story. I've decided to tell you."

Conrad stared at her, his lips parted. "You've decided . . ." And his mind was racing: What is the number? Does it have to do with this, with Robert Rostoff, is that it? Why my daughter, Elizabeth? Why me?

He did glance down at his watch now: it was 7:46. He wiped his lips dry. *Talk to her. Just like you usually do. Talk to her, get her to relax.*

"Well . . . yes . . . ," Conrad said slowly. "I . . . I want to hear about that, Elizabeth, of course."

He turned away from her, setting his face. He walked to the wooden chair in the far corner. He brought it back, placed it backwards in front of her.

Just like you usually do.

Casually, he stripped off his trench coat and laid it on the bed. He saw Elizabeth look at him with surprise.

"Saturday," he said with a smile. But he did feel a little naked without his suit and tie.

He straddled the chair. Folded his arms on the back. He thought he looked composed and attentive now. He tried to hold on to that. "Go ahead, Elizabeth," he said.

But she hesitated, searching his face. And then she said, "The thing is . . . I've decided . . . you're not one of them. That's the thing, all right? I didn't mean to . . . suspect you but . . . you have to understand: it's so hard to tell . . . I never know. People are nice and then all of a sudden they . . . change. Do you understand?"

Conrad nodded solemnly. "Yes. I understand."

"All right then." She made a determined little motion with her chin. "All right." She glanced up at him. "Don't you want to turn on your machine?"

"What? Oh." *Shit,* he thought. He unwound himself from the chair. He retrieved his recorder from his coat and set it on the table. "Go ahead," he said. He straddled the chair again.

"All right," she said. "All right."

I'm giving you maybe a half hour. Conrad heard Sport speaking almost as if he were there.

Eight-thirty, he thought. By eight-thirty, I've got to be out of here.

It was seven forty-eight.

"Tell me," he said.

Elizabeth started talking.

The Murder of Robert Rostoff

He's always different. The Secret Friend, I mean. I guess I told you that already, but it's an important thing. He's never the same. You've got to understand that. Dr. Holbein didn't understand. He was my doctor at the state hospital. After the Secret Friend hurt the sailor—the sailor who touched my . . . touched me, or whatever . . . after that, I was sent to the state hospital. They gave me medicine there and Dr. Holbein worked with me. Dr. Holbein was good, he was nice. He was like you a little, only older and he had a gray beard. And he didn't have a sad face like you—he laughed all the time. Anyway, he was from California so I can't see him anymore. But I liked him.

His medicine made me sleepy, but it made me feel better too after a while. I wasn't so confused anymore. And the Secret Friend stopped coming—at least, I thought he did. I mean, you never knew for sure. I tried to tell Dr. Holbein that: you never knew, because he was never the same.

But Dr. Holbein said I could live outside the hospital. Lucy—my social worker—she helped me get a job at the Liberty Center for Children. It was for poor children, a day-care center. My job was to clean the place up in the evenings. The cafeteria and the rooms and the windows. It was a big job. There were a lot of things to remember. But I liked it. I liked being near children, even though they'd usually left by the time I got there. I just liked being where they were. I liked going into the classrooms sometimes when

123

no one was around and just sitting, you know? I would sit and think about, you know, being in school, the Sunshine School. But not in a crazy way or anything. It was nice.

Then, the other thing, the best thing, was that I got a room—an apartment—all to myself. It was in a brownstone up on Eighty-first Street, off Columbus Avenue. A social worker lived downstairs, on the ground floor. Ronnie. He would come up and visit me a lot. But the rest of the time, I was by myself. It was just one room, but it had a kitchenette and a bathroom, and a couch that I could fold out into a bed at night. I *loved* that. I wish I was still there now, I really do. I guess after what happened, though, I won't ever get to go back.

But that was, like, the happiest time of my life. Maybe seven or eight months. I just worked at the center in the evenings and lived in my apartment. I felt good. I wasn't confused. In fact, the only trouble was that I felt so happy that, you know, I worried . . . I worried that the Secret Friend *would* come back. I mean, you never knew, he was always . . . Well, I told Dr. Holbein. But he said I should stop worrying. He said he thought the Secret Friend was gone forever.

But I did worry. I thought about it a lot. I thought about it all the time.

Anyway, the Liberty Center, the place where I worked, was on a little lane in the Village. A narrow, cobbled lane with one sort of old-fashioned streetlamp on it. The center was a brick building that took up one side of the lane, and across the street was the brick wall of a church. Sometimes, when I was out in the lane, the church's bells would chime or even play a carol.

When I left work, about eleven o'clock, the lane would be dark and empty. Just the one streetlamp burning across the street. And there would be no one in sight, except over on MacDougal Street where the lane ended.

Then, one night, I stepped out of the center and there *was* someone there. I thought . . . I remember, I stepped out the door, and the church bell was chiming eleven, and I thought . . . I saw someone. A figure, standing behind the lamp, hiding in the glare of the lamp. I could feel him though. Standing there. Looking at me . . .

Well, I . . . I was scared. I was scared, but I tried to ignore him. I started walking away from him, toward MacDougal Street. I took about—I don't know—four steps. And just then, the church bell stopped tolling the hour. And the echo of it died away, and it was so quiet. And I heard a man's voice right behind me, right in my ear. And it said, "Elizabeth."

I stopped and turned around.

124

"Go away," I said—loudly. "Go away. I don't want you here."

But he *was* there. He was there, coming toward me. I saw his face. His red hair, his white skin, his freckles. He was wearing a dark overcoat and he had his hands hidden in the pockets.

"Go away," I shouted. "No."

But he kept coming toward me. And I heard his voice again: "Elizabeth." I turned again and ran.

I ran down the lane as fast as I could. I ran to MacDougal. There were people there, young people from the university and the neighborhood. And there were lights from streetlamps and from restaurants and stores. I ran toward the lights as fast as I could. I glanced over my shoulder to see if he was behind me . . . and as I did, I stepped off the curb.

There were screeching brakes to the left of me. A horn blared. I remember I turned around and saw the front fender of a cab like the teeth of some giant creature about to eat me. I screamed and threw my hands up in front of my face.

And suddenly, someone grabbed me. An arm wrapped itself around my waist. It pulled me backward, back to the sidewalk. The cab went rushing past me.

But the arm kept holding me. And I thought: It's him. You see? I kept thinking: It's him. He's got me. So I hit at him. I punched his arm. I kicked and struggled and I shouted at him, "Let go of me. Please."

"All right, all right," he said. He lowered me slowly to the ground. I turned around and faced him. He laughed. And he said in this sort of laughing voice, "I guess that's New York gratitude for you."

Because, you see, it wasn't him at all. It was another man. A young man, handsome. With a sort of round, boyish face. Brown hair falling into his eyes. And he had a nice smile—even though I knew he was laughing at me—a nice smile.

I looked past his shoulder, down the alley. The red-haired man was gone. I stood in front of this new person, this stranger, panting, embarrassed.

"I'm sorry," I said. "I didn't . . . I'm sorry . . ."

I didn't know what to say. I was all confused. I started to walk away from him, but he followed after me.

He said, "Hey, wait a minute. I've been standing at this corner all day waiting for a pretty girl to step out in front of a cab so I could save her life. Don't tell me it was just a waste of time."

Well, that was a funny thing to say. I didn't . . . I didn't know what to answer. I kept hurrying to the corner.

And he said, "No, wait. Really." He took hold of my arm. I stopped and looked at him. He said—he said, "You know, the Japanese say that when a man saves a woman's life, he has to buy her an automobile dealership. Or maybe it's a drink. Who the hell can speak Japanese?"

I didn't. . . . I just said, "Japanese?"

He laughed again—he had this very nice laugh. He shook his head. And he explained that he wanted to buy me a drink; that's what he was saying.

Well, I . . . I just looked at him. I said, "Why?"

And he said, " 'Why?' " He said, "Well, let's see. Because you're one of the most beautiful women I've ever seen in *my* entire life and I just saved *your* entire life. And that might not happen to me again for hours. I mean, it's the least I can do by way of thanks."

Well, I said . . . I told him, "I don't drink." I didn't want to tell him, you see, that I was on medication. So I said, "I could have a soda, though."

And he said, "Well—I don't know. It *is* Thursday and the rules on these things *are* pretty strict. But hell, if it's just this once. The Central Committee will never find out."

"The Central Committee?" I said.

He laughed. He said, "Come on, spacegirl."

He took me to a little café called The Alamo on Sixth Avenue. We had Cokes together and one of those—what do you call it?—a guacamole dip. It was very good. And he told me then—he told me his name was Terry Somerset. He was an actor, he said. He said he was in a play at the MacDougal Street Playhouse. I knew that theater too. I walked by it every day on my way to the subway. I'd always wanted to go in. He said he worked there and then sometimes did word-processing work for money. I told him I worked at a day-care center. I guess I made it sound like I was one of the children's caretakers, you know. I guess I was trying to impress him.

Well, he said, "You're working kind of late tonight, aren't you?"

And I said, "Yes." I said, "Yes. I work late a lot."

And he said, "You came out of that lane like there was someone chasing after you. . . ."

And I said, "Well . . ." I said very quickly, "Well, it was dark." I said, "And there *was* someone there. I guess I got frightened, that's all."

Terry said you couldn't be too careful in New York. Then we talked about other things.

When we were finished at the café, it was very late. Terry put me in a cab and paid the driver for me. I was happy driving home. I'd never met a man like Terry before. I mean, I'd never even had a date or anything really. It was fun. I had a good time.

I didn't hear from Terry for a few days, but he called me on Monday. He invited me out to dinner. I lied and said I had to work late again. I didn't want to tell him that I worked late every night; I mean, that I was just the cleaning lady at Liberty. Anyway, Terry said he would meet me at The Alamo after work.

All that day, I was worried. Dr. Holbein had told me that the Secret Friend showed up whenever I got anxious about . . . you know, like, sex things. Whatever you want to call them. But I kept telling myself, you know, this was just a soda. I mean, Terry didn't try to *do* anything to me. Why should the Secret Friend be angry? But all the same, I was worried.

I left work a little early that night—around ten forty-five. I stepped out the door into the lane—and the red-haired man grabbed me.

He caught me by the arm. I tried to pull away. But he leaned his face into mine. And his voice was everywhere, inside my head, all around me.

"Keep away from him, Elizabeth," he said. "He just wants to take your mother out. You have to understand that. He's just trying to take your mother out. Keep away from him."

I cried out, "No!" But he kept saying things, terrible things about Terry, about my mother. He kept saying them. I cried out again and pulled away from him. I ran—I ran down the lane as fast as I could.

I went to the café, I went to see Terry, but I was very upset. Terry kept asking me what was wrong. I just said it was nothing. I changed the subject. I told him how I'd always wanted to go to the MacDougal Street Playhouse. And he said, you know, well, why don't we? So after we had a soda, he took me over there. The place was locked up by then, but he had a key. We went inside and he showed me where his picture was on the wall. There was a sign for a play called *Shadows,* and there were pictures of the cast tacked to a bulletin board in the lobby. Terry's picture was right in the center of them. He was the most handsome, I thought.

Then he took me inside and we stood on the stage together. It was very exciting. It was all set up to look like a living room, except the furniture was covered with sheets. Terry read some of his lines to me as if I were in the play. He made me laugh a lot.

But then he said, he asked me, "What *is* the matter, Elizabeth? What's been bothering you all night?"

Well, I had to say something, so I said, "Oh, you know, it's that man again. That one who was in the alley before. He's been bothering me, saying nasty things."

Terry looked really angry. He said he would meet me right at the door of the center from now on. He said he better not catch that man bothering me. I was sorry I'd told him, but it was nice to have Terry talk that way, about protecting me and everything. Then he took hold of my shoulders and he kissed me. Right there on the dark stage. It was very romantic. As if we were lovers in the play.

The next day, I was supposed to go to the clinic to get my medication. The doctor there asked me if everything was all right, if I was hearing voices, if I was seeing things.

I wanted to tell him the truth. But I was afraid. I was afraid he would put me back in the hospital and I wouldn't see Terry anymore. I told him everything was fine. He gave me the medication and let me go.

Then, that Saturday, Terry and I had a date for dinner. He took me to a steak house in Chelsea. We went to see a movie and then had coffee at a café and talked about it. Terry talked about all the different actors and whether they were good or not. After that, we went for a walk.

It was pretty late by then, I guess. Around eleven or so. And we walked into a neighborhood that wasn't very nice. There were big empty buildings—warehouses—everywhere. And there were men gathered together in the shadows of doorways. And there were homeless men standing around trash-can fires. It was late September and it had gotten chilly, especially where we were, over by the river.

Finally, we stopped in front of an old brownstone just a block before the Hudson on a little street called Houses Street. It was very dark there. I could just see the shadows of a big warehouse and the brownstone and a vacant lot. There were no streetlamps and the house we were in front of, the brownstone, was the only place with a light on.

Terry said, "This is me. I live here. Would you like to come in?"

He looked at me, waiting to see what I would say. I was nervous. I was scared. I was scared something bad might happen. But I wanted everything to be nice. Like it is for normal people, you know? So I said all right. I said I'd go inside.

We went inside. The light was out in the hallway and I was very nervous. But then—once we got upstairs—once we got into Terry's apartment, I thought: It's going to be all right. I thought: Everything is going to be just fine.

The apartment was on the second floor. It was a small studio and it wasn't nice. It was . . . I don't know: seedy. But . . . it was manly, sort of. You know what I mean? I mean, there was this tatty old sofa and a couple of worn-out armchairs. Magazines about sports and electronics lying around all over the place. And there was one of those little Hollywood beds against one wall.

Terry said, "One day, when I'm a big star on Broadway, I'll look back at this and weep uncontrollably."

But I liked it. I liked being there.

There was no kitchen, just a little half-sized refrigerator and a hot plate. But Terry found a can of Coke in the fridge. We sat on the sofa and passed the can back and forth. Then, Terry put the can aside and moved close to me. We began to kiss again. Hard, a lot. He put his tongue in my mouth. He put his hands on me, on my breasts, whatever. But I didn't mind. Really. It felt good. I was feeling all right about it. After a while, he even put his hand inside my skirt. He put his fingers inside my underpants.

That's when I opened my eyes and saw him.

He was at the window—the red-haired man. He was staring in the second-story window at us. His eyes were wide, crazy. His face—all white, all freckled—it was wild and mad.

I screamed and jumped up, away from Terry.

"What?" he said. "What's the matter?"

"We have to go! We have to get out of here!" I screamed the words. "Please! I have to leave!"

"Leave? Elizabeth, what's the matter?" Terry got up. He took me by the shoulders. "Elizabeth, for God's sake, you have to tell me what's wrong!"

"You don't understand. You're in danger. You're in terrible danger. . . ."

"Danger? What are you talking—"

"The red-haired man. It's him. It's him."

I pointed to the window. Terry turned and looked. "Who? There's no one there."

"Please." I had started crying. I couldn't stop. "Please, you have to take me home. You have to get away from me right now."

"Damn it, Elizabeth, you have to tell me what's the matter."

"I can't," I screamed. I cried harder. "I can't."

And then I ran away. I was so afraid. I was so afraid the Secret Friend would hurt him. I ran out of the apartment. Down the stairs. I pushed out the door. I stumbled down the stoop to the sidewalk.

I heard Terry call out behind me, "Elizabeth!" But I didn't stop. I ran. Through the dark, past the dark men. I don't even know how I got home. I guess I just kept running until I found a subway. I remember riding on a subway and then . . . Then the next thing I remember is being inside, being home. I turned the light on, locked my door. I lay down on the bed. I lay there trembling, crying.

After a long time, I guess I went to sleep.

Elizabeth paused here for a moment. Conrad looked down at his watch. It was eight oh four now. He had to stop her soon. He couldn't let the story go on much longer.

But he kept thinking—listening and thinking: maybe there's something. Something here. About the number. About my daughter. About a man named Sport. Maybe there's something that will help. Something that I'll need.

What is the number, Elizabeth? Why me?

He lifted his eyes to her. He smiled gently. He nodded his encouragement.

Elizabeth went on.

I sat up, suddenly, my heart pounding. There had been a noise. It sounded again. The buzzer to the downstairs intercom. It was loud as a fire alarm.

I looked around, blinking, confused. The room was dark. I wasn't even sure where I was.

And then the buzzer sounded again. I got out of bed. The clock on my bedside table showed it was after two A.M. I couldn't think. I stumbled to the intercom. Pressed the talk button.

"Yes? What?"

"Elizabeth. Elizabeth, it's me." It was Terry. "Are you all right?"

"I'm . . . fine. I was sleeping. What are you . . . ?"

"Let me in. Let me come up. I have to see you."

I was about to answer him—when a hand wrapped itself around my mouth.

I was pulled back from the intercom. I saw a pale white hand reach out in front of me. I grabbed for it. I tried to stop it. But he was too strong. He pressed the button that opened the downstairs door.

I struggled. I tried to scream. But he grabbed me around the waist and dragged me backward. I heard his voice, hoarse and breathless in my ear.

"It's all right, Elizabeth. I'll protect you from him. I'll take care of you. I'm your friend."

I scratched at his hand. I tried to shout, "No! Please! Let me go!" But the hand around my mouth muffled my screams. The hand around my waist held me tight. I was dragged toward the bathroom.

Now there was knocking at the door. I heard Terry's voice outside: "Elizabeth? Open up, it's me. Are you all right?"

"Terry! Run!" I tried to shout it. I did. But he muffled me. His hand muffled me.

And then I was thrown into the bathroom. I fell to the hard floor. The door was closed. I scrambled to my feet. I rushed at the door again. I tried to open it. It was stuck. Something had been shoved against it. I pounded on the door with my fists.

"Terry! Oh, Terry! Please, God, no! Don't hurt him! Jesus Christ, Terry, run!"

I clutched my face in my hands. I tore at my forehead with my nails. I wanted to rip the madness out of me. I had to stop it, stop it before Terry got hurt. The blood ran down into my eyes. I kept screaming, "Terry! Don't come in! Run!"

And then—it was like it came from another world—from some other country or something, far away, through a fog—I heard a man shriek: "No!" And there was a terrible noise. A terrible—I don't know—*strangling* noise. And I looked down. I looked down and there was blood on my hands. Blood. Blood all over. And I wasn't in the bathroom anymore. I was out, I was out in the darkness. And I was crying, and the blood and the tears were running down my cheeks. And then suddenly . . . suddenly I could feel him there. I was lying on the floor somehow and I could feel him under me. And I felt the blood. The blood all over. Oh, blood. Oh, it was everywhere. And there were people screaming. There were people screaming my name. And then the lights came on. I was blinded. Lights in my eyes. And people were screaming. And I was covered, I was covered with blood all over.

I looked down. He was there. He was lying under me. He was cut, all over. . . . His eyes. Jesus Christ. His eyes. He was dead, I knew he was dead. And I knew what had happened. Finally. I knew everything now. You see?

Because it wasn't Terry. It wasn't Terry lying there dead, Dr. Conrad. It was him. It was the red-haired man. It was Robert Rostoff.

Terry had killed him. Terry was the Secret Friend.

What Is the Number?

Conrad looked up from his watch. "What?"

Elizabeth sat before him, crying quietly. Her head was bowed. The tears fell onto her lap, onto her clasped hands.

Conrad shook his head, trying to clear it, trying to focus. It was so late, he kept thinking. It was all he could think about. Eight-twelve now. Eighteen minutes left. He had to question her. He had to get the number. He couldn't concentrate on anything else, think of anything else.

Still, when she finished, he blinked at her. "What did you say?"

Elizabeth spoke through her tears. "I said, it was the red-haired man. Not Terry."

"But how is that possible? I thought . . ."

"They told me . . . the police, I mean . . . they told me he was some kind of clerk, a token clerk, in the subways. They said he'd taken me for a date and that I'd . . ." Her tears were slowing. She raised her head. She held him with her damp eyes. "I tried to tell them about Terry. I took them to the MacDougal Street Playhouse. I tried to show them his picture . . . on the wall, you know?" She swallowed, shook her head. "But there *was* no picture of him. And the other people, the rest of the cast . . . they'd never heard of him."

"Oh . . . Elizabeth." Conrad stopped himself from saying more.

She bowed her head again. "Then . . . I told them I'd been to his house.

132

I told them the address. They just looked at me. They said the houses on that block were all abandoned. They even drove me there. They showed me. There's the brownstone, they said. Number two twenty-two. And the house was—empty . . . nothing in it but trash."

Conrad looked at the young woman, shook his head again.

"He's always different," she said miserably. "The Secret Friend. He's never the same."

For a few seconds more, he watched her. Her eyes were turned down. Her red-gold hair spilled over her cheeks, almost to her lap. The tears fell more slowly now. Conrad watched her, and his throat went dry. He heard his pulse hammering at his temples. He knew he had no more time.

"Elizabeth," he said gently. He pushed off his chair. Swung his leg around it and stood over her. Without looking up, she brought one hand to her eyes and swiped at her cheek. He heard her sob quietly. He cleared his throat. "Elizabeth," he repeated, "I have to ask you a question."

Slowly, she raised her face to him. Even through tears, her big eyes seemed to go down into the heart of her. He saw the appeal in them. He looked away.

"Oh, shit," he whispered. He took a breath. Faced her again. "Listen to me. I can help you. Okay?"

"Oh . . . can you?" Her hands went out to him. She took hold of his. "Can you?"

"Yes. And I'm *going* to help you, Elizabeth."

"Because I know that bad things have happened. But there could be good things too," she said. "I was all right for a while. After the state hospital. At the Liberty Center. I was better. I was. I tried to tell Dr. Holbein: He's always different. He can come back because he keeps changing. You see? He wouldn't believe me. You believe me. Don't you?"

Conrad held her hands tightly. He moved closer to her. "Listen to me. Please."

"You'll keep him away. I know you will. I could do good things too. I know it . . ."

"Elizabeth."

He spoke sharply. His patient stopped babbling. She continued to gaze up at him expectantly. He went on, as gently now as he could.

"Elizabeth . . ." He kept holding her hands. "I can help you. I *will* help you. All right?" She nodded eagerly. "But today," he went on, "today I have to ask *you* to help *me*. I have to ask you a question, Elizabeth. And it's very important that you try to answer it as best you can. Do you understand? I need . . . for you to answer it carefully, all right?"

Again, she nodded. "What?" she said. "What is it?"

Conrad took another deep breath. It wasn't easy with his heart going the way it was. "Elizabeth," he said finally, "what is the number?"

The appeal in the depths of her eyes held him. He saw the tears roll quietly down her white cheeks. A faint smile of hope played at the corner of her lips.

And then the words struck her.

"What is the number?" he said. And her face went ashen. She recoiled against the back of her chair. Her eyes grew turbulent, dark, and flat. Her mouth opened. He could hear the breath whistle in and out of her.

"Elizabeth?" he said.

"My God," she whispered. She yanked her hands away from him. "My God."

Oh . . . boy, Conrad thought. "Elizabeth, listen . . ."

She brought her fingers to her mouth. She shook her head. "Oh, no. Oh, my God, no." And suddenly, she cried out, "No!" She jumped back. Her chair fell over. It struck the edge of the bed and clattered to the floor.

Conrad approached her, his hands out. "Elizabeth, it's all right. Please . . ."

But she backed away from him, shaking her head, edging toward the window. "No. Oh no, oh God, oh God."

"Please, Elizabeth, if you'll just listen to me . . ."

The metal grating shook as her back hit the window. She looked to the right, to the left, as if searching for a way to escape him, a way out. Her hands went up in front of her to ward him off.

Conrad took another step toward her.

And she spoke again—and his heart went cold. The sound of her voice—it was distant and tremulous. Her eyes flickered about the air as if she were searching for an unseen face.

"No, he's not," she rasped, drawing out the words. "He's good. He's good. Really."

She was talking to the Secret Friend.

Oh, thought Conrad. He stopped in his tracks. He stared at her. *Oh, I am so, so badly fucked.*

Elizabeth started whispering now, babbling in a whisper. "Oh no, oh

God, leave him, oh don't, please . . ." She seemed pinned to the window behind her. She was shaking her head back and forth rapidly. White froth bubbled at the edge of her lips. It flew off as she shook her head. "Oh, God, please don't, I just, God, no . . . one of them . . . stay away . . . stay away . . . You're all . . . all one of them. They all are. They all are, you're right. I know." Her head swung back. Her eyes rolled. She grunted.

Conrad looked over his shoulder. . . .

One time, she beat the living shit out of a Dutch sailor. Broke both his arms and stomped one of his testicles to pudding. And she's just a little thing. . . .

He figured he was four strides away from the door. And he'd have to unlock it once he got there.

Elizabeth shrieked, "All of you! All of you! You're all in it!"

She came off the wall. Her eyes burned into him. The froth burbled over her lower lip, dripped to the floor.

Conrad backed away from her. He held up his hands. "Uh . . . please. You've *got* to listen."

"Please. You've got to listen." Elizabeth echoed him in an eerie whisper. She looked to the left and the right. She waved her hands in front of her wildly. "Got to listen. Dr. Conrad, he'll help me. He's going to help . . ." But then she was snarling, stalking him, her hands curled like claws. "No. No. No. He's like the other one. Just like the other one. What is the number? First they pretend, first they say, 'Yes, Elizabeth, talk to the doctor,' then they ask you, they ask you . . . They're all in on it."

She came toward him slowly. Conrad took another step back. He glanced back at the door again. Another step—maybe two—and he could reach it—maybe jam his key in. He reached into his pocket. "Elizabeth," he said quickly. "I do want to help you. I'm trying to . . ." Then he faltered. He slowed. He faced her.

"The other one?" he said. *How did she know? How did she know I was coming?*

"Just like the other one," Elizabeth echoed. She came closer to him, her hands raised. Her eyes were flat and hard.

"The other doctor?" Conrad asked her. *She got dressed up for me. How did she know?*

"They say they're doctors," she said. Her voice broke with pain and sorrow. "Oh, they say they're nice. They say, they say they're good. Then they ask you. They ask you."

"Another doctor asked you about the number," said Conrad.

"'What is the number?'" She stepped closer to him, growling the words. He could smell her. He could feel the heat of her breath. "'What is the number?' he asked me."

Conrad halted, a step from the door. "The other doctor," he said. "Dr. Sachs. Jerry Sachs?"

"Sachs. Yes," she said. "'What is the number?'"

"He asked you that? He did, didn't he? That's why you went wild. That's why you wouldn't talk at first. My God, you were right. Sachs *is* one of them."

And Elizabeth began shrieking again: "I'm going to kill you! I'm going to kill you!"

Conrad took another step backward—and hit the door. His back was pressed to it. Elizabeth moved in on him.

"I hate you for this," she screamed. "I hate you, hate you for this!"

"Elizabeth, no, damn it!"

But she wouldn't stop. She was almost on him. She thrust her hands out at his throat.

"Elizabeth!" He threw his hands out desperately. He grabbed the front of her shift. "Please! For God's sake!" he shouted. "Help me! *Help me!* They've got my daughter!"

She had him now. She had her hands on his neck. He could feel the hot fingers tightening on him. The nails digging into his flesh. He tried to hold her back. He shook her, his face against hers. Tears were in his eyes.

"For God's sake, for God's sake, please!" he shouted. "Please help me!"

Elizabeth blinked. She stared at him.

"They've got my little girl," said Conrad. "You have to understand. Please. You have to. They took my daughter."

Elizabeth stood still, her head lolling, her eyes vague. Her lips worked silently in confusion. She reached up and put her hand roughly against Conrad's mouth.

"Please," he said. He tasted her fingers.

"Your daughter?" said Elizabeth.

"Please. I need your help."

"My help?"

"Yes."

"Because of them. Because of the bad men?"

"Yes."

She stumbled back from him. "You mean . . . They're real?" She put her hands to the sides of her head as if to hold it together. "I don't . . . I don't . . . I don't . . . They're real, you mean?"

Breathless, Conrad staggered forward. He leaned weakly against the edge of the table. "Yes," he said. It was barely a whisper. "Please. You've got to tell me who they are. You've got to tell me what they want."

Elizabeth shuddered. She hugged herself. "I don't understand this. I don't understand what's going on now. At all. At all."

"My little girl . . . ," said Conrad. He looked at his watch. It was eight twenty-six. "Oh, Jesus. My little girl."

He looked up at her. She stared at him, hugging herself, shaking her head. She had to understand, he thought. There had to be time, more time to make her understand.

All at once, there was a heavy pounding at the door. A voice called into them.

"Hey, Nate? Nate? Everything all right in there?"

Conrad spun around. He saw Sachs's huge egg of a face pressed against the door's thin window.

He closed his eyes.

And the next moment, he heard the doorknob rattle as Sachs's key slid into the lock.

D'Annunzio

Agatha lay on the couch. She stared at the ceiling. It was a white ceiling. There was a long, Y-shaped crack in the paint just above her.

Agatha lay with her right arm draped over her forehead. Her left arm lay across her stomach. The old teddy bear, White Snow, was tucked into the crook of her left arm. She stared at the ceiling, imagining the police.

It was half an hour since Billy Price had left. Since she had told him to call the police. Since she had shoved him out and shut the door on his blank, stupid face. It was half an hour since she had stood in the nursery closet, clutching the gray bear; since she had heard the phone ringing and ringing in the other room.

She had heard the phone and she had tasted her fear. A coppery spurt of it had come up from her throat onto her tongue. She had been certain—she had known—that she had lost everything. There *were* microphones. They *could* hear her. They *had* heard her—they had heard what she'd said to Billy Price.

Now they were calling to tell her they had killed her daughter. They were calling to make her listen to Jessie scream as she died.

She had time to think about that as she went to the phone. She had time to think about more than that. That trip, those several steps, from one room into the other—it seemed to take her forever. The phone kept

138

ringing and ringing. Aggie walked toward it. She clutched the teddy bear under her arm. She thought about how she would hear Jessie scream.

Why had she thought there were no microphones? Because that man—that terrible, vicious man Nathan had called Sport—because he had not heard Billy Price's name? For Christ's sweet sake. Was that all? Was that everything? Why hadn't she realized: Billy Price could've been one of them? They could've been testing her. Or there could've been a malfunction in their listening equipment. There were so many other reasonable deductions she could have made. How had she decided in the space of a few seconds to risk her daughter's life—to lose her baby's life—on a guess, on a bet, on a stupid gamble?

The phone rang again and Aggie stepped toward it. And then her hand was on it. And then she was lifting it to her ear. She could hear Jessie crying out to her—Mommy! She could hear her muffled wail as they closed their hands around her. She could hear it all clearly in her mind.

Then she pressed the phone to her ear.

"Yes," she whispered.

It was the same voice as before. The kidnapper's voice. But it was softer now. The rage was gone. It was composed and smooth, almost friendly.

"Well done, Mrs. Conrad," it said.

Agatha did not answer. She did not breathe.

"You did that just right," said the man.

"Yes," Aggie whispered. "I did just what you told me."

"That's right. That's just right. And your daughter's glad you did, Mrs. Conrad. Believe me. She's very, very glad you did."

"Oh . . ." The small sob of relief broke from her. She bit it off. No microphones. She had been right. No goddamned microphones.

"Now you just keep playing straight with me, baby, and everything's going to be all right, understand?"

"Yes," said Agatha. "Yes."

"Who knows—if you're real good, maybe I'll even come over there myself and pay you a little visit. How would that be? You'd like that, wouldn't you?"

The man gave a wicked little laugh—and Aggie thought crazily: like a movie, like a villain in a movie. Like he's playing a part . . .

Then the line went dead again.

Aggie set the phone down slowly. Oh. Oh, boy, she thought. It was then that she had moved to the couch. That she had lain on it, one arm over her brow. She had stared up at the ceiling. The white ceiling with the Y-shaped crack.

She had begun to imagine the police.

She kept replaying the scene in her mind. Nathan was there. He was standing on the rooftop of a high-rise apartment. The kidnapper and his faceless accomplices were holding Jessie out over the edge. They were threatening to drop her. Suddenly, shouting curses, the police burst through the rooftop door. Nathan rushed forward. Heroically, he snatched the child out of the kidnapper's hands. And then—and then the police opened fire.

She couldn't stop thinking about it. She kept imagining the police opening fire. She imagined how the kidnappers would stagger back. How the impact of the bullets would make them dance. Blood and bits of flesh would fly from them. There would be pain in their eyes—pain and this searing, ceaseless, unbearable terror. They would fall, screaming, over the edge of the roof. It would take a long time for them to die.

Aggie lay on the couch and imagined it. When she was done, she went back to the beginning and went through it again. She went through it slowly. She built slowly up to the part about the police and the gunfire. About the kidnappers' spattering blood and their pain—and the terrible fear that would be like her fear now.

Aggie lay on the couch and stared at the ceiling. She imagined the police and the gunfire. And she smiled thinly.

And then someone unlocked the front door. The door swung open. A man walked in.

Aggie gasped and sat up. She began to say "Nathan?" But the word died on her lips. She looked over the back of the couch and saw the man enter. He closed the door behind him.

He was a young man, maybe thirty, maybe even less. He was dressed in green overalls. He was carrying a toolbox in one hand.

When Aggie sat up, he turned and saw her. He stopped, startled.

"Oh—jeez, I'm . . . sorry," he said. "I . . . Roger, the super, he said no one was up here. He gave me the key. I'm . . . I'm the plumber."

Aggie stared at him, her mouth open.

"The Coleman apartment downstairs . . . ," he went on. "They got a leak in their bathroom. It could be coming through your walls. I wanted to check. You mind? Roger said the apartment would be empty."

Aggie stared at him another moment. She turned and stared at the phone. She looked at the phone a long time. But the phone didn't ring.

"Uh . . . you mind?" the plumber said again. He gestured toward the hall with his thumb.

Aggie raised her eyes to him. She gazed at his face, dumb. It's not a plumber's face, she thought vaguely. He had a rough, working-man's voice, but it was not, she thought, a working-man's face. The young man's face was round and smooth and boyish. He was handsome, with a mop of brown hair that tumbled into his eyes. And those eyes: they were intelligent, watchful, witty. Not a plumber's eyes. Something else . . .

She looked at the phone again. It did not ring. She opened her mouth. "I . . . I don't . . ."

"It'll take me just a minute," the young man said. And he started walking down the hallway.

A second too late, Agatha called after him, "They didn't ring me. Usually they ring up. The doormen."

"What's that?"

Agatha stood off the couch. The teddy bear lay where she had been. Agatha crossed her arms under her breasts. She looked at the phone.

"It's . . . it's so late," she called. She glanced at her watch. "It's after eight."

"What's that?" the plumber called back again. A loud hammering sound—metal on metal—started to come from the bathroom.

Aggie moved across the room. She moved to the end of the hallway. She stood there staring down the hall toward where the bathroom was. She saw the light shining out through the open door. She heard the metallic hammering. She ran her hand up through her hair. She glanced back at the phone. Why didn't it ring? Why didn't he call?

The hammering stopped. Agatha's breath caught. She put her hand to her breast and stared down the hallway.

"Mrs. Conrad?" the plumber called.

Agatha didn't answer.

"Excuse me." He called louder: "Mrs. Conrad?"

"Uh . . . yes." Agatha's voice quavered. "Yes, what is it?"

"You think you could come here for a second, Mrs. Conrad?"

Agatha stood where she was. She shook her head: no. She wiped the sweat from around her lips. "I . . . I don't . . . They didn't call up," she said weakly. "Usually they ring before anyone . . ."

141

Her voice trailed off. There was a pause, a silence. Then the plumber said, "Mrs. Conrad. I really think you better come here."

There was no mistaking the tone of this. It was a command. A cold, undeniable order. As Aggie stood there, conscious of every breath, a strange snatch of memory floated across her mind. Her social studies teacher—Mrs. Lindsay—the seventh grade, Great Neck North Junior High: an aging spinster with a froggy face and dyed-red hair. She was standing before an enlarged replica of the United States Constitution. It was pinned to a bulletin board and she was pointing back at it. She was gazing froggily at the class. And she was proclaiming tartly, "Freedom is harder than slavery. No-choice is the easy choice."

Agatha nearly laughed at the memory. She let out a shaky breath. She put her hand to her mouth to stifle the miserable little noise it made. No-choice is the easy choice, she thought again. She walked down the hall to the bathroom.

She came into the doorway and she could see him. He was on his knees by the side of the bathtub. His back was toward her. She could see he had a wrench in his hand. He was knocking it against the inner rim of the drain.

She stood there, looking at him, saying nothing. Then her eyes lowered to his toolbox.

The toolbox was sitting on the white-tiled floor, just by his feet. It was open. It was empty. There were no other tools in it. Not a screwdriver, not even one of those "snakes" she'd seen plumbers use to unclog drains. There was nothing.

"Oh . . ." Aggie covered her mouth again. She looked at the man. He continued to tap, tap, tap.

A moment later, he turned to look at her over his shoulder. He noticed her eyes flick back to the open toolbox. He smiled at her. It was a charming smile. It seemed almost to sparkle.

"You're right," he said. "I don't know what the hell I'm doing." He turned back to the drain. "The thing is," he said, "I'm not really a plumber." He tapped the wrench against the drain uselessly. "My name is Doug D'Annunzio," he went on. "Detective D'Annunzio, Midtown South. I'd show you my shield, but your neighbor, Billy Price, he says the bad guys are watching. Is that right?"

Agatha didn't answer. She shook her head slightly. She looked down the hall. The phone did not ring. She looked at the man kneeling on the floor. It was not the same voice, she thought; it was not the kidnapper's voice. And why should he pretend to be a police officer? The kidnappers could come over here anytime they wanted. They could do anything they wanted. They had her daughter. Why should they pretend?

"You're the police?" she finally asked him. "You're . . . ?" She stopped. Somehow, all at once, this did make sense to her. It fit the man. The worker's voice, the intelligent, witty, and watchful eyes. Not a plumber's face. A cop's.

The man kept tapping at the drain. "You want me to show you the shield or not?"

"No," she said quickly. "No, no. You can't."

D'Annunzio grunted, shifting his position on the floor. "Christ. What'd they do? Rig the place with cameras?"

Agatha nodded at his back. "Yes. Cameras. They told us there are cameras." She raised her eyes to the bathroom ceiling. She could not see the cameras. "They can see us," she said. She looked down at him again. She massaged her forehead with her fingers. "You shouldn't have done this. You shouldn't have come here like this."

"Yeah, well . . . We had to do something, lady," D'Annunzio said. "I mean, these guys sound very serious. Cameras and shit—excuse my language. But I mean, I've seen this kind of thing before. When they take the trouble to use cameras, you know you're dealing with serious people."

Agatha looked down the hall. She wrung her hands in front of her. "You shouldn't have. I . . . I . . ."

"All right, all right, don't panic," said D'Annunzio. With another grunt, he climbed to his feet. He began to run his hand up the shower wall as if he were feeling for something. "This has got to look good. Smile. We're just having a friendly conversation with the plumber."

Agatha did not smile. She looked at the man. She studied his back. Yes, she thought. He could be a cop. He *could* be.

"I shouldn't stay too long either," D'Annunzio said. "Just tell me whatever you can, as fast as you can."

Agatha kept wringing her hands. Her hands felt cold and damp. Once more, she glanced down the hall. She drew a deep breath. All right, she thought. All right. No-choice is the easy choice.

She nodded. She smiled—sweetly—the way she had smiled at Billy Price. She swallowed hard. "They took my daughter," she said, smiling. "Last night. They just came in. . . . They're watching us. They can talk over our phone. They say they're listening, that they have microphones, but I don't think they do. But they can definitely see us. They've got me trapped here."

143

"Keep going," said D'Annunzio. "What's Jessica look like? How old is she?" He kept feeling the walls.

Agatha forced her smile up again. "She's five. She has long sandy hair, blue eyes, round cheeks. She's very pretty. She was wearing a nightgown with valentines . . ." She couldn't go on. She would've started crying.

"How about the kidnappers?" D'Annunzio said. "You've talked to them?"

"Yes. One of them. He's very . . . cruel. Angry."

"Anything that indicates where he might be? A noise on the line. A slip of the tongue."

She thought a moment. She glanced down the hall toward the silent phone. "No. Look, you shouldn't stay anymore. You should go. I mean it."

D'Annunzio turned to face her. He looked at her with kind, melancholy cop's eyes. He nodded once. "Okay," he said.

He knelt down and placed his wrench back in his toolbox. He closed the box and latched it.

"Where's your husband?" he said.

"I don't know. He had to go out. He said he had to do something and then they would give our daughter back. They wouldn't let him . . . They told him not to tell me where he'd be. . . . But he said he would meet with them"—she had to clear her throat—"at nine."

D'Annunzio nodded. He smiled and winked. He could've been saying: No leak in the plumbing here, lady. Everything's copacetic. A-OK.

But what he said was, "Good. We'll track him down."

Agatha nodded, smiling back at him. "Be careful. For God's sake, please."

D'Annunzio left the bathroom first. Agatha followed him down the hall. He opened the front door and lifted a hand to her. He grinned.

"We'll get her back for you, Mrs. Conrad. You have my word. Don't do anything suspicious. And try to stay calm."

Tears flooded Agatha's eyes. She said nothing. She kept her stupid smile plastered in place. She moved to the door as D'Annunzio stepped into the hall.

She looked out into the hall as he moved away from her. One step, she thought. One step over the threshold, and she would be free.

She smiled once more at D'Annunzio as he walked away. Then she pushed the door closed, shutting herself into her apartment.

She turned to the phone again. It didn't ring.

Plumber's Helper

The moment he was out of the Conrads' apartment, Sport began to strip off the plumber's overalls. He hurried down the hall to the far apartment, 5H. He glanced back over his shoulder to check the empty hall. To make sure Aggie Conrad stayed safely out of sight.

Oh, he thought, there's a smart cunt all right. He peeled the green suit off his arms. There was no question about it. She was one smart little mommy. Pretending to be a sweet little hausfrau who wouldn't hurt a fly. And all the time the wheels are turning. All the time she was thinking how to get you, how to get at you, go for your balls. Sport knew that type; he hated that type. He hadn't minded the doctor so much. He liked the doctor in a way. The doctor was tough. Sport could respect that. But this one . . . She was just smart and tricky. Just playing on a man's mistakes. No, he had no time for that at all.

Well, he thought. It was his own fault. It was his own damn mistake that gave her the leeway. He had known he'd fucked up the minute he hung up on her that first time. The minute he calmed down a little, he realized he had given himself away. He had watched her through the binoculars, waiting to see if she'd noticed it. And she'd noticed it, all right. Smart, sneaky little cunt. Sport could see it on that punk's face, that Billy Price. She was telling him everything, telling him to call the cops. She had realized that there were no microphones.

He reached the door of 5H now, knocked quietly. As he waited for an answer, he finished taking off the overalls. His lips were moving silently as his angry thoughts raced.

This was what he'd wanted to avoid all along. The whole point had been to avoid personal contact with anyone, so that even if he got caught, there'd be no one to identify him. But he'd had to find out what the Conrad bitch knew—and now she'd seen him.

"Shit," he whispered aloud.

Now they'd have to move too. A smart cunt like that, once she knew there were no microphones, she might begin to wonder why she couldn't see any cameras either. She might figure out that they were watching her from across the courtyard. Then—if she did manage to contact the cops—then they'd have real problems on their hands.

No, they would wait a bit, give Sport time to get on the road—then Maxwell would take the kid back to the old place.

He knocked at the door again, louder. His overalls were off now. He was in his jacket and tie again. His D'Annunzio outfit. A navy sports coat, a blue shirt, a striped tie. Classic American cop. He had used this earlier to talk his way into Price's apartment. He wrapped the overalls around his work box. He tucked the bundle under his arm. He shook his head.

Never should've happened, he thought. The whole thing never even should have started. All he'd wanted was to get out of the Correction Department, stop being a goddamned guard, take his crack at a singing career, a new life. That was all. And there'd been money enough for that. After his accident, after his settlement with the city, there'd been money enough for that and more. But he had to get smart. He had to start listening to Eddie the Screw. Christ! What could've possessed him? That old man, that old rummy: Eddie. He'd been sitting in the old Harbor Bar, where the Rikers guards gathered, for three straight months—ever since he'd gotten out of jail. He'd been telling the same story over and over again to anyone who'd listen, to any Rikers guard young enough or polite enough or drunk enough to listen: "Oh, when I was a CO like you, I was no fool, not me. I *ran* the drug trade in the department, made myself a little fortune, that's right. And when the feds came after me, did they get a piece of it, did they get any of it? No, sir. No, sir, I outsmarted them all." Every night, night after night, he went on and on about it. No one really *believed* him, no one really paid attention to him. Until Sport suddenly had his brainstorm, suddenly decided—hey, maybe he's serious. And after that, it was all this goose chase, this bullshit scam, this treasure hunt. . . .

He heard the peephole cover slide back. He took a deep breath, composed his features. Then Billy Price's door opened a crack. Sport stepped in.

Maxwell closed the door behind him. The big man stood over him, his great shoulders hunched, his small, babyish face jutting forward. It was that guilty-little-boy look he always got afterward. As jumpy as Sport felt, he could not really get mad at the guy.

"Did he call the cop back?" Sport asked.

"Yeah," Maxwell said. He gave a little laugh when he said it. His eyes shone. "Yeah. D'Annunzio was still there too. He told D'Annunzio not to come. He told him they'd found the girl."

"Good," said Sport.

Maxwell laughed again. It was almost a giggle. "I took his pants off. I held his balls."

Sport snorted. "I guess that would convince him."

"I said I'd leave him alone if he did it right." A childish laugh burst from him machine-gun style.

Sport smiled with one side of his mouth. He looked at the monster and shook his head. What a fucking character, he thought.

Almost reluctantly, Sport moved out of the foyer, deeper into the apartment. He thought, might as well see what we've accomplished here.

The apartment was not yet fully furnished. There were no pictures hung on the walls. There were no carpets on the parquet floor. Some boxes still sat unopened in the corners. But the glass and metal bookcases had been set up. There were photographs on them, and books and knickknacks. And there was a sitting area by the far windows: a coffee table, a wicker sofa, some Breuer chairs.

Billy Price was sitting in one of the Breuer chairs. He was wearing a black sweatshirt. He was naked from the waist down. His mouth was taped shut. His hands were taped behind his back. His head flopped to one side like a rag doll's. His eyes were open.

His throat had been crushed—really crushed. Sport gave a soft whistle when he saw it. It looked as if a train had run over the guy's neck or something. Sport lowered his eyes to Price's crotch. Jesus Christ, he thought, shaking his head. That crazy, crazy Maxwell.

Maxwell still hovered behind him, shoulders hunched, face jutting. He watched Sport eagerly, expectantly. Sport turned to him, gave him a big smile and a wink. He reached up to pat his thick shoulder with his hand.

"Way to go, big guy. Looks good," he said.

Maxwell nodded and smiled. Sport took one more quick look around the room.

"Okay. Let's go."

Maxwell's smile faltered. "What about the Conrad woman? Shouldn't we do her too?"

Sport shook his head. "She doesn't know anything. She doesn't know where we are. She still thinks we got cameras in there."

Maxwell sighed and straightened. He nodded somberly.

Sport gave a sympathetic laugh. "That was the whole point, see? Now she thinks the cops have been there. Now she'll just sit tight. She won't do anything till we're done."

"She won't do anything if she's dead either," said Maxwell.

Sport laughed again. Thank you, Professor Pinhead, he thought. "No, no," he said. "See, then we'd have to worry about the doctor, okay? He's smart, see, and he knows what's happening. He got me to let him talk to the kid before. He could pull something like that again. You know? If he finds out his wife or the kid are hurt, we lose him, then we're screwed. You see what I'm saying?"

Maxwell hung above him, looking down at him. Does he see what I'm saying? Sport thought. What a stupid question. The guy couldn't pull the wings off a fly without an instruction manual.

Sport gave Maxwell a playful slap on his meaty arm. "Hey," he said. "Hey. You wanna be rich, don't ya? You wanna go away?"

Maxwell wagged his head.

"You wanna have all the boys and girls you want and not have to go to jail anymore, right?"

"Yeah," said the big man sullenly.

"Well, then we gotta get on the horn here, pal. I'm gonna need time to get down to the clocktower. And you gotta pack up. We're moving you back to the old place."

"Aww," Maxwell said.

"For Christ's sake, it's just for a few hours. Just in case the woman figures things out. She was smart about the microphones."

"She wouldn't be smart if she was dead," Maxwell muttered.

Sport laughed and shook his head again. He kept shaking his head as he walked to the door. Maxwell shuffled after him.

The Kid

They had left Jessica lying on the bed. They had taped her hands behind her back. They had taped her ankles together. They had taped her mouth shut. They had left the television on. "It'll give her something to do," Sport had said. The room was dark except for the TV's flickering light.

The little girl lay on her side. She was trying to keep her eyes open. They kept sinking half closed though. The blue of her eyes seemed foggy, as if the light in them were going out. Her face, her round cheeks, were mottled, red in patches and then chalky. Her mother had braided her hair to keep it from getting tangled at night, but the braid had started to come undone.

Jessica felt sick and bad. The chloroform had made her stomach hurt. She was scared of vomiting. She thought she would have to swallow the vomit because of the tape over her mouth. She had peed on the mattress too and she felt bad about that. She couldn't help it. She had held it in as long as she could, but it had finally come out. Now she had to lie there on the wet bed. And there was pee all over her valentine nightgown, her favorite. After a while, she started to cry again. It felt like she was suffocating. It made her feel dizzy. Sleepy. She closed her eyes.

She slept, but even then she felt hot. When she woke up, there was sweat on her forehead. It felt like the time she had had chicken pox, like that bad fever she had then. It made her want to sleep again, but she was too sick.

She stared at the TV. There were two men talking there. She hoped her

149

daddy would come soon. He had told her on the phone: *You'll be home soon.* She thought he must be coming to get her now. She thought he would knock on the door very loudly—so loudly that the bad men would be scared and have to let him in. And then the bad men would see him and they would be *really* scared because he would be very, very mad. He would look all dark and growly the way he did that time she stood up on the big rock in Central Park when he'd told her not to. And Daddy would hit them. (Daddy did not think hitting was right—that's why he never hit her—but would make an exception in this case.) He would punch the bad men right in the nose. He might have to hit the big one with a stick or shoot him with a gun. And then Jessica would go over and hit them too.

Oh, but now she felt sick. She felt so sick. She really was going to throw up. The tape over her mouth seemed to be choking her. Tears sprang to her eyes. *Mommy!* she thought. Suddenly, in a fit of frustration, she tried to pull her hands apart. She rolled frantically back and forth on the bed. She was crying. She tried to breathe in and couldn't. Her eyes rolled in her head. She lay still. She felt hot and far away.

A little while later, she was awake again. She felt even sicker than before, even hotter. She was starting to cry though, and she couldn't breathe. Oh, Mommy, she thought. She gave one of her hands a sharp, short pull upward.

The hand came free.

For a second, Jessica didn't even think about it. She just reached up and picked at the tape on her mouth. It hurt but she didn't care. She had to get it off. She had to breathe.

She peeled the tape off. She lifted herself up a little. She thought she was going to throw up. She gagged. Her tongue stuck out of her mouth. But there was no vomit. She settled down on the mattress again, moving away from the wet part. She lay still and took deep breaths.

And then it occurred to her: her hands were free.

She brought her arms around in front of her. They were stiff, sore. She rubbed her wrists. She still felt sick, but she didn't feel as hot or dizzy as before.

As she looked at her hands, she began to get worried. She glanced up at the door. Maybe she should try to put the tape back on, she thought. The bad men would be angry if they saw she had taken it off. She hadn't meant to do it really. It had just happened. Because she couldn't breathe. But they might not understand that. They might think she was being bad.

Maybe, though, she could wait. She had heard the bad men go out a while ago. Maybe she could wait until they got back and then put the tape on real quick before they saw her. It was still wrapped around one hand. She could just slip the other hand into the loop. And put the tape over her mouth again too.

Moe, the Turtle Tot, was lying on the bed next to her. Sport had left it there. "That'll keep you company," he'd said, after he'd taped her up. Jessica reached out and took hold of Moe. She pulled him close and leaned her cheek against him. She began to suck her thumb. She knew it was a babyish thing to do, but she couldn't help it now. She stared at the television. A commercial had come on now. Little boys and girls were running in a playground. One of the boys fell and got his shirt all dirty. His mommy had to wash it in the laundry.

Jessica wished her mommy was here.

Jessica slept for a little while—she didn't know how long. When she woke up, there were more commercials on the television. She was glad for a second because she did not feel as nauseated as she had before.

But then she thought, What if the bad men had come back while she was sleeping? She looked at the door. She listened. She couldn't hear anything besides the TV.

At first, she thought she should put the tape back on just in case. But she did not want to put the tape on her mouth again. Maybe, if she was very quiet, she could peek outside and make sure the bad men were still gone.

That was what she decided to do.

She sat up, glancing at the door to make sure no one came in. She slowly scraped the tape off her ankles. It didn't hurt as much there as it had on her mouth. When the tape was off, she put it on the bed so she could use it later when the bad men came back. Then she climbed off the bed. Hugging Moe under one arm, sucking her thumb, she started walking to the door.

She walked very quietly, on tiptoe. Blue light from the TV danced over the door. She felt the wet spot on her valentine nightgown against her leg. She hated that. She had tried so hard to hold it in. Mommy would understand that when she told her, but she hated it all the same.

When she reached the door, she pulled her thumb out of her mouth and took hold of the doorknob. She turned it slowly, slowly—as quietly as she could.

The door clicked and swung in. Jessica pressed her face to the opening. The room outside was dark. There didn't seem to be anyone in it. She pulled the door in a little more, stuck her head out. She looked to the right, down the length of the room. It was dark and quiet. She saw the dim outline of chairs here and there. She saw the glass doors to the balcony. The curtains were drawn across it.

She turned to the left. There was nothing moving there either. She was about to pull her head back into the room when she saw the front door.

She knew it was the front door because it looked just like her front door at home. It was big and solid and it had two locks and a chain on it. It was not far away. She might've run right to it. She *could* run right to it, she thought. She could pull it open and go out. Then she could take the elevator downstairs and ask the doorman for help. The doorman would call her daddy and tell him where she was. That was probably why Daddy hadn't come yet, she thought. He probably didn't know yet where she was. The doorman could tell him.

That's it! she thought. (In the cartoons she saw on television, there were always little girls who had adventures and got into trouble. Just when everything looked bad for them, they always had an idea. They would snap their fingers and say, "That's it!" But Jessica didn't know how to snap her fingers.)

So she just thought: That's it! And she slipped out of the bedroom.

But it was dark out there. She pulled up short just beyond the bedroom door. It was very dark and big. She looked at the shapes of the furniture in the shadows. What if the bad men *were* here? she thought. What if they were hiding in the darkness? Or what if they had left a big dog behind to watch her and it jumped up suddenly from behind something and roared at her and had red eyes?

Hugging Moe, Jessica backed up a step toward the bedroom. But she kept looking at the front door. It was right there, just a few steps away. And her daddy really might not know where she was. If he had known, after all, he would have come to get her.

She stopped backing up. She looked around at all the shadows. She was not nauseous anymore, but her stomach felt bad in a different way. She shivered and clutched the pink turtle tighter. Then she gritted her teeth and scrunched up her shoulders to make herself small. She started tiptoeing to the front door.

She tiptoed slowly. The wood felt cold under her bare feet. Her stomach felt cold and airy. She looked back over her shoulder. She thought something might be creeping up in back of her out of the dark. She looked at the front door again. Somehow, it did not seem so close now. It seemed to be taking her a long time to get there. And when she glanced back at the bedroom, *it* seemed to have gotten very far away too. Too far anyway to run back to through the dark.

She tiptoed on faster. She covered the final distance. She reached the front door. The knob was just about at her eye level. Holding Moe hard under one arm, she reached out with the other and took the knob in her hand. She turned it. It went a little way and stuck. She turned it harder, jiggled it. It wouldn't go. It wouldn't open.

The little girl groaned. "Oh, no." The door was locked.

She lifted her eyes. She looked up at the door towering above her. The chain hung loose beside it. The two other locks were high up. One was just a sort of windup key coming out of the door. The other was a big brass plate with a knob on it. They looked hard to work, but she did know how to work them. She'd done it at home a few times. Usually, though, Mommy had to help her.

She reached up to the lower one, the key. She tried to twist it. It was too hard. She wasn't strong enough. She bent down and set Moe on the floor. She tried the key again with both hands. This time, it went over. She heard it click.

"Yay," she whispered.

She knew she could do it now. She reached up to the second lock. Her fingers touched the bottom of the brass plate. The knob, though—she couldn't reach the knob—it was too high. She stood on tiptoe. Her fingers touched the edge of the knob. She tried to push it, to turn it, but she couldn't get a grip. . . .

Then, outside the door, out in the hall, she heard the deep whoosh of the elevator door opening. She heard men's voices.

". . . just make sure you take the phone with you, all right? Will you remember that?" one of them said.

Jessica knew it was the bad men.

She reached for the lower lock to lock it again so they wouldn't know. But they would hear that. She had to leave it.

"Yeah, I'll remember," the bad man said. He was right outside the door.

Jessica turned and ran back to the bedroom. She had to put the tape back on so they wouldn't know she'd done anything wrong. They would be so angry if they found out she'd been bad. She hadn't meant to be. She just couldn't breathe. . . .

As she slipped through the bedroom door, she heard a key slip into the lock. She glanced back and saw the knob on the high lock turn around.

Then she looked down and saw Moe. The pink Turtle Tot was still lying on the floor. She could see the shape of it.

Jessie screwed her face up. She didn't know what to do. Both locks were unlocked now, the door was about to open. But if they saw Moe lying there . . .

She dashed back out of the bedroom. She ran on tiptoe back to Moe. She heard a key going into the second lock. She bent down and picked up the pink turtle. The lock above her went around. She heard the bad man push at the door.

Then she heard his voice: "Shit. Did you forget to lock this?"

He had locked it again. Because he hadn't known Jessica had turned it the other way.

Jessica ran back toward the bedroom. She heard the lock turning again, unlocking for real this time. Running, she looked back behind her.

And she hit the edge of the bedroom door and fell.

The door hit her in the ankle. There was a loud thump and she went down face forward.

"Ow!" she cried out.

Moe flew off in front of her. She hit the floor hard, breaking the fall with her hands and arms.

The front door opened. A light went on. Crying, lying facedown, Jessica turned. She saw Sport looking down at her. Maxwell stood behind him, looking down over his head.

Now my daddy's going to come, Jessica thought. My daddy's going to come and hit them.

Sport's face twisted. His eyes seemed black. "Fuck!" he said. He spit the bad word out. "Fucking cunt. Fucking, fucking cunt."

He stepped toward her. Maxwell shut the door.

Jessica was crying hard. "I didn't mean it," she said.

Sport reached down and grabbed her arm. He pulled it.

"Ow!" Jessica cried.

He dragged her up off the floor. He slapped her, hard, in the face. The blow knocked her back to the floor. Jessica screamed and sobbed.

Now Daddy, Daddy, come, Daddy, Daddy, she thought.

"You and your fucking mother, little bitch," said Sport. "I fucking killed her, what do you think of that? Your mother's dead, you little cunt!"

"She is not!" Jessica sobbed.

"She is. Too smart for her own fucking good, that's why."

"My daddy will come!" Jessie screamed at him, choking on her tears.

"He's going to come and hit you! He's going to come and throw you out the window!"

Sport looked over his shoulder. Maxwell was standing there. He was staring down at Jessica.

"Get the chloroform," Sport said.

Jessica screamed, "No!" And then she wailed it: "No . . . Mommy . . ." And then she could only sob, putting her hand up in front of her face as Sport came toward her again.

The Painful Chair

"Heighdy-ho, psychiatry fans," said Dr. Jerry Sachs. He stepped into Elizabeth's isolation room and shut the door behind him. "Everything all right in here?"

Conrad could only stare up at him.

He is one of them.

He could only stare up at him and think: *I've got to . . . I've got to . . . do something.*

But there was nothing to do. He still didn't have the number. And Elizabeth was still agitated, maybe on the verge of a violent episode. . . . And it was eight twenty-six and now Sachs . . .

Sachs glanced over at Elizabeth through his thick black glasses. His eyes moved rapidly, to her, back to Conrad. He went on in that jovial tone, but there was something quick and shaky in it. His smile—his damp red smile—seemed crooked; it seemed on the verge of failing him. "Are we having a problem here? Is something wrong here? We don't want anything to go wrong between two old chums like you, do we?" He faced Conrad eagerly. His eyes, distorted by the thick lenses, looked as if they were drowning in their own fluid. "Do we, Nate?" he said desperately.

Conrad stared up at him, at the big pink head glistening with sweat, pouring sweat.

Eight twenty-six. I've got to . . .

The words went through his mind like black streaks; vanished. Without thinking, he whispered, "You son of a bitch."

But Sachs just went on over him. He glanced at his watch and said, "I mean, it's getting kind of late around here, isn't it? I mean—whoa! look at that—it's about eight-thirty. It is just getting really, really late." Again, the drowning eyes appealed to Conrad. "I'd hurry if I were you, Nate. I definitely would."

And with that, he turned quickly back to the door.

Conrad's hand shot out. He grabbed Sachs by the elbow. "You son of a bitch," he whispered. He couldn't stop staring at him. "You're one of them, you . . . Do you know what they did? Do you know?"

The bigger man's damp lips parted. His wide eyes shifted back and forth with fear. "Hey, now. Hey. I mean, no one said anything about . . . I mean, who told you that? They weren't supposed to tell you that. They weren't supposed to tell anyone."

"For Christ's sake, Jerry, how could you?"

Sachs's mouth closed. It pulled into a damp frown. With an angry flick of his arm, he shook Conrad's hand away. "Listen, don't give me that stuff, all right? I mean, not everyone's the mayor of Central Park West. You know? Not everyone is so highfalutin he can afford to turn down a good offer, good money." He was growing breathless. He swallowed once. His eyes shifted again, to Elizabeth, back to Conrad. He spoke in a half whisper, confidentially. "Look. I didn't know they were going to do this, all right? I mean, I told them you wouldn't take money but . . . I didn't know they were going to do this." He glanced down at his watch again. He shook his head. "I mean, listen. . . . You really do have to hurry. These guys are molto seriose-o, okay? We have got to stay on schedule here." He reached for the doorknob.

"You!"

The word stopped him; the deep, guttural sound of it. His hand went slack on the knob. His lips went slack. He turned around. Conrad turned, too. Both men looked at Elizabeth.

Until now, she had stood there stunned. Her hands to her head, her mouth open, her eyes wild. She had stood and looked from one doctor to the other. Her head had gone back and forth as if she were saying, No, no, no.

But now—now she had lowered one arm, leveled one finger at Sachs's face. Her other hand was still at her head, her fingers clutching her red-gold hair.

157

"You," she growled again. "You're real."

They froze there for a second: Elizabeth pointing like that, Sachs looking down at her, rivers of sweat running down his cheeks. Conrad felt something like an icy breath on the back of his neck.

I've got to . . . do something . . . I've got to . . .

Sachs finally gave a brisk nod. "Well, Elizabeth, uh . . . I see you're . . . making great strides," he said. "And now, uh, I think I'll do the same. So long."

She stepped toward him, still pointing. "*You're* the bad one. You *are* one of them."

Sachs's eyes went wider and wider. He flicked a glance at Conrad. "You told *her?* Oh, Christ."

Conrad held his hand up. "Elizabeth. Don't."

She didn't even look at him. "Dr. Conrad is the good one," she said. She took another step toward Sachs. Sachs stood where he was, dazzled, like snake meat. "I knew that. I was right. Dr. Conrad is good and you . . . you took his daughter. You took his little daughter to make him do things."

Sachs's mouth opened. "Oh . . . oh, Christ . . ."

"You stole Dr. Conrad's daughter. And it's all real. And . . . It's not me. It's not just me."

"Elizabeth, that's enough." Conrad stepped between them. He took hold of Elizabeth's arm. He stroked it. He spoke to her gently. "That's enough. Please."

"But you're good," she said softly. "You told me: they're bad, they're real."

"Please," said Conrad. "Please. Be quiet now."

He backed her toward the bed. She was shaking her head again. She brought her hand to her lips. Her eyes filled. "I don't . . . ," she said. "I can't . . ."

Conrad sat her down on the bed. "It's all right," he told her. "It's going to be all right."

And then Sachs repeated, "My God, Nathan . . . You told her. You told her everything."

Conrad swung around to face him. The big man stood before the door. His mouth was still open. He was staring at Conrad.

"I mean, shit, Nathan, shit," he said. "You weren't supposed to tell anyone. No one was supposed to tell anyone. That was the idea."

Conrad felt sweat breaking out on his own forehead now—sweat and a chill that now seemed to blow all over him. He straightened beside the bed. "Jerry . . . ," he said.

Sachs stepped toward him, away from the door. "For Christ's sake, Nathan. You weren't supposed to tell fucking *anyone*."

"Jerry, listen, we can get out of this if we stick together."

"I mean, isn't that what they said? Don't tell anyone?"

"We can get out of this if—"

"*I* can't!" His eyes bugged behind the glasses. "*I* can't get out of this. She'll tell. *You* could tell. And them . . ."

"Christ, Jerry," Conrad said.

"I mean, never mind the fucking police. Never mind my job. What about *them*? I mean . . . they'll be *mad*." Sachs brought a huge hand to his sweaty head. "I mean, holy shit, Nathan. I mean holy *shit*, do you understand what I'm saying? You were just supposed to ask her the fucking question. Why couldn't you just ask her for the fucking number and get the fuck out?"

"Jerry," said Conrad carefully. "They have my daughter. We have to stick together. We can't tell them about this."

"Not *tell* them?" Sachs's voice became high and thin. "Not tell *them*? They're going to *call* here. They're going to call here to make sure you're gone. I've *got* to tell them. They've got to deal with this or . . . the police, my job, I . . ."

"If you tell them . . . If you tell them," Conrad said, "they'll kill my daughter."

"Oh, fine."

"They'll kill her, Jerry."

"Oh, fine. Fine. You mean you want them to kill *me*? You want them to think *I* held something back, *I* betrayed them? I mean, huh uh, buddy. I mean, no way. The day that happens I want to be in somebody else's body altogether, you hear what I'm telling you?"

"Damn it," Conrad said. He stared at Sachs. *I've got to,* he thought. *I've got to . . .* "Damn it," he repeated softly, "they'll kill her, man. She's only five years old. She's just a little girl. She's in kindergarten. She's five."

"Fuck *her!*" Sachs leaned his face down toward the smaller man. Conrad felt his sour breath. "You should've thought of that when you started talking, when you started telling everyone." His hand to his head, he turned away. He looked around the room as if searching for a way out. "Maybe we can dope her," he muttered. "That's it. We'll tell them

. . . We'll dope her up until everything's over. They might go for that. Maybe they'll go for that. Then they can have her. They can just . . . deal with her."

Conrad took a step back, away from him. *I've got to . . . I've got to . . .* He wiped his mouth with his hand. The cold sweat seemed to be coming out everywhere. *I've got to stop him,* he thought. He backed up again. The back of his leg hit his chair, the wooden chair he sat on when he spoke with Elizabeth.

Sachs kept babbling. "Look, Nathan, this might work. Okay? Maybe they'll even let the kid off the hook, you don't know. You can't tell. But the main thing is, we can't get them mad. We have to play straight with them and hope they'll deal with this. Okay? When they call, we'll just say, 'Well, yeah, okay, he told her, but we doped her up and you can come by later and . . .' That's all. Okay? We'll just tell them."

Conrad looked down. *I've got to . . .* His hand was resting against the back of the chair. *I've got to hit him,* he thought wildly. *I've got to hit him with this chair.*

Amazed, he looked at Elizabeth. She stared back at him from the bed. Her eyes were enormous: she seemed amazed too.

With this chair? he thought. *How do I . . . ? How am I supposed to . . . ?*

Sachs looked at his watch. "Oh, Jesus. Almost twenty-five of. They're gonna call in five minutes. Okay. Okay. You gotta go. Do you have the number? You gotta get outta here. I'll go downstairs, get the call. All right? That's what we'll do."

Conrad gripped the back of the chair with both hands. He stared down at it. *Chair,* he thought. *Got to . . . uh . . .* He lifted it off the floor.

"Come on!" said Sachs. "What're you doing? Have you got the number? Let's go!"

And Conrad rushed at him.

He lifted the chair high. He took two steps. His bad knee buckled. He grunted in pain. The ache twisted through his leg. The joint seemed to collapse. He lunged forward clumsily with his other leg. Clumsily, he brought the chair crashing down on top of Sachs.

Elizabeth cried out once. Sachs said, "Hey!" Sachs stepped back. He threw his arms up in front of his face. The chair thudded weakly into his shoulder.

"Ow," he said. He tottered back against the wall. "What the hell are you doing, Nathan?"

The impact knocked the chair out of Conrad's hands. It dropped, smacking the floor. It lay there, faceup.

Conrad stood there breathless. He grimaced at the throb in his knee. His arms hung down at his sides. His head hung down, his chin on his chest.

What *am* I doing? he thought. What the hell am I doing?

"Jesus, Nathan." Sachs straightened off the wall. He rubbed his shoulder. "I mean, Jesus! You could've killed me."

Conrad ran his hand up over his thin hair. He shook his head. He looked at the floor, dazed. "I'm . . . sorry. I don't know what I'm . . . I'm upset, I . . ." Automatically, he reached down and picked up the chair. He set it straight in front of him. "Christ, I'm at the end of my rope here. I don't . . ."

"Yeah," said Sachs, rubbing his arm. "But—ow! Jesus. I mean, that really hurt. I mean, is this the way a couple of doctors are supposed to behave?"

"No, no, I . . . I must be crazy." Conrad looked down at the chair. He couldn't believe what he'd done.

Stretching his arm, massaging it, Sachs looked at his watch again. "All right. Ow—damn it. All right, lookit, we gotta move. If we're gonna do this the way they want, we gotta really go."

Conrad nodded wearily. He picked up the chair and hit Sachs again.

He brought it straight up from the floor this time. Grabbed it by the back and the seat. Whipped it around in a swift, wicked arc. The heavy legs struck Sachs full on the side of his big pink head. His head snapped to the side sharply. Sweat flew off it into the pale-purple light. His glasses flew with it. They hit the wall and dropped to the floor.

Conrad lost his grip on the chair again. It tumbled and spun, fell over onto its side. Conrad stumbled, caught himself, stayed on his feet.

He looked up. Sachs was still standing too. The big man's naked eyes were blank and motionless. His mouth was opening and closing like a fish's mouth. There was a raw, open gash on one side of his head.

As Conrad watched, the gash turned scarlet. It flooded with blood. The blood ran thickly over Sachs's eye, his cheek.

"Really, Nathan. Really . . . ," Sachs said.

Then he crumbled to his knees. Then he pitched forward. He hit the floor with a thud and lay there motionless.

He's on His Way

Elizabeth was on her feet. She was staring down at Sachs. She held her cheek with one hand. She pointed at Sachs with the other.

"You hit him with the chair," she said.

Panting, Conrad stared too. His mouth was open. His eyes were wide. "I . . ."

"You hit him over the head with the chair," said Elizabeth.

"I had to stop him. He was going to tell, they'd have . . . killed her."

"But you hit him with the chair. You hit him over . . ."

"For God's sake, Elizabeth, I know that."

Elizabeth recoiled from his bark. Her hand dropped. She hugged herself. She gazed at him silently.

Still breathing hard, Conrad wiped the sweat off his face. "Come on," he said, more gently. "Help me tie him up."

He went to the bed. Tossed his trench coat to the floor. Stripped back the blanket, pulled up the top and bottom sheets. He pulled the pillowcase off the pillow. He carried the sheets and the pillowcase to Sachs.

Sachs lay twisted on the floor, his head to one side. The blood had coated the exposed side of his face. It was dripping down onto the floor in a sticky pool. It made a *pat-pat* sound.

Conrad knelt down beside Sachs, flinching at the pain in his knee. He pulled Sachs's right arm behind his back. The arm was heavy. The hand was slippery with sweat. He tied the sheet around the wrist. Then he pulled the left arm up. The slippery hand snaked out of his grasp. The arm flopped back to the floor. Conrad let out a breath and grabbed hold of it again. He tied the other wrist. He didn't know how to make any special knots. He just kept tying the sheet again and again.

He glanced at the door, at the thin window in the door. No one was looking in. He glanced at Elizabeth. She stood over him, hugging herself, watching him. Maybe this isn't the best course of treatment for her, he thought. He smiled thinly. He moved around Sachs's body to his feet. He took hold of his ankles and pulled his legs straight.

He tied Sachs's ankles with the bottom sheet. Then he took a deep breath, a shaky breath. He had to tie the pillowcase around Sachs's mouth: a gag. He turned Sachs's head to get the pillowcase under it. Blood smeared over his hands and the cuffs of his shirt. The blood was warm and sticky. When he turned Sachs's head, blood that had pooled in the ear spilled out. It pattered rapidly on the floor. Conrad swallowed hard. Even in medical school, he hadn't liked blood. He wrapped the pillowcase around Sachs's face. It wouldn't go into his mouth. Conrad pushed on the case, forcing it between Sachs's teeth. He felt Sachs's wet teeth on his knuckles. He pulled the pillowcase tight and tied it.

"Will he choke?" Elizabeth whispered.

"Huh?" said Conrad. "What?"

Elizabeth didn't repeat it.

Conrad stood up.

"Doctor!"

He reached out for her, falling. His knee had given out. At the same time, a hot pain sliced up through his forehead. Explosions of red went off in his right eye. He saw the familiar shapes of the sunset clouds off Seminary Hill.

He felt Elizabeth catch his arm in her two hands. He took hold of her shoulder, supported himself.

"I'm all right," he said quickly.

"Are you all right?"

"What? Yes. I'm all right. I'm fine."

The red bursts were subsiding. His knee throbbed dully. He straightened, letting go of Elizabeth. She let his arm slip through her hands.

Moving slowly, he returned to Sachs's feet. He bent at the waist and picked them up. He turned the heavy body in a circle until its feet were facing the bed. Then, grunting, he dragged the body to the side of the bed.

Sachs's head went through the thick pool of blood. It left a smeared trail as Conrad dragged it.

Now Sachs was beside the bed. Conrad knelt down next to him, letting out a groan of pain. Sachs's bloody features were turned toward him. His eyes were half open. His teeth bit on the pillowcase gag.

Is this the way a couple of doctors are supposed to behave?

Conrad shoved at Sachs's shoulder. The gelatinous mass of flesh didn't budge. Conrad shoved harder. He turned to look at Elizabeth. She stood behind him, wringing her hands.

"Help me," he said.

For another second, she only stood, her hands moving. Then she knelt down beside Conrad and pushed too.

They shoved together at Sachs's shoulder and torso, then his legs, then his shoulder and torso again. Bit by bit, Sachs's body slid under the metal bed; when it was under completely, Conrad had to bend the legs so the feet wouldn't stick out.

Then Elizabeth stood up. She helped Conrad stand up also. He clung to her shoulder and pulled himself erect, letting his leg straighten slowly.

"Thanks," he said. "See if you can clean up that blood."

Elizabeth nodded and went to the washbasin. She dampened her towel. She knelt down on the floor and began scrubbing at the smeared trail of blood. Her gold-red hair, tied with the black ribbon, fell forward. She brushed it back quickly over her shoulder.

Conrad, meanwhile, put the blanket back on the bed. He tried to make it look as if the bed were made, but he hung the edge of the blanket over the side to hide Sachs.

"I can't do this," said Elizabeth.

He looked down and saw her kneeling there, looking at him. She had cleaned away the trail of blood easily. But she hadn't touched the place where the blood had pooled.

"It'll just smear," she said. "I need a mop."

"Uh . . . all right. Just put the towel over it and let's get out of here," said Conrad.

He glanced at his watch. It was eight-forty.

"All right," Elizabeth said.

He heard a key slide into the door's lock.

"Oh, God," he said.

He looked up. Elizabeth froze. The door opened and the therapy aide peeked her head in. She was smiling.

"Everything is all right in here now?" she asked.

Conrad stared at her from the bed. Elizabeth stared at her from the floor.

"Fine," Conrad croaked. "Fine."

"Did Dr. Sachs, he leave?"

"Yes." Conrad quickly put his hands behind his back to hide the bloodstains.

"Okay. I am just checking," said the aide cheerfully.

She started to pull the door closed. Then she stopped. She put her head back into the room. She peered sharply at the floor. Her eyebrows came together.

"Are those your glasses?" she asked.

"Oh," said Conrad. His voice cracked. He looked down at the far wall where Sachs's glasses lay. "Oh, there they are."

"Have to be careful with those," said the aide. She backed out and shut the door.

Conrad bent down and swept up his trench coat. He put it on. Elizabeth got to her feet. She kept watching him.

"Come on," he said.

Elizabeth stared at him. "Me?"

"I can't leave you here. You've got to come with me. Hurry."

He took her by the shoulder. He led her to the door. He glanced back one last time.

The glasses.

He went to them, picked them up, slipped them into his pocket. He stood up. And he saw the cassette recorder sitting on the table.

"Oh, great," he said.

He snatched it. Dumped it in his pocket.

He took Elizabeth by the arm and led her out of the isolation room.

He hurried her down the hall. He held her by the elbow and walked quickly. Elizabeth had to run every few steps to keep up with him. He had to limp a little on his right leg to rest his knee. Aides glanced at the two of them in the dim corridor. The ward nurse looked back over her shoulder at them as they passed.

When they went out the door, the correction officer was at her desk. The wide woman glanced up from a newspaper. She looked at Conrad's face and nodded once, unsmiling. Then she looked down at the newspaper again.

Conrad led Elizabeth to the elevators. He pressed the button. He waited with her, listening to the guard turn the newspaper's page.

When, at last, they got in the elevator, they were alone. Conrad stood beside Elizabeth holding her by the arm. He faced the door. He felt her turn to him. He felt her studying his profile with her green eyes. He thought of how Sachs's face had looked when he shoved him under the bed. The door opened and he hurried her out.

The downstairs hall was quiet. Conrad took Elizabeth's hand and pulled her along. He had to skip on his right leg. He ran to Sachs's office.

It was eight forty-two when he came to the doorway. The door was open. The room was quiet. Sachs's phone sat at the front edge of his desk. It was right beside the long sign that said, JERALD SACHS, M.D., DIRECTOR. There were papers lying all around it.

Conrad watched the silent phone a moment.

"All right," he said. "We can't wait."

The phone rang.

Conrad limped forward quickly. He caught the phone before it rang again. He spoke very quietly, in a high murmur from the corner of his mouth.

"Sachs," he said.

"Where the fuck were you?" Conrad straightened. He recognized the voice. It was Sport, all right. "I had to call twice, you dumb fuck."

Conrad's heart beat hard. He spoke even more softly. "It's all right," he murmured. "He's on his way."

"Dumb fuck," said Sport. He slammed the phone down.

Conrad hung up with a trembling hand. He stood for a second looking down at the phone. He could pick it up, he could call the police.

There's no time. Too much could go wrong. There's no time even to explain.

He turned. He saw Elizabeth, still in the doorway.

She was staring at him. She had one hand raised to her forehead. She was massaging her brow.

"Is it you?" she said.

Conrad shook his head. "What?"

"Are you, I mean, him? The Secret Friend, I mean. Are you the Secret Friend?"

Conrad laughed. He stepped to her quickly. He was still laughing—giggling a little wildly—as he took her by the arm.

"Let's go," he said.

He had eighteen minutes to get to the clocktower.

Time to Kill

Nine o'clock. That's when you have to be back. Not a minute after nine. Not a second.

It was Saturday night. Traffic was thick but moving fast downtown on the FDR. The Corsica cut and darted through it like a fish through weeds. Conrad gripped the wheel hard. His head ached. His knee throbbed. The glare of headlights hurt his eye. He steered quickly, kept his foot pressed to the gas. He kept his eyes moving—to the windshield, the rearview, the sideview, the dashboard clock.

Underneath him, the pavement was rough and uneven. It dipped and heaved. The Corsica sank and rattled. Cars stopped ahead of him suddenly. Red brakelights suddenly burned and the traffic packed and slowed. Conrad didn't brake. The Corsica dodged and wove. His eyes burned through the windshield, flicked to the rearview, the sideview, the dash—the clock: ten minutes to nine. He was only now coming down across Forty-second Street.

What is the number? he thought. What is the number?

From the seat beside him, there came a soft sound. Elizabeth was singing to herself in an undertone.

"Forty-nine bottles of beer on the wall, forty-nine bottles of beer. One of those bottles should happen to fall, forty-eight bottles of beer on the wall. . . ."

She had a sweet, clear voice.

Conrad glanced over at her. She was sitting as she always sat. Erect, composed, her eyes forward, her hands folded in her lap.

What is the number?

His lips parted. He was about to ask her again. If she reacted now, if she went wild and attacked him at this speed, in this traffic . . .

". . . one of those bottles should happen to fall, forty-seven bottles of beer on the wall. . . ."

He faced front. The road was open for a stretch. At his window, the East River glittered with the lights of Brooklyn. On the far shore, the faint, chill mist gave the small lights halos. The clouds were white and purple with the city's lights.

". . . one of those bottles should happen to fall . . ."

The sound of her voice made him shiver.

Are you the Secret Friend?

Conrad's eyes went to the rearview, to the headlights reflected there. Were they following him still? Had they seen him leave the hospital with Elizabeth? Conrad didn't think so. He thought maybe they had left him alone for a while. Why would Sport have called in to the hospital if he'd had anyone to tail him? No, he'd had to check with Sachs. There was a good chance, Conrad thought, that he was alone for now. But still . . .

Still, even if they weren't tailing him, they would be at the clocktower, they would be waiting. They could spot her there. They could grab her. They would torture what they wanted out of her. They would kill her. Then him. Then Jessica.

". . . Forty-five bottles of beer. One of those bottles should happen to fall . . ."

"Elizabeth," he said.

Her singing stopped. He couldn't look at her. He worked the wheel as the black pavement raced at him, under him. "Elizabeth," he said again, "can you help me? Can you help me now?"

There was no answer. He just couldn't look.

"You have to tell me what they want from you. You have to help me get my daughter back. This number they want—is it a phone number? An address? A . . . a safe combination? Do these people know you? Do you know who they are or . . . ?"

"Does your daughter have a nice room?" Elizabeth asked suddenly.

"What?" Conrad stared ahead as the red taillights of a speeding Cadillac swung in front of him, pulled away.

"Are there pictures on the wall? I'll bet she has pictures on the wall. I bet she has pictures of Mickey Mouse. Or Big Bird. Now they like Big Bird, the children, don't they?"

Conrad nodded slowly. "Yes. Big Bird. She has . . . there are Big Birds on her quilt, her cover. I don't . . ."

"Mother is nice now," Elizabeth said. "Now she comes in and says good-night. Now mother is nice."

Conrad waited. He didn't say anything. In another moment, he heard her voice again:

"Forty-four bottles of beer on the wall, forty-four bottles of beer. . . ."

Now, finally, he did look at her again. He saw her sitting erect and empty eyed. Staring out at the weaving traffic and the night while her own reflection stared back at her from the windshield. It was strange, he thought. Yesterday, last night, less than twenty-four hours ago, he had fantasized about her while he was making love to his wife. He had fallen asleep thinking about her. He had looked forward to more sessions with her; to the sound of her laughter, the sudden sanity in her eyes.

I'm still in here.

And now it was all gone, all cold. He could remember that he had felt that way, but he could not remember what it had been like. He couldn't remember what it had been like to feel anything besides the crush of this terrible vise of fear. For a moment, he thought of Timothy, his patient with AIDS: he was alone, scared, and made of flesh—and there was nothing else to him. That was like this, Conrad thought: the nausea of time, of the presence of time, of time running out.

I won't wait one second, Doctor. Nine o'clock and you're through, your daughter's through. Remember that.

Conrad rubbed his knee. He had to hold his foot steady on the gas. It made the knee hurt more. He worked the wheel, worked the car. Into the left lane as traffic gathered to the right for the Fourteenth Street exit. Into the middle as the left lane slowed. Dodging through the racing traffic. Checking the mirrors, the clock. Six and a half minutes to nine. . . .

"Forty-three bottles of beer on the wall, forty-three bottles of beer. . . ."

Elizabeth sat erect and gazed out the windshield. She sang without emotion. Her voice was as pure and clear as an electronic tone.

He had four minutes left when he hit Canal Street. And the traffic there congealed. Saturday night in Chinatown. Thick lines of cars coughed forward under green lights or jammed together at the reds. Out on the street, people strolled past banks and restaurants with pagoda roofs and Chinese facades. Young Chinese couples, old Chinese women, old men; groups of white teenagers in from the boroughs, young black families—all strolling casually on Saturday night. Time to spare, time to kill.

Three minutes to nine.

"Thirty-two bottles of beer on the wall, thirty-two bottles of beer. . . ."

"Goddamn it!" Conrad cried out.

But then there was Lafayette. An easier flow of cars. He turned downtown. Turned on his emergency lights. Honked his horn. Pushed through intersections against the lights. He had MD plates, and he knew the cops wouldn't stop him. He just hoped everyone else would get out of his way.

The car sped on. Past the young crowd bopping down the broad avenue. Past the husky rococo office buildings, the little appliance stores, the walls sprayed with curling graffiti. Past the clusters of people gathered round the three-card-monte players and the black marketeers hawking sweaters and watches and radios: "Check it out." Then, to his left, there was the Tombs. The prison's limestone ziggurat stared down at him over its four concrete towers. He had two minutes left.

He turned right, the wrong way, onto Franklin Street. It was a dark, thin lane under the flat-black granite wall of the Family Court building. There was no traffic. One couple passed by them, taking a shortcut toward Chinatown. Then the street was empty. Conrad hoped he could hide Elizabeth here. The Corsica screeched to the curb next to a NO STOPPING sign.

Then Conrad's hands were flashing everywhere. Pulling out the ignition key, turning off the lights, undoing his seat belt . . .

Elizabeth turned to him slowly and blinked. "Are we here?"

"Just wait for me," he said. "Don't move. Don't talk to anyone. If the police come by, say you're waiting for a doctor on an emergency call. Do you understand?"

"You're going?"

"I have to. They'll hurt my daughter. I have to meet with them."

She gazed at him silently.

He threw open the door. The toplight came on, and he saw her face clearly. The look in her eyes.

He stopped, one foot on the pavement, the other still inside.

"Elizabeth," he said. She waited. She looked at him. He shook his head. "I'm sorry."

She didn't move. Softly, she told him, "Five fifty-five, three-thirteen."

"What?"

"Five fifty-five, three-thirteen."

Conrad pressed his lips together. He reached out, touched her arm. Elizabeth looked down at his hand.

"I'll be back," he said hoarsely.

He got out of the car and slammed the door.

He had just about sixty seconds.

Elizabeth watched him go. A small, slender figure, limping quickly into the misty darkness. He looked kind of silly, she thought, running along like that. She did hope he found his daughter, though.

She smiled, laughed silently. He had hit Dr. Sachs with the chair. She was pretty sure that had really happened. He had hit him right on the head with it. He was just like the Secret Friend. He *was* the Secret Friend. Only he was real. She was pretty sure of that too.

She watched him limping off. She thought about his face. He had a sad face, she thought. A sort of saggy, hangdog face. His eyes were like an old man's, sad and tired. His brow was furrowed, his sandy hair was almost gone. Elizabeth sat in the car, her hands folded on her lap. She watched him go and thought about his face. She smiled. It gave her a warm feeling.

He was going to help her, she thought. He had said so. Things would not be so cloudy anymore. She would feel better, the way she had when she worked at the day-care center. She had liked that. Dr. Holbein had done that for her. Dr. Holbein had been good too.

And Dr. Conrad was good. She felt sure of that. The feeling made her calmer, happier. It was like a warm light around her.

Then she saw his figure limp around the corner and the light went out. She stopped smiling. She was alone here suddenly. All alone in this dark car on this dark street. . . .

Don't talk to anyone. Don't move. Just wait for me.

Elizabeth shivered. There were goose bumps coming up on her arms. She rubbed at them with her hands until she felt warmer. She gazed through the windshield at where Dr. Conrad had been. She sang to herself softly.

"Twenty-six bottles of beer on the wall, twenty-six bottles of beer."

A man sat up on the seat in back of her.

Elizabeth sensed him. She started to turn. She caught a nightmare glimpse of a face stretched tight, of corded tendons, twitching lips, eyes bulging and white. She tried to cry out but his hand flashed at her, clapped over her mouth. He pulled her back, hard, against the seat. Elizabeth's arms moved wildly, helplessly. She heard a high, screaking giggle behind her: Hee hee hee.

And then she felt something cold pressed against her throat.

She had time to realize it was a knife.

Time Runs Out

The Criminal Court Annex was an ornate and massive building. An entire block long, its white marble facade swept up over the purple sky. It was a long wall of high, arching windows and chiseled filigree. At its top, stone eagles squatted along a balcony, glaring north toward the Empire State Building, south toward the twin towers and Wall Street. Above them, almost shabby atop all the rest, was a square, off-white tower with a clockface on two sides. That was the clocktower.

Conrad ran toward it, limping, practically skipping. The damp air blew back his open trench coat. He could feel the seconds being used up like the oxygen in a locked room. He turned the corner onto Leonard Street.

The narrow lane was deserted. The surge and tilt of the pavement's old flags glistened and faded beneath a streetlamp's gleam. The building hung above him. In all that wall of arching windows running up the side of the sky, not a single light was burning. The place looked desolate and empty. Locked.

He ran to the door and yanked it back. It opened easily. He stepped into the lobby.

The wide space was full of shadows. The grandiose sweep of two marble staircases. Shapely balusters striping the dark. A tawdry spherical chandelier hanging above him. All still and cold. Conrad thought he could feel the chill coming off the stone in waves.

He ran under the stairs to the elevators. He knew the way. Aggie and he had come to the Clocktower Museum often before Jessica was born. They had climbed up to the top and kissed and pawed each other . . . but he couldn't think about that now. He ran.

He pressed the elevator button. A door broke open. The sharp light inside the box spilled out onto the floor. Conrad got in and pressed the top button, number twelve.

His time ran out as the elevator rose. He looked down at his watch and saw the minute hand lean over past the twelve. He felt his throat close as he saw it. They had to wait.

Not a minute after nine.

Yes, wait.

Not a second.

The elevator rose quickly. A bell rang as it reached each floor. Seven . . . eight . . . nine . . . Conrad raised his face to the ceiling and brought his hands to his head.

Nine o'clock and you're through, your daughter's through. Remember that.

Please, he thought. Please.

The elevator door opened. Conrad rushed out.

There was now a winding stair, a wooden balcony coiling upward. Conrad clutched it, dragging his leg, climbing up quickly into the high dark. He crested the landing. Stumbled down a hallway of closed gray doors. He could feel the minute hand tilting farther past the hour as if the mechanism were inside him. Panting, coughing, he ran toward the door at the end of the hall. It came out of the shadows at him. The gray paint on it was chipped. The sign read NO ADMITTANCE. He pushed through.

A cluttered stairwell. Another flight of stairs, this one a short series of wooden steps. He climbed toward a red metal door at the top. More than the chill of the concrete walls, he could feel the cold of the outside seeping in to him now. He wheezed and coughed.

"Jesus."

He pushed the red door open. He stepped through it onto the roof.

There was a shock of air and noise. The sough of wind, the susurrus of traffic on the streets far below. The faint, intermittent honking of horns down there.

He skittered up a small metal ramp to the balcony. The stone eagles squatted on the wall all around him. The white, red, and green lights of the city stretched out in the mist below. The golden crown of the municipal tower rose up in front of him, scraping the starless sky.

Gasping, he looked at his watch. His stomach turned. Three minutes past nine.

He took a step across the balcony. He heard a gong.

It rang out solemn and loud. The sound of traffic vanished under it, rose up beneath it as it faded away. Conrad lifted his eyes and saw the clocktower.

It was right in front of him, right above him. A sculpted marble block with the illuminated clockface peering out at him. And on the face, the great black hands on the roman numerals. And the hour hand was on the nine, and the minute hand was directly on the twelve.

The clock was slow.

The second gong sounded.

Still time! Still time!

Then, as he stared, a black silhouette—the black silhouette of a man—passed behind the lighted clock. The gong sounded a third time.

Conrad stumbled toward the clocktower door.

The gong sounded again. Conrad pulled the door back, charged into the tower blackness. A narrow, winding staircase twisted up into nothing. The gong sounded a fifth time. The air in here shivered with it. Conrad grabbed hold of the banister and began to climb.

He hauled himself upward, straining, gritting his teeth against the pain. The gong sounded. He dragged his right leg after him. It felt like a concrete block with a lightning bolt trapped inside. The gong sounded again, a seventh time. It got louder as he neared the top. His head was aching with it.

Not a minute. Not a second.

Still time! he screamed in his mind. Still time!

He swung around the stair's final arc. There was the opening above him that led to the clockroom. The gong sounded the eighth time. He was up, he was through the hole. He took another step, another. He came off the stairs onto the floor.

There, inside the cramped chamber of the mechanism, the last gong rattled the air like the bars of a cage. Conrad felt the vibrations go through him. The red sunset clouds broke over his vision, shimmered, floated. He closed his right eye, fighting them back. Slowly, the sound of the gong faded. Conrad stood slumped, wheezing softly. In front of him, at the center of the tiny room, gears and cogs and wheels rose in a turning, shifting tangle of machinery. They hummed and whispered. A shaft running from them to the clock's hands turned. The minute hand keeled past the hour with a buzz and a click.

Against the white of the clockface, a man's shadow moved out from behind the mechanism.

In the Clocktower

"You cut it awfully close there, Doc," he said. "My watch shows almost five after."

"Your watch is fast, Sport." Conrad was still breathless. But he tried to keep his voice steady. Calm. Authoritative. The doctor is in.

Sport chuckled easily. "My watch is fast," he said. "I like that. My watch is fast."

There was a sudden flash of red light. Conrad felt the pain of it piercing his right eye. He turned his face half away. The light faded to a yellow glow. The man called Sport had lit a match. He was holding the flame to a cigarette.

As the match flared again, Conrad saw the kidnapper clearly. Jesus, he thought, he's so young. In his late twenties; thirty, at most. Lean and fit in jeans and a patched tweed jacket. And handsome too, with a round, boyish face, a shock of brown hair falling into his eyes. And those eyes; there was a fierce black fire of intelligence in them. They were an artist's or a student's eyes or . . .

Sport waved the match out. His face was blanketed with shadows.

"What's the matter, Doc?" he said. "You look a little worn out. You weren't hurrying on my account, were you?" He laughed. Conrad didn't answer. Sport waved the cigarette at him. "Just kidding. Just kidding, Doc.

177

Don't get all bent out of shape. I told you before: you're all right with me. Really."

Conrad kept his silence. Fought to breathe more slowly. Straightened his shoulders. The doctor is in.

Sport laughed again—a little nervously, Conrad thought. "All right, all right, so you're not talking to me. Big Mr. Shrink. I'm crumbling. I can't deal with your silence. So, uh, let me ask you this: Just what *is* that ker-azy old number anyway? I mean, if you're not talking to me, let's get down to it, right?"

Now Conrad spoke; slowly, steadily. "Where is she? Where's my daughter, Sport?"

Through the dark, he saw the other man shake his head. He heard him chuckle again. "Psychiatrists," Sport said. "Always answering questions with questions." Conrad saw the red glow of the cigarette pointed at him. "First, we talk about the number, then we talk about the kid. Follow? First the number, then the kid. It's really simple once you get the hang of it."

"No." Now the sweat began. Conrad felt it gather in his hair, felt it rolling down his back, from his armpits, down his sides. "No, you said she would be here. I would give you the number, you would give me my girl. That was the agreement."

"Oh," said Sport. "Oh, Doctor. Doctor, Doctor, Doctor. Am I a bozo? Am I a chucklehead? No, no, no, my friend." He put one hand in his pocket. He made an elaborately casual gesture with his cigarette hand. "It's going to take me several hours to check out whether this number is the one I want. When I'm sure that it is, you get your daughter back. By midnight, I'd say, at the latest."

"No," said Conrad again. His breathing was regular now, but the pulse in his temple was hard and fast. "I'd have no guarantee that—"

"Doctor." All at once, Sport's voice stretched tight. He was talking through gritted teeth. He took a step forward. "I must not be explaining this well. Okay? The thing is: I'm a decent guy. I don't *want* to kill anyone. Not at all, okay? But I do want that number. Oh, yes. I want that number so very badly that I would happily cut your child to pieces to get it. See? I would kill her, your wife, your whole family: in-laws, that annoying uncle with the palm-tree tie, the whole lot. Okay? So—you're thinking, well, you bluffed me out once before. Maybe it'll work again. And hey, I respect you for that. Really. I told you so. But we are now at a whole different place in the proceedings. Understand? We are now smack-dab at the center of things and I have to move one way or the other. The question before the committee is simple: What's the fucking number? You have thirty seconds to answer it. That's nonnegotiable. No slow clocks, no refunds. Thirty seconds and then I'm walking out of here and your daughter is suitable for dog food."

Conrad licked his lips. He took one shaky step toward the other man. "That's no good. You could've killed her already." He tried to control his voice.

And Sport said, "Twenty-five."

"Or you could kill her afterward. It's no good, Sport."

"Twenty."

"Up here, hell, you could kill me," Conrad said.

"You're right. I could. Fifteen."

Conrad's eye fluttered closed again. His temple throbbed. I've got to call him, he thought. I've got to turn and walk out of here. "You've got to let me talk to her at least or no deal," he said.

"Ten seconds, Doc," said Sport. His teeth showed gray in the dark as he sneered.

Then, suddenly, Conrad's fists were clenched in front of him. He was screaming, the spit flying from his lips. "You piece of shit! You demented piece of fucking garbage! You scum! You scumbag! You scum!"

"Five—four—three . . ."

"All right," said Conrad.

"One."

Conrad's hands fell to his sides again. He looked away from the other man. "Five fifty-five, three-thirteen," he said. "That's what she told me. Five fifty-five, three-thirteen."

The clockwork hummed. The minute hand buzzed as it moved imperceptibly. For a long, long moment, both men could be heard breathing hard in the little room.

"All right," Sport said then hoarsely. He dropped his cigarette, crushed it under his foot. He stepped forward until he was standing next to Conrad. Conrad turned to him, faced him. They were inches apart. They were about the same height and their eyes met directly. Conrad could see the younger man's eyes glittering. He could see his lip curling.

Sport let out a soft snort. "Who's the piece of shit?" he said. "Who's the piece of garbage? Right? Big man. Big cock. I thought you were tough. Big shrink, big Mr. Psychiatrist. Big fucking cock with your smart cunt of a wife. Without your bullshit and your money, your fancy degrees, just man on man—what are you then? You follow? What are you?"

Sport spit at him. Conrad recoiled but the spittle hit him on the cheek, just under his right eye. Conrad wiped it off with a trembling hand.

"Who's a scumbag?" Sport said softly.

He walked away. He walked to the top of the spiral stairs. Slouching, his hands in his pockets, he paused there. He glanced back.

"Wait here five minutes," he told Conrad. "Until fifteen after by the big clock. Remember: we're still watching you. At fifteen after, go downstairs, get back in your car, and drive to your office. Go inside and don't leave. If you do leave, we'll see you. If we see you . . ." He drew a hand across his throat. "It'll be coitens for da goil." He laughed. He had to fight to stop the chuckling. "But seriously: If you're a good boy, you can come out at twelve o'clock. The kid'll be on the sidewalk right in front of your building."

With a swift, agile movement, he lowered himself onto the stairs. He climbed down until only his head still showed above the opening.

Then he paused. He grinned.

"Remember," he said. "Wait five minutes. Until nine-fifteen. By the clock."

Alone, Conrad remained motionless. Stared at the place where Sport had gone.

I'm scared, Daddy.

He listened to the hum of the clock, the sound of his own breathing.

I don't want to stay here. I'm scared.

Minutes passed and he didn't move, just stood, just stared.

Daddy?

He shuddered convulsively. He blinked, looked up, looked around him. For a moment, he thought there were tears on his cheek. He raised his hand to wipe them away. But it was just the place where Sport's spittle had hit him. He could still feel it, though it was gone now.

He watched the hands of the big clock. Seen from behind like that, the clockface was reversed. The minute hand moved counterclockwise down toward the Roman three. It seemed to move slowly.

Daddy, I'm scared.

"Jessie," he whispered. "I'm so sorry."

The minute hand touched the three. Conrad turned away. He went to the stairway. He started down.

He had decided to call the police.

If they had really followed him, why had Sport checked in with Sachs? If they had really followed him, why hadn't Sport known about Elizabeth—that she was out, that she had come here with him?

Conrad limped down the shadowed hall. He stood at the elevator, resting against the wall, waiting for a car.

And if they weren't really following him, he had to call the cops. He had to. It was the only way he might still save her. He could not handle this alone.

As he rode down in the elevator, he stared at the red lighted numbers. The numbers kept blurring. Conrad had to keep wiping his eyes. The door opened and let him out into the lobby. He walked under the marble staircases. He pushed out onto Leonard Street, into the night.

They did not know about Elizabeth, he repeated to himself. And since they did not know, they must not be watching him. And since they weren't watching him, he had to call the police.

I'm scared, Daddy.

He had to. He had to help her somehow.

He went hobbling around the corner, breathing hard, glancing around to see if he was being pursued. He saw no one. He came up Lafayette where the traffic sped by, the lights blinding. He kept moving. He could feel the dampness of the air on his face, the cold of it on that same spot on his cheek. He grit his teeth. He turned onto Franklin. He worked his way into the quiet under the courthouse's black wall.

The Corsica was parked just where it had been. It still sat dark and silent on the dark and silent street. He hurried across to it. He had to call them. He had to risk it. And they had to save her. Someone had to. If they didn't, if no one did, if she died . . . oh, Christ, if she died . . . then Aggie and he and everything . . . everything would be . . .

He stopped in the middle of the pavement. He let out a small, miserable little noise.

He saw that the car was empty.

Staring—gaping—he stepped forward, stepped stiffly. He stepped to the door, shoved the key in.

"Oh . . . ," he whispered.

The door swung open. Conrad stared. He saw blood—a long swath of blood—running down the back of the passenger seat. He turned. He saw something lying on the dash. His eyes moved over it. It was long seconds before he could comprehend what it was.

It was paper; a crumpled piece of notebook paper. He stared and stared at it until he understood.

There were words on it. Words written in red ink:

We are still watching you. Go to your office. Wait.

PART THREE

Ten

Sparrows and chickadees were singing in the ivy. Agatha was in the kitchen, at the stove. She was wearing an orange-and-white apron, the one her mother used to wear. She was stirring a bowl of batter with a wooden spoon. She was humming, smiling to herself. The birds seemed almost to sing along.

Outside, though, the white carnation was lost in a field of wildflowers. The thought of it nagged at her. Finally, she set the bowl down and went to the cottage door. She stepped outside into the field.

Very quickly, she was in the midst of it. The cottage was far behind her. The wildflowers were thick around her everywhere. She could feel their soft petals tickle her instep, their cool stems beneath her toes. She wished she had not left the house, that the house was not so far away.

Then, there was the white carnation. At her feet, just beneath her. She was frightened because she had almost stepped on it. She reached down to pick it up. . . .

But as she did, the white carnation turned pink. The color seemed to rise up from within it. The pink darkened to red, and then to scarlet. And then the scarlet thickened, and as Aggie watched, horrified, the thick scarlet began to drip from the carnation's petals, falling to the earth below, seeping into the earth, which seemed already choked with red, gagging the red back up in viscous pools. . . .

* * *

185

"Jessie!" Aggie sat up on the sofa. She looked around her with wide eyes. Her daughter's teddy bear lay on its side next to her. "Jesus," she whispered. She had fallen asleep. How could she have fallen . . . ? She looked quickly at her watch. It was nine-fifty. Only for a minute . . . She had only dozed off for a minute. She turned her head, looked around the long room. Her worktable by the door, the dinner table against the wall, the empty playspace . . . Nothing had happened, nothing had changed. No one had come in, the phone had not rung.

But why didn't it? Why didn't the phone ring?

Aggie rubbed her eyes. She shook her head quickly to clear it. She had to get up, move around. She had been sitting on the couch, sitting still for a long time. Ever since D'Annunzio left—the man she thought was Detective D'Annunzio—ever since he'd left about ninety minutes ago, she'd been trying to keep her movements to a minimum. She was afraid she might do something that would somehow arouse the kidnappers' suspicion. She was afraid she might make some gesture of hope or eagerness or anticipation. Do something that would make them suspect that the plumber—D'Annunzio—had really been a cop; that she had managed, right under their noses, to notify the police; that now the police were out there, after them.

It was a sweet—a comforting—image: the police, on the job. Their army of professionals. Out there. They know what they're doing, she told herself.

But why didn't . . . ?

She forced the irritating little voice down. She stood. She ran her hand up through her hair. She was still a little foggy.

She went into the kitchen. A city kitchen, narrow, white. Still, it brought part of her dream back to her. She had been in the kitchen wearing her mother's apron. . . . She could not remember the rest of it.

She filled a glass with water from the tap. She stood pressed to the sink, drinking it down.

Why didn't the phone ring? When D'Annunzio was here? Why didn't it ring the way it did with Billy Price?

She gasped out of the water. She shut her eyes tight.

Stop it, she told herself. It's going to be all right now. The police are out there. Detective D'Annunzio. He's out there. All his tough detective friends. Come on, guys—she could hear their deep voices—let's find that kid. That's what they were saying. She could imagine their chairs scraping as they pushed them back. She could see them purposefully jamming their pistols in their shoulder holsters.

She set the glass down on the countertop. It clattered against the vinyl as it shook in her shaking hand.

But why didn't . . . ?

Freeze! She could hear their tough, their manly, voices. *Blam! Blam!* The kidnappers reeled back, their jaws slack, their eyes hollow. *Rescue!* said the headline of tomorrow's *Daily News.* And there was a photo on the front page of Aggie on her knees, Jessica in her arms, Jessica clasped tight in her arms, the small, living warmth of Jessica pressed against her breasts, sheltered in her arms and . . .

Agatha sobbed. She raised her trembling hand to her mouth, wiped her lips slowly.

Yeah, but, excuse me? Excuse me—Mrs. C? Uh—why didn't the telephone ring?

"Shut up," she muttered.

She started out of the kitchen. The kitchen had begun to seem too close, too tight. She walked quickly into the living room. She paced across it to a bookcase. She turned to pace back—but then stopped.

Stand still . . . Don't let them see any . . . Don't . . .

She stood where she was. The thing that wanted to pace was still moving in her, jumping around, pushing at her. She took a deep breath, trying to quiet it.

It's just that they weren't watching, that's all, she thought. That's why the goddamned phone didn't ring. They weren't home when D'Annunzio came. They'd stepped out, they were glomming some tube, I don't know. Or the cameras malfunctioned. Or they didn't get suspicious about a plumber. That's why. There are plenty of reasons, good reasons why they didn't call, why they didn't threaten me like they did with Billy Price. . . .

Like, you mean, that D'Annunzio's not a cop at all? Like, for instance, that D'Annunzio is really one of them? That Price—maybe Price—is also one of them?

She brought her hand to her temple, massaged it. Her head hurt. Where was Nathan? He was supposed to meet the kidnappers at nine. Why hadn't he come home? Why didn't he bring Jessica home?

Good questions. And another thing, since we happen to be on the subject: Why didn't the goddamn phone ring?

"Oh . . . ," she said.

The thing that wanted to pace jumped and babbled and ricocheted off her insides like that Mexican mouse in the cartoons Jessie watched. Aggie wanted to hit at her stomach to stop it. She wanted to tear at her hair. She wanted to tear the little questions out of herself. D'Annunzio's out there, she repeated. He's out there with the other detectives. They're going to rescue my baby. *Freeze,* they're going to shout. *Blam.*

She stood shakily by the bookcase. She tried not to cry. She didn't want them to see her cry. She was getting hysterical, she thought. She had to focus. She tried to think about D'Annunzio. His youthful, intelligent face. His watchful, trustworthy eyes. His cop's voice, his cop's questions.

What's Jessica look like? How old is she? How about the kidnapper? Anything that indicates where they might be? A noise on the line? A slip of the . . .

"Tongue," Agatha whispered aloud.

How had he known her name was Jessica?

There was a flutter in her stomach. Her knees went soft. She reached out and grabbed hold of a bookshelf.

Had she told him Jessica's name? She couldn't remember. No. No. Or maybe yes, maybe she had, she couldn't remember. Maybe she had told Billy Price. Yes, of course, that was it. She had told Billy Price only . . . only she hadn't, not just now, not as she was pushing him to the door. She had been in too much of a panic to think of it.

My daughter's been kidnapped. My apartment's being watched. Call the police.

No, but . . . Agatha thought frantically.

Yes, she thought. Yes, of course. Price had met Jessica by the elevator. She had introduced them. This is my daughter, Jessica, Aggie had said. Sure. That's it. And when Price called D'Annunzio, D'Annunzio would've asked, "And what's the child's name?" And Price would've said, "Let me see. She's told me once before. . . . Oh, yes: Jessica. That's right. Her name is Jessica."

But wouldn't D'Annunzio have asked *her* too? Wouldn't he have confirmed it with her? Wouldn't he have said, *And her name is Jessica, is that right?* Wouldn't he?

And hey, that brings up another interesting question: Why didn't the fucking phone ring while he was here?

The thing that wanted to pace was going wild inside her. Agatha couldn't stand still any longer. She started walking, as slowly as she could.

She walked toward the bedroom. Her eyes flicked from place to place as she walked: the table, the standing lamp, the door, the phone . . .

"Nathan," she said softly as she walked.

Where was he? Why hadn't he come back? He was supposed to meet with them at nine. He was supposed to tell them what they wanted at nine and then they were going to . . .

Freeze! Blam.

. . . they were going to give him back her baby. That should've happened by now. He should've been back by now. It was almost . . . She looked down at her watch. It was almost . . .

Agatha stopped walking.

She was standing at the entrance to the hallway. Before her were two doorways: the bedroom to her right and to her left . . .

Ten, she thought. It was almost ten. Almost ten o'clock. Ten o'clock even now, the minute hand moving up to the twelve.

Agatha started down the hall. She tried to go steadily. One step, two steps, don't run . . . Any minute now.

She turned left. Into the bathroom. She flicked on the light, stood before the sink. She stood before the sink and she . . . She had to do something. Something so they wouldn't be suspicious. She took a washcloth from the rack on the wall. She ran some water on it, dampened a corner of it. Any minute now. She looked up at herself in the mirror.

Jesus, she thought.

Her face was drawn, almost ashen. Her auburn hair hung down around it in sweat-damp tangles. Her round cheeks looked splotchy and sunken. Her lips were almost white.

Like a fever victim, she thought. Like I've been sick for weeks with fever.

With a trembling hand, she began to wash her face. She concentrated on a corner of her eye, as if something were irritating her there. She worked the spot carefully. She had to take time, enough time until . . .

Come on, she thought. Come on. It's just about right. It's just about now.

She worked the washcloth around her eye. She leaned into the mirror and studied the spot. Come on, she thought. Come on. She worked the washcloth around the spot carefully.

And then she heard it. It was right on the button: 10:01.

It started as a low, wet rumbling. Next came a series of thick, phlegmy hawks. Finally he spat—she could hear him through the heating grate. He spat and the thick gob splashed into the toilet bowl.

She closed her eyes with relief. "The ten-o'clock *cheh,*" she whispered. She had to choke down her wild laughter.

Mr. Plotkin was starting up again. A groan came through the heating duct followed by more of that low, wet rumbling.

Agatha kept washing her eye, kept washing that spot at the corner of her eye.

"Mr. Plotkin," she said aloud.

He was hawking again: *cheh, cheh, cheh.* That third time he got it up. Spat. She heard the splash in the toilet water.

She suppressed a giggle. "Mr. Plotkin," she said. The washcloth trembled at the corner of her eye.

Again, the old man was rumbling away. "*A-chah-chah-chah* . . . hanh? Hanh?" he said. "What?"

Aggie took a deep breath. Her hand shook so violently she had to lay it down on the sink. "Mr. Plotkin . . ." She swallowed. Her voice was shaking too.

"Hello? Hello? What?" came the answer from the grate.

"Mr. Plotkin, can you hear me?" Aggie said. There was a long silence. She forced herself to lift the washcloth again. She brought it to her lips. "Can you hear me?" she repeated more loudly.

"Can I hear you? What is this, a test of the emergency communications system?" The old man's raspy voice had lost its Yiddish accent, but the old intonations were still there. "I can hear you. You can hear me. We can listen to each other in the bathroom. Who is this?"

Aggie let her breath out. She felt she had been holding it for minutes on end. She stared at herself in the mirror, at her glassy, frightened eyes.

"Hello?" said Mr. Plotkin. "Hello?"

"This is Aggie Conrad," she said.

There was another pause. Then: "Oh." It was a flat, hard sound. It called the old man's round, hairless face to her mind. The way he stood in silence when they met in the elevator. The thin smile he spared Jessica when she said hello to him. "What? You're going to bother an old man because he spits? Believe me, Mrs. What's-your-name, it's no fun for me either."

"Mr. Plotkin," Aggie said. "I need help." Tears sprang to her eyes. She dabbed them away with the washcloth. "I need help. Please."

The old man's tone changed on the instant. "What? Are you sick? What's the matter? You can't get to the phone, you need a doctor? What?"

"I need the police," Aggie said. The tears came more quickly now. She covered her eyes with the cloth. "Call Detective D'Annunzio, at Midtown

South. Please. If he's not there, ask for someone else. My daughter's been kidnapped. The kidnappers are watching my apartment. Tell Detective D'Annunzio I have to talk to him . . . he may already know, I'm not . . . Just . . . Tell him not to come here, tell him to come to your place, to talk to me through the duct like this. . . . And Mr. Plotkin . . ." She had to stop for a moment as she cried into the washcloth. "Mr. Plotkin, be careful, all right, because I don't know what's happening, I don't know whom to trust, and these are dangerous . . . men, they're . . ."

She couldn't go on. She cried into the washcloth. No answer came from above her, from the grate. It seemed to her as if whole minutes passed in silence while she cried.

Then, she lifted her face. She raised her eyes to the high corner of the white-tiled wall. Tears were streaming down her cheeks now. She gazed through them, up at the grate. She gazed at the darkness beyond the gray checkerboard of metal. She peered *into* the darkness, as if trying to see the old man on the other side.

Finally, she heard him speaking to her. He murmured to her softly, gently.

"Hold on, Ag-ela," he said. "Help is on the way."

Prince of the City

Detective Doug D'Annunzio leaned back from his typewriter. His swivel chair screaked with his weight. D'Annunzio tilted his big body to one side and squeezed out a fart. Goddamn fives, he thought.

He'd been filling out the DD-5 forms on the garment center stickup for an hour and a half. He was sick of it. He wanted to get out, get something done. He glanced at the digital watch on his thick wrist: 10:06. He had just enough time to run up to the Deuce and shake down Snake-Eye Jones, if he was quick about it.

"Jesus Christ, D'Annunzio." Sergeant Moran was standing by the filing cabinets. He waved the air in front of his face. "They oughta run a pipeline up your ass and provide free heat to millions."

"Eh, G.F.Y.," D'Annunzio muttered. He pushed his chair back and stood up.

He waddled across the dingy squad room to the coffee machine. He poured the dregs from the pot into a fresh Styro. He sipped at the grainy black mess, gazing thoughtfully across the long room: the scattered gunmetal desks, the torn swivel chairs, the stripped wooden walls plastered with notices, the windows blanketed with filth. It'd been a while since he'd gone after Snake-Eye, he thought. The little nig oughta be worth a few bills by now, at least. He practically had a monopoly in the back of the Deuce's biggest porno shop. Peddling hits of crack to the johns at the peepshow. Hell, he oughta be worth a K after all this time.

He sipped his coffee, eased out another silent fart. All that sitting with the DD-5s—it made the gas build up. Not to mention the veal hero he'd had for an after-dinner snack. But it was the sitting down that really did it to you.

"Oh. Oh, Jesus Christ, D'Annunzio, have some mercy here," cried Moran. He and Levine were the only others in the room. Levine was at a desk in the rear, talking on the phone.

D'Annunzio ignored Moran. He set his Styro down, started back to his desk to get his jacket. He could take care of Snake-Eye and be back to finish the fives before his shift ended. Or maybe he'd take it slow and make a little overtime too. He walked across the room slowly. He breathed loudly, hard.

His gut surrounded him as he went like an entourage; at the age of thirty-eight, he was bloated and gnarled. His brightly checkered shirt bunched and overflowed at the waist of his tent-size blue pants. His neck was a column; his collar button couldn't close around it, and the knot in his gold tie had gone slack. His face was round, his cheeks ballooned, but his skin was still mottled and sandpaper rough. Short brown hair capped a stony brow. Marbly black eyes peered out from grainy folds of flesh.

He reached his desk. He wrestled his jacket off the back of the chair.

The phone rang.

Moran glanced up from the files. "Hey," he said, "Suburban Propane. Quit farting a minute and get that, willya."

D'Annunzio let out a heavy sigh but he didn't say anything. You didn't fuck with Moran. Not with the mick master of the flashy arrest; the precinct whip; the commander's darling.

Shit, he thought. So much for Snake-Eye. He worked his sausagy arms into his corduroy jacket. The phone kept ringing. He gave another sigh, louder this time. He snatched up the receiver.

"Detective D'Annunzio," he said.

"Good evening to you, Detective D'Annunzio. Leo Plotkin here. I have a job for you."

D'Annunzio raised his eyes to the ceiling. He perched his huge ass on the edge of his desk. "How can I help you, sir?" he said.

"Well . . . frankly, unless you know a cure for angina, there's not much point in discussing it. My neighbor Aggie Conrad: her, you could help."

"Aggie Conrad," D'Annunzio said. It only took him a second to place it. "The one whose kid was supposed to be kidnapped."

"You know this already?"

"Yeah, yeah, I got a call about two hours ago. They thought the kid was gone, then they found her hiding in the stairwell, right?"

"This would come as a surprise to me," said the raspy voice on the other end. "Also to the child's mother, who's telling me not two minutes ago through the heating duct no less: Help, help, call the police, my child is kidnapped."

D'Annunzio shook his head wearily. Fucking Poppi-luv. He hated these old ziptops. "You're telling me she's still reporting the child missing?"

"I'm telling you she's weeping into my toilet, does this sound like a happy woman? She says her apartment is being watched, you shouldn't come there, you should come to my apartment upstairs and then *you* can talk through the heating grate. It's a thrill you won't forget."

"Wait a minute." D'Annunzio scratched his putty nose. "I don't get this."

The man let out a breath of exasperation. "For him she asks specifically," he muttered. "You don't get this. Let me make a suggestion, Mr. Sam Spade here. You'll come by and investigate. It'll be like a 'case,' your friends should know you're a policeman. Then you'll get this. How would that be?"

After the old man hung up, D'Annunzio sat on the desk, staring at the linoleum floor. He remembered the first caller—Billy Price—had said the child's father was a psychiatrist. Maybe this was some kind of EDP thing: one of the shrink's emotionally disturbed patients playing games or something. If it wasn't, though . . . If the kid really had been missing all this time and he'd been drawn off the trail by a phony phone call . . .

"Uh, boy," he groaned as he stood up. Christ on the cross, it was always something.

"I'm goin' out," he grumbled.

"Praise God," said Sergeant Moran. "And say hello to Snake-Eye Jones."

D'Annunzio took his own car to the East Side. He parked the five-year-old Pontiac on Thirty-sixth, just off Madison. He walked the half block to the Conrads' building.

As he waddled along, wheezing, he glanced up and saw the Morgan Library. The Greek facade through the autumn sycamores. The frieze of Lady Truth Leading the Arts by the hand. The gentle play of the spotlight on the marble.

Oh, yeah, he thought. This is near where that old gash got slaughtered. Mrs. What's-her-name. Sinclair. Now there was a shitcan of a case. No motive, no leads. And it was Moran's. Boy, he came up with nothing on that one.

He smiled to himself. He turned under the building's awning, pushed through the glass doors.

He didn't flash his shield at the doorman. Might as well take care until he found out where all this stood. He just said he was Doug D'Annunzio for Leo Plotkin. The doorman gave Plotkin a buzz, then sent D'Annunzio up to the sixth floor.

When he got off the elevator, D'Annunzio plodded heavily to Plotkin's door. He knocked and waited, trying to tuck in his shirt. A moment later, Plotkin opened up.

He was a typical old Yid, D'Annunzio thought. Cut from the mold. Small, thin, bent. About seventy. A round head completely bald, and only the faintest trace of gray beard stubble on the wrinkled chin. Rheumy eyes blinking out at you. Damp, red lips in a slight quizzical smile. He was wearing a white shirt open at the neck to show grizzled chest hair. His gray slacks had gotten too big for him as he'd shrunk with age.

Now D'Annunzio did lift his shield and ID card. "Detective D'Annunzio, Mr. Plotkin," he said.

The old man said nothing. He bent forward. He peered at the badge. He stayed like that for a long time, just peering. As if he were reading the shield over and over. Then he turned around and started walking away.

"Over here," he said.

D'Annunzio shrugged and followed.

The apartment smelled of old man: that stagnant, musty smell. The upholstery on the bergères was shiny. The gold rug on the floor was practically worn through. There was dust, plenty of dust, on the mantelpiece and the shelves and the tables. And there were ancient yellow photographs: a woman in a shawl; a woods; the old country.

What do they do with all their money? D'Annunzio wondered as he tailed after Plotkin's bent back. He thought the old Jew probably had hundreds of thousands of dollars stashed away in cookie jars and mattresses and places like that.

Plotkin led him into the bathroom. The smell was worse here. Tart medicine, dull pain; decay. D'Annunzio passed his eyes briefly over the stained tub and the vaguely fuzzy sink. Then, following Plotkin's gesture, he looked up at the heating grate.

"Go ahead," said Plotkin. "Don't mind me."

D'Annunzio glanced at Plotkin. Plotkin shrugged. D'Annunzio glanced back at the grate, then back at Plotkin, then back at the grate. Finally, he shrugged. He cleared his throat.

"Mrs. Conrad?"

He waited. No answer. He glanced at Plotkin. He felt like an idiot: talking to a fucking heating grate.

He took a breath, tried again. "Mrs. Conrad?"

"Yes?" The voice that came back was tremulous and low, but he could hear it clearly.

This time, when he looked at Plotkin, the old man made a gesture that said, Didn't I tell you? D'Annunzio nodded. He shoved his hands in his pockets. He spoke up at the grate.

"Mrs. Conrad, this is Detective D'Annunzio, NYPD. Have you been trying to get in contact with us?"

There was a brief pause. Then the low voice said, "Is Mr. Plotkin there?"

"I'm here," Plotkin said. "He's here, I'm here. The whole neighborhood is in my bathroom."

"Mr. Plotkin, could you tell me what he looks like?" the woman's voice said. "The detective? Can you tell me . . . describe him for me?"

Plotkin looked at D'Annunzio, wagged his head back and forth, shrugged again. "What's to describe? He's a big fatso with a face like knuckles."

"Oh, Jesus," she said. Her voice got muddy. D'Annunzio could tell she was starting to cry. "Oh, God, there was another man . . . Another man who said he was you. He must've been . . . Oh, God . . . I'm sorry. I'm so frightened. My baby . . ."

D'Annunzio heard her stifled sobs very clearly. Boy, he thought, you get great reception on these things, no question.

"Mrs. Conrad," he said. He lifted one hand in a gesture to the grate. "It would help me if you could give me a general idea of what this is all about. You think you could do that?"

"I don't know." She had to fight the tears to speak. "I . . . They just came in here. At night. They just . . . they took my little girl. They sent my husband off to do something. He couldn't tell me what. He just said he would meet them at nine. But now it's so late, I . . ." She was overcome.

"Okay, okay." D'Annunzio tried to make his voice soothing. "Let's go to the part about surveillance. Okay? You say they're watching your house?"

He heard the woman gasp through her tears. "They say . . . they say they put microphones here. And cameras. They say they're watching us, listening. . . . I think they were lying about the microphones but I don't . . . I'm not sure of anything now."

D'Annunzio snorted. Stupid broad, he thought. "They say they put cameras in there? Ma'am, can you see any cameras? Any wires? Anything?"

"Well . . . no."

A laugh riffled through D'Annunzio's lips. "Uh . . . ma'am, I . . . I think they may be lying about the cameras too here."

"No, but . . ."

"Hiding microphones is hard," D'Annunzio said. "Cameras are, like . . . I mean, they'd need a whole hidden room practically. They're not gonna plant cameras and no microphones. That just doesn't make sense."

"But they can see us," the woman said rapidly. "I know they can see us. They've told me, they've seen . . . what we're doing, wearing . . ."

"Well, isn't there some kind of window? Could they just be looking in a window there?"

"I . . . I don't . . . I don't know. I suppose if they . . ."

D'Annunzio shook his head, smiled with one side of his mouth. Stupid, stupid broad, he thought. Tell her you've got "Candid Camera" running in her apartment, she buys that wholesale. Never thinks about the goddamned windows. Probably some six-foot-five nigger hanging from her ledge staring in at her right this minute.

"My God," the woman gasped suddenly.

Oops, he thought; she must've found him.

"My God," she said again. "Mrs. Sinclair."

The half smile faded quickly from D'Annunzio's face. "What? Mrs. Sinclair? You mean the old . . ."

"The old woman who was killed," said Aggie Conrad through the grate. "You know?"

"Yeah, hell, yeah. What's that got to do with . . . ?"

"Well, I just . . . I mean, you asked about the windows, windows that look into our apartment and . . . her window looks right in and . . . a little while ago, my husband saw someone . . . in her apartment . . . in Mrs. Sinclair's apartment . . . he thought he saw someone in there. I didn't think . . . But I mean, the window. The window is right across from us, directly across, and it's been empty ever since and . . . Oh, God."

Her voice trailed away. But he could still hear her making the small, wet crying noises. The fat detective looked up at the grate, his mouth crooked. He licked his lips. He thought: Mrs. Sinclair.

His heart was beating hard. But he thought, well, now, just hold on here. The woman is obviously hysterical. She doesn't know what she's talking about. Still . . . If the Sinclair apartment really was empty, and if it really was right across from her like she said. It *was* possible. It could be.

Oh, thought Det. Doug D'Annunzio. Oh, to crack the Sinclair case after Moran had shitcanned it.

"So what about this Billy Price character," he asked the heating grate. "I mean, he calls me up, he says there's a kidnapping, then he calls me back, says it's all off. I mean, what's that about?"

"I don't . . ." He heard her fighting back her hysterical sobbing. "I don't know. I don't know, he . . . Maybe he's one of them. I told him to call you and then this man showed up, this other man, and he said he was you, I don't . . . I don't . . ."

Uh-oh, thought D'Annunzio. This did not sound good. This sounded very much like the opposite of good.

He wheezed out a bellyful of air. He looked up at the grate as the sounds of the crying woman reached him.

"Mrs. Conrad," he said. "I want you to hold on there a few minutes. I'll be right back, all right?"

"Please find my little girl," she said, sobbing. "Please. Just don't let them hurt her. She's only five, she's . . ."

D'Annunzio tried to think of something reassuring to say. All he could come up with was another "Hold on." He turned and nodded to Plotkin. "Wait here," he said.

The old man nodded. Then he wrinkled his fuzzless face. "Whew," he said softly. "Is that you?"

Nobody answered D'Annunzio's ring at the Price apartment downstairs. The detective stood before the door a long time. He walked down the hall and stood in front of Aggie Conrad's door. Then he walked back to Price's door and rang again and waited while no one answered. Of course, it was Saturday night, he thought. The man could be out.

But he decided to go downstairs and get Price's key.

The doorman didn't give him any trouble about it. He was a big, tall, handsome Hispanic with thick black hair and a thick mustache. He said he had a cousin on the Job down in Brooklyn. D'Annunzio told him he was worried about the tenant in 5H. The doorman gave D'Annunzio the key right away.

D'Annunzio lumbered back to the elevator. He traveled up to five.

Lumbered down the hall. He fit the key in the lock, turned it. Then he pushed the door in, pocketed the key, and entered the apartment.

Billy Price was not sitting in the Breuer chair anymore. He had fallen out of it. He lay on his side on the bare wood floor. His face had gone bluish gray. His eyes still stared out at nothing. The white strip of tape was still tight across his mouth. Lying as he was, his head was visible now from the foyer.

D'Annunzio stopped when he saw it. He drew his pistol out of his belt holster. He came forward slowly, carefully. But the place was empty. He could feel that.

Holding the gun up in the safe position, he stopped again. His eyes traveled over Price's half-naked body. When he saw the mass of what had been the man's genitals, he looked away. He whistled softly, fighting down his gorge.

After a moment, he looked back again. He looked at Price's face. He saw the strange shape of his neck, the way it had been crushed.

Don't get excited, he told himself. There's no proof. There's still no proof of anything.

But as he looked down at the dead man, his gravelly face broke slowly into a rough grin. Something—some sixth sense—told him that he had just cracked open Moran's Sinclair case.

He chuckled out loud in the quiet apartment. "Son of a bitch," he said.

Tale of the Tape

Conrad's silver-blue Corsica moved slowly up Lafayette Street. Sleek cars and yellow cabs whipped by on either side of it. Over and over came the glare of their lights in the rearview, a rush of wind, the red taillights receding fast up the wide avenue. The Corsica moved on slowly. Colonnade Row passed on the left with its long line of crumbling columns. The Public Theater passed on the right with its airy arches, its little intermission crowd milling in the mist. The Corsica continued at its slow, stuttering pace.

The car reached Astor Place. The sidewalks were crowded here. Seedy peddlers lined the sidewalks. Their old clothes and books and magazines were laid out on worn blankets on the ground. Crew-cut young men bopped east toward St. Mark's Place, leaning back on their hips, rhythmically stretching their legs. Young women, dyed blondes, all in black, traveled at their sides.

The Corsica stopped at the red light there. On the sidewalk across the street, two policemen were rousting a peddler. The peddler, a young white man, sat propped against a building's low wall. He was drugged or drunk. He stared up, stupid and openmouthed, at the cops. The cops talked down at him, quiet and implacable.

From behind the Corsica's wheel, Conrad gazed at the patrolmen. He was clutching the wheel and leaning forward, bent forward. His face was

200

pasty and gray, clammy with sweat. His mouth was hanging slack. His eyes yearned across the plaza toward the two officers.

There was still blood on the seat where Elizabeth had been sitting. The note, the crumpled note, still lay on his dashboard.

We are still watching you. Go to your office. Wait.

The light changed from red to green. Conrad saw it from the corner of his eye. He slowly pulled his eyes away from the policemen. He looked straight ahead. He shifted his foot to the gas pedal and pressed it down.

The Corsica moved slowly through the intersection.

It took Conrad a long time to reach the Upper West Side. It was close to ten when he parked the car on Eighty-second Street. He walked around the corner to Central Park West. He shuffled wearily, staring at the ground. His back was bent. His right leg dragged a little. He reached his office building, pushed in through the revolving doors.

The doorman glanced up as Conrad went past.

"Hey, Doc," he said.

Conrad flashed a thin smile at him. He limped through the lobby, down the hall to his office.

The moment he pushed the door open, he stopped short, stood frozen in the doorway. His mouth was pulled down in a tired, miserable frown. He shook his head weakly, back and forth.

The light was on in the consulting room. He could see it, bleeding through the bottom of the closed connecting door. Still shaking his head, Conrad shuffled in, his head bowed. The door closed behind him. The waiting room slipped into deep shadow.

Conrad limped slowly toward the consulting room. He was going to open that door and find Elizabeth. Elizabeth would be lying there dead. He could already see her sprawled on the floor, her red-gold hair splayed around her head like a halo. He limped toward the door. Not Elizabeth, no. It was Jessica there. The little girl was lying on her stomach in her valentine nightgown. Her face was turned toward him. Her glassy eyes stared.

Why didn't you come, Daddy?

Conrad reached the consulting-room door. He swallowed and pushed it open.

All the lights were on: the toplight, the standing lamp, and the desk lamp. But the place was empty. He moved into the center of the floor, scanned the room slowly. The analysis couch, the therapy chair, his own leather recliner. The rolltop desk with the mess of papers on it. The bathroom. He moved to the bathroom door and looked in. No one was in there either.

He turned around and faced the room again. He looked at his rolltop desk. He understood what had happened.

The phone was gone. It had been taken out. The papers and journals that had covered it now surrounded the empty space where it had been. Conrad moved toward the desk, shaking his head. He stood and looked down at it. He shuddered. *They've been here,* he thought. And it was as if he could still smell them. It was as if their dark shapes were still hunkering in his peripheral vision.

He reached down and moved some of his papers aside. He uncovered his answering machine. He held his breath. The machine's light was blinking.

Conrad's fingers trembled as he pressed the playback button. He watched the machine as it clicked and whizzed. Then the voice began. A new voice, not Sport's. It was high and breathy and frantic.

"Welcome, welcome, Doctor C." Then there was a high giggle: Hee, hee, hee. "Now you're here. And we're here, man. We're fucking everywhere. Booga-booga!" Hee hee hee. Conrad turned his face away, closing his eyes. "So anyway, uh, you gotta stay here, okay? Till twelve o'clock. Witching hour. Dum! Dum! Duuuum! Otherwise—you know what. So don't walk out of that door, Marshal Dillon, because we have got you covered. Uh, abudyuh, abudyuh, abudyuh, that's all, folks." Hee hee hee. And the machine clicked off.

Conrad let his breath out in a sigh. He took off his trench coat. He draped it over the back of the recliner. He walked over to the couch and sat down on it. He put his head in his hands and began to cry.

He cried hard. He sobbed. He rocked back and forth. The tears spilled into his hands. He sniffled.

"My little girl," he said softly. "My little girl."

For half an hour, he lay on the couch. He stared up at the ceiling dully.

Without your bullshit and your money, your fancy degrees, just man on man—what are you then? You follow? What are you?

He felt the dried tears on his cheek where Sport had spit at him. He closed his eyes.

With his eyes closed, he saw his daughter. He saw her lying dead on the floor. He saw her glassy stare.

Why didn't you come?

He imagined then—he saw before him—the child's small coffin being lowered into its open grave. He heard her voice from inside the little box.

Daddy?

He pressed his lips together tightly.

Then, for a moment, he saw his daughter alive. He saw her lying on a bed, her hands tied behind her. The man who called himself Sport was coming toward her. He had a knife in his hand. Jessica was screaming. . . .

He gasped and his eyes came open quickly. He coughed and wiped his cheeks with his hands. Trembling, he stared at the ceiling.

He stared up at the glow of the toplight on the white plaster. He saw the arc of shadow near the wall. He saw a small section of water damage in the corner. He saw the box being lowered into the ground. The child's body was inside the box, rocking from side to side as the box went down. Her hands were crossed on her chest. It was dark in the coffin. She would want a night-light, Conrad thought. He heard the sound of dirt hitting the lid of the casket.

Daddy?

But now his face was hard, his eyes were cold. When the dirt hit the casket lid, he even sneered a little. He stood on the manicured grass. He looked over the edge of the open grave. Shovelful by shovelful, the coffin disappeared beneath the earth. Agatha said later that his eyes looked like stones as he watched it. She hugged herself and shuddered. "Like stones, Nathan."

But that had been his father's funeral, hadn't it? And by that time, he'd been estranged from the old man for years. At the end, he had gone to see him in the hospital only because Aggie had insisted. When Nathan had come into the hospital room, the old man was lying in the bed under a single sheet. His face, once round and pale, was now thin and very, very white. With the sheet over it, his body seemed like nothing.

"Nathan," he had said weakly. He had lifted his hand. Nathan had stepped forward and taken it. His father had smiled with white lips. His hand was cold. "Thanks . . . for coming."

"It's all right, Dad," Nathan had said. He had gazed down at the old man without expression.

His father had taken a laborious breath. ". . . wanted the chance to tell you . . . ," he said, ". . . love . . . I love you."

"I love you too, Dad," Nathan answered automatically. He knew he'd feel bad later on if he didn't say it. What was the point of making the old man sad now? He gazed down at him.

His father closed his eyes. "Couldn't . . . ," he whispered. Then he let out a low whistling moan of pain. "I couldn't . . . help her, Nathan. Couldn't . . ."

Conrad gazed down at him. One corner of his mouth lifted in a hard, ugly smile. He was thinking about his mother. About her lying on the kitchen floor. About her struggling and screaming, her nightgown on fire. The silk nightgown with the purple chrysanthemums. He was thinking about all the times his father had told her: "All right, take the bottle to your room; but just this once." Or: "All right, here's the money, but only so you won't go out and steal it." Or the ever-popular: "Look, don't try to quit it all at once. Just ease off, stop a little at a time."

"Couldn't help her," his father whispered again.

Conrad's mouth twisted. He held his father's cold hand. He gazed down at him.

"Your eyes were like stones," Agatha said after the funeral. She had hugged herself and shivered. "Like stones."

Conrad sat up. He got off the couch. He walked unsteadily into the bathroom. He bent over the toilet, his stomach churning. He gagged; gagged again. Then he threw up, a trickle of thin vomit. He'd hardly eaten anything all day.

He wiped his mouth with his hand. He straightened. He moved to the sink and splashed water on his face. He lifted his head. He looked into the mirror.

Couldn't help her. I couldn't help her.

The sad brown eyes looked back at him out of a pasty face. His cheeks sagged, the wrinkles stood out on them. With his sandy hair plastered down by sweat, he looked almost bald. He looked old, like an old man.

Couldn't help her.

His eyes filled with tears again. One tear spilled over, ran down his cheek. He couldn't bear the sight of it. He lowered his head. "I couldn't help her," he said softly. He shuffled back into the consulting room.

He limped slowly to his recliner. He dropped down into it. He closed his right eye. It had started to flare again when he threw up. The red clouds played and drifted over his vision. The same old sunset from Seminary Hill.

He leaned back in the chair, closed both eyes.

I couldn't help her.

He thought of Elizabeth. The way she had been tonight. So proud of her pretty clothes, almost giddy. Proud of her makeup and the black ribbon tying back her hair.

I can help you. That's what he'd said to her. He remembered the way her hands had reached out to him. The desperate way she'd gripped his hands in hers.

Can you? Can you help me? Because I know that bad things have happened. But there could be good things too.

"Oh . . ." Conrad moaned aloud. He covered his eyes with his hand. Rocked back and forth in the chair in his pain.

There could be good things too.

"Ah, blood, the blood." He clenched his fists in front of him. He just sat like that, bent forward, his whole body clenched, his face. "I couldn't help her."

Then he sagged. He fell back against the chair again. The red clouds swam before him. His hands fell to his sides.

His trench coat was hanging from the back of the chair. When his hands fell, his knuckles brushed one of the pockets. He felt the weight there.

Conrad shifted. He reached into the pocket and took out his cassette recorder. He pressed the rewind button. Stared at the little box as the tape rolled back.

When it was near the beginning, he pressed the button. Tinny and distant, Elizabeth's voice rose up to him.

He's always different. The Secret Friend, I mean. I guess I told you that already, but it's an important thing.

Conrad leaned back in the chair. He held the recorder lightly on his stomach. He listened to her soft murmur.

I liked being near children, even though they'd usually left by the time I got there. I just liked being where they were.

He thought of her face. That rose-and-alabaster painting of a face framed in the gold-red hair.

. . . the place where I worked was on a little lane in the Village. A narrow, cobbled lane . . .

He thought of her hands reaching out for him. Desperate. Desperate for help, for hope. Her voice went on. It hurt him to hear it. It was a burrowing pain.

Then, one night, I stepped out of the center and there was someone there. . . .

He thought of her as she'd been in the car, the way she'd been as they

205

were driving into Manhattan. He thought of her flat, clear, crystal voice singing about the bottles of beer. The dead sound of her voice, like wind whistling through a ruin. Her voice on the tape continued.

I saw his face. His red hair, his white skin, his freckles. He was wearing a dark overcoat and he had his hands hidden in the pockets. . . .

The tape played. He held it steady on his stomach. He thought of Elizabeth in that last moment. That moment when he had paused in the doorway of the car. When she had looked up at him and he had found her again deep inside those eyes. Like a specter standing in the ruin of herself. A solitary soul trapped in there.

And yet she had reached out and given him what he needed. She had given him the number. Her voice went on:

. . . I turned again and ran. I ran down the lane as fast as I could. I ran to MacDougal. . . . And suddenly, someone grabbed me. . . .

He lay like that in the chair with his eyes closed. And he thought of the blood. The line of blood on the seat where Elizabeth had been. That hurt too. To think of that and to hear her voice. He smiled grimly. It hurt; yes. He kept his eyes closed, kept thinking of the blood. Kept making it hurt and hurt more. That was what he had turned the tape on for.

Elizabeth's voice continued:

I kept thinking: It's him. He's got me. So I hit at him. . . . I kicked and struggled . . .

He lowered me slowly to the ground. . . . He laughed. . . .

Because, you see, it wasn't him at all. It was another man. A young man, handsome. With a sort of round, boyish face.

Conrad let her voice work at him, dig at him. He saw what she described. The Village street. The dark alley behind her. The sudden arm around her waist and then: that face. That round, boyish face. It appeared before him; familiar somehow. . . .

Brown hair falling into his eyes, said Elizabeth. *And he had a nice smile—even though I knew he was laughing at me . . .*

The face became clearer in Conrad's mind. He saw it coming toward him as if out of deep shadows.

I looked past his shoulder, down the alley. . . .

And then, all at once, as with the flaring of a match, the face was illuminated in an orange glow: his brown hair falling into his eyes, his charming smile. . . .

I stood in front of this new person, this stranger, panting . . .

Conrad sat up quickly.

"What?" he said. "What?"

He stared down at the recorder. Suddenly, his fingers were fumbling over its controls. He hit the stop button. Elizabeth's voice went off.

He hit the rewind button. The playback.

I ran down the lane . . .

"Shit!"

He hit fast forward. Play again.

. . . it wasn't him at all. It was another man.

Conrad held the recorder up to his ear.

A young man, handsome. With a sort of round, boyish face. Brown hair falling into his eyes. And he had a nice smile . . .

"My God," said Conrad. Terry: the young actor. The man she had fallen for. The man who had vanished. Her imaginary lover.

He turned the tape off again. He lowered the machine to his lap. He looked at it, stared at it sideways, as if he expected it to leap at him.

A young man, handsome. With a sort of round, boyish face.

"It was Sport," Conrad whispered.

Sport was Terry. Her Secret Friend.

Island in the Mist

The mist drifted and coiled over the water of the sound. The water was black out there, black and unsettled. The cold October air was whipping up into a wind and whitecaps licked up out of the waves. Sport could hear them slapping against the pilings of the old pier.

The Correction Department shack sat on a lot just before the pier. It was a battered blue trailer, dark but for the flickering light of a television set at one window. Huddled in his windbreaker, Sport stood at the door and knocked lightly.

The television set went off inside. The shack windows went dark. Sport waited, hearing shuffling steps inside.

A moment later, the shack door opened. A tall, broad figure stood in the shadows, a man with a crew cut over a square, flat, brutal face. He was wearing his gray-blue uniform pants, but his shirt was open and his undershirt swelled with his huge potbelly.

Sport shivered in the cold wind from the sound. "You guys ready?" he said.

"Sure, Sporty," said the man in the doorway.

Sport nodded. "Let's go."

They rode out on the Department's cruiser: Sport, the guard, and the machinery man. The machinery man sat inside in the cabin. He was a little

man with slumped shoulders. His face was all wrinkles and frowns like a
basset hound's face. He sat inside and smoked a cigarette nervously.

The guard was at the wheel, guiding the cruiser over the waves, over the
short distance out to Hart Island. Sport stayed outside, out by the stern rail.
He squinted through the wind, peered back at City Island, at its pier, its
white houses; at the ragged black outline of its trees fading into the mist.
Sport's foot pattered nervously against the deck. His fingers raveled and
unraveled. The wry, easy look in his eyes, his easy smile—they were both
gone. He stared intently at the disappearing shore. The wind made his hair
dance on his brow.

"All or nothing at all," he sang tensely to himself. "La-da-da. Da
da-da-daa . . ."

He paused. He took a deep breath. He wiped his mouth with his hand.
All or nothing at all, he thought. All or fucking nothing at all . . .

He mumbled the old song until it was just a tuneless noise lost under the
grumble of the ferry's engine and the hiss of the wind.

". . . la-da-da-da . . . nothing at all."

You fuck-up. You fuck-up, he thought.

Fucking Freak, he thought. It was the Freak's fucking fault, all of it. It
wasn't supposed to have come to this: all this bullshit with the kid; fucking
murder . . . The whole thing was just an idea, just a joke, that's all. . . .

Sport hummed another bar of the song. Then he let the rest of his breath
out silently into the wind. He shook his head.

"Fucking Freak," he muttered.

It was all the Freak's fault. His fault that things had gotten so fucked up.
His own damned fault even that Maxwell had had to kill him. First, he'd
started fagging around with Dolenko. And then, with Elizabeth, he just
went nuts. Everything was all his fault from the beginning.

They were supposed to get the number from her, that's all. It was going
to be funny. It was going to be something to do. The plan was, Sport would
arrange to meet her, then pull his famous Handsome Guy routine on her.
All the little mousies went for his Handsome Guy routine. Next, they
would go to an old abandoned brownstone that Dolenko knew about.
Dolenko said he and some of his friends used to use the place for parties. He
said he knew how to get the electricity working there; he'd done it before.
They would fix one of the rooms up and pretend it was Sport's apartment.
Then Sport could bring Elizabeth back there and fuck her till her brains
melted. After that, he'd get her talking, ask her about her past. . . .

Finally, he could casually ask her about her mother and about the number. By the time it was over, he'd have what he wanted and she wouldn't even know he'd gotten it. Then, when she tried to find him, he'd be gone-a-roo without a trace.

Even if they didn't get the number, it was bound to be a barrel of laughs. And that was the whole idea. That was as far as it was supposed to go.

But then the Freak saw her. And from that moment on, everything started to go wrong.

They'd found her listed in the phone book. Sport and the Freak had gone to her brownstone on the Upper West Side. They waited across the street for about an hour. All they knew about her was the color of her hair.

But the second she walked out the door, they knew it was she.

"Is that her?" said Sport.

"Christ," the Freak said. "Look at her. Christ, look at her, willya."

"That's gotta be her."

"Good Christ," said the Freak. "I mean—Jesus. Jesus, look at her. She looks like a fucking angel."

That was all it took. That one glimpse. After that, the Freak wouldn't stop talking about her. They followed her down to the Village, down to the day-care center where she worked. Even after they went home, the Freak just went on and on.

"Christ, the look of her. I mean, the way she—looked. You know?"

Sport got annoyed. "What're you, in fucking love with her?" he said.

The Freak shook his head. He ran his fingers through his thick red hair. "Look," he said. "I don't know about this. Okay? I don't know I wanna do this. I mean, look: it's probably all bullshit anyway, you know. The stuff Eddie the Screw told us. . . . I mean, think about it, Sporty. Okay, so he was a big-time drug dealer when he was with the Correction Department. Okay. But you're gonna tell me that old piss-drunk rummy has got a fortune—half a fucking million? And he hides it away before the feds catch him and it's *still there?* I mean, why doesn't he get it himself? It's out of a storybook, for Christ's sake. We should forget about it, that's what."

"I don't believe this," said Sport. "You take one look at some little cunt, all of a sudden you got a bone on or something? You really are a fucking faggot, you know that?"

The Freak hadn't said anything after that. Not for a while. He just hung around the house all day, sulky, irritable. Then, that evening, he suddenly piped up and said, "Look, just forget this, all right? Just deal me out. I don't want any part of this."

Sport had screamed bloody murder at him. Ditching his friends for some little cunt like that. Ditching his own fucking roommate for some pretty slash. But the Freak would not reconsider. When they moved into Manhattan and set up operations in the brownstone, the Freak stayed behind.

Or so he told them anyway. In fact, while Sport was trying to figure out a casual way to meet up with the girl, the Freak was visiting her in secret, trying to warn her about the whole thing. Unfortunately for the Freak, Sport got lucky. One day, just as he was about to walk down the alley to the place where she worked, the girl came tearing past him and stepped in front of a cab. Sport pulled her out of the way: a perfect accidental meeting. He couldn't have planned it better. Then he went into the routine he'd worked out about being an actor and all. He even took her into a nearby theater and showed her his picture on the wall (he'd sneaked in and tacked up one of the publicity shots he'd had taken for his singing career). She came to trust him very quickly.

When Elizabeth told him a man had been bothering her, Sport didn't even think of the possibility that it might be the Freak. The Freak might want out of the project, but he wasn't going to betray them, for Christ's sake. Not the Freak. Not just for some little slash.

But when the girl said the man had shown up again, Sport did begin to wonder if someone was trying to cut in on the action. Then came Sport and Elizabeth's tender love scene in the brownstone on Houses Street. Elizabeth had flipped out. Started screaming. Told Sport he was in danger. Then ran off into the night.

That did get Sport worried. Worried and pissed. What the hell was going on here? What kind of danger was he in? Danger from whom?

Sport called Maxwell, who'd been hiding upstairs. Together, they headed off to the Upper West Side, to Elizabeth's apartment.

It had been hard getting the girl to buzz him up. When she did, Sport went to the apartment door while Maxwell waited in the hall. Sport knocked on the door. The door opened . . . And Sport's jaw dropped as hard as a baby tossed off a rooftop.

There was Freak. Fucking Freak. Standing right there in the girl's apartment. He had a butcher's knife in his hand, and a look in his eyes like his guts were on fire.

"That's it, Sporty. It's over," he said. "I'm sticking to her. Wherever she is, I'll be there. Understand? Just leave her the fuck alone, all right?"

Meanwhile, he had the girl barricaded in the bathroom, a chair propped against the door. She was pounding on the door and screaming. And the Freak kept carving the air with the butcher's knife and saying:

"Just stay away from her, Sport. I'm sticking to her. Just stay away."

Sport was pissed, out-of-his-mind angry. This was the Freak talking to him? The fucking Freak?

He reached out and tried to grab the Freak's arm. The Freak actually tried to cut him. The Freak lashed out at him with the butcher knife; almost cut Sport's arm right off.

But then Maxwell came charging to the rescue.

The giant creature lunged through the door. He grabbed the Freak's wrist and Sport heard the bone snap. In another moment, Max had the knife. With one powerful slash, he cut so deeply into the Freak's neck that Freak's head fell back as if he were examining the ceiling. A geyser of blood shot out into the room.

And Maxwell didn't stop at that either. Oh, no. It was Slaughterhouse City then. Sport stood by with his mouth open, watching what Max did. It was just like with the kitten: Max was just too excited. There was no stopping him now.

And in fact, Sport wasn't sure he *wanted* to stop him. The Freak *had* betrayed them, after all. And for some cunt? Just because some slash had sweet-looking eyes or something? It was total bullshit, as far as Sport was concerned.

Anyway, the whole thing was over in seconds. The Freak fell to the floor jerking and dancing around. His arm went out and knocked the chair from the bathroom door. Out tumbled the girl, falling across the dying Freak.

But Sport and Max didn't stay around to say their how-de-do's to her. By then, the whole building was awake. People were shouting out in the halls. It was panic central. Sport knew they had to get out of there fast. He had to get back to the brownstone and clean the place out before the cops came. He had to take his picture down off the theater wall. And then he had to get home to Flushing so that when the cops came by to tell him his roommate—Robert Rostoff, aka the Freak—was dead, he would be fast asleep, like any good boy in the middle of the night.

Sport practically had to drag Maxwell out the window to the fire escape.

The big idiot was too busy watching the Freak die. Rubbing his hard-on and watching the Freak kick and tremble and die.

And so they had to get the number then. It was the only way they could escape, blow the country. With the number—with the money, that is—everything would be all right, they'd be able to do anything they wanted. He talked it over with Dolenko and Maxwell and they agreed with him. Hell, they were more scared than he was. Maxwell was practically crazy with fear. He didn't want any part of going to jail again. And Sport told them, their only chance to get out of this clean and safe was to get the number. With the number, they'd be free.

Even then, it looked as if it were going to be easy. The girl was put in the loony bin, and when Sport made overtures to the director there, Sachs, the guy rolled over immediately. Some cash, the promise of a lot more cash—that was all it took to get him going. Unfortunately, the guy turned out to be a prize asshole in the end. When he asked the girl for the number, she flipped out again. She wasn't talking to anyone, Sachs said. She wasn't talking at all.

Sport was pissed. He took Maxwell to see Sachs. The girl better talk, and fast, Sport explained. Sachs was in a panic. He said the only guy he knew who might be able to get her talking again in a big hurry was the famous Dr. Nathan Conrad. . . .

"Yo!"

The guard's low cry brought Sport back to the present. He looked over his shoulder and saw the guard at the cruiser's wheel. The guard tilted his head forward slightly. Sport came around the boat's cabin and looked up along the rail.

He took a deep breath at what he saw. He stuck a cigarette in his mouth but he didn't light it. He stood with the cigarette dangling from his lips, one hand in his pocket, one hand on the rail. He watched as the mist parted before the cruiser's prow, as the black shadow of Hart Island grew steadily closer.

Skeeter and McGee

"Now," said D'Annunzio.

The long-haired plainclothesman threw open the door and jumped back. D'Annunzio pressed himself against the wall, out of sight. Behind him, the plainclothesman named Skeeter did the same. All three of them had their guns drawn and lifted in the safety position.

They waited, listening. From inside the apartment, there was darkness, silence.

"Okay," said D'Annunzio in a harsh whisper.

Breathing heavily, he went tromping into the apartment. He leveled his thirty-eight. Skeeter and the long-haired plainclothesman—McGee— came in behind him. Skeeter went to his left, McGee to his right. Both swept the space before them with their pistols. They held their pistols in two hands. They peered into the dark.

The shapes in the room before them were motionless. Standing shadows and crouching shadows: they seemed to be peering back at them.

"Get the lights," whispered D'Annunzio.

McGee backed up until he reached the wall switch. Then the lights came on, dazzling all three. They blinked, keeping their guns leveled.

But all they saw was furniture. A table, two sofas, a few director's chairs. The wooden floor gleamed brightly under the toplight. It was discolored in places as if a rug had recently been removed.

214

D'Annunzio edged in farther, huffing and wheezing. Skeeter and McGee fanned away from him on either side.

They saw a door on the right wall. D'Annunzio jerked his head at it. Skeeter peeled off. He was a young guy and his eyes were very wide and white. He was wearing shabby clothes and three days' growth of beard. He had been undercover as a bum in Grand Central Terminal when McGee had come by to pick him up.

Skeeter pushed the door in with his fingers. Then he charged through it, disappearing into the other room. D'Annunzio and McGee waited.

Then Skeeter called out, "Empty."

D'Annunzio holstered his gun at once. McGee moved more slowly. He scanned the room once more before replacing the pistol under his sweatshirt at the navel. He was young too but he seemed weathered and calm. He had long black hair and a handlebar mustache. He was wearing jeans and a khaki windbreaker. He had been driving a cab when he'd gotten a radio call to phone Moran.

His gun holstered, McGee stretched his face and pulled at his nose. "Whew," he said. "Smells like farts in here."

D'Annunzio cleared his throat and looked away.

Up until now, he'd been playing it very cautious. Even after he'd found the body of Billy Price, he'd been careful to keep the lid on things. He'd left Price's apartment and returned to Plotkin's. He'd used Plotkin's phone to call in to Moran.

"I just want a couple of guys to check things out," he'd said. "No uniforms. And landlines only. I don't know what these guys have." He hadn't said anything about the Sinclair apartment. He hadn't wanted Moran to come horning in.

After hanging up on Moran, D'Annunzio went around the corner. He had a little chat with the doorman at the Sinclair building. Until D'Annunzio mentioned the Sinclair apartment, the doorman was a tall, thin black man with bad teeth. Afterwards, he was a tall, thin green man who was sweating very hard.

"I don't know shit about what's going on in that place," he'd explained. "I don't *know* shit, and I don't *wanna* know shit. I don't *give* a shit, you dig? Because it's bullshit. Shit."

"Is there anyone up there now?" D'Annunzio asked him.

"No—and even if there was, I wouldn't give a shit, you see what I'm saying? I don't give a shit if there is, I don't give a shit if there ain't. It's *all* shit, if you ask me."

"Gimme the key," said D'Annunzio.

"Shit," said the doorman. "I'll give you the key. You can *take* the fucking key. Shit on this."

D'Annunzio took the key. Which was when Skeeter and McGee showed up in the taxi. Then the three of them had gone upstairs to check the place out.

Standing in the apartment now, D'Annunzio realized he was going to have to call in the cavalry. The thought made his mouth turn down at the corner. Once Moran got wind of this, he'd be over here like a fucking bullet. Then there'd be task force techs and brass and shiny suits. And finally, the feds, who were the worst of all of them. D'Annunzio had worked with the feds after the Castellano killing. They let the cops do all the legwork so they wouldn't have to soil their pretty fingernails roughing up street scum. Then when it came time for press conferences, suddenly it's Efrem fucking Zimbalist starring in "F.B.I." D'Annunzio shook his head and gave a little shiver. Moran and the feds and the whole lot: they were the last thing he needed.

Off to his left now, McGee had pulled open the door of a small closet. He had his head inside it.

"Pile of clothes in here," he called.

D'Annunzio glanced over. He caught a glimpse of the laundry in a messy mound on the floor. The closet was empty otherwise.

"Don't touch anything," he said.

He looked away. In front of him, in front of the glass doors that led out to the balcony, there was a canvas chair. As he stepped toward it, D'Annunzio saw a pair of binoculars lying on its seat. He waddled over to them. He stood above them, hung over them, not touching them, just looking down. It was a nice pair, a real piece of work. It must have cost someone hundreds of dollars, at least, he thought.

Hitching up his pants, he started to bend down to pick them up.

"Hey, D'Annunzio."

The fat man straightened and turned. Skeeter had come out of the other room. He was holding up a pink stuffed animal. He was pinching its ear gingerly between his thumb and forefinger.

"I found this on the bed. It's a Turtle Tot. My kid's got one too."

D'Annunzio nodded. "Yeah, great, well, put it back. You'll shvitz all over it and ruin it for CSU."

"Yeah," said McGee, looking up from the closet. "One drop of stuffing from that, and the lab can tell us who its father is and everything."

Skeeter laughed. He carried the stuffed animal back into the other room.

"Now let's see what we got here," said D'Annunzio softly.

With a soft grunt, he pulled his pants up over his waist. Then he was able to bend again and pick up the binoculars. He held them carefully in two fingers, but the black tubes were pebbled: he knew there would be no prints on them. He lifted them to his eyes, peered out through the balcony's glass doors.

"Man, oh, man," he said. "Are these fucking things powerful or what."

He was looking, he found, right into the Conrads' apartment. He knew it was the Conrads' apartment because he could read the address on an envelope sitting on the windowsill. Still holding the binoculars tenderly, he swung them a little to the right.

"Okay," he muttered to himself. "Okay. Mrs. Conrad, I presume, right?"

By looking straight through the bedroom, he could see her standing out in the hall. She was in the bathroom doorway. Probably waiting for him to come back and talk to her over the heating duct some more, he thought.

She was standing with her arm raised, her hand braced against the doorframe. Her head was lowered, her red hair hanging down in damp strands, hiding her face.

D'Annunzio pursed his lips as he looked at her.

"Nice tits," he said.

Skeeter came hurrying back out of the bedroom. "What? What?"

McGee came out of the closet, moved toward D'Annunzio. "Let me see," he said.

Specter

Aggie had not expected the buzzer. She'd been standing in the bathroom doorway, waiting for D'Annunzio to start talking through the heating duct again. She was still standing there when the front-door buzzer sounded. She was still standing with her arm raised, her hand braced against the bathroom doorframe. Standing with her head hung and her hair falling in tangles about her face. She was staring at the doorsill, not crying anymore, just staring, feeling wrung and dry. Her anxiety—the thick, twisting grip of her constant anxiety—had wrung her and wrung her inside. She could not cry anymore. She could just stare, just waiting, while it kept twisting her. And then the buzzer rang.

She closed her eyes at the sound. She shook her head. Wearily, she blinked and lifted her eyes. She looked up at the high corner of the bathroom wall, at the heating grate, as if toward heaven. Her lips trembled, but her eyes were dry.

The buzzer stopped. A fist rapped against the door sharply. "Mrs. Conrad. It's Detective D'Annunzio. It's all right. You can open up now."

She swallowed hard but the thing in her throat would not go down. Her heart was hammering so fast she thought it would kill her. She straightened, letting her hand slide off the jamb. She brushed the hair off her forehead. She looked around her as if she did not know where she was.

She moved slowly out of the doorway. She shuffled slowly down the hall.

D'Annunzio kept knocking. "Mrs. Conrad?" He kept calling to her. He had a rough rumble of a voice. She recognized it from the heating duct. He kept calling and calling.

But all the same, she hesitated for a long time. She stood for a long time confronting the door as if it were an adversary. She was looking up warily from under her eyebrows at the thing.

D'Annunzio kept knocking and calling. "Mrs. Conrad? You can open up now. It's all right."

Only after a while, only slowly, did she raise her hand. She watched it rise and move forward as if it didn't belong to her. She wanted to call out to it, to tell it to stop, be careful. But it rose all the same, gripped the doorknob.

She turned the knob and pulled it. The door swung open.

She was looking at a man, a man standing out in the hallway. He was obese; sloppily fat, overflowing with fat as if his body had been crammed full of food until it just couldn't hold it anymore. Checked shirt and blue pants both ballooned toward her as if they would burst. His jacket dangled at his sides as if it had been blown apart.

Aggie peered at him. She blinked and squinted, her mouth hanging open, her face turned half away. She saw his round, gnarled face with the hard little eyes in it. She smelled him: his gas, his unwashed sweat, his corruption.

The man was standing still, but he was breathing as hard as if he were running. He lifted one meaty arm. His jacket rose from his side as he did. He had a badge in his chubby paw, a badge and an ID card.

"Detective D'Annunzio, Mrs. Conrad," he said. "The kidnappers have vacated the Sinclair apartment. They're not watching you anymore. You can come out now."

Aggie just stood there. She blinked at him again. "Come out?" she said. Her voice sounded very weak to her. Very weak and far away.

The fat man nodded. Uncertainly, Aggie stepped toward him. She stepped across the threshold of her apartment. She stepped out into the hall. She turned her head and looked down the hall. She saw the row of brown doors on the right. The elevator doors on the left. She turned back and looked at the fat man.

She was very close to him now. The smell of his old sweat and his old farts was like a cloud around her. She smelled his breath. It was hot and sour. She looked in his eyes. She knew he was mean and small.

She took another step and laid her head against his chest. The smell of him surrounded her. It was warm. She closed her eyes.

She felt D'Annunzio's chubby hand as it patted the back of her head.

Then she was sitting in an armchair. There were men all around her, and there were men's voices. She had a glass of water in her hands. Someone had given it to her and she held it tightly. She liked the cool feel of it against her palm. She sipped at it now and then. She liked the touch of the ice against her dry lips.

She listened to the burr of the men's voices. The voices were deep and solid. She found them comforting. They reminded her of when she was a child, when she would sit in front of the TV in the living room and hear the grown-ups talking at the kitchen table. Daddy and Mom and Uncle Barry and Aunt Rose. She would stare at Heckle and Jeckle chasing around before her on the television, and she would hear the low rumble of the grown-up voices, and she would sense important events and bask in the serenity of her own helplessness. Whatever it was, she knew, they would take care of it. . . .

She sipped her water. Her eyes moved vaguely over the men in the room. She watched them talking. She watched their serious lips, and their sharp jaws, the dark shadows of their beards. Two of the men were patrolmen in uniform. They kept coming in and going out. They were both very young, just boys really, but they looked grim and strong and busy. They wore heavy utility belts on their hips and their heavy guns hung from them. All of the other men were wearing jackets and ties, which made them look business-like and capable. Aggie turned to watch as one of them put his hand on his hip and brushed back his jacket, exposing the gun on his belt.

Her eyes came to rest finally on D'Annunzio. D'Annunzio was standing by the nursery door. One of his shirttails was almost entirely out of his pants now. Aggie could see a patch of the white skin near his navel. His gold tie was pulled open to reveal a thick, hairy neck. Aggie remembered the stench of him, and the hot damp of his shirt against her cheek. What was he like? A man who smelled like that, who let himself smell like that? She watched him and thought: He did not care. He lived alone and he did not like anyone and he did not care. She imagined that he would do filthy things and not care at all about them: sleep with a whore or steal money. Or even kill someone. He would kill someone and then spit on the ground, she thought.

She hoped he would not leave her. She wanted to be able to see him. It made her feel a little calmer to have him near.

D'Annunzio was talking to another man, a tall man in a black suit. That was the special agent, she remembered. Special Agent Calvin. She remembered he had introduced himself and asked her questions. He had been very intelligent and grim, but he was a little too pretty. He had wavy blond hair and a cleft, jutting jaw that seemed chiseled from stone. D'Annunzio was talking to him and she imagined D'Annunzio was telling him how things were.

And then someone inside the nursery took a picture. A flash went off as Aggie watched. She saw an arc of the rainbow she had painted on the wall starkly illuminated. For a moment, her anxiety broke through again. It washed over her. It choked her. Maybe the kidnappers were still watching, she thought, maybe they saw what she'd done, how she'd called the police and maybe . . .

She bent forward a little and shuddered and fought for breath.

Oh, Jessie. Oh, Nathan, our poor baby.

She let her breath out slowly. She straightened. She lifted her water glass to her mouth. The rim of it pattered against her teeth as her hand trembled. She sipped the water. She listened to the men's voices. She let the low, strong murmur of them envelop her, the steady hum that only sometimes broke into words:

". . . his bare hands?"

". . . what the doctor said."

". . . some kind of monster . . ."

". . . looked just like the Sinclair case. I remember they were saying that . . ."

"Look what we found."

This last was a little louder than the rest. Aggie lifted her eyes toward the voice. There was a young man standing in the doorway. He was holding up a small plastic bag with something inside it.

"It's a transmitter. It was hooked up in the box downstairs," he said. "Has the phone been dusted? Try the phone."

One of the other men picked up Aggie's phone. He listened. "Yeah, it's working now."

"Can't even trace it," said the man in the doorway. He chuckled with wonder, shaking his head. Then he moved away, down the hall, out of sight.

"Mrs. Conrad?"

She knew by the sour smell that it was D'Annunzio. She turned to him, smiling dimly.

The fat man was trying very hard to kneel by her chair. He was wheezing with the effort. Finally, his face was level with hers. She looked into the gnarls and crags of it. D'Annunzio had a slim notebook opened in one of his hands. He looked down at it. As he did, she saw his marbly eyes flick over her breasts and then away quickly. She felt something rise in her throat.

"Uh . . . listen, uh, ma'am," he said. "Do you know a doctor by the name of, uh, let's see: Jerald Sachs? He's the . . . director at Impellitteri Psychiatric Facility."

Aggie nodded. "Yes. Nathan knew him. He knows him. Why?"

"He was a friend of your husband's?"

"No. No, Nathan didn't . . . doesn't like him. He's too . . . political, he said."

"What about a woman named . . . here it is: Elizabeth Burrows? Ever hear of her?"

She shook her head.

"A patient at Impellitteri."

"No," she said. "I mean . . . well, Nathan doesn't tell me patients' names. But it . . . I don't know, it does sound familiar somehow."

"Yeah. You probably read it in the papers."

"That's right. That's right. A murder in the newspapers."

D'Annunzio's round head bobbed up and down. He stroked his chin with one hand, looked down at the notebook. "I don't know what any of this means, all right? But I'll tell you what's happening up to this point. Dr. Sachs was found about a half hour ago. He was tied up under a bed at Impellitteri. The bed was assigned to this Elizabeth Burrows woman, in the forensic ward, where they keep the prisoners. Sachs had been knocked unconscious, with a chair it looked like. And your husband was seen leaving the hospital with Miss Burrows . . . ." He turned his arm and looked at the watch squeezed around his thick wrist. "It's after eleven now so it was over two hours ago."

Aggie shook her head again. "Nathan wouldn't hit someone with a chair. He wouldn't hit anybody."

"Well . . . you know . . . Well . . . okay," said D'Annunzio. He flipped the notebook closed. He stuffed it into his jacket pocket. Cleared his throat, brushed back his hair. "The thing is, this Sachs character is refusing to talk, won't tell us a fuh . . . uh, you know, anything. He's still pretty punchy but . . . I mean, he's already looking to get himself lawyered-up, you know? So there's not much chance we'll get anything out of him tonight, you see what I'm saying? I don't . . ."

His voice trailed away. He was silent for a moment. Then, with a deep grunt, he hoisted himself to a standing position.

"You mean, you think Nathan helped her escape?" Aggie said suddenly.

"Well, we don't . . ."

"You think they took Jessie so that Nathan would help a murderess escape?"

D'Annunzio shrugged his big shoulders. "What can I say? Could be. We don't know."

Aggie looked up at him. She caught his eyes flicking away from her chest again. She held his eyes with her own and he looked at her. He looked, she thought, as if he knew something about her.

"He would, you know," she told him quietly.

"Ma'am?"

"Hit a man with a chair," she said. "If he had to. He would kill him, if he had to, or anything. He would do anything."

D'Annunzio nodded. "Yes, ma'am," he said.

"D'Annunzio."

It was Special Agent Calvin, calling from the nursery door. His eyes were sharp and bright. He beckoned D'Annunzio over. The fat man waddled over to him.

Aggie turned away. She sank away from him into herself. She sat still, trying not to shiver, trying not to let the fear break through again. She held her glass of water tightly. She listened to the voices of the men: ceaseless, deep, hypnotic.

". . . the super around the corner . . ."

"Yeah, he was sweating like a pig."

"Get this. He says, 'I thought they were only drug dealers.'"

". . . one sorry mick, I'm telling you . . ."

". . . help Dr. Conrad . . ."

". . . you hear about that . . . ?"

". . . found another stiff downtown . . ."

". . . was it, downtown . . . ?"

". . . just on the radio . . ."

". . . got to help him—Dr. Conrad . . ."

". . . they think it's connected with this. The girl, the patient . . ."

"You've got to help Dr. Conrad."

". . . and the guy is crying, can you believe . . . ?"

". . . really cut up . . ."

". . . Dr. Conrad. Help him."

". . . the dead one . . . ?"

". . . under a Dumpster . . ."

". . . who says there's a connection . . ."

"Someone has got to help Dr. Conrad! You've got to help him! Please!"

The men's voices ceased altogether. The shrill cry hung in the air. It was a woman's cry. It brought Aggie's face up, made her look around, startled, through the figures of the men.

"Please," the woman cried to them again. "Please. Please listen to me. Someone has to help him. Dr. Conrad. They took his daughter. And now they're trying to take my mother out. Please."

Then Aggie saw her. She was passing among them like a specter. Staggering forward stiffly, ghostly, step by step. The men stood where they were, struck silent, unmoving. They stared at her as she walked through the middle of them as if down an aisle. Her hands were held as if bound behind her. Her eyes were so large and white they seemed to take up most of her face. And there was blood, Aggie saw now. Blood all over her. Drenching and staining the wrinkled pink shift she wore, streaked down her cheeks, matting clumps of her strawberry-blond hair.

"You've got to. Got to help him. Please. Someone—you've got to help Dr. Conrad. It's Terry. He's real. He's going to take out my mother. Please."

"Hey, miss—damn it—hold on just a minute there."

The command—the deep male sound of the voice—seemed to wake the room up. The murmur of voices began again.

"What'd you bring her in here for?"

"Hold on there, miss."

"Hold on to her. Someone get her."

"Hey, you can't just come in here."

The aisle that had seemed to open for her closed suddenly. Men moved in on either side of her, taking her by her bare and bloody arms. Her hands still behind her, she struggled against their grips. Aggie saw the handcuffs around her wrists.

The woman cried out. "No! You've got to listen! You've got to help him."

"All right, all right, just take it easy, lady. Just hold on."

224

"Hold her."

"Please!" The cry seemed to have been torn from deep in her throat. Her arms held fast by men on either side, she threw her head back and howled at the ceiling. "Please."

"Wait." Aggie tried to set her water glass down. It tipped over on the side table. It rolled off the table, smashed on the floor. "Stop that, for Christ's sake!" she said. She was on her feet. She was holding her hand out. "Stop."

The sound of her voice, the shattering glass, stopped everything again. The room went quiet. The men's faces turned. Aggie felt their hard eyes on her. She glanced at D'Annunzio. He was looking at her too, waiting.

She looked at the others, at all of them. "Well, let her talk," she said to them softly. "Let her go. Let her talk."

The men turned from Aggie to the other woman. Slowly, the hands on her arms relaxed. The men released her, stepped back a little. The woman stood swaying on her feet, her head still thrown back, her eyes still raised toward the ceiling.

Then her chin came forward. Her face lowered. She looked through the men. She looked straight at Agatha.

Agatha brushed the hair out of her own face, looked across the room at the other woman. The woman stared at her with wild confusion, her mouth open, her head shaking.

"Who are you?" she said. .

Agatha answered gently, "I'm his wife. Who are you?"

The woman shook her head another moment. Then she said, "I'm his Elizabeth."

And she collapsed to the floor.

Eddie the Screw

The Correction Department cruiser bounced against the Hart Island pier. Sport went over the side with the line and held the boat close. The machinery man came out on deck. He climbed over the rail unsteadily. When he was standing on the pier next to Sport, Sport threw the line back onto the cruiser. The guard waved down at him from behind the wheel. He called out to Sport in a harsh whisper.

"Eleven-ten at the latest, Sporty. Gotta be back for the change of shift."

Sport waved back at him. "An hour and a half. I'll be here. No sweat."

The cruiser pulled away from the dock. It turned in the water and buzzed back toward City Island. A minute later, the mist closed over it. The sound of its engine faded.

It was quiet on the island, except for the plash of waves against the beach.

Sport took a flashlight out of his windbreaker pocket. He played its beam briefly over the area around. In the distance, beyond a stand of trees, he could just make out the silhouette of the modules: the old gray barracks sitting behind a barbed-wire fence. In the old days, when Sport had been here, the prisoners who volunteered to work the island had lived in those modules around the clock. Now, the city saved money by driving them out here from Rikers every day.

226

Now, at night, Hart Island was completely deserted.

A thin asphalt road wound away from the pier. Sport and the machinery man started along it. Autumn trees, rattling their last leaves in the wind, quickly grew thick at the road's edges. Massive old buildings, their brickwork crumbling, hunched amid those trees, peered out through the branches. Sport's flashlight played over the jagged glass in their empty windows.

"Spooky shit," he said.

The machinery man said nothing.

They walked on under the trees.

Sport knew the way to the graveyard. This place was written on his memory—as his home ground was, like the streets of Jackson Heights. The jungly summer heat among the trees, the bitter winter wind off the water—he could feel these sometimes, like a memory in his flesh. He could see the heavy-hanging sky—misted and colorless by day, starless by night—he could see it pressing down over the long trenches, the white headstones. He could see the skells, the prisoners in their greens, shambling from their gray barracks to meet the latest load of coffins at the pier. He could hear them laughing among themselves, glad to be out in the open air. Glad to be free of Rikers and the boredom and the stench of sweat and the prospect of stone. Hell, they were the privileged few, these gravediggers—you had to be inside for under a year and have no outstanding warrants to get this spot. Yes, these guys were *privileged* to be hauling the pine boxes from the truck to the trenches; to be piling up the bodies of broke whores and homeless drunks, of newborns who'd bought it in foaming seizures 'cause their mommies pumped their wombs too full of drugs. . . . They were honored and privileged, happy and proud to be here.

But not Sport. Sport wasn't any of those things.

This had been the bottom of his life, this place. This place and Rikers. He had reached the very rock bottom here. With no training but years of imitating the Frank Sinatra cassettes he played on his Walkman, this was the only decent job he could get. And he could only get this job because his mother had a friend (the walking penis who'd been giving her booze money for the last five years) who worked for the city Correction Department.

And so Sport, the next Sinatra, the next Julio, had become, at the age of twenty-six, a prison guard on Rikers Island. A correction officer, as they preferred to be called. And because he was such a good boy, he had soon been able to transfer over to Support Services out on Hart Island, at Potter's

Field. He had been put to work burying what department regulations referred to as "the indigent and the unclaimed."

Oh, yes, he remembered this place; he would always remember it. It wasn't only the dead, he remembered thinking, who get buried here. Out here, on Hart Island, he'd had a vision of his life stretching out before him; a life that could have been drawn wholesale from one of his mother's screeching prophecies. Out here, among the graves, Sport had heard his mother cackling with triumph unto eternity.

And then, out of nowhere, the accident saved him.

It had happened in a moment. He had been overseeing the work in the trench. One prisoner was in there attaching a hook and chain to the heavy bulkhead that was used to hold yesterday's piles of coffins steady overnight. The civilian machinery man was positioning his backhoe so it could draw the line up, lift the bulkhead out. Two other prisoners, meanwhile, were using a rake and shovel to drain off the groundwater that was continually seeping up into the trench's bottom. The rest of the prisoners were behind Sport, carrying coffins toward the ditch.

Many of the dead were infants that day. Their boxes were hardly bigger than shoe boxes. The cons were making jokes as they took them off the dump truck.

"Looks like my Adidas finally came."

"Hey, homes, here's the carton of cigarettes you ordered."

"It's the new fast food: MacBaby in a Box."

And as one of the men turned back to shout to another, he dropped his coffin. It tipped over the edge of the ditch, splashed into the puddle on the bottom, and cracked open.

The box lay on its side. The small plank that covered its top had sprung off. A white plastic bag had tumbled out and lay in the muddy groundwater.

The skells fell silent. There was no sound but the rumble of the back-hoe's engine. The prisoners at the edge of the ditch stared down at the white plastic bag. It lay at the feet of the kid who had been working the rake.

"Go on," someone said from the top of the ditch. "Put it on back in, Homes, t'ain't no thing. It's dead."

The skell in the trench shook his head. He stared down at the white bag. He kept shaking his head.

"Go on, nigger," another con shouted at him.

"That's your lunch, man, pick it up," said another.

All the prisoners were laughing now, shouting to the con in the ditch. The con in the ditch just stood there, staring, shaking his head.

"Go on, man, do it. Do it. Pick it up."

"Oh, fucking Christ," Sport muttered finally.

He jumped down into the trench himself. The skells applauded: "Sport-man to the rescue. Go get 'em, Sport."

Sport crouched down, ankle-deep in water. He lifted the plastic bag. It was so light; it shifted in his hands as if it were full of twigs. He put the bag in the box. Then he fit the lid back on and pressed its nails home with his palm.

And as he did, the backhoe lifted up the hook and chain, the bulkhead was drawn up out of the ditch. The wet bottom of the ditch gave way and the piles of yesterday's coffins toppled over.

Crouched down as he was, Sport was flattened when the coffins hit him. He fell to the earth and the boxes rolled over on top of him, pinning him in the muck. For a moment, he felt nothing but the mud and water rushing into his mouth, the suffocation, the panic . . .

And then the pain exploded inside him and he gagged and choked as he tried to cry out.

His appendix had ruptured. The doctors at Bronx Municipal later said they had gotten him to surgery just in time.

Sport immediately got himself a lawyer who loudly proclaimed that the city's negligence took this incident beyond the bounds of mere workman's compensation. The city responded by offering Sport a settlement of thirty thousand dollars above benefits. Sport accepted and quit his job at once.

He resolved to take a shot at show business. A real shot this time, no fooling around. Even his mother's obscene phone calls in the dead of night could not dissuade him. He had new photographs taken. He prepared to hire a recording studio.

And then he had his brainstorm. His great idea about Eddie the Screw.

For three months before the accident, the drunken ex-guard, ex-con had been telling his story down in the Harbor Bar where Sport liked to meet his CO friends. The story was always the same: how Eddie had run the drug trade in the city prison system; how he had stashed away over half a million dollars in cash; how the feds had come after him and how he had outsmarted them, by converting the cash into diamonds and hiding the diamonds away.

"It was nine years ago," the old man would say. "The investigators were closing in on me, see. But I still had my diamonds. Half a million dollars' worth—then—though I wouldn't care to estimate their value now." He would tilt his round head so that his liver-spotted pate caught the tavern's yellow light. He would screw up his skewed face until his enormous right eye seemed ready to pop out onto the table. And he'd say: "I was working the Potter's Field detail out on Hart Island at the time, ya see. And I thought to myself, I thought: If I can just get two minutes alone with one of these here coffins, I'll slip this safebox of diamonds into it and it'll be buried safe and sound until the heat's off. And then, one day, what should happen, but an opportunity arose too beautiful, too perfect, to pass up. A little girl—Elizabeth Burrows was her name—stowed away on the meat wagon. Yessir. She wanted to see her mother buried, the poor thing did, so we pretended one of the Jane Does was hers and we held a little funeral for her. It was downright moving. Yes, it was. But the point is, the point is, while everyone else was busy attending to the kid, I climbed into the truck, cracked open the Jane Doe's lid, and slipped my package inside it. It was buried right there in front of everybody, and nobody knew a thing."

Now, he would point a finger at his bald crown, wink his huge eye, and say, "Soon as I get the backing to pull it off, I'm gonna dig those diamonds up too. No one else can do it, see, 'cause no one else knows the number of that coffin but me."

And then he'd cackle and say, "No one but me and Elizabeth Burrows, that is. No one but me and that little girl."

When had it occurred to Sport to believe that horseshit? He couldn't remember now. It had just suddenly seemed to him that he was in a perfect position to pluck those diamonds from the earth, to make a real fortune, have a real stake for his new career. He had money, he had Correction Department contacts, and he knew the Potter's Field burial system.

Soon after he got out of the hospital, he wandered over to the Harbor Bar. Eddie the Screw wasn't there anymore. He'd died, the bartender said. While Sport was in the hospital, the old man's heart had given out and he'd died in bed in an old hotel just around the corner.

Sport could've called it off right there. Christ, he wished he had. But oh, no. He found Elizabeth Burrows in the phone book—and then he got a friend to make him some copies of the Hart Island burial records for the year Eddie was arrested. . . .

* * *

Now, he withdrew those records from his windbreaker pocket. He and the machinery man had reached the graves.

They were just off the road in a little field of blackened earth. Small white headstones, gleaming even in the moonless mist, rose from the ground at intervals of about eighty feet. At the near end of the field, right in front of Sport, was the new ditch, an open pit. There were unused coffins at the edge of it. One of these, Sport knew, would be full of digging tools. A backhoe also stood at the ditch's edge. It looked, in the shadows, like an animal come to drink.

Sport stood where he was a moment. He hunched his shoulders and shuddered. Behind him, the cold wind came off the water. The water slapped the shore, rattling the carpet of mussel shells there. The wind moved on and stirred the mist that lay atop the field of headstones. The wind moved on, and on the far side of the field the dense, dead trees creaked and swayed.

"Okay," Sport whispered.

He left the machinery man standing on the road and walked into the field.

Sport had overseen exhumations before. There were about a hundred of them on Hart Island in any given year. As crafty old Eddie had made sure to bury his Jane Doe at the top, this one would be relatively easy, he thought. He just had to find the right location.

Sport moved slowly through the mist, bending down in the dark here and there to shine his flashlight on a headstone. Each headstone marked a trench, and each trench held the bodies of a hundred and fifty paupers. They were buried in three sections of forty-eight, forty-eight, and fifty-four boxes: they were stacked up in two piles of three and so had to be sectioned in multiples of six. Sport moved on, drawing farther and farther from the road behind him, closer and closer to the woods up ahead.

When he reached the far edge of the field, he paused. The overgrown woods were right beside him. He heard the dead leaves skittering in the dark. He shone his flashlight over the stone at his feet. He read the number on it. He had found the one he wanted.

Sport braced his heels against the stone and began to pace off the distance. The number Conrad had given him corresponded with another number on his records: 2-16. The coffin he wanted was the sixteenth one in the second section. He paced the number off.

When he found the place, he reached down and drew an X in the dirt with his finger. He walked back to the road, to the sad-faced machinery man.

"X marks the spot," he said.

The machinery man nodded. Without a word, he walked over to the backhoe by the open ditch. He climbed up into its cab.

A moment later, the backhoe's engine started. Its headlights went on. It rumbled away from the open trench.

Sport walked over to the unused coffins by the trench's side. He sat down on top of one of them and watched the backhoe moving out across the field.

The machinery man positioned his machine at the place Sport had marked for him. Sport heard the machine's shovel chunk into the earth.

Marshal Dillon

Conrad was pacing back and forth now, ignoring the pain in his knee, staring into the empty space before him, gripping the recorder in his right hand. He could be wrong, he kept telling himself. The description could fit a million people. He could be completely wrong about the whole thing. . . .

But he stared into the empty space before him, and the face of Sport was there. The young, handsome face with the artist's eyes. The same face that had leaned sneering into his, that had cursed him and spit at him. And he paced back and forth gripping the recorder tightly. And he did not think that he was wrong at all.

It must have been Sport. It must have been Sport all along. Sport must have been Terry, the struggling actor. The man who had kissed Elizabeth. The man who had murdered the red-haired man, Robert Rostoff, in her apartment. That was it, he thought. That was what must have happened. She had assumed he was a hallucination, her Secret Friend, but he was real. He was real and he had tried to seduce her. But somehow, for some reason, the red-haired man had gotten in the way. The red-haired man had known Sport was coming to her apartment. He had hidden there, he had grabbed Elizabeth, locked her in the bathroom. He had been trying to keep her away from Sport. Maybe he'd even been trying to protect her. Then, while

233

Elizabeth was locked in the bathroom, while she was confused, hysterical, maybe even hallucinating in fact, Sport must have burst in and overcome the red-haired man. He must have murdered this person who had managed to interrupt him as he kissed Elizabeth, who had frightened the girl away after Sport had succeeded in enticing her home, bringing her back to . . .

Conrad stopped pacing. His eyes went wider. He looked down at the recorder in his hand.

. . . to his apartment.

Sport had taken Elizabeth back to his apartment. She had told him that. She had told him where it was. He remembered . . .

He moved quickly to the recliner again. Sat down quickly. He held the recorder between his knees. He pressed the fast-forward button. He tapped his foot convulsively on the ground as the tape spun ahead.

He stopped it. He hit playback.

. . . *looked really angry. He said he would meet me right at the door of the center from* . . .

"Shit," Conrad said.

He hit fast forward. He looked at his watch. Five after eleven. He felt the press of time in his stomach. It had been gone for a while; that pressure, that urgency. For a while, here in this little room, it had been as if time had ceased—or simply ceased to matter. But it was moving again now, moving too fast again. He could feel it, burning in him.

He hit the playback button.

. . . *late by then, I guess,* Elizabeth's voice went on. *Around eleven or so. And we walked into a neighborhood that wasn't very nice.*

That was it. There it was. He let the tape roll on.

. . . *we stopped in front of an old brownstone just a block before the Hudson on a little street called Houses Street.* . . .

"Houses Street," Conrad whispered.

He spun the chair around, rolled it to his desk. He pushed the papers there aside, found a pen. He pulled an old envelope out of the pile. The tape was still rolling.

There were no streetlamps and the house we were in front of, the brownstone, was the only one with a light on. . . .

Impatiently, Conrad reached out and jabbed fast forward again. He let the tape scramble on a long time. He had to stop and check it twice. Then, the third time, he found what he was looking for.

They even drove me there. They showed me. There's the brownstone, they said. Number two twenty-two.

Conrad shut the recorder off. He scrawled the address on the back of the old envelope: 222 Houses Street.

He rolled the chair away from the desk. He stood up.

It could be wrong, he thought.

He laid the recorder on the desktop. Bent over the desk, he pawed through his papers. He had a map somewhere. In one of the compartments. There it was. A pocket atlas of the city. He pulled it out, threw it open. He found the index and ran his finger down the street names.

"Ach!" He had to shake his head, close his eyes to clear the red clouds from them.

He looked again. Houses Street. He flipped to the map of Manhattan. It was there, down in Tribeca. The Broadway local would get him close.

But it could be wrong, it could be wrong. Hadn't the police checked the building out? Hadn't they shown Elizabeth it was abandoned . . . ?

He straightened. He turned. He looked across the room. He looked at the shuttered window.

Don't walk out of that door, Marshal Dillon, because we have got you covered.

He reached up under the shade of the desk lamp. He snapped it off. He looked at the window.

Don't walk out of that door . . .

He moved to the patient's chair. He turned off the lamp that was standing beside it. His head throbbed as the red clouds drifted in front of him. He went to the door, to the light switch beside the door.

It could be wrong, he thought. He would not be able to call the police because it could be wrong, and if Jessica was not there, if Sport saw them but Jessica was not there . . .

He pulled the switch down. The consulting room went black. Even then, even in the darkness, the red splotches swam and spread and contracted in front of him. He peered through them in the direction of the window.

And if he was wrong, he would have to get back in time too. If he was wrong, if it was all a mistake—then he had to get there and back here by midnight. He had to go and return without being seen, return in time to take that last, small chance that the kidnappers would really return her to him as they'd promised. And even if it was right . . . Well . . .

If it was right, if Sport was holding Jessica there, then Conrad had to get to her now and fast. He had to get to her before Sport could check out the number, before Sport had time to decide that he did not need a hostage anymore. Only if he did that, if he found her there in time, only then could he call the police and finally get someone to help her. . . .

But the time was passing and it burned at him, ate at him. He had to do something in either case. He had to do something fast.

He came forward. Nursing his weak leg only a little, he moved slowly forward through the dark. The red clouds were thinning from before him, they were getting fainter, they were fading away. He inched through the dark with his hands out in front of him. He moved around the analysis couch. His fingers touched the wall, passed along the wall until they brushed the window's wooden shutters.

He unfastened the shutters, folded them open. He looked out at the airshaft.

They wouldn't be watching this, he thought. Hell, with the shutters closed in here, most people didn't even know this window existed.

Don't walk out of that door, Marshal Dillon.

And even if they knew, it just led to an airshaft: a closed alleyway between this building and the one on the corner of Eighty-third Street. The wall of the neighboring building ran up high, at least twenty stories. And while there were small airshaft windows in that wall too, the lower ones were all shut tight. It would be tough. Just to get himself through this window would be tough. And then, to somehow break into one of the windows of the neighboring building . . . without being seen, without being caught . . . The kidnappers wouldn't take the trouble to guard against that, he thought.

He licked his dry lips. His stomach churned. He thought of the blood on the passenger seat of his Corsica. Elizabeth's blood. He had not thought the kidnappers were watching him then either.

And so he stayed at the window. He did not move. He breathed through his mouth and gazed out at the airshaft.

Could be wrong, he thought again.

He stood in the dark and gazed at the airshaft. He saw Jessica. He saw her lying on the floor in her valentines nightgown. He saw her hair—the same color hair as his—tangled and matted about her face. He saw her glassy eyes staring at him through the strands of hair.

Why didn't you come, Daddy?

He thought of Elizabeth's blood.

Daddy?

Conrad nodded. He whispered back, "I'm coming."

Aggie and Elizabeth

The policemen surged toward Elizabeth. They surrounded her. Aggie lost sight of her in the crush of them. She moved slowly toward the closing circle of dark suits.

"Give her air," one of the men said.

"She's coming back around," said another.

Aggie was now at the edge of the circle. Men's backs blocked her way. Across from them, she saw men's faces, stern and thin-lipped. They called to each other curtly.

"Hold on to her."

"Watch she doesn't hurt herself."

Then, from the midst of the circling men, from beneath the sound of their voices, Aggie heard the woman's voice rise to her. It started softly, thinly. "What? What? Please, please, I . . ."

"Please," said Aggie. She reached out and touched a man on his shoulder. The man turned to her, an olive-skinned detective with carefully waved hair. "Please," Aggie said. The detective stood back to let her pass. Aggie pressed into the circle of men. She heard the woman's voice growing louder.

"I can't . . . I can't deal with this. I can't deal with this, please, I can't deal with this, please . . ."

The words came faster and faster. The same thing over again: "I can't deal with this." Aggie heard it rising to a shrill note of panic.

"Please," Aggie said. "You're scaring her. Let me . . ." She tried to shoulder her way between two men, to get deeper into the cluster.

The woman's voice grew still more shrill. "Oh, God, oh, please, I'm scared now, I'm scared now, right now, please . . . please . . ."

Agatha touched the man just in front of her. He moved aside and she pressed in toward the circle's center. She could see the woman now—Elizabeth, *his* Elizabeth—she could see the top of her head, her golden hair, then part of her face, her blood-streaked brow. She was thrashing around, pulling back and forth. Her eyes were wide, darting everywhere as the men pressed in close to her.

"Please," Agatha said loudly. "Please. Give her some room. You're terrifying her. Can't you take those handcuffs off?"

As she pushed finally into the center of the men, Agatha saw the woman fully. She was on her knees, the skirt of her shift spreading out around her. Men were holding her upper arms, their fingers pressing into the flesh. Her head was lashing from shoulder to shoulder in her panic. Her hair whipped about her cheeks and eyes.

"I'm scared now, I'm scared, I can't deal with this, I can't, please . . . ," she kept saying.

"Oh, for God's sake," said Agatha.

She knelt down in front of the woman. One man moved toward her as if to stop her. Another touched her shoulder, then let his hand slide away.

"Please," Agatha said. And then she spoke more sharply, "Please! Someone take these handcuffs off her."

The policemen looked at each other over the head of the struggling woman. Then they looked over Agatha's head, up at D'Annunzio. D'Annunzio shrugged.

One patrolman knelt down behind the woman. Agatha heard the cuffs come loose. Other cops still held the woman's arms firmly. Her hands were still forced behind her back.

Now Agatha reached up to the woman's left shoulder. A burly plainclothesman had his two hands wrapped firmly around the upper arm. Aggie touched his hands, pushing at the fingers gently. The plainclothesman looked down at her. His grip on the woman loosened. Slowly, the woman's arm came free. It settled beside her.

Elizabeth's thrashing began to subside. She made frightened grunts, her eyes lowered.

Agatha turned and looked up at the man who was holding the woman's right arm. It was one of the young patrolmen. He looked down at her.

"Please," Agatha said.

The patrolman glanced around at the other men. No one said anything. The patrolman let the woman's right arm go. The woman brought it around in front of her. She clutched her right wrist in her left hand.

She had stopped thrashing altogether now. She was breathing hard. Her chest was heaving. Her chin had fallen forward. Her face was hidden in her hair. She hunched her shoulders and rubbed her wrist and sat quietly.

After a while, she raised her face to Agatha.

"We've got to help him," she whispered.

Her face wrinkled. She began to cry.

She cried like a child, her face contorted, her mouth opened wide. She bawled loudly, holding her wrist in front of her. Christ, Aggie thought. She put her arms around her. The girl let out a wet gasp and leaned toward her. She lay her head against Agatha's breast. Aggie looked up at the ceiling. Jesus, she thought, where the hell did you get this one, Doc? She was just a kid, just a teenager.

The girl cried and Aggie held her. The men hovered above them in a circle, looking down.

"All right," Agatha said after a moment. "All right. That's enough now. Listen now. Listen . . ." The girl sniffled against her. She trembled in Aggie's arms as she cried. Agatha shook her head, touched the girl's hair. She felt the stiffness of the dried blood in it. "All right," she said gently. "Listen to me. Tell me about Dr. Conrad. How can we help him? Try to tell me."

The girl sobbed. She struggled to sit up. She pulled away from Agatha's hold. Her face was mottled, painted with blood, shiny with tears. She waggled her hands in front of her urgently.

"You have to find Terry," she cried. "Terry's real. Dr. Conrad said so. I *saw* him."

"Who's Terry?" said Agatha.

"I don't know. He was the Secret Friend but then he wasn't. The Secret Friend was with me but Terry was real. He was the one who wanted the number, just like the red-haired man said. But he wasn't magic. Only the Secret Friend was magic."

Oh, boy, thought Aggie. She glanced up. The faces of the men hung over her. They turned and looked at each other. They looked down at her. Oh, boy.

"All right," said Agatha. "Come here. Come on, stand up, sweetheart. Your name's Elizabeth? Come over here, Elizabeth."

She took the girl by the elbow. She helped her to her feet. The crush of men opened a little as they stood.

"Excuse me," Agatha said.

She started walking the girl over to the sofa. The men stood aside to let them pass. Then they edged after them in a half circle.

"Look at you," Aggie said softly as she guided the woman across the room. "You're covered with blood. Are you bleeding? Are you hurt?"

"No. I don't think so."

"Are you hungry?"

"No. I'm thirsty, though."

"You're scratched. You have scratches all over you. Look at this. What happened to you?" She looked up and saw D'Annunzio. He was watching her, his hands in his pockets. He was standing next to Special Agent Calvin. "Would you get me a damp washcloth please," she said. "And a glass of water."

"You can't wash her, ma'am," Calvin said. He had a sharp, thrusting voice, ridiculously forthright. "We'll need to take samples from her face and clothing for evidence. We'll have to have one of our team examine—"

"All right, all right," said Aggie. "Just bring her some water then."

Calvin fell silent. D'Annunzio went tromping away.

Aggie sat the girl down on the sofa and sat down next to her. The girl stared at her with big green eyes. Aggie wasn't sure she knew where she was.

She took both of Elizabeth's hands in hers. "All right," she said. "Elizabeth. Now, tell me. You were in the hospital, weren't you?"

She nodded. "Yes. That's right."

"And you left the hospital with Dr. Conrad."

"Yes. Yes. He hit Dr. Sachs with a chair."

Aggie almost laughed. It was an odd sensation. "All right," she said. "Do you know where Dr. Conrad is now?"

Elizabeth shook her head. "No. No. He . . . He went around the corner. He didn't come back. Terry came."

"Terry."

"Yes. He's real. He's not the Secret Friend. He took Dr. Conrad's daughter, your daughter, so Dr. Conrad would ask me for the number. They knew I would give him the number because I . . . I know him. Dr. Conrad. We . . . I know him."

Aggie narrowed her eyes. "Know him?"

D'Annunzio came back with a glass of water. He handed it to Agatha. Agatha handed it to Elizabeth.

"Drink it slowly," she said.

Elizabeth put the glass to her lips. She raised it quickly, sucked off a long draft. Agatha had to pull the girl's hand down finally.

"Elizabeth," she said. "Do you know where Terry is now?"

She nodded quickly. "Yes, yes. He went to take my mother out. Now he has the number."

Agatha took the water from her and put it on the coffee table. Goddamn it, she thought as she turned away. She couldn't make any sense of this. The girl was crazy.

Goddamn it, Doc. What did you do? What did you get us into?

She took a breath against the tightness in her stomach. When she looked at Elizabeth again, she continued to speak calmly.

"Where is your mother, Elizabeth?" she said.

"She's dead."

"She's dead?"

"Yes. And worms are coming out of her."

"And Terry wants to take her out."

"Yes. Yes."

Agatha looked into the girl's earnest eyes. "You mean, he wants to take her out of her grave," she said.

"Yes. Yes."

"Why the hell would he want to do that?" asked D'Annunzio. He was still standing beside them.

"What?" Elizabeth looked up at him. Looked back at Aggie. "What? Why . . . ? I mean, I don't . . . What?"

"Never mind," Agatha said. "Just never mind that now, all right?"

"All right," said Elizabeth. Her eyes moved over Aggie's face frantically. "All right. Is it all right?"

"Ssh," said Aggie. She patted the girl's hand. "It's fine. Just tell me now: Do you know where your mother's grave is?"

"Yes. It's on the island. Where they take the poor people."

"Hart Island?" said D'Annunzio.

"Yes."

"That's a big place," he said. "A hundred acres. A lot of people buried there. How would he know where your mother is?"

Elizabeth pulled her hands away from Aggie. She shook them up and down. "The number!" she said. "I had to tell Dr. Conrad the number!"

241

"The number of your mother's grave," said Aggie.

"Yes! Yes!"

The rest of the men in the room had now moved close to them. They were pressing up against the back of the sofa, grouped together. They were watching the two women.

"So now he's going out to Hart Island to take your mother out of her grave?" Aggie asked.

"Yes," said Elizabeth.

"Did you see him go out there?"

"Well . . . yes. I mean, I saw him leave. He came out of the big building with the clock on top. I hid. I was looking for Dr. Conrad. You see, first, Dr. Conrad went around the corner; and then the man was in the back of the car—he put a knife on my neck, a knife. . . . And then, after that was over, after the man was . . . gone, I . . ." She swallowed hard. She talked faster and faster, moving her hands. "After the man was gone, I was scared and I went around the corner where Dr. Conrad went. There was a building. A big building with a clock and I saw Terry coming out of it. I hid behind the other building, the big black building. And I watched him. Terry. I saw him get in a car and drive away. But Dr. Conrad didn't come. He didn't come."

Aggie felt something drop inside her. She had to steady herself before she could speak again.

"What did . . . ?" D'Annunzio began.

But Aggie was already saying it. "What did the car look like, Elizabeth?"

"Uh . . ." She lifted her eyes to the ceiling. "It was white. It was white, like, a big white car with four doors. And it had a big long scratch on the side of it, and one of its back lights, the red lights in back, was broken, smashed."

"Put it on the radio," said D'Annunzio.

Agatha felt a small flurry as the men in back of the sofa started to move. She kept her eyes on Elizabeth. The girl looked at her eagerly.

"Now you said a man put a knife on your neck," Aggie said.

"Yes," she said. She nodded.

"Do you know where that man is now?"

"He's . . . there was a big . . . one of those garbage things . . ."

"A Dumpster," said D'Annunzio. "Jesus Christ."

Elizabeth glanced up at him. "He put a knife on my neck and he said he would kill me. But then he didn't kill me, he . . . he came up into the seat, the seat next to me, Dr. Conrad's seat. He had a piece of paper, a note for

Dr. Conrad, he said. He put it . . . he put it on the front, on the dashboard of the car. . . . And then he said, he said, 'Now we're, we're just gonna tilt the bucket seat back here and have some fun.'" She nodded. "And then . . . He said that and then he . . . he put his hand on me, on my breast, or whatever." Elizabeth looked up at the men standing behind the sofa. She looked at D'Annunzio. And finally she lowered her eyes and looked at Aggie. She shook her head—almost sadly, Agatha thought.

"That," she said softly, "made the Secret Friend mad."

Digging

In the end, Sport's face showed no trace of emotion. As the cruiser cut back toward City Island, he was expressionless. He stood at the stern again, at the rail again. He peered out over the turbulent sound. His eyes were dull, his mouth was slack. His hands rested on the rail and were still.

When the machinery man had finished with the backhoe, Sport had gone out to the spot with a pick and shovel. He had set his flashlight at the edge of the fresh hole. He had stepped into the hole himself and started digging.

He had dug quickly but gingerly, using the shovel to scrape off the top layer of the earth beneath him. He had stared intently at the earth as he lifted it. He had not looked up at the bending trees. He had not heard the wind in their branches or the waves lapping on the beach. He had heard that chuck and scrape of dirt and pebbles, over and over in the freshly dug hole. He had heard that, and he had heard a voice in his head, repeating: All or nothing at all. All or nothing. All or nothing at all.

He kept turning the earth over. Chuck and scrape. There would be nothing left of the pine box now, not after nine years. There would only be bones. He kept digging.

What were you, crazy? he thought. *You crazy, stupid fuck. How could you*

244

have believed this? How could you have believed in this, you brainless toad?
You murdering piece of nothing. You're nothing.

All or nothing. All *for* nothing.

He dug in the earth. The shovel chucked and scraped.

Nothing is what you are! Nobody, what you always are! Mr. Big Superstar,
and you're shit, you're nothing, you're nobody, a dead man standing in a dead
man's hole.

He kept digging. The hole had been six feet wide and two feet deep when
he started. He was down almost three feet now. And all the while he was
thinking:

All for nothing. All for nothing.

All for nothing at all.

When the cruiser returned to City Island, Sport went into the
Correction Department shack. He used the little bathroom inside to clean
up and change his clothing. He washed the dirt off his hands and sprayed
himself with deodorant. He stuffed his old clothes in a garbage bag. He put
on a denim jacket, a blue-and-white striped T-shirt, and fresh jeans. Then
he combed his hair carefully. Only a faint trace of dirt ground into the flesh
of his fingertips showed that he had been digging.

When he came out of the shack, he found the guard and the machinery man waiting at the edge of the pier. He handed each of them an
envelope with a thousand dollars in it. Each of them shook his hand
solemnly.

"So long, Sporty-boy," the guard said. "Hope you found what you were
looking for."

The machinery man said nothing.

Sport left them and walked off the department lot to Fordham Street.
His white Chevy was parked there, just beyond the fence. He loaded the car
with his things and slipped inside behind the wheel. He drove up to the
corner and turned onto City Island Avenue.

The Chevy moved slowly down the empty thoroughfare. Sport stared out
through the windshield at the boatyards, the seafood restaurants, the
sailors' clapboard homes—all standing dark by the side of the avenue. The
red and green of the traffic lights seemed very bright up ahead of him. He
stared at them blankly, his lips parted.

"Jesus Christ," he whispered after a while. "Jesus Christ."

* * *

245

At three feet, he'd begun to hit the bones. The shovel gave a squeaky thud and the earth went hard with them. Soon, Sport was turning over broken chunks of dirty ivory; unrecognizable shards; a sudden section of arm or leg. The earth was suddenly thick with worms and centipedes. They wriggled in and out of the black loam.

Dem bones, dem bones. Sport was sweating hard. The sweat carried grime down the sides of his face. The shovel kept spearing the earth, bringing it up. Sport kept thinking: All for nothing, all for nothing at all . . .

And then the shovel hit something that would not yield.

Sport stopped, staring down. In the outglow of the flashlight, his eyes burned. He worked the shovel around the hard object, cutting it out of the earth. Then he dug down again, furiously now, grunting with the effort.

Look, he was thinking suddenly. Look, look, look. Look at this!

The shovel pried at the object and suddenly, out of the earth sprang a grinning death's head. A human skull, packed with dirt, crawling with centipedes.

"Ah!" Sport cried.

The head rolled off his shovel. Dropped to the ground. It rocked there gently. Then it lay still as the worms burst out from under it.

Up ahead now, Sport spotted a Sunoco station. There was a pay phone at the edge of its open lot, near the street.

Sport pulled the Chevy into the station and parked it beside the phone. He turned off the car and sat still. He stared out through the windshield. There was no expression on his face.

After a moment, he bent forward. He reached down under the car seat and took hold of the safebox there. He brought it up and held it on his lap.

"Jesus Christ," he said quietly again. "Jesus fucking Christ."

He had found the safebox just underneath the skull. It was the next thing his shovel hit when, in frustration and anger, he had jabbed it into the earth again. The metallic chink that had answered him from down there had made him let go of the shovel handle as if it were electrified. The tool had pitched over to lay sidewise against the edge of the hole. Sport, almost awestruck, had knelt down and wrestled the box free with his two hands.

They were worth half a million dollars—then. I wouldn't care to venture an estimate of their value now.

It was a cheap box. Eddie the Screw could've bought it in any office supply store. His hands shaking, Sport sprung the lock with the blade of the shovel. He opened it and looked down.

Even in the dark, in only the flashlight's pale glow, the diamonds glittered. They skittered back and forth across the box's metal bottom and glittered up into the starless mist. There were so many of them. So many . . .

Sport had shut the lid quickly. He had stood up quickly and motioned to the machinery man, who was sitting by the roadside on an unused coffin, smoking a cigarette.

"You can fill it up now," he'd called.

The machinery man had risen wearily and moved to his backhoe without a word.

Now, sitting in his Chevy in the Sunoco parking lot, Sport caressed the box's metal top with one hand.

"Jesus Christ," he whispered to it, his face expressionless. "Jesus fucking Christ."

He got out of the car. He carried the box to the back, opened the trunk, and set it in there, hiding it under the flap for the spare tire. Then he walked over to the pay phone.

He dialed the portable cellular. A computer with a woman's voice told him to feed the phone forty cents for the first five minutes. Sport put the change in, coin by coin. He wiped sweat from his mouth while the phone rang on the other end.

"Yuh." It was Maxwell.

"Maxie," said Sport. He had to clear his throat and start again: "Max?"

"Yuh, Sport. Yuh."

"I got it, buddy."

There was a pause. Then a single sodden laugh: "Huh. You got it?"

"Yeah. Yeah." Sport wiped the sweat off his mouth again. "Okay," he said. "Do the kid and get out of there. Okay? Meet me and Dolenko at the Port Authority like we said. And Maxie . . ."

"Yuh, Sport, yuh."

"Do her quick and get out of there, all right? Just kill her and blow. This is no time to mess around. Understand?"

There was no answer at first.

247

"You hear me, big guy?" Sport said. His voice was perilously close to cracking.

After a long moment, Max finally answered, "Yuh, Sport. I hear you. Yuh."

"Good boy," said Sport. "Go to it."

He hung up the phone. He turned around.

A police car had pulled into the gas station behind him.

Stupid Chloroform

Maxwell hung up the phone. His small, square face was taut and tense. Under the deep brow, his eyes shifted back and forth nervously. What was he going to do now? he wondered.

Do the kid. That's what Sport had said. *Do her quick and get out of there.*

Maxwell walked over to the mattress against the wall. The girl lay sleeping on it. Maxwell looked down at her. He dragged a big hand across his mouth.

The trouble was, she wouldn't wake up. That was the trouble right there. He'd been trying to get her to come around for almost an hour now. But she just lay there. She lay on her side. Her legs came naked from the warm flannel of her nightgown. Her hands were taped behind her back. Her mouth was taped over. Her eyes were almost closed. He could see a little bit of eye like dull glass peeking out under the lids. She was breathing very small, shallow breaths.

Maxwell bent down, reached down and poked her shoulder with one thick finger. The girl rocked back and forth a little. But she did not stir, she did not wake up.

Chewing his lip, Maxwell lumbered away from her. He ran his hands up through his hair. He went to the canvas chair in the corner. He sat down, his thick arms hanging heavily between his legs. He sat there, staring at the girl.

Too much of that stupid chloroform, he thought. Stupid, he thought, you gave her too much of that chloroform.

Well, it had been an accident. He couldn't help it. He had had to move the girl all the way from the Sinclair apartment to here and he had been worried, that's all. He had had to carry her the whole way in a duffel bag: out past the doorman, all the way downtown in a cab. He had been worried she would wake up on the way. So . . . he had doused the rag with plenty of the stuff before he'd put it over her mouth. It was just an accident, that was all.

Maxwell rubbed his forehead. He hated it when he got like this, all clogged and confused inside.

The thing was, the problem was, he thought . . . After he'd poured the chloroform, when he'd come into the bedroom where the little girl was . . . Well, the way she had looked . . . She had been lying on the bed curled up on her side. She was sucking her thumb and staring at the television. She looked almost peaceful, almost dreamy. Just like she was watching TV at home, like any little girl. And there were those black bruises on both her cheeks from where Sport had slapped her when she tried to get away. Those looked good too. Maxwell liked those.

When Max had come toward her with the chloroform rag, she had started crying. But she hadn't tried to get away. She just lay there on the bed and her face had gotten all scrunched up. She had cried and she had trembled too. Maxwell had been breathing hard as he sat down on the bed next to her. Then he had grabbed her hair . . .

Now, Maxwell stirred on the canvas chair. Remembering that—grabbing her—it made his penis start to uncoil in his pants.

He remembered: He'd grabbed her. He'd grabbed her and the little girl had cried and said softly, "No." Weakly, she had tried to turn her face away from the rag. But Maxwell had held the rag over her mouth. That was very good. He had watched her body, warm and twisting, like a little animal. . . .

He stared now at the bound child on the mattress. His erection pressed up hard against his khaki pants. He put his hand on top of it. He rubbed it with his palm, staring at the girl. He remembered:

He had held the rag over her face. He had held it there and held it there. Too long. That was the problem. Even after she stopped twisting and struggling, he had held it there. He had gripped her hair and felt the weight of her body in his hands and he had kept holding it there. That was why he couldn't get her to wake up now.

Look at her. Lying there. Her face was practically gray.

Do her. This is no time to mess around.

Maxwell sat in the canvas chair and rubbed his cock and stared at the little girl. He knew he had to do what Sport said. He had to do it soon too. He knew that.

But it wouldn't be any good if she didn't wake up for it.

He sat in the canvas chair and watched her.

This is a smelly old place, Maxwell thought after a while. He was sorry he'd had to come back here. It was smelly and it was dirty. And it was dark too. There was just the one old lamp that Dolenko had rigged up. It stood in the corner. It threw off a weak, yellow glow. In that glow, Maxwell could make out the cracked walls, the old, gray, rotten wood flooring, the two filthy windows on the wall across from the mattress. He could see roaches up near the ceiling and in the corners of the floor. And right under the window, he could see a water bug practically as big as his hand.

After they'd killed the Freak, Sport and Maxwell had hidden all the furniture upstairs. But when Maxwell brought the girl here, he'd dragged down the mattress and the canvas chair and the lamp. He sat in the canvas chair now and looked fretfully at the girl on the mattress. Her face really was a bad color. Kind of gray but chalk white at the same time. And before, when he'd first got her here, she had been breathing very strangely too. She would not breathe at all for a long, long moment. And then her whole body would get stiff and she would take a sudden deep breath. She had to take it through her nose because of the tape on her mouth.

Do her. Just do her and blow.

But Maxwell sat. He watched her. He tapped his foot against the floor. He *had* to do what Sport said, he thought. He *wanted* to do what Sport said. Sport was going to give him lots of money so he could do whatever he wanted. He could have boys and girls, Sport said, and he would never have to worry about going to prison again. Maxwell wanted that a lot. He had not liked prison. Not at all. Not one bit. The only good thing that had happened to him in prison was that he'd met Sport.

He tapped his foot rapidly on the floor and he tapped his hand rapidly on his knee. Maybe she would wake up soon, he thought. Maybe he could wait just a little while and she would wake up. She was already breathing better than she had before. She was taking those small breaths now, but at least she didn't stop and start the way she'd been doing. She was breathing steadily.

251

Maybe he should take the tape off her mouth, Maxwell thought. Maybe that would help.

But no. He didn't want to do that. Even though the building was empty, he didn't want her to start screaming suddenly. Not until it was just the right time.

Maxwell tapped his foot and patted his knee—and then started nodding his head to the same rapid rhythm.

That's what he would do, he thought. He would wait just a little while. See if she woke up. See if she came around.

He would wait just a little while longer.

PART FOUR

Breakout

There was about a ten-foot drop to the airshaft outside Conrad's office. From where Conrad stood at the window, he could barely see the pavement below. Light from apartments in his building and the building next door fell down over the little alleyway in isolated patches. The rest was in deep shadow. Some of the first-floor windows—all of them dark—glinted out of the black places.

"All right," Conrad whispered.

He closed his eyes and shook off the image of his daughter lying dead. He shook off the memory of Elizabeth's blood on his car seat. He opened his eyes. He unlocked the small window and pushed it up.

He felt the damp air blow in over his face.

What if they're watching? What if they're out there?

He shook that off too, shuddered it off. He had to move. It was eleven-ten. If he was wrong, he had to be there and back by midnight. He had to move fast. Now.

He went out the window.

It was tight. He had to snake his way out, first an arm, then his head, then the other arm. There was no room to bring his leg out after. He twisted around until he was facing up. He pushed against the sill. The metal frame scraped his sides as he came through. His hips stuck. He pulled hard, twisting, grunting. Finally, he could sit on the ledge, holding on to the sill. He maneuvered his right leg out until he was straddling the ledge. He tried to work his left leg around. . . .

"Jesus!"

He slipped off. He clung to the sill by the tips of his fingers. His legs dangled beneath him. Then he fell.

The airshaft pavement slanted into the gutter. His feet hit it at an angle. He felt the jolt slice up through his right knee. The knee collapsed and Conrad went down, his hand against the wall.

There was water in the gutter, old rain. He felt it seep through the leg of his pants as he knelt in it. Breathing hard, his breath rasping, he worked his way up, pushing against the wall with his palm.

He looked up. He looked up and all around him. And he let out a sobbing laugh.

Nice going, shithead. You lost us the game.

His own window was high above him. The other windows were all dark, all shut. Could he even reach them, could he even reach any of them?

Nice going, shithead.

He sobbed again but the laughter seized in his throat. An old nausea swept over him, an old panic. Like being nine years old again, cowering in left field, praying for an easy end to the game. And then seeing the long fly ball sailing out to him; hearing the shouts of "Move back, go back," and being washed by the claustrophobic nausea of being trapped inside this stoop-shouldered, stumbling body that was sure to reach the ball only to feel it strike his mitt and plop weakly into the grass.

Nice going, shithead. You lost us the game.

Good Christ, he was going to spend the rest of the night stuck here. Trapped in the fucking airshaft. Wandering back and forth in it like a rat in a cage while his daughter . . .

Nice going, Daddy.

"Oh, God . . ." It was a low moan. He raised his hand and wiped the miserable sound of it off his mouth. He forced himself to move away from the wall. He looked up at the windows of the neighboring building.

All dark, all shut. All at least ten feet off the ground, barely within reach of his fingers. Grimacing with pain, he limped across the alley until he was standing underneath one of them. He reached up, grabbed hold of the ledge. Stood on tiptoe. Working his fingers under the frame, he pushed up. The window only rattled against its lock. He moved down along the alley and tried another. It was also locked. Well, what else? These were offices; doctors' offices, dentists', other shrinks'. They would all be locked. Conrad leaned against the wall, his cheek pressed to the cold stone. His lips were trembling. The dim light in the alleyway blurred before him.

Nice going, shithead.

He thought: Something. He had to do something. Anything. He looked up at the window just above his head. He cursed.

He bent down, lifted his foot and took off his shoe. He made a face as he lowered his stockinged foot into the cold gutter water.

He slipped the shoe over his hand. He reached up as high as he could. He thrust his arm up and pushed the shoe through the window.

Until that moment, he had just been thinking about getting through the window. No one, he'd thought, would hear the breaking glass. This was New York: no one who did hear the breaking glass would care.

Until the moment he actually shoved the shoe through the pane, he never even considered the possibility of an alarm.

There was, after all, no alarm in his own office. He didn't need one: there was nothing of value there except maybe his prescription forms. But other doctors, of course, kept drugs around and expensive equipment. He hadn't even considered that until the moment the glass shattered.

Then the thought was like a thing exploding. The world was like a thing exploding inside his mind. There was the glass, the glass shattering with a kind of violent music; there were the shards flashing dangerously in the half-light as they tumbled down around him in a daggerlike rain; and at the same moment, there was that explosion of thought: My God, *an alarm, what if there's, my God, there must be, alarm, alarm!*

And then the alarm started ringing.

The bell pounded into him like a shrill jackhammer. The night shook with it. His mind, his thoughts, were shivered to pieces and he stood in the alley below, gaping up, thinking: *Bell! Alarm! Alarm!*

Lights went on in the windows above him. Windows already lighted started to rumble open.

Alarm! Christ! Oh, Christ!

The air kept bursting with the sound.

Quickly, Conrad wrestled his shoe back onto his foot. Then he crouched down, staring at the window above. Jagged shards of glass stabbed up from the sill, out from the jambs. Conrad leapt toward them.

He sprang toward them, grabbed hold of the window frame. The glass stabbed into his palms. The bell, the ceaseless bell, screamed and screamed into his ears.

He dragged himself up. His teeth were gritted, his eyes were closed against a pain in his hands like fire. He threw his arm over the sill, felt the glass snagging at the soft upper flesh. He dragged himself up, pulled his torso through, struggled into the dark on the other side. The glass was clawing at him, snagging his shirt, his flesh. He felt the hot blood on his arms, on his belly. The bell shrieked and shrieked at him.

And then he was through. Tumbling headfirst into the blackness. Hitting the floor blind, his hands out in front of him, his feet dropping in after. His body ached and bled. The pain in his knee screwed deeper into him. He lay on the floor, the red flashes bursting before his eyes, the sound of his heart drowning out everything.

And then the bell again. The bell rose through it, over his heart. He had to move. The bell screamed it at him. He had to get up, get out, move now before they came.

He reached up into the blackness. Felt something—a countertop. He took hold of it. Grunting, he hauled himself to his feet. He clutched his side, felt the damp blood through his shirt. Tilted over toward the pain, he staggered forward, one hand on his belly, one hand stretched out, feeling his way.

He stumbled through the room. Touched one wall, moved away from it. Bumped into an equipment tray and heard it rattle as it rolled back. He felt his way through a door, into a hallway. Squinting against his scintillating vision, he saw the door—the light from the outside hall etching the rectangle of the door. He hobbled toward it, reached out for it.

The bell kept hammering at him. Conrad neared the door. And now, under the sound of the bell, he heard other sounds. A bass voice, calling out. A jingle of keys. The doorknob rattling.

He halted, staring. Someone was there, coming. A doorman probably. A maintenance man. Not the police, not yet. But someone . . .

The door cracked open. A shaft of light dropped into the hall before him.

Conrad threw himself back, pinned himself back against the wall. The shaft of light got wider and wider. It spread like a yellow stain down the wall in front of him, down over the floor, out across the floor toward his feet.

The door opened wider and Conrad saw the shadow of a man.

He was a big man. Tall, square shouldered. A black man in a purple doorman's uniform.

Aching, bleeding, Conrad pressed tight to the wall as the doorman peered cautiously into the hall. The doorman pushed the door open a little farther. The stain of light spread toward Conrad's feet, stopped an inch from the toes of his shoes. The alarm bell blasted the shadows. The doorman stepped into the hall.

Conrad saw his dim silhouette as he slowly moved forward. He saw him running his hands along the opposite wall, looking for the light switch. Another step and the doorman loomed directly in front of him. If Conrad had breathed out, the doorman would've felt it on his cheek.

Then the doorman took another step and went past him. Under the constant bell, Conrad heard him say, "Here it is."

Conrad bolted. He ran for the door. The doorman flicked the switch and the office lights went on. But by then, Conrad was out the door, rounding the corner, half running, half staggering down the outer hall. Behind him, the bell kept ringing and ringing. The doorman never even turned around. He never even saw him go.

He was a wild figure; his hair wild, his eyes wild. His orange shirt was stained at the sleeves with blood. His hands were running with blood. Blood was dripping off the tips of his fingers. He came around the corner into the lobby at that hopping, staggered pace. It was a broad lobby. Mirrors on the walls. A chandelier hanging from a high ceiling. The front door, a revolving door, was to his left. He limped toward it.

"Hey!"

He looked around. On the wall far to his right were two elevators with golden doors. One of those doors had just slid back. A man had just burst from the car and was running toward him. He was a small, stocky Hispanic man in khaki, his round belly stretching his shirt buttons. The maintenance man.

"Hey!" he said again, pointing at Conrad.

Conrad stopped where he was. "Quick," he said. He pointed back down the hall whence he'd come. "In the office right next to mine. Quick. Hurry. The doorman . . ."

The man's eyes narrowed with determination. He swerved in his course, raced bravely away from Conrad, down the hall.

Conrad limped to the revolving door. Shouldered it around. Tumbled out onto the sidewalk and stood there unsteadily, dazed and blinking in the night mist.

He was on Eighty-third Street. Central Park West was to his right. That was where they were, he thought. The kidnappers. They were watching the exit to his building around the corner. They would not be watching this street, this door. They would not, he told himself.

He panted hard. Every breath made his abdomen sting. He put his hand to the bloody place. He groaned at the pain there, at the pain in his knee.

Let them not be, he thought. Please. Please. Let them not be watching.

He turned away, toward Columbus Avenue. He cried out once in pain as he began to run.

In the Nursery

By the time the police brought in their prisoner, Aggie and Elizabeth were in the nursery.

"The stars," Elizabeth was saying. "Did you paint the stars?"

The two women were alone in Jessica's room. The policemen were all in the living room outside. Elizabeth was gazing up at the ceiling, her lips parted.

"Did you paint the stars?" she asked again.

Aggie only nodded. She found it hard to talk about Jessie's stars. "Yes," she finally managed to say.

"They're so beautiful," said Elizabeth.

"Thank . . ." But Aggie couldn't finish.

Elizabeth lowered her eyes to the older woman. Hesitantly, she raised her hand, touched Aggie's shoulder. Then, quickly, she dropped her hand to her side.

"It will be all right," she said, looking down. "She'll come back. I know it."

Aggie nodded, tried to smile.

Elizabeth turned away. With one slow sweeping look, she took in the whole room. The stars on the ceiling, the rainbow on the sky-blue wall, the crystal palace painted there among drifting clouds. "Really she will," she added helpfully. "She has such a beautiful room."

Elizabeth was wearing one of Aggie's old dresses now. The police technicians had taken her other one, the bloody one. They had taken it away in a plastic bag. They had also scraped flakes of blood off Elizabeth's cheeks and dug under her fingernails for other samples. They had done this in the bedroom while D'Annunzio and Special Agent Calvin asked her questions.

Aggie had been there too. Elizabeth had asked her to stay there with her. Aggie had sat on the bed next to Elizabeth and held her hand. She had listened to Elizabeth's story about the man in the car with the knife. She had listened and she had thought: *My God, she killed him. Is that what she's saying? Yes, she killed him. With her hands . . .*

She had stopped patting the girl's thin hand then. She had simply stared down at it. She had stared down at it and an image of her little girl's face had risen before her: Jessie, with her small lips trembling, her blue eyes frightened and bewildered.

Aggie had swallowed hard, fighting down the nausea, staring at Elizabeth's hand.

Aggie had made the policemen leave the room before Elizabeth took her dress off. Then she'd handed the dress to one of them through the door. She had picked an old dress out of her closet, a flower print on a cream background. Elizabeth had had to pull the belt tight, and the hem ended above her knees, but it fit well enough.

Then Aggie had taken the girl into the bathroom. She sat her on the toilet and cleaned her face with a washcloth. She worked around the cheeks and eyes, stroked the blood away gently while Elizabeth gazed up at her. Aggie thought about washing Jessica's face. Jessica would never stop talking and asking questions: "What am I doing today? Will Daddy be home before I go to bed? Can I watch TV after school?" Sometimes Aggie would lose her patience: "Jess-i-ca! How can I clean your face if you keep moving it around like that?" Jessica would giggle, which only made things worse.

But Elizabeth Burrows did not talk or move as Aggie cleaned her face. She sat very still, her back straight, her hands folded on her lap. And she gazed up at Aggie. She gazed up at her steadily with big green eyes and parted lips. Aggie wanted to say, "Stop that." But she didn't. And Elizabeth gazed and gazed.

When Aggie was done, she put the washcloth in the sink. Elizabeth kept looking at her, her head tilted slightly to one side.

Aggie could see now how beautiful she was. Like someone in a painting. Like Botticelli's Venus. God, Aggie caught herself thinking, what she would have been if only . . . She stood at the sink and looked down at Elizabeth. Elizabeth, her head tilted, gazed up at her.

She must have just torn that man apart with her bare hands, Aggie thought.

"Let's go back in the bedroom," she said gently.

"No . . ." Elizabeth blinked, as if Aggie's voice had awakened her. "I mean . . . I mean . . . Could I see her room?"

"Her . . . ?"

"Your daughter's."

Now she stood next to Jessica's loft bed, gazing with that same stupid wonder up at the painted stars, the crystal palace, the painted rainbow, and the clouds. She wandered dreamily away from Aggie. Over to Jessica's toyshelf in the far corner. She touched a little music box there, a tiny carousel. She touched the horses on it, the cloth flags waving from their golden poles.

Aggie watched her. She saw her smile down at the painted horses. Through the walls, she could hear the low murmur of the men talking.

"I thought about this room," Elizabeth said suddenly. "Your daughter's room. I wanted to come here."

"Did you?" said Aggie. She shivered a little. The thought of this woman, this madwoman, sitting in a madhouse, thinking of her daughter's room . . .

Jesus, Nathan! Do you just tell them all about us?

"Yes," said Elizabeth. "After the man . . . there was the man with the knife and then . . . then the policemen. They found me with him when he was . . . After he was dead, you know, because of the Secret Friend and . . . And the policemen put me in their car and I told them, I said, 'You've got to help Dr. Conrad. You've got to help him.' And I kept saying that, and they called in on their radio, and they said they would bring me here and I . . . I was afraid. I was afraid but I thought . . . I thought, 'Now I'll see her room.' That's what I told myself so I wouldn't be afraid. 'Now I'll see what her room is like.' I kept telling myself that."

Aggie offered her a kind smile as she fought down another shiver. "I understand," she said.

"And then I . . . ," Elizabeth began. And then she stopped. "Oh," she said, breathing it out on a long sigh. "Look." Her eyes were bright now, her lips parted and turned up gently. She was looking into Jessica's closet. "Look. She has so many . . . You know . . ." She moved her hands in front of her. "Animals. Toys and animals."

"She calls them her friends," Aggie said. And her voice became hoarse again.

"Friends," Elizabeth repeated. "They're so sweet." She stepped into the closet.

Aggie hesitated. She did not think she could go into the closet again. When she did step toward it, she felt leaden; in her throat, in her chest, in her stomach. Thick and heavy.

She came to the closet door and looked in.

Elizabeth was in there with the animals. She was on her knees and they surrounded her. The alligators and the martians; Goofy and Miss Piggy and Kermit the Frog.

But of course, she was holding White Snow, the old teddy bear. Holding it against her breast, her arms wrapped around it.

Christ, thought Aggie, blinking her tears back. She would pick him.

Hugging the teddy bear, Elizabeth looked up at her. "I'm going to disappear," she said softly. Her voice sounded oddly unclouded, oddly strong. "Did Dr. Conrad tell you that?"

"No," Aggie managed to say. "No. Of course not."

"Well, it's true," said Elizabeth sadly. "I know it is." She rocked White Snow in her arms. "It's like, I'll be in here, stuck in here. With all these friends. And . . . the friends will be talking in here and I'll . . . have to listen to them. I'll have to listen to them and then slowly, slowly . . . I'll just be gone." She raised her eyes to Aggie. Aggie saw how deep they were, how clear. "I've seen them like that, you know. The ones who've disappeared. In the hospitals. They sit there. They stare into space. They stare at the wall." She shuddered. "You can almost see, you can almost look into their eyes and see it. It's like a funeral: the room in-side is full of all the person's friends, but the person himself isn't there anymore. Only the friends are in there, talking and living inside. But the person is just . . . gone." She smiled slightly, snuggling against the teddy bear. "It's worse than a funeral," she said. "I think it must be worse than dying."

"Don't say that." Aggie stepped toward her.

Elizabeth clutched the bear tightly, rubbed her cheek against it. Her eyes swam and her lips grew thick and she blurted out, "This is such a nice room! I wish I had a room like this one!"

"Oh, hell," said Aggie. There were tears in her eyes too. She stepped forward, reaching down toward the girl, reaching down to touch her cheek.

But that was when they brought in the prisoner.

The two women could hear him the moment he came through the front door. He was screaming.

"Fuck you people! Fuck *you* people! This is so fucking illegal. This is so fucking incredibly illegal. You assholes. You think this isn't illegal? You think you can just get away with this? You guys are in for the big surprise-a-roo. Motherfuckers! Assholes! You didn't read me my ri-ights," he sang out. "You guys are about to get your fat blue asses in a big sli-ing. Hey. Hey! Get your fucking hands off me. Brutality! Fucking brutality. Get the *fuck* off me."

"Oh, Jesus," Aggie whispered.

Then she was running out of the nursery. Around the corner of the hall. Into the living room. Into the crowd of men in ties and men in uniform. The men parted to form a corridor to the door. And Aggie looked down the corridor of men and saw the prisoner.

It was the man who had pretended to be Detective D'Annunzio. He was pinned between two patrolmen. They were holding him by his elbows. His hands were secured—handcuffed, she saw as he twisted this way and that—behind his back. His brown hair flopped and tossed as he struggled in the patrolmen's grip. His eyes were bright and he was smiling so that his white teeth flashed in the toplight. He laughed wildly. His voice cracked as he spoke.

"You guys are soooo fucked. You are so fucked you don't even begin to know the meaning of the word *fucked*. They are going to have your pictures next to *fucked* in the fucking dictionary, dickheads. Assholes. Nobody even read me my rights, nobody said a fucking thing to me, they just . . ."

And then, before Aggie knew what was happening, she was on him. She was clutching at his jacket, pulling at it, clinging to his neck, his hair. The tears were pouring down her cheeks; they were hot, they were burning into her skin. Her voice was a hoarse wail. She hardly recog-

265

nized it. She hardly realized she was screaming into the man's startled face:

"Where is she? Please, please, tell me where my baby is! Oh, please, Jesus, you've got to tell me where she is, please, please, I swear, I'll do anything . . ."

Vaguely, she felt the hands grabbing at her, prying at the arms she'd thrown around the prisoner's neck. Vaguely she heard the deep voices shouting, "Mrs. Conrad!" And she felt their strength pulling at her shoulders, at her waist.

But she held on to the prisoner. She held on and kept crying, screaming, "Please. Oh, please, in the name of God, in the name of Jesus, please tell me, tell me she's alive, just tell me she's alive. . . ."

And then they had her, the policemen had her, they were pulling her back, pulling her away from him, and he hadn't told, he hadn't told her. Agatha fought against the hands that held her, fought to get back to him.

"Please," she screamed, she wailed it. "Make him tell, oh, Jesus, please make him tell, make him tell me. . . ."

But now they were pulling the prisoner away. Someone was barking out, "Take him in the bedroom." Aggie could hear her own hoarse sobs. They sounded faraway and terrible, as if they belonged to someone else. Held back by the powerful hands of the men, she looked up and saw the prisoner being pulled away toward the hall. He was laughing again, his hair falling into his eyes. He was looking back at her and laughing.

"Hey, sorry, Tits," he called to her. "So sorry, baby, your friends here fucked up. They got the wrong guy here. I don't know nothin' about stealin' babies. All I want is my lawyer, you hear what I'm saying? Why don't you tell your friends: Better get Mr. McIlvaine his lawyer, boys."

Aggie sagged limply in the men's hands. "Please," she said. She sobbed helplessly.

As the man disappeared into the bedroom, she felt herself being released. The policemen lowered her slowly, gently to the floor. She went down on her knees, her head hanging, her hair hanging down around her face.

"Please. Make him tell." She heard herself crying. "Make him tell me where my baby is. Please."

Then, a moment later, she felt warm arms around her, holding her. She

266

felt soft hands in her hair, stroking at her hair. She heard a soft, smoky murmur in her ear.

"It's all right. It's all right, really. It's going to be all right now."

Crying, Aggie rested her head against Elizabeth's breast.

"It's going to be all right now," Elizabeth said again. "Everyone can see him now. Don't you understand? They can *all* see him. Everything is going to be just fine."

222 Houses Street

The subway car was brightly lit. It rattled loudly, rocking back and forth as it headed downtown. There were four people on it. There was a couple murmuring to each other in one front corner: a young black man in a leather jacket, a young white woman with bleached-blond hair. There was a Con Ed worker reading the *News* in a middle seat: a stocky black man in his work overalls, carrying his hard hat resting on his thigh.

And lastly, there was a man huddled alone in a rear corner. His head hung forward. His large bald spot glistened in the fluorescent light. His arms were crossed on his lap, hands clutching forearms as if he were holding himself together. His shirt was torn and there were patches of blood on it. There were pats of blood that had dripped from him onto the linoleum between his feet.

The subway slowed as it came into the Canal Street station. The Con Ed man folded his paper and stood. He carried his hard hat under his arm as he went to the rear door. Holding the metal pole with his free hand, he glanced down at the huddled, bleeding figure.

"You need help there?" he said quietly.

The bleeding man did not look up. He shook his head. The train's dark windows became bright as the subway passed into the station. The yellowed tiles on the station wall went by in a blur, then focused as the train gradually came to a stop.

"You oughta get yourself to a hospital," murmured the Con Ed man.

The man who was bleeding glanced up at him. "I'm all right," he said.

The Con Ed man shrugged and sighed. "Suit yourself."

The train's doors slid open. The Con Ed man stepped out. The doors closed. The train moved forward again, rattling, rocking back and forth.

Conrad raised his head then, looked out the window, trying to spot the Con Ed man. Had he walked on to the exit? Had he stopped at a telephone to call the other kidnappers? Conrad couldn't find him.

Then, for a moment, he saw the Con Ed man standing still on the platform, looking this way and that. But in a moment more, the train shot into the tunnel. The windows went dark. The man was out of sight.

Bent over, hugging himself, Conrad took a painful breath. He stole a glance at the couple in the opposite corner. Flashes of red obscured them. He squinted until his vision cleared. He saw the girl whispering in the young man's ear, stroking his cheek with her finger. The young man was looking straight ahead, smiling to himself.

Conrad bent forward again. "They didn't see me," he whispered. The words were washed away under the roar of the subway. "I got away. Let me get away. Please." He clutched his forearms, rubbing his palms against his sleeves to wipe the blood off. He thought he could still feel bits of glass eating into his flesh.

The subway pulled into the Franklin Street station. Conrad started to work his way to his feet.

Eleven-forty now. No chance anymore, he thought. No chance to get back to the office by midnight. Only one chance to help her: the chance that she would be there, that they were holding her at 222 Houses.

He limped and stumbled down a small street, a small, deserted night street in Tribeca. Long loft buildings hung dark against the mist-gray sky above him. In the distance, a fire flickered up out of a garbage can. He saw the shadows of hunched men crowded around it, holding out their hands for warmth. He felt the chill, the night's damp chill, crawling over his skin.

He limped on, steadily working his leg forward against the barrier of pain. Anything could stop him now, he thought. A Good Samaritan; a cop; a mugger could lay him out in a minute, leave him on the street for dead. He coughed, steadily limping.

Should have waited for them, he thought. Should've done what they said, waited till midnight like they'd told him to. He should've called the police when he'd gotten out. He should've trusted the Con Ed man, asked him to get help. . . . He should've done *something*. . . .

Nice going, shithead.

. . . something instead of this. This last, terrible mistake.

Houses Street. Greenwich and Houses Street. He looked up and there it was. He could hardly remember guiding himself to it. He stood on the corner under a streetlamp. He blinked up at the small sign. He turned his head, looked down the road. Two short, dark blocks. The irregular line of buildings in the mist, no lights in any windows. The highway and the Hudson at the far corner. He could see the cars shooting past down there. He could see the black river sparkling with shore lights. He'd made it.

He started down the street, leaving the streetlamp's glow behind.

He was walking faster now. He grunted with every step. His right knee was locked. His leg was stiff as a board. As the streetlamp fell behind him, the dark of the little street closed over him like a boy's hands closing over a moth. One chance, he thought. He pushed on, dragging his leg. One chance. That she's there. She has to be there. Jessie. The mist was at his side, the dark before him. He kept limping on.

He limped past an empty lot grown high with weeds. It came clear to him out of the mist as he hobbled past it. The weeds were littered with silver soda cans and stone debris and paper flapping on the earth in the chill breeze from the river. He went past it, grunting; went on to the next building, a looming silhouette: a hunkered pile of brown stone that seemed to be pitched forward, as if it might collapse at any minute and shatter to rubble on the street.

He reached it. Stood, panting, in front of it. Squinting up through the night, through the flashes and drifting red clouds before his eyes, he could read the number on the chipped lintel: 222. He raised his eyes a little farther.

"Oh," he said softly.

There was a dim light burning in the second-story window.

She had said that, hadn't she?

The apartment was on the second floor.

Hadn't Elizabeth said that? Yes. Yes, he was sure she had. The apartment was on the second floor. And the red-haired man's face had been at the window. It had been hanging, ghostly, at the window, like a phantom, like her Secret Friend.

But it was not her Secret Friend. It was a man. It was Robert Rostoff, the man whom Sport had killed. And if Robert Rostoff had been peering in through a second-story window then there had to be . . .

"A fire escape," he croaked.

He started limping back toward the empty lot.

Standing at the edge of the lot, he could see the shape of the fire escape zigzagging up the side of the building. He could see it passing underneath the lighted window on the second floor.

One chance, he thought.

He stepped into the weeds. The weeds were about knee-high. He looked down as his feet disappeared into them. He took another step—and the weeds became alive all around him.

He stopped. The weeds rattled and swayed. Rats—he could see them—a dozen rats—were wobbling away from him, weaving into the grass.

Conrad started limping forward again. He traveled slowly. He watched his feet.

Fucking rats, he thought.

He shuddered. He glanced up from his feet at the brownstone for a moment. He stepped on something . . .

Jesus, shit, a snake.

. . . something lying in the weeds. He gasped, jumped back. He looked down—and saw a long, thin shape lying on the earth.

. . . snake . . .

But the shape lay lifeless. He bent down toward it. It was not a snake. It was a broom handle that had been snapped in half. One end of it was rounded, smooth. The other end, the broken end, came to a jagged point.

Conrad reached down and picked up the handle. He weighed it in his hand. He gripped it. He hissed as his fingers closed on it, as the rough wood scraped against his wounded palm.

He started limping again toward the brownstone. Now he was carrying the broom handle.

One chance, he thought.

One chance. Jessica.

The fire escape's ladder was already down. Conrad put his hand on the rung before him. The rusted iron seemed to bite into his flesh. He held on to the broom handle, put his other hand through the rung, braced his wrist against it. That felt better. He hoisted his left foot onto the lowest rung. Brought his right leg up stiffly until his two feet rested together. And that was how he climbed, one rung at a time, first his left foot, then his right dragged up behind it. One chance. One chance.

He climbed up to the first landing, crawled up onto it, panting, the air whistling in and out of him. The cut in his side ached, but he could feel that the bleeding had stopped. Nothing vital damaged, he thought, no chance of bleeding out. Gripping the thin banister, he started up the stairs to the second landing. He raised his eyes to the lighted window. Even that dim light hurt his eyes as he got closer to it. The old red clouds kept bursting and spreading and fading on the surface of his vision. He came up onto the landing by the window.

He pushed his head through the landing hole. Crawled up onto the little grated space there. He crowded himself onto that small space, crouched on all fours, coughing and wheezing. Shaking his head once, he looked up, looked through the window, peered through the filthy pane of glass.

And he saw her.

"Jessica."

She was there. Not twenty feet away from him. She was lying on a mattress on the floor. Lying on her side, her valentines nightgown bunched around her knees. He thought she was dead at first. She was so stiff, so still. He felt everything drop inside him. He stared through the window at her, holding his breath.

Her hands were bound behind her somehow. A strip of white tape was plastered brutally over her mouth. Her hair—her pretty, curling, sandy hair, the same color as her father's—was tangled and matted around her chalky face. Through her hair, her eyes were wide, staring emptily into some section of the room that he couldn't see. And she was so pale, so pale. . . .

Oh, God, he thought. Dead? Had she died like that? Staring like that? Gagged. Terrified.

Waiting for her Daddy.

He raised himself to his knees for a better look. He peered in at her, oblivious to the pain, to everything.

"Baby?" he whispered, barely whispered. "Sweetheart?"

His eyes filled with tears as he looked. His hand shook as he lifted it, as he placed it against the window. He tried to clear the dirt away but the blood from his fingers streaked the glass.

"Jessie . . . ?"

And then his daughter moved.

It was sudden. A sudden, whipping motion, her whole body coming to life at once. Snaking back on the mattress, coiling back and back until she was pressed against the wall. Still snaking back, still trying to retreat farther. Pressed against the wall, sitting up against the wall, kicking at the mattress to try to go farther. And her eyes went even wider still, and tears poured from them. And she shook her head: no, no, no. He saw her mouth moving behind the tape. . . . He could *feel* her screaming.

She was alive. He had to get help. . . . She was still alive. He had to climb down, get the police. Alive. Jessica. She was . . .

And then a shadow passed into the corner of his vision and he saw . . .

"Oh, shit, oh, holy shit, oh, God. My God."

He saw Maxwell, moving toward her.

Lewis McIlvaine and His Constitutional Rights

"Now, Mr. McIlvaine . . . Lewis . . . things can go easy for you, or they can go very hard," said Special Agent Calvin. "Do we understand each other?"

The prisoner, whose name was Lewis McIlvaine, was sitting on the bed. His hands were still cuffed behind his back. He was looking up at Special Agent Calvin. He was nodding.

"Good," Special Agent Calvin said. He was standing in front of McIlvaine, leaning down toward him, pointing at him with his sharply chiseled chin. "I want you to tell me now," he went on. "Just exactly what you've done with the little Conrad girl?"

Lewis McIlvaine continued nodding. He smiled. He said quietly, "Special Agent Calvin. Special Agent, that is to say, Asshole. For the hundredth time, I would like to talk to my lawyer, please. I am not going to say anything to anyone until I talk to my lawyer. And when I do talk to my lawyer, what I am going to say is, 'Oh, Mr. Lawyer, please bring me the testicles of Special Agent Calvin on a tray, so that I may eat them.' You dig?"

Detective D'Annunzio sighed heavily. He was leaning against the bedroom wall, leaning on his hands, bouncing his expansive ass against his knuckles. He yanked one of his hands—his left hand—out from under himself. He glanced at his watch. It was eleven forty-five. D'Annunzio

274

looked up again and watched Calvin hovering over the suspect. Calvin looked lean and intense in his tailored black suit.

D'Annunzio watched him and thought about Mrs. Conrad. He thought about her soft, smart, tearful blue eyes. He thought about the shape of her breasts under her sweatshirt. When she had hugged him—when he had first come in and she had fallen into his arms—he had felt those large breasts pressed against him. This Dr. Conrad, he thought with an interior groan; this is one very lucky man. What must it be like to have a woman like that under you? A sensitive, intelligent woman like that, screaming and thrashing under you, with those breasts naked?

"Lewis," Calvin was saying. "Lewis, I'm sure you realize that time is of the essence here. If anything should happen to that little girl, no lawyer on earth is going to be able to help you, do you understand me? Now don't you think you'd feel better if you got this off your chest?"

McIlvaine sniffed the air. "Did someone fart in here?" He turned to D'Annunzio. "Hey, you. Fatso. You cut the mustard? What is this, some kind of interrogation technique?"

Special Agent Calvin rolled his eyes. Slowly, shaking his head, he strolled over to where D'Annunzio was leaning on the wall. He spoke softly, out of the side of his mouth, so McIlvaine wouldn't hear him.

"I think we should bring Mrs. Conrad in here," he said.

"What?" D'Annunzio blinked out of his fantasy. "Uh . . . I mean, what for?"

"Well, to *appeal* to him," Calvin whispered. "To make a personal appeal."

D'Annunzio stared at the FBI man. He didn't know what to say.

Special Agent Calvin nodded confidentially. "Go on," he said. "Go ahead. Bring her in."

Mrs. Conrad was in the living room. She was still kneeling on the floor, looking forlorn. Elizabeth was kneeling next to her, touching her shoulder. When D'Annunzio came waddling in, Mrs. Conrad looked up at him. She looked up at him with hopeful, trusting eyes. It made the flesh under D'Annunzio's collar prickle.

"Did he tell?" she asked. There were still tears in her voice. Her voice trembled. "Has he told you anything?"

D'Annunzio took a deep breath. "No, ma'am," he said. "Special Agent Calvin thinks it might be helpful if you came in and talked to him again. Sort of made an appeal." It sounded stupid when he said it too.

275

But the woman nodded uncertainly. Trustingly. D'Annunzio's eyes automatically flicked down over her sweatshirt. What must it be like, he thought; a woman like that.

He reached down and took hold of the woman's upper arm. He felt the ample flesh under his fingers as he helped her to her feet.

When D'Annunzio brought Mrs. Conrad into the room, the prisoner looked up at her from the bed. He grinned.

"Hey there, ho there, Tits," he said. "Howya doin'? You know, I wouldn't come in here if I were you. Fatso over there's been farting the place up but good."

D'Annunzio felt his face get hot. He quickly handed Mrs. Conrad's elbow to Special Agent Calvin. He walked back to the wall and leaned against it again. From the wall, he looked at McIlvaine: at his merry eyes; at his white smile.

D'Annunzio watched as Special Agent Calvin led Mrs. Conrad closer to McIlvaine.

"Now, Lewis," Special Agent Calvin said softly. "This is the mother of the little girl we're talking about. I just want you to listen to what she has to say, all right?"

Lewis McIlvaine gave her a big silly grin.

Mrs. Conrad looked down at him a second without speaking. She was obviously trying hard not to cry. McIlvaine kept grinning, bouncing on the bed like a toy monkey.

D'Annunzio looked down at his feet. Jesus Christ, he thought.

"Please, Mr. McIlvaine," the woman said then. Her voice shook badly. "Please. If you'll tell us where my daughter is, I swear . . . I'll do anything. . . . I'm sure I could talk to your judge or . . . or testify at your trial. . . . If you could just . . ."

McIlvaine let out a high-pitched laugh. He rolled back on the bed with glee. "Sweetie pie—Titskies—there's not going to be a trial," he said. "Aren't you listening here, honeypot? They *fucked up*. See? They haven't read me my rights. They haven't let me call my lawyer. Sweetie darling . . . I'm going free, I'm walking away from this."

Mrs. Conrad looked down. She couldn't continue. Special Agent Calvin glared at McIlvaine very sternly indeed.

Breathing hard, Detective D'Annunzio moved away from the wall. Humphing loudly, he walked over to the bed. He felt the gas twisting in his stomach but he held it in. He did not want to pass one next to Mrs. Conrad.

"Detective?" said Special Agent Calvin.

"I am going to read the prisoner his rights," said Detective D'Annunzio. He glanced quickly at Mrs. Conrad. She was looking up at him. A single tear was rolling down her cheek.

D'Annunzio turned to McIlvaine. He reached down and took hold of McIlvaine's arm. With a quick, rough jerk, he hauled the prisoner to his feet.

"Detective . . . ," warned Special Agent Calvin.

McIlvaine grinned uncomfortably. "Careful now, Mr. Blubber Guy," he said. "You don't want to get in any more trouble than you're in already, do you? Just my rights, if you please."

D'Annunzio nodded for a long moment. "You have the right to bend over double and say 'oof,'" he said.

McIlvaine laughed. "What the fu . . . ?"

D'Annunzio pulled his hand back, then drove it forward, shooting his stiffened fingers into McIlvaine's solar plexus.

McIlvaine bent over double. "Oof," he said.

"Detective!" Special Agent Calvin said. "Detective . . ."

McIlvaine was bent over so far that D'Annunzio could see the handcuffs behind his back.

"You have the right to fall to the floor like a sack of potatoes," D'Annunzio said.

He raised his fist over his head and quickly brought it down like a hammer. It hit McIlvaine square on the back of the neck. McIlvaine dropped to the floor like a sack of potatoes. His legs seemed to just turn to spaghetti under him, and slam, down he went.

"Detective!" Special Agent Calvin cried out. His voice cracked as he said it. "Detective! Detective!"

Detective D'Annunzio reached around to the small of his back. His service piece was there in its holster. He drew it out. It seemed very small in his pudgy hand.

"Detective! My . . . Oh . . . Detective!" cried Special Agent Calvin.

At Calvin's cry, McIlvaine looked up. Lying there on the floor, he turned his head and peered woozily at D'Annunzio. His face had gone gray and his lips were snowy white. His eyes were moving strangely, as if they'd come loose in his head.

Then he saw the gun. His eyes stopped moving. They went wide. They stared into the gun's muzzle.

"That's enough!" said Special Agent Calvin. He stepped toward D'Annunzio.

But in another second, Mrs. Conrad was between them. She was standing between Calvin and D'Annunzio. She had her hands up on Calvin's shoulders. She was grabbing the lapels of his black suit.

"No!" she said.

The young agent looked down at her. His mouth moved as if he would say something. He did not say anything.

"No," Mrs. Conrad said again very clearly. "No."

She turned and looked over her shoulder at D'Annunzio.

And D'Annunzio looked into those eyes of hers. Blue and tearful, wide and deep. He smiled a little.

Then, as Special Agent Calvin stared, D'Annunzio knelt down next to McIlvaine, his gun in his big paw.

This kneeling down thing: it wasn't easy. He had to tug his pants up on his stubby legs. He had to lower himself carefully. He breathed hard with the effort. But finally, he was kneeling on the floor in front of McIlvaine. McIlvaine kept gaping at him, gaping at his revolver.

D'Annunzio pressed the barrel of the piece against McIlvaine's left knee.

"You have the right to scream in unbearable agony," he said. "And then writhe around the floor and whimper."

He pulled back the gun's hammer.

"Two twenty-two Houses Street," McIlvaine said. He spoke in a dull voice that seemed to rise up, echoing, from the bottom of him. "Two twenty-two Houses."

It was now five minutes before midnight.

Maxwell

At just that moment, the little girl finally woke up.

Maxwell sat in the canvas chair and watched her.

First, her eyelids lifted, but her eyes were white. She made snorting noises. Her body stiffened again. Maxwell licked his lips. He leaned forward in the chair, waiting to see what would happen.

Finally, though, the child's eyelids had fluttered closed, then open. Her blue eyes had reappeared, staring out at nothing.

Maxwell smiled.

He shifted in his chair, braced himself to stand up. But in a moment, the little girl went under again. Her eyes rolled up again so that only the whites showed. Her eyelids fluttered down over them.

Maxwell lowered himself into his chair and waited. He had his hands still braced on the chair arms. He had to work to swallow. His throat was tight with the suspense.

The child opened her eyes. She stared at nothing. This time, Maxwell waited. A minute. Maybe two. A long time, it seemed to him. The girl's eyes shifted. She stared at Maxwell. She stared at him but she didn't move or react. She seemed, Maxwell thought, to be looking right through him.

So Maxwell waited. Just to make sure. Just to give her a chance to come all the way around. The man and the girl stared at each other across the gloomy little room. The air was thick around them and smelled of dust.

The little girl took a deep breath through her nose. Then another. She did not close her eyes. She lay on the mattress and stared at him dully. After another minute or so, Maxwell nodded to himself. She was definitely awake now. He stood up.

Uh-oh, she didn't like that, he thought.

The moment he stood up, she just went crazy. Thrashing around on the mattress. Kicking her little legs at him. Backing away, up against the wall, making muffled noises under the tape: Uh, uh, uh.

Maxwell was startled at first—just by the suddenness of it. But then it was good. His penis stirred again and hardened. He began lumbering toward her.

The girl cried out again behind her gag. She kicked her naked legs. Her nightgown rode up around her thighs. Maxwell could see her thing, her crack. It made his breath rasp in his throat. He touched his cock through his pants.

He lowered himself to the mattress. He sat next to the girl. Tears were pouring down her cheeks. Her round baby cheeks.

Maxwell reached out and grabbed one of her kicking legs. He wrapped his hand around her soft calf. He felt the warmth of it. He dragged her toward him.

"Mmp, nmp . . . ," the child said behind the tape. Her chest heaved. The tears kept streaming down her cheeks.

Holding on to her leg with one hand, Maxwell took hold of the tape on her mouth with the other.

"It's all right," he cooed to her in his dull voice. "It's all right."

With one quick motion, he tore the tape off her mouth. The girl sucked in the air greedily. She coughed. She twisted away from Maxwell on the bed and made harsh retching noises.

His fingers massaged her calf as he watched her. His eyes were bright.

After a moment, the girl's retching subsided. She turned and looked up at Maxwell. She was crying hard now. A sickly red had risen to her cheeks under the black bruises. She kept shaking her head—no—her sandy hair whipping back and forth. Her whole body shivered with crying. Maxwell watched her shivering with his bright eyes.

"Please . . . ?" the girl managed to whisper.

Maxwell let out a low moan. He released her leg. He touched his cock with one hand. He reached out and put his other hand around the girl's throat. He felt her pulse. It seemed to beat right into his hand, right up his arm, right into his own heart. He sucked in a breath.

The window behind him shattered.

Maxwell swung around where he sat. A voice went off in his head like a siren.

Police. Police. They're going to jail I shouldn't have don't wanna police jail . . .

The window burst in at him in a sparkling spray. The body of a man came hurtling through it. The glass, the man, seemed to explode into the room and then hang there a second before Max's terrified eyes.

Then the glass rained down upon the floor. And the man fell.

He fell with a thud. He lay on the floor. He did not move. His shirt was covered with blood. Glass sparkled on it. It glittered in his thin, sandy hair.

Police, po . . . isn't prison is it shouldn't have?

The voice in Maxwell's head was starting to grow fainter. It was starting to subside.

Slowly, painfully, the man on the floor shifted. He was just a little man, Maxwell saw now. He glanced up at the window. There was no one else there with him. It was just him, just this little man.

The little man raised his head off the floor and looked at Maxwell.

Wait a minute, that's, it's that, what's his, that guy, the guy . . .

He heard a noise behind him. He turned and looked at the little girl.

She had rolled onto her side. She was looking at the man on the floor. She was gazing at him dreamily. Her lips were parted. Tears kept streaming down her cheeks, but she was no longer sobbing. She licked her lips. She shook her head as if she could not believe what she was seeing.

And then, as Maxwell watched, she smiled weakly.

"Daddy?" she whispered.

Maxwell turned around again. He looked down at the little man lying on the floor. The little man was staring up at him. His legs and hands were moving around in the broken glass. He looked like a baby trying to crawl.

Maxwell laughed heavily at that, his shoulders moving up and down.

Then he began to stand.

Midnight

Oh, God, thought Conrad, it's standing up.

Frantically, he moved his hands through the litter of glass around him. *Broomstick . . .*

He had lost his weapon, his broom handle, in the fall. He moved his hands back and forth, looking for it. He peered up through the spangles and blotches that burst and played upon his vision. This thing, this creature, was rising off the mattress like a pillar of smoke: up and up, the shadow of him climbing the wall.

"Shit," Conrad whispered.

Forget the broom handle.

He had to get up.

Get up now!

His leg burned with pain as he bent it toward him, as he tried to rise onto his hands and knees.

Oh, Christ, he thought wildly, after this, no more windows.

Letting out a groan, he got his knees under him. He pushed up off his hands.

"Daddy!"

At his daughter's hoarse cry, he raised his eyes again. The thing was towering over him, the black pillar of him blotting out the dim light. It stepped toward him.

Conrad got his left foot on the ground, pushed off his knee. He started to wobble upright.

And then the creature grabbed him around the throat.

Conrad had not seen the body of Billy Price. He had not seen the way Price's neck had been flattened as if in a steam press. If he had, maybe he wouldn't have been shocked by the inhuman, the machinelike, pressure that began to strangle him. A black suffocating cowl dropped over him with such suddenness that his limbs were going slack, his bowels loosening even before he fully understood what had happened.

"Daddy Daddydaddy Daddydaddy . . ."

Jessica's hysterical shriek pierced his brain like a dagger—but only for a moment. Then it seemed to fade into a vast silence that was bleeding in toward him from the edges of the room. Everything seemed to be fading into that silence, into the darkness that crept in with it. Everything—except the weirdly small, blocky face of the animal that had him. That face—it filled Conrad's vision as Maxwell lifted him off the ground, as Conrad's legs dangled and kicked in the empty air. There was nothing but silence and darkness gathering in on him—and that face, bright at the center of the closing aperture: that face with its thick, dreamy smile, its heavy brow, its deep bright eyes . . .

. . . *bright eyes* . . .

Conrad lifted one of his rubbery arms. It jerked up into the air like the arm of a marionette. He struck out at one of those eyes with it. Two of his fingers found the mark.

"Ow!" said Maxwell.

His hand opened. Conrad spilled out of it to the floor.

The psychiatrist tried to stay on his feet. But he couldn't find his feet. His feet, the floor, the world—he couldn't find any of it. That silence, that darkness still closed in on him as he wobbled there. Then a single sound crashed in to him.

"Daddydaddydaddynononononono . . ."

Jessie . . . ? Baby . . . ? Baby . . . ?

He saw her there, bound on the mattress. He saw her in the glare of the bare bulb in the corner. He saw her through the red clouds drifting and exploding. And then she was gone.

She was blotted out. Everything before him was blotted out as this giant man, this creature, lumbered in front of him again.

Maxwell was holding his eye in one hand. He was frowning severely with his thick lips.

"That hurt," he said. And he struck Conrad down.

It was a single wild blow, thrown out in rage. Maxwell's anvil-heavy hand slammed into Conrad's face full force. Conrad's head snapped back. He went flying backwards, his arms pinwheeling in the air.

"Daddydaddy . . . Ohnoohnodon'thurtmydaddy . . ."

Conrad heard his daughter's scream become a wild, inarticulate wail. Then he slammed into the wall. The air rushed out of him. Something swelled up inside his head: he felt the thing would burst out through his eyes.

"Daddyhelpmydaddydaddypleasepleaseplease . . ."

Jess . . .

There was a roar. An animal's roar. As Conrad, stupefied by the blow, looked on, Maxwell stamped across the room at him. The hulking beast moved with uncanny quickness. Before Conrad could even push himself upright, before he could clear his head, it was on him.

"Fucker!" Maxwell shouted.

He clubbed Conrad with his fists. Swung them like mallets from either side. The first blow knocked Conrad over. Before he could tumble to the ground the second caught him in the face. He felt his jaw crack. He felt his nose burst. He tasted a gush of thick blood. The fists hammered down on top of him as he crumpled to the floor.

"*Aaaaaaaah . . .*" The five-year-old girl kept screaming wordlessly from the mattress. Again, the scream faded from Conrad's consciousness. Consciousness itself began to fade. Vaguely, through fog, through a dream of fog, he saw the massive figure of the beast lumbering away from him.

Jessica kept shrieking.

Baby . . . , Conrad thought weakly.

"Shut the *fuck up!*" Maxwell roared.

And he stomped across the room to get her.

Stairs

D'Annunzio grabbed McIlvaine by the lapels. He dragged him off the floor to his feet. McIlvaine's legs were rubbery under him. D'Annunzio held him upright. He jutted his leathery face close to the prisoner's.

"There are rooms on Rikers Island that no lawyer's ever seen," he growled into McIlvaine's eyes. "*I've* seen them. I'll see *you* in them if you lie to me now."

"Two twenty-two Houses," McIlvaine repeated quickly. "I swear. The second floor. He's gonna kill her. He's crazy. He's gonna kill her."

"Oh, God," Aggie Conrad cried out.

D'Annunzio looked at Special Agent Calvin. "Let's go," he said.

The fat detective burst into the living room shouting.

"We need units at two twenty-two Houses Street in Tribeca. Tell 'em to use caution, we got a possible hostage situation on the second floor and the bad guy's armed and dangerous." He glanced at a patrolman as he went past. He pointed back at the bedroom. "Bring the skell so I can blow his nuts off if he lied."

"Right," the patrolman said.

Yes, thought D'Annunzio. Yes. He felt good. Like a train. Like a steamroller. Going to get the man. Yessir. He could feel Aggie Conrad behind him. He could feel her tagging after him like a lost puppy.

He glanced back, and sure enough, there she was. Rushing along behind him, her tits bouncing under that sweatshirt. This was great.

"You can come with me," he said.

She nodded and kept following.

D'Annunzio marched down the hallway swiftly, his head erect, his belly out before him. He huffed and wheezed in time to his step. Behind him came a small parade of people. Aggie Conrad followed him. Elizabeth Burrows followed her. Special Agent Calvin was trying to catch up with all of them. And the patrolman, doing his best to tag up, was dragging Lewis McIlvaine along.

D'Annunzio marched in the lead proudly. He was panting as hard as if he were tugging the others on a rope.

He reached the elevators. Both doors were closed. The police had commandeered one of them but some tech had just taken it downstairs. D'Annunzio stopped. He cursed. He was about to reach out and push the call button.

But he felt Mrs. Conrad's eyes on him. He cleared his throat.

"Okay," he barked breathlessly. "We'll have to take the stairs."

Jesus Christ, he thought.

And he led the way to the stairway door.

The Broom Handle

"Daddydaddydaddydaddyaaaaaaaaah . . ." That long, mindless wail broke into Conrad's darkness.

. . . baby . . . ?

The wail seemed to go on and on endlessly, breathlessly. Conrad could not tell whether it was coming from the outside world or from somewhere inside him. He pushed himself off the floor. He peered through a dim, shifting corridor of vision.

. . . baby . . .

He saw the hulking bear of a man starting to kneel down on the floor beside his daughter. He saw his daughter . . .

Oh . . . oh . . . oh . . . my baby . . .

The child was backed up against the wall, frozen against the wall. Her face was scarlet. Her mouth was wide open as she bawled and bawled. . . .

Conrad blinked away the red clouds and black fog for a moment. And in that moment, he saw the broom handle.

It was lying on the floor. The thin, dark shape of it. It was lying amid a sparkling pile of glass. It was not far from him. He could get there, he could reach it.

"Shut *up!* Shut the fuck *up!*" he heard Maxwell shout.

Conrad began to drag himself across the floor.

He pulled himself with his hands. He tried to push with his legs too. The electric pain in his knee shot up his thigh, into his crotch, into his balls. The pain jolted him awake, and as he came around, he became aware again of his broken jaw, the searing agony: it ballooned inside his head. His head felt as if it were all one raw and open nerve. He was aware suddenly of blood spilling from his open mouth, running down his chin. Of glass cutting into his belly. Of the wound in his side opening again, bleeding again. He dragged himself forward. And he reached out. . . .

And he had it. His hand closed around the raw, splintery wood.

Have to get up . . . have to . . .

"Come here!" Maxwell was shouting angrily. He snatched at Jessica's leg. He grabbed hold of her ankle. He dragged her toward him.

"Pleeeeeease," she howled.

Conrad got up.

In a single excruciating motion, he pushed to one knee and launched himself. He stumbled toward Maxwell, the broom handle gripped in his hand.

Maxwell was only half turned away. He caught Conrad's movement in the corner of his eye. He let Jessica go and spun around. He rocketed to his feet. . . . Christ, it was like a demon shooting up out of the earth. Before Conrad could reach him, the whole massive weight of the man was driving into him full force. The broom handle flew out of Conrad's hands. It clattered to the floor in the far corner. Conrad himself was flung backwards, knocked down hard. He hit the floor like deadweight. And then Maxwell was on top of him, Maxwell was pounding at him, his daughter's wild cries were surrounding him, filling him, there was nothing but those cries and Maxwell's animal roar and Maxwell's fists. . . .

Conrad was hit in the belly. He doubled over, vomit spurting up into his mouth, mixing with the hot blood. Another fist drove into his balls. He curled up on his side. Another blow struck him in the face and then another. He was driven onto his back. He lay there, spread-eagle, limp.

Jessica wailed and wailed without ceasing.

Maxwell roared. He stood up, one fist pounding wildly at the air, the other pounding heavily against his chest. His mouth was contorted with rage, his lips white with froth. His eyes were rolling crazily. He roared and roared over the sound of Jessica's wailing.

"Fucker!" he roared. *"Motherfucker!"*

He kicked Conrad hard in the side. The doctor's body lifted a little, slid a little across the room. But Conrad didn't feel the blow. He did not hear the roaring. He lay on his back in a warm blackness, a deep nothing.

"Shut *up*. Bitch!" Maxwell screamed. He started for the child again.

"No! Please! Mommy! Mommy! Mommy! Pleeeease!" Jessica shrieked.

Conrad lay still on his back, his arms out, his legs spread.

"Pleeeeease . . ."

. . . baby . . .

Ho Sung's
Chow Mein Palace

By the time D'Annunzio reached his old Pontiac, he was gasping for breath. He coughed deeply and thick phlegm rose up in his throat. Aggie Conrad and Elizabeth Burrows were still behind him. The others—Calvin, the patrolman with McIlvaine—had tailed off. They had gotten into other cars, their own cars, to head to the scene.

D'Annunzio unlocked the driver's door first. He squeezed his huge body in behind the wheel. He put the key in the ignition and switched on the engine. Only then did he lean over—grunting loudly as he did—to unlock the passenger side.

Aggie Conrad got into the car beside him. She unlocked the rear door. Elizabeth Burrows got in back. D'Annunzio, meanwhile, was turning up the volume on the police radio under the Pontiac's dash.

He heard Aggie Conrad's door thunk closed.

"All right," he said.

He wrestled the wheel to the right. He heard the back door thud shut also. He hit the gas.

The Pontiac's tires screeched as the big boat screwed out of its parking space. Already, ahead of him, a blue-and-white cruiser was pulling out into the swift Thirty-sixth Street traffic. Its siren whooped, its beacons spun. An official black car—Calvin's—pulled out after it, a red beacon spinning on its dash. Its siren joined the call. D'Annunzio reached under the seat and brought up his own beacon. He stuck it to the dash, hit his siren toggle.

The swiftly moving cabs on the street slowed and pulled to the side. The blue-and-white shot past them, Calvin's black car followed, D'Annunzio's came next. They raced past the Morgan Library, its marble stately against the dark, its spotlights swallowing the red light of the beacons. Then, with a wicked shriek, the Pontiac cornered onto Park. It shot downtown, cutting neatly through the traffic ahead.

D'Annunzio stole a sidelong glance at Aggie Conrad on the seat beside him. She had one arm around herself, the other propped on it, her hand covering her mouth, rubbing her mouth. She stared out through the windshield.

"There should be downtown units almost there," he told her.

She nodded, but she didn't turn. She kept rubbing her mouth.

There was a burst of static from the radio. The fragments of a report.

"Central . . . we don't find any hostage situation in progress at this location, over."

D'Annunzio glanced at Mrs. Conrad. She had turned to stare at the radio now.

Another burst of static. ". . . confirmation . . ."

"Affirmative, Central. . . . Second floor two twenty-two Houston is Ho Sung's Chow Mein Palace. Excellent hot-and-sour soup, Central, but definitely no hostages, over."

With a guttural curse, D'Annunzio reached down and grabbed the microphone. He held it to his mouth, pressed the button, shouted into it.

"Central, you dip, this is D'Annunzio, advise all idiot units that hostage situation is at two twenty-two *Houses* Street. That is negative *Houston*. Two twenty-two Houses Street."

There was a short lull. D'Annunzio glared out through the windshield. The Pontiac was now approaching a red light. The civilian cars ahead were not pulling over. A couple of them were trying to use the police sirens as an excuse to sneak through the intersection. Horns were sounding on the cross street. Brakes were squealing. D'Annunzio maneuvered the wheel with one hand, followed Calvin's black Chevy through a crevice in the bottled traffic. The Pontiac snaked through, sped on.

There was a burst of static from the radio.

"All units be advised of wrong address . . ."

A burst of static. "Uh . . . shit, Central."

291

"We copy, Central . . ."

A burst of static. "Where the hell is Houses Street?"

"Houses Street?"

D'Annunzio replaced the microphone on its hook. He glanced over at Aggie Conrad again.

The woman looked up at him, her lips parted.

"Don't worry . . . ma'am," he said.

Aggie Conrad laughed dismally. She hugged herself even tighter. She shuddered.

Death

Conrad saw nothing, knew nothing. He floated on his back in that black sea. He bobbed and drifted.

It was a place without change, without horizons. There was only the element itself, the plash of the element rising and falling under him, rising and falling within him.

"Mom-my. Mom-my. Mom-my."

The sound of it swelled and fell away and swelled again. It seemed to him almost a part of himself. He was the element in which he floated, the element of a cry:

"Mom-my."

Two heaving syllables, sobbed out of his daughter's chest:

"Mom-my. Mom-my. Mom-my. Mom-my."

. . . *baby* . . .

Conrad could feel the thoughtless terror in that shriek. Feel it rising and falling within him in that cry.

"Mom-my . . ."

He could feel the confusion in it, the last, the dying, confusion. He could feel her wondering wildly what was happening to her. Why? Why wasn't she with her mother, pressed against her mother?

"Maaaamaaaaaa . . ."

. . . *baby* . . . , Conrad thought.

And he got up.

He was not sure at first that that was what he was doing. He felt himself shift somehow in the blackness. He felt an intolerable weight of pain, he felt as if he were trying to lift this intolerable weight of pain with arms made out of paper, with legs made out of sand.

. . . *baby* . . . *baby* . . . *my* . . .

Jessica's wail became a long shriek of terror. "Nooooo. . . ."

And the shabby room was spinning around Conrad. He was on his feet. Tumbling forward on his feet. The room was stretching in and out of focus. And there was Maxwell, growing tall as a building, shrinking to a point of darkness.

"Noooooooooo . . . Mommeeee . . ."

There was Maxwell, down on his hands and knees, crawling toward his daughter. . . . And Jessica was cowering against the wall and Maxwell was moving across the mattress toward her. . . .

Conrad staggered forward. The room pitched and dipped. Bent over, his arms swinging, Conrad stumbled the last few steps across the room. He dropped on top of Maxwell. He threw his arms around Maxwell's neck.

"Fuck!" Maxwell said.

He rose to his feet. Conrad clung to him, his arms thrown weakly around his neck. He rode up into the air on Maxwell's back. The great, roaring creature grabbed at him, swatted at him. Conrad clung to him as he floated above the floor, as the room tilted and spun.

"Fucker! Fucker!" Maxwell screamed.

He reached around and got a purchase on Conrad's neck. He grabbed hold of one of his arms, his left arm. That was all he needed. With a wordless shout, he wrenched the little man off him. He hurled him down to the floor.

Even under the child's wail, even under his own animal snarl, Maxwell heard Conrad's arm snap. Conrad let out a single high-pitched shriek. His body stiffened, then went limp.

Maxwell stood over him. He roared curses down into his face. Flecks of foam flew from his mouth. He tore at his own hair.

"How do you like that? How do you like that, you fuck, you fucker! Now you're dead, now you'll be dead. Huh? Huh?"

His eyes rolled so wildly that for a moment only the whites gleamed under that heavy brow.

And then Maxwell reached down and grabbed Conrad by the throat and squeezed. He grabbed him by the belt buckle and lifted him into the air.

Conrad went up like a doll, his arms dancing in air, his broken arm jouncing in unnatural directions. Maxwell lifted him higher, up to his shoulder. Blood belched from Conrad's mouth in a great gout.

"Now you're dead!" Maxwell roared. And he flung the doctor's small body across the room.

Conrad went through the air like a rag doll. His daughter watched it in wild, stupid fright. She was screaming and screaming. Her father hit the far corner of the wall and dropped to the floor face first. The blood fanned out quickly around his head in a scarlet pool. He lay with his legs bent under him, his left arm splayed at a strange angle.

He did not move again. He saw nothing. He heard nothing. He did not hear his daughter screaming and screaming. He did not hear Maxwell laugh or see him turn away. He did not lift his head as the giant started moving, more calmly now, to the little mattress, to the little girl.

Maxwell knelt down beside her. He grabbed her by her ankle as she screamed and screamed for her mother. He laughed again, breathing hard, as he circled her throat with his one hand. He began to squeeze her. Slowly. Almost tenderly.

Jessica cried out one last time.

A Bum in a Doorway

A bum in a doorway out on Houses Street heard her. That last ragged
shriek: "Mom-my, mom-my. Mommy!" It got under his skin like wriggly
worms. It made him stir in the doorway where he was sleeping.

He lifted his head, looked around him. He shivered and grumbled, "Eh,
shit. Wha' wazzat?"

The bum was a long, thin white man, about forty. He was wearing a
filthy overcoat over filthy rags. He was lying in the doorway across the street
from 222. He had his back propped against one side of it, his feet against
the other. He had been sleeping soundly until the shriek woke him. He
had, in fact, been sleeping off a snootful of very bad bourbon.

He had worked long and hard for that bourbon. Well, not long, but hard
enough, he felt. He had spent the better part of the lunchtime hours
panhandling over on Broadway, in front of Broadway Audio. He had a
theory that people felt guilty whenever they thought about making big
luxury purchases. He believed it made them more charitable.

Today, the strategy had paid off. Between twelve-thirty and two o'clock,
he had made twenty-five bucks in quarters and singles. He closed shop for
the day and rewarded himself for his labors with a full quart of Kentucky
Best whiskey. By rush hour, he was sitting with some friends on a
comfortable bench in the Spring Street subway station arguing over the

296

lyrics to "What Kind of Fool Am I." Shortly after nightfall, he was lying alone at the edge of the platform, puking over the side.

It was late—after ten—before he made his way to this doorway and went to sleep. He had plans to sleep here the rest of the night. He surely did not want to be bothered now.

But Jessica's last scream had awakened him for sure. He sat up. He listened. Had he dreamed it? Of course he had but . . .

But the ugly chill of that sound stayed with him. Under his skin, wriggling, crawling. He cocked his ear again to the city silence: the hiss of traffic, the thrum of underground pipes and wires . . .

And then, from far away at first, there was another scream. Closer, louder. Another scream rising over the steady city throb, taking up where the last one had left off. Closer. Louder until he could hear: it was not a scream. . . .

Sirens, he thought. *Cops. Shit.*

He grabbed hold of the side of the doorway. Grunting and spitting, he pulled himself to his feet.

Cops. Fucking cops.

The first red-and-white beacons came flaring around the corner. The sirens grew louder, bearing down on him. More cars appeared, more beacons, an entire army of whirling lights.

"Ach," the bum said.

He started moving away, hobbling toward the river as fast as he could, his back bent, his legs bowed. He waved his hand at the onrushing cruisers behind him.

"Ach," he muttered again, disgusted. "Whadda fuck izzit to me? Whadda fuck? Whadda fuck izzit?"

Maxwell Again

D'Annunzio's car took the last corner fast. It plunged into a night blown black and scarlet by flashing beacons.

Aggie sat rigid with a premonition of despair. For a moment, she closed her eyes, held her breath. The flashers pulsed behind her eyelids like red clouds. She felt the sirens throbbing in her temples like the heavy pulse that clogged her throat.

The Pontiac screeched to a stop. Aggie opened her eyes. There were police cars scattered over the small street. Cruisers and unmarked sedans with beacons in their windshields. Men were pouring out of them: men in uniform, men in suits and ties. All of them were crouching down. All of them were gripping pistols. All of them had their eyes turned upward toward a single building.

Aggie looked up too. The building stood dark in the marble glow of a police spotlight. It was a brownstone, standing alone beside a vacant lot. Crooked and crumbling, its black windows stared stupidly. Its chipped and rotten stone, its scarred door, its sagging stoop—its aura of decay—gave it the idiot malevolence of a human skull.

Aggie's breath came shuddering out of her.

"Wait here," said D'Annunzio.

He threw open his door. He grunted as he wrestled his way outside.

298

But Aggie waited only a moment. She waited to check the backseat over her shoulder. Elizabeth sat there, dazed, it seemed, and baffled. She was watching the flashing red lights, gazing at them dreamily. When Aggie turned around, Elizabeth blinked and faced her. She smiled—sweetly, distantly.

Aggie tried to smile back. Then she pushed open her own door. She stepped out into the whirling night.

She was shaking. Her legs were weak. She wanted this not to be happening. She wanted that so much. To be home with her family, to be home with her husband and child and this would not be happening . . . To have it be yesterday, just yesterday . . . She kept one hand braced against D'Annunzio's car as she looked over the scene.

The other cars, she saw, were spread irregularly on the pavement before her. A new cruiser had just moved into the crush, and for a moment, the red flash of its spinning beacon blinded her. She raised her hand to her eyes. Under her hand, she saw the shadows of men. They were everywhere, running forward, crouching behind their cars, looking up over their guns.

Aggie did not crouch. She stood by D'Annunzio's car. She looked up from the men to that dead brownstone.

Oh, she thought. *Oh, Jessie . . .*

D'Annunzio's great bulk passed in front of her. He was crouching like the others, as best he could. He moved to the window of the cruiser right in front of her.

"This is it?" he said.

Aggie saw McIlvaine's face come to the cruiser's window. She saw him looking up fearfully at D'Annunzio. He was nodding.

"Yeah, yeah, yeah," he said quickly. "But he's crazy, man, I'm telling you. He might've done her, he might've, no one could've stopped him, I'm telling you."

Now Aggie saw Special Agent Calvin run up beside D'Annunzio. He had a bullhorn in his hand.

"We're gonna call to him," he said sharply. But it was a question really.

D'Annunzio turned to him and nodded. "Yeah," he said. "Try calling to him." He glanced back at McIlvaine. "What's his name?"

"Maxwell. Max Duvall," McIlvaine said.

D'Annunzio glanced at Calvin and nodded: Go ahead.

Calvin nodded nervously. He looked over the cars, over the flashers, up at the brownstone. He raised the bullhorn to his lips.

But before he could speak, the brownstone's door began to open.

No one moved. The cops stood frozen at their positions, their guns raised. Their eyes were bright and unblinking in the flasher light. Their eyes and guns were trained on the brownstone's door. The brownstone's door opened wider.

Aggie stood rigid, staring at the door. Her lips moved silently. *Hail Mary, full of grace, Hail Mary, full of grace, Hail Mary, full of grace, Hail Mary . . .* The world seemed strangely clear beyond the deafening hammer of her heartbeat, the foggy nausea of her fear.

The heavy wooden door swung open. And through it, as Aggie watched, a monster stepped into the glare of the spotlight.

He was massive. Blinking and stupid and huge. His arms hung heavily down at his sides as he shuffled forward on columnlike legs. His shoulders seemed to brush the doorway on either side as he moved out onto the stoop.

The door swung shut behind him. He stood where he was. He peered down at them, at all of them. His small, blocky face contracted as if he could not quite imagine who they all were, or why they had come. He stood and stared from small, hard eyes set deep in a protruding brow. And then he started forward again.

"Freeze!" someone shouted.

And there was another shout: "Freeze!"

"Hold it!"

The men were standing up behind the cars, bracing their guns on car rooftops, coming out from behind the cars and kneeling with their guns held steady on the approaching man.

"Just stay right there!"

"Put your hands over your head!"

"Put your hands up now!"

McIlvaine's voice rose babbling out of the car in front of Aggie.

"See, he did it! I couldn't stop him. No one could stop him! It's him, he's crazy, I swear, I didn't . . ."

Aggie stared up at the man on the stoop. Until this moment, she had hardly known that she'd had any hope left—until this moment, that is, when it all collapsed inside her and she was hopeless. Standing behind the phalanx of men and guns, staring over the car roofs up at the stoop, up at that creature, she felt as if her body were about to tear open with a cry, as if from now on there would be nothing to her but a long unthinking cry of black grief.

She made no sound. Her hand moved to her stomach. She pressed it there gently. She stared up at the man on the stoop.

The man on the stoop looked down at the lights, down at the policemen and the guns pointed up at him. He smiled dreamily at them. He nodded and laughed a little and smiled.

And then he swayed where he stood. And then, without taking another step, he pitched forward like a felled tree—dropped headlong onto the stone steps beneath him—and lay there dead.

And still, for long seconds, no one moved. For long seconds, they did not understand what they were seeing. Aggie did not understand. She kept staring at the stoop. She kept shaking her head and staring.

A moment ago, the man was there—a massive, powerful thing standing there, seeming almost defiant against all those lights and men and weapons. And now a moment later, he was splayed on the steps, his head pointing down toward the sidewalk, his arms limp, still at his sides—and the back of his shirt, exposed in the spotlight, soaked through everywhere with rich, black blood.

Aggie looked at him. The police looked at him without moving.

And then the door of the brownstone began to open again.

It swung out in stages this time, a little bit and then a little more. Everywhere on the bright street, the policemen tensed. They raised their guns again, trained their guns again on the door. The door opened a little more, a little wider. Aggie lifted her eyes to it, shaking her head, uncomprehending.

The door jerked open wider, and a battered little man staggered through it into the night.

Aggie didn't recognize him at first. The bottom half of his face had been shattered. His mouth was a ragged hole, his nose was flattened. His eyes stared dull and white through a mask of blood; forehead to chin, he was all blood. And his shirt and his pants were dark and rusty with it: it was their only color.

"Aiieee . . . ?"

His voice came to her. It was deep and hollow. It seemed to echo up from the bottom of him.

301

"Aiieee . . . ?"

He stared blindly into the beam of the spotlight. He lifted one hand as if feeling his way. His other arm dangled crooked at his side.

"Aiieee . . . ," he called again.

And now Agatha's hand left her belly, reached out trembling in front of her. Her lips parted.

"Aiieee . . ."

"Nathan?" she cried out wildly. "Nathan, I'm here!"

"Aiieee . . ."

"I'm here, Nathan! Oh, Jesus!"

She took a stumbling step forward.

Suddenly, all around her, there were other shouts: guttural barks from one cop to another. Above them all, she heard D'Annunzio screaming, a hoarse basso:

"Put 'em up, put your guns up, for Christ's, he's got her, put up your, don't shoot, hold your fire, hold your fire . . ."

Then he had grabbed the bullhorn from Calvin. His voice was booming over them as if from everywhere:

"Hold your fire, hold your fire, he's got the kid, put 'em up everywhere . . ."

With her lips parted, her hand reaching out, Aggie looked down and saw the small figure by Nathan's side. The child was clinging to his bloody pants with her fingers, pressing close to his pants, her cheek to his leg; looking out into the bright lights with dazzled eyes.

"Jessie?" Agatha whispered. "Jessie?" She started moving forward more quickly. "Jessie?" she called.

The child blinked. Her mouth pursed, small and trembling, she leaned forward a little. "Mommy?"

Agatha rushed between the cars. Past the men.

"Jessie!" she cried out, her voice breaking.

Clinging to her father's pants with one hand, the little girl reached out into the bright lights with the other.

"Mommy!"

Aggie ran toward her.

What Conrad Remembered

Later, they would ask Conrad about the end of it. D'Annunzio, sitting by his hospital bed with a notepad open in his pudgy paw, would ask him several times: How did it happen, what exactly did you do? So would other detectives from the district attorney's office; lawyers, too; and the hospital doctors—to get a sense of his injuries, at first; then later, Conrad felt, just to satisfy their own curiosity. Even Frank Saperstein, an old friend and the doctor who was to put him more or less back together, insisted he try to remember those final moments. And he did try. He tried hard. But they were gone; blacked out. Pain and shock had erased them. His mind had filed them away as secrets from itself.

"What I want to know," Saperstein would say later, "is where you come up with the strength at that point to drive a broom handle into a man's kidney."

"Wha' I wanna know," Conrad answered, speaking with his jaw wired shut, "is how I wemembuh wheah da kidney is."

Saperstein laughed. "You can take the boy out of med school . . . ," he said.

And Conrad simply nodded, trying not to smile too much. That was all he had to say on the subject. He had forgotten everything.

Or not everything. Not exactly. There was one small moment that he did remember, that he would always remember.

In the end, in the room with Maxwell, he had been beyond thinking. What he considered thinking anyway—he was no longer capable of that. He had simply lain unconscious where Maxwell had thrown him and felt his daughter dying. He felt it inside him. It was like a sort of antipregnancy: something in the belly—something he loved—being slowly squeezed into nothing, into lifelessness. He had had to stop it, to try to stop it. It hurt so much, too much. So Conrad had gotten up one more time.

He did not realize that he'd been thrown into the room's far corner—where the broom handle also lay. He touched the handle though as he shifted on the floor, and then it was in his hand. He strained upward against the crying weakness of his one good arm and his stiffened legs. He thought he would drop to the floor again, but the dying of his daughter inside him seemed to lift him. He just seemed to keep rising after his physical strength had failed.

All the same, he barely made it to his feet. Just close enough. Just close enough to stagger forward, bent double, across the little room. If Maxwell had been standing then, he could not have attacked him effectively. But the giant was on his knees, stretched out over the mattress, clutching Jessica's leg in one hand, reaching out to strangle her with the other. Conrad simply fell on top of him. He lifted the stake into the air like a dagger. And he drove it home with surgical precision.

Maxwell should have dropped right then. The blow should have killed him outright. Instead, he rose off the bed like a wave, roaring. Conrad rolled off him onto the mattress. He groped for his daughter, found her, held on to her . . .

. . . baby . . . baby . . .

. . . while Maxwell towered and raged above them. Jessica was not screaming anymore. She was leaning against her father's chest, staring up at the spectacle and crying.

Maxwell beat his hands back and forth in the air as if to shoo away the thing that had him. He lifted his face to the ceiling and cried out, foam and spittle flying from his lips. Finally, he reached around in back of him. Conrad heard a wet, sucking sound. Maxwell retched with pain as he drew the broom handle out of his flesh.

. . . die . . . , Conrad thought.

Maxwell had to die then. There was no way he could survive anymore, not with the stake pulled free. Conrad wrapped his good arm tight around his daughter, held her close against his chest . . .

. . . *baby* . . .

. . . and stared up at the raging man.

. . . *die* . . .

And still, the man stood. He hurled the broom handle at the wall. He growled after it. He looked down at the bloody figure on the mattress at his feet: the bloody figure and the little girl cowering under his arm.

. . . *baby* . . . , Conrad thought, holding her close, staring up at Maxwell.

Maxwell looked down at him and shook his head sadly. And then he turned. Silently, he lumbered away from them. His feet shuffling, he moved to the door.

Conrad and Jessica lay on the mattress and watched him go. They saw the dark blood spreading up through his shirt, down over the seat of his pants. Maxwell reached the door and pulled it open. Ducking his head, he went through, out into the hall. And he was gone.

Conrad didn't know how he got the tape off his daughter's wrists and ankles. How he got out of the room, down the hall, out the front door. He just knew he had to get out, get away, get Jessica out and away. Find Aggie. He had to find his wife, that was it.

. . . *wife* . . .

She would help them. She would take care of them.

He stumbled down the hall with the child clinging to his pants leg, with his bloody hand touching her hair, pressing her face close to his hip. Then, all at once, he was out on the stoop, and there were lights everywhere. Bright white light and flashing red lights that seemed to blend in with the red clouds floating and dancing before him.

. . . *wife* . . . , Conrad thought, standing on the stoop.

He was calling her then, but he didn't know it. He only knew he had to keep standing. Stay on his feet. Keep moving until he got Jessica away, until he found Aggie.

. . . *wife* . . . , he thought.

"I'm here, Nathan!"

. . . *wife* . . .

"Mommy!"

Nathan closed his eyes, shook his head. He felt the world swaying around him.

305

. . . *have to* . . .

Stand. He had to stay on his feet, keep standing. He pried his eyes open and stared into the light. Stared down the steps. He saw now: Maxwell's body lying there. Maxwell's body and . . .

. . . *wife* . . .

Aggie. Aggie was there running toward them, reaching out. And then the child, the girl, was gone from beside him, was running down the stairs, running past the great body of the dead man. She ran to the edge of the sidewalk, where Aggie met her, where Aggie fell to her knees in front of her, wrapped her arms around her, pulled her close . . .

Conrad, swaying precariously on the stoop, nodded slowly.

. . . *wife* . . . , he thought. . . . *baby* . . . *wife* . . .

And it was over. He knew he could let go. He knew he could go down.

He released himself into the darkness at his feet. He let himself spill into it. But he did not fall then. His body did not drop. There were people around him. People holding him. Holding his arm. Shouting into his ear.

"You're all right. We got you, pal. You're gonna be all right."

. . . *man* . . . , Conrad thought. . . . *fat, smelly man* . . .

The fat, smelly man's growly voice kept booming in his ear. "You're gonna make it, buddy. You're gonna be okay. You're gonna be okay now, hang on."

And that was the moment that Conrad remembered—just then. Just as he began finally to sink into the pool of darkness around him. There was one sudden moment then of comprehension, of bright, crystal understanding.

He saw everything: the policemen running toward him, the cars in the street, the lights everywhere, the dead man underneath him on the steps, his wife holding on to his daughter on the sidewalk below. He saw everything etched in finest detail upon the night.

And he thought: *I'm going to live.*

With perfect clarity, he thought: *I'm going to live to see my grandchildren.*

306

The End

"Is Daddy going to be all right?"

"I hope so," said Mommy. Mommy was crying. "I think so, sweetheart."

They had taken Daddy away to the hospital in an ambulance. Now she had to go to the hospital too, but she was going with Mommy. Mommy held her by the shoulder. They walked together across the street. There was an old navy-blue car on the far side of the street. They were going to drive in that.

Jessica felt strange. She felt dizzy and faraway. Her stomach hurt and her feet were cold and tingling. She wished she didn't have to go to the hospital. She wished she could go home and go to bed.

"Will Dr. Saperstein be at the hospital?" she asked.

"Yes," said her mother. She wiped her eyes.

"He never has lollipops."

Mommy laughed even though she was crying. "I'll get you a lollipop later, sweetheart. I promise."

As they walked, Jessica saw a policeman move to the navy-blue car. He opened the door and a woman stepped out. She was a beautiful woman. Her face was as beautiful as a princess's face. Her hair was dirty though. And she was wearing one of Mommy's old dresses—the one with the purple flowers on it. It didn't fit her very well: she was too tall and thin.

The policeman held the woman by the arm. He walked with her to one of the police cars nearby. He helped her get into the backseat, then closed the door. Then the policeman got in the front door and sat behind the wheel.

The woman in the backseat turned and looked out the window. She looked directly at Jessica's Mommy. She lifted her hand to the window, pressed it to the glass.

Agatha stopped walking. She raised her hand and waved back. Then, just before the car drove away, the beautiful woman looked at Jessica too. She looked right at her with the strangest look. It was a kind of a sad look, but a soft look too. It was the way Jessica looked at something like Gabrielle's dollhouse, or Lauren's kitten—something she wanted really badly but couldn't have.

Then, while the woman was still looking at her, the police car backed up. It swung around and went down the street to the corner. It turned the corner and the beautiful woman was gone.

"Who was that, Mommy?" Jessica asked.

Mommy shook her head. "Just a girl. One of Daddy's patients."

Jessica knew about Daddy's patients. "Is she sad?"

"Yes. Yes, she is."

"But Daddy will help her?"

"I don't know. Yes. He'll try."

Jessica thought about it. They started walking to the car again.

"Daddy fought with the bad man," Jessica said finally.

"I know," said her mother. Her voice sounded strange—she was crying again.

"The bad man was a *giant*," Jessie said.

"Yes, he was. Almost a giant."

"Did Daddy kill him, Mommy?"

"Yes, sweetheart."

"Because he had to."

"Yes."

They reached the car. Jessica's mother stopped and looked around her.

"Is Daddy the strongest man in the whole world, Mommy?" Jessica asked her.

Mommy laughed. "I don't know." She made a gesture in the air. Then she nodded and laughed. "Probably," she said. She wiped her nose with her hand.

Jessie stood beside her mother and looked around too. Many of the cars in the street were beginning to pull away now, to move down to the corner, to turn and move out of sight. Some of them—some of the police cars—still had their red lights spinning on top of them.

"Why aren't we going?" Jessica asked.

"We have to wait for the detective," her Mommy said. She pointed to him. "He's going to drive us."

"That fat man?"

"Ssh, sweetie. Yes."

Jessica watched the fat detective. He was leaning down next to a nearby police car. In another moment, he stood up. He walked over to them. He looked down at the little girl.

"Hello there," he said to her.

Jessica moved closer to her mother's leg. The fat detective smiled. He had a gravelly face. It looked strange when he smiled. He looked up at Agatha.

"Well . . . ," he said.

"Thank you," Agatha started to say—but she couldn't finish it. She bowed her head, crying hard.

The fat man's smile grew even wider. "Well, whattaya know, huh?" he said. "Whattaya know?"

The nearby police car was backing up now. It was turning around. As it turned, it pulled forward. It stopped right in front of Jessica. Jessica's eyes went wide.

"Mommy!" she said.

She pulled even closer to her mother's leg. She stared at the window of the police car. The window was open, and there, staring out of it, was the bad man, the man called Sport. He was looking out the window and right at her.

"What?" said Jessica's mother.

"Look, Mommy," Jessica said. "That's the bad man."

"Oh . . ." Her Mommy held her more tightly. "It's all right," she said. "He's going to jail now. He can't hurt you. Come on."

She tried to pull Jessica toward the navy-blue car. But Jessica hung back. She looked up at the fat detective's gravelly face.

"He's the one who told everyone else what to do," Jessie said.

The fat detective inclined his head. Then he turned and gave a big grin to the bad man. "Well, that's very interesting," he growled. "You and me are going to have a long talk about that, okay?"

"Okay," Jessica said uncertainly.

"Come on, sweetheart," said her mother again. "Get in our car and we'll go see Daddy."

Her mother turned to open the car door, but again, for another moment, Jessie remained where she was. She stood very still and looked at the face of the bad man called Sport.

The man called Sport looked back at her. His lip curled up. He snorted.

The little girl shook her head at him almost sadly. "I told you," she said. "I told you he'd come."